MAGIC HIGH School

Nine School Competition Arc (II)

4

Tsutomu Sato

Illustration Kana Ishida

Illustration assistants Jimmy Stone,
Yasuko Suenaga

Design BEE-PEE

"I...I think I want to fight. I don't know how many more chances I'll have to seriously compete with Miyuki... I don't want to let this chance go."

Shizuku Kitayama

Miyuki's classmate in Class 1-A. Specializes in high-power vibration and acceleration magic. Cool and collected at a glance, her personality is the opposite of Honoka's.

"If Kitayama wants to have a match with me, then I have no reason to refuse her."

Miyuki Shiba

The younger sister of the Shiba siblings. Part of Class 1-A. An elite who entered Magic High School as the top student. A Course 1 student, called a "Bloom," whose specialty is cooling magic. Her lovable only flaw is a severe case of a brother complex.

"This is exciting!"

Erika Chiba

Tatsuya's classmate. Has a bright personality; a troublemaker who gets everyone involved. Her family is large and famous for *kenjutsu*—a magical technique that combines swords and magic.

"It's finally Shizuku's turn!"

Honoka Mitsu

Class 1-A. Miyuki's classmate. Specializes in controlling light-wave vibration magic. Rather subjective in her outlooks.

"Yoshida, is something the matter?"

Mizuki Shibata

Tatsuya's classmate. Sits next to the main character in class. Plain, but very popular among some upperclassmen as the "healing little-sister character." Because of her pushion-radiation sensitivity, she wears glasses, which is unusual in this day and age.

Mikihiko Yoshida

Tatsuya's classmate. Belongs to a distinguished family of old magic. An accident in his past forced him to be a Course 2 Weed, but he's strong enough in magical techniques to rival the Course 1 Blooms.

"N-no, I'm fine."

"Don't run away, Shiba. You may be a substitute, but now you've been chosen, and you will do your duty."

Katsuto Juumonji

A senior at First High. Central member of the competition's male players. Also the club committee chairman, who is involved in overseeing all club activities. Strong enough to be counted as one of the three giants of First High, along with Mayumi and Mari.

"...!"

Tatsuya, I'll prove
what you said is true!

"I wouldn't have any
options in a normal
fight, but now that
Ichijou seems to be
overly sensitive to
me, maybe..."

Tatsuya Shiba

The older brother of the Shiba
siblings. A new student of the
National Magic University
Affiliated First High School.
Part of Class 1-E. One of the
Course 2 students, mockingly
called "Weeds." Specializes in
designing Casting Assistant
Devices (CADs).

"Waaarrioooorrrrr!"

Leonhard Saijou

Nicknamed "Leo." Part of Class 1-E, like Tatsuya. His father is half-Japanese and his mother a quarter. Specializes in hardening magic.

"Why don't you show us why you're using multiple devices at once?"

Masaki Ichijou

A freshman at Third High and an athlete competing in the Nine School Competition as the freshman ace. Can use advanced magic freely and is also known as the Crimson Prince. Next leader of the Ichijou, one of the Ten Master Clans.

"Masaki!"

Shinkurou Kichijouji

A freshman at Third High and an athlete competing in the competition. Also Masaki's good friend and adviser. A boy genius who discovered the first Cardinal Code of magic programs at the young age of twelve. Given the nickname Cardinal George for his achievements.

Various Modern Spells

• Flight Magic

A spell that uses gravity manipulation to move through the air. Long thought impossible to realize, it continuously activates magic with the interspell connection time set to an extremely small interval (0.5 second by default), thus clearing the obstacle of needing stronger magical interference whenever changing one's flight path. It is possible for a caster to continue flying until their magic power runs out.

• Mist Dispersion

A spell that disintegrates physical objects down to their constituent atoms or ions by exerting influence on the construction information of said objects. Spells that directly influence an object's construction information belong to the most difficult type of magic.

• Program Dispersion

A spell that dismantles magic programs (other spells) back into inert clusters of psions. When magic programs are used on information bodies, their information makeup is exposed, and the eidos themselves do not have any method of preventing outside interference, so in theory it's easy to disperse a spell. However, one needs to be aware of a spell's makeup in order to dismantle it, which requires a special information-processing ability that allows one to recognize a magic program's structure just by observing it. Before Program Dispersion can be used, one must analyze the spell target, but in modern magic, spells complete in mere tenths of a second. Experiments with this magic have been successful when the caster knows the spell being used beforehand, but practical usage of this ability is thought by most to be impossible.

• Program Demolition

A typeless spell that rams a cluster of compressed psions into a target object without going through the Idea, thus causing it to explode down to the atomic level. Also, all the psion information bodies within the target are blown away, along with any other magic programs that may be present around it. Though Program Demolition is magic, as this psionic bullet is not structured like a magic program to alter events, anti-magic (like Information Boost and Area Interference) doesn't affect it. In addition, the density of the bullet itself turns away any effects of Cast Jamming. Because it has absolutely no physical essence, no physical obstacles can block it.

• Inferno

A spell that reverses heat entropy. It splits a target area in half and then decreases the kinetic energy of every object in one part while evacuating that leftover energy to the other part, heating it up and thereby obeying the law of conservation of energy. Essentially, the spell creates two adjacent areas, one scorching and the other freezing, at the same time.

• Niflheim

An oscillation/deceleration-type area-of-effect spell. Cools all physical matter in an area evenly, regardless of specific heat or phase. As an application, a caster can create a large mass of cold air from diamond dust (ice crystals), dry ice particulates, or sometimes even liquid nitrogen fog, and then use it as a ramming force.

• Dry Blizzard

A spell that gathers carbon dioxide in the air, creates particles of dry ice from them, then converts the heat energy left over from the cooling process into kinetic energy. That energy sends the dry ice particles flying at a high speed.

• Slithering Thunder

A combination spell that freezes the water vapor from Dry Blizzard into pebbles of dry ice while also creating a high-conductivity fog from the vaporized carbon dioxide. Static electricity, created from the fog through an oscillation spell and an emission spell, then strikes an enemy with lightning. The friction for the lightning uses either the fog itself or water droplets merged into the carbon dioxide gas as a conductor.

• Burst

A divergence-type spell that vaporizes the liquid inside a target object. When used on a creature, the bodily fluids vaporize and the body ruptures. When used on a machine driven by internal combustion, the fuel vaporizes and explodes. The same result happens with fuel cells as well. Even without flammable fuel on board, all machines have some amount of fluid in them, whether battery fluid, hydraulic fluid, or lubricating liquid. Because of this, Burst can stop and destroy virtually every single kind of machine.

The Irregular at Magic High School

NINE SCHOOL COMPETITION
Part II

4

Tsutomu Sato
Illustration Kana Ishida

YEN ON
NEW YORK

THE IRREGULAR AT MAGIC HIGH SCHOOL
TSUTOMU SATO

Translation by Andrew Prowse
Cover art by Kana Ishida

© TSUTOMU SATO 2011
All rights reserved.
Edited by ASCII MEDIA WORKS
First published in Japan in 2011 by KADOKAWA CORPORATION, Tokyo.
English translation rights arranged with KADOKAWA CORPORATION, Tokyo,
through Tuttle-Mori Agency, Inc., Tokyo.

English translation © 2017 by Yen Press, LLC

Yen On
1290 Avenue of the Americas
New York, NY 10104

Visit us at yenpress.com
facebook.com/yenpress
twitter.com/yenpress
yenpress.tumblr.com
instagram.com/yenpress

First Yen On Edition: April 2017

Yen On is an imprint of Yen Press, LLC.
The Yen On name and logo are trademarks of Yen Press, LLC.

The publisher is not responsible for websites (or their content) that are not owned by the publisher.

Library of Congress Cataloging-in-Publication Data
Names: Satou, Tsutomu. | Ishida, Kana, illustrator.
Title: The Irregular at Magic High School / Tsutomu Satou ; Illustrations by Kana Ishida.
Other titles: Mahōka kōkō no rettosei. English
Description: First Yen On edition. | New York, NY : Yen On, 2016–
Identifiers: LCCN 2015042401 | ISBN 9780316348805 (v. 1 : paperback) |
    9780316390293 (v. 2 : paperback) | 9780316390309 (v. 3 : paperback) |
    9780316390316 (v. 4 : paperback)
Subjects: | CYAC: Brothers and sisters—Fiction. | Magic—Fiction. | High schools—Fiction. |
    Schools—Fiction. | Japan—Fiction. | Science fiction.
Classification: LCC PZ7.1.S265 Ir 2016 | DDC [Fic]—dc23
LC record available at http://lccn.loc.gov/2015042401

ISBN: 978-0-316-39031-6

10 9 8 7 6 5 4 3 2 1

LSC-C

Printed in the United States of America

The Irregular at MagicHigh School

NINE SCHOOL COMPETITION
PART II

An irregular older brother with a certain flaw.
An honor roll younger sister who is perfectly flawless.

When the two siblings enrolled in Magic High School,
a dramatic life unfolded—

Character

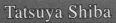

Tatsuya Shiba

Class 1-E. One of the Course 2 (irregular) students, who are mockingly called "Weeds." Sees right to the core of everything.

Miyuki Shiba

Class 1-A. Tatsuya's younger sister; enrolled as the top student. Specializes in freezing magic. Dotes on her older brother.

Leonhard Saijou

Class 1-E. Tatsuya's classmate. Specializes in hardening magic. Has a bright personality.

Erika Chiba

Class 1-E. Tatsuya's classmate. Specializes in *kenjutsu*. A charming troublemaker.

Mizuki Shibata

Class 1-E. Tatsuya's classmate. Has pushion radiation sensitivity. Serious and a bit of an airhead.

Mikihiko Yoshida

Class 1-E. Tatsuya's classmate. From a famous family that uses ancient magic. Has known Erika since they were children.

Honoka Mitsui

Class 1-A. Miyuki's classmate. Specializes in light-wave vibration magic. Impulsive when emotional.

Shizuku Kitayama

Class 1-A. Miyuki's classmate. Specializes in vibration and acceleration magic. Doesn't show emotional ups and downs very much.

Shun Morisaki

Class 1-A. Miyuki's classmate. Specializes in CAD quick-draw. Takes great pride in being a Course 1 student.

Subaru Satomi

Class 1-D. Frequently mistaken for a pretty boy. Cheerful and easy to get along with.

Eimi Akechi

Class 1-B. A quarter-blood. Full name is Amelia Eimi Akechi Goldie.

Mayumi Saegusa

A senior and the student council president. One of the strongest magicians ever to grace a magical high school.

Azusa Nakajou

A junior and the student council secretary. Shy and has trouble expressing herself.

Suzune Ichihara

A senior and the student council accountant. Calm, collected, and book smart. Mayumi's right hand.

Hanzou Gyoubu-Shoujou Hattori

A junior and the student council vice president. Very serious and a good student.

Mari Watanabe

A senior and the chairwoman of the disciplinary committee. Mayumi's good friend. Good all-around and likes a good fight.

Koutarou Tatsumi

A senior and a member of the disciplinary committee. Has a heroic personality.

Midori Sawaki

A junior and a member of the disciplinary committee. Has a complex about his girlish name.

Kei Isori

A junior. Top grades in his class in magical theory. Engaged to Kanon Chiyoda.

Kanon Chiyoda

A junior. An energetic, vivid girl. Engaged to Kei Isori.

Katsuto Juumonji

A senior and the head of the club committee, the unified organization overseeing all club activities.

Takeaki Kirihara

A junior. Member of the *kenjutsu* club. Junior High Kenjutsu Tournament champion within the Kanto Region.

Sayaka Mibu

A junior. Member of the kendo club. Placed second in the nation at the girls' junior high kendo tournament.

Yakumo Kokonoe

A user of an ancient magic called *ninjutsu*. Tatsuya's martial arts master.

Haruka Ono

A general counselor of Class 1-E.

Masaki Ichijou

A freshman at Third High. Participates in the Nine School Competition. Direct heir to the Ichijou family, one of the Ten Master Clans.

Shinkurou Kichijouji

A freshman at Third High. Participates in the Nine School Competition. Also known as Cardinal George.

Retsu Kudou

Renowned as the strongest magician in the world. Given the honorary title of Sage.

Harunobu Kazama

Captain of the 101st Brigade of the Independent Magic Battalion. Ranked major.

Shigeru Sanada

Executive officer of the 101st Brigade of the Independent Magic Battalion. Ranked captain.

Muraji Yanagi

Executive officer of the 101st Brigade of the Independent Magic Battalion. Ranked captain.

Kousuke Yamanaka

Executive officer of the 101st Brigade of the Independent Magic Battalion. Medical major. First-rate healing magician.

Kyouko Fujibayashi

Female officer serving as Kazama's aide. Ranked second lieutenant.

Glossary

Magic High School

Nickname for high schools affiliated with the National Magic University. There are nine schools throughout the nation. Of them, First High through Third High each adopt a system of Course 1 and Course 2 students to split up its two hundred incoming freshmen.

Blooms, Weeds

Slang terms used at First High to display the gap between Course 1 and Course 2 students. Course 1 student uniforms feature an eight-petaled emblem embroidered on the left breast, but Course 2 student uniforms do not.

CAD (Casting Assistant Device)

A device that simplifies magic casting. Magical programming is recorded within. There are many types and forms, some specialized and others multipurpose.

Course 1 student emblem

Tatsuya Shiba's CAD

Miyuki Shiba's CAD

Four Leaves Technology (FLT)

A domestic CAD manufacturer. Originally known more for engineering magical products than for manufacturing finished units. The development of the Silver model has made them much more widely known as a maker of CADs.

Taurus Silver

A genius engineer said to have advanced specialized CAD software by a decade in just a single year.

Eidos (individual information bodies)

Originally a term from Greek philosophy. In modern magic, *eidos* refers to the information bodies that accompany events. They form a so-called record out in the world, and can be considered the footprints of an object's state of being in the universe, be that active or passive. The definition of *magic* in its modern form is that of a technology that alters events by altering the information bodies composing them.

Idea (information body dimension)

Originally a term from Greek philosophy; pronounced "ee-dee-ah." In modern magic, *Idea* refers to the *platform* upon which information bodies are recorded—a spell, object, or energy's *dimension*. Magic is primarily a technology that outputs a magic program (a spell sequence) to affect the Idea (the dimension), which then rewrites the eidos (the individual bodies) recorded there.

Activation program

The blueprints of magic, and the programming that constructs it. Activation programs are stored in a compressed format within CADs. The magician sends a psionic wave into the CAD, which then expands the sequence data there and uses it to convert the activation program into a signal; that signal, in turn, returns to the magician as a magic program.

Psions (thought particles)

Massless particles belonging to the dimension of spirit phenomena, they record awareness and thought information. While eidos are considered the basis of modern magical theory, activation programs and magic programs form their practical usage. Both types of programs are information bodies made up of psions.

Pushions (spirit particles)

Massless particles belonging to the dimension of spirit phenomena. Their existence has been confirmed, but their true form and function have yet to be elucidated. In general, magicians are only able to sense energized pushions.

The Nine School Competition

Officially dubbed the Magic High School Goodwill Competition Magic Tournament.
    As its name suggests, student teams from First High through Ninth High gather from all over the country to compete in heated magical competition.

There are six events: Speed Shooting, Cloudball, Battle Board, Ice Pillars Break, Mirage Bat, and Monolith Code.
* Monolith Code is a male-only event, and Mirage Bat is a female-only one.

Each school can enter three people in a single event, and a single person can compete in up to only two events. Teams of athletes generally consist of ten male and ten female students with twenty athletes for the main events and twenty for the rookie events.

The competition takes place over the course of ten days, and it includes a rookie competition where only freshmen compete (the main competition has no class restriction). The rookie competition is held from day four to day eight.
    Victory in the Nine School Competition and rankings are based on the total number of points earned from each event. First place gains fifty points, second gains thirty, and third twenty. For Speed Shooting, Battle Board, and Mirage Bat, fourth place gains ten points. In Cloudball and Ice Pillars Break, there is no fourth through sixth place; the three teams that lose in the third round are granted five points each. The most popular event of the Nine School Competition, Monolith Code, grants one hundred points to the winning team, sixty points to second place, and forty to third place, making it the most heavily weighted event. (Points in the rookie competition are halved and added on to the total scores.)

Date	Category	Events
Day 1 August 3 (W)	Main (All classes)	Speed Shooting: men's and women's qualifiers to finals tournament Battle Board: men's and women's qualifiers
Day 2 August 4 (R)	Main (All classes)	Cloudball: men's and women's qualifiers to finals Ice Pillars Break: men's and women's qualifiers
Day 3 August 5 (F)	Main (All classes)	Battleboard: men's and women's semifinals and finals Ice Pillars Break: men's and women's qualifiers to finals round-robin
Day 4 August 6 (S)	Rookie (Freshman)	Speed Shooting: men's and women's qualifiers to finals tournament Battle Board: men's and women's qualifiers
Day 5 August 7 (S)	Rookie (Freshman)	Cloudball: men's and women's qualifiers to finals Ice Pillars Break: men's and women's qualifiers
Day 6 August 8 (M)	Rookie (Freshman)	Battle Board: men's and women's semifinals and finals Ice Pillars Break: men's and women's semifinals to finals round-robin
Day 7 August 9 (T)	Rookie (Freshman)	Mirage Bat: women's qualifiers to finals Monolith Code: men's qualifiers round-robin
Day 8 August 10 (W)	Rookie (Freshman)	Monolith Code: men's finals tournament
Day 9 August 11 (R)	Main (All classes)	Mirage Bat: women's qualifiers to finals Monolith Code: men's qualifiers round-robin
Day 10 August 12 (F)	Main (All classes)	Monolith Code: men's finals tournament

Event

Speed Shooting

Sometimes called "quick-draw" by competitors.
 Competitors use magic to destroy targets fired into the air, like in skeet shooting. One hundred targets each of red and white are prepared, and competitors try to destroy more of their own color targets than their opponent. During the qualifiers, a single competitor will aim to destroy as many targets as possible within five minutes, and each is scored individually. From the quarterfinals onward, the matches are one-on-one.

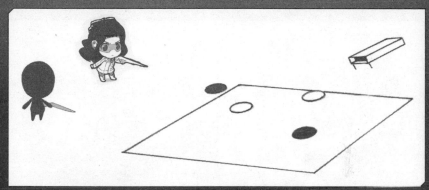

Cloudball

Sometimes shortened to "cloud" by competitors.
 A compressed-air shooter fires bouncy balls two inches across onto a court inside a transparent box where two players use either a racket or magic to keep as many balls as they can on the opposing player's side. Each set lasts three minutes. An additional ball is fired onto the court every twenty seconds, and in the end, the players chase nine balls around. Girls play three-set matches, while boys play five-set matches.

Event

Battle Board

Sometimes referred to simply as "surfing."

Originally an activity conceptualized for magic training in the navy, competitors ride a flat surfboard-like sheet and make three laps around an artificial waterway two miles in length, utilizing things like acceleration magic to make them go faster. As a rule of Battle Board, directly interfering with another competitor using magic is forbidden. The qualifiers consist of six races of four players each; the semifinals are two races of three players each; third place is decided between the four losers from the semifinals; and the finals is a one-on-one competition.

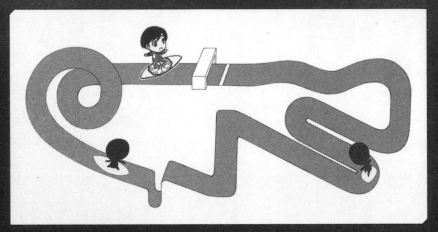

Ice Pillars Break

Each player stands on a thirteen-foot-tall tower on their own side and aims to knock over or destroy the twelve ice pillars on the opposing side, forty feet square, while defending his or her own twelve ice pillars on his or her own side. Players compete only with distance magic, with no need to use physical means. Because of this, competitors don't have a set uniform; they're free to wear what they want to within the bounds of public decency. As a result, the girls' Ice Pillars Break event is sometimes called the "fashion show" of the Nine School Competition.

Mirage Bat

A women-only event sometimes abbreviated to "mirage" by the competitors.

The players set their eyes on holographic balls projected into the air, and use magic to leap up and hit them with sticks. It has the least number of matches of all the events in the competition, but it lasts the longest. Because the players have to continuously use magic to keep leaping into the air throughout the match, some say the event rivals a full marathon in how difficult it is.

In the Nine School Competition, since only girls participate, some call the competitors flitting about in elaborate outfits "faeries."

Monolith Code

A men-only event sometimes abbreviated to "monolith" by the competitors.

On the match field, called a "stage," each three-man team fights using magic to protect their monoliths. Victory is decided either when one team is no longer able to fight or when one team splits the other's monolith in half and transmits a code to it. Direct attacks against the opposing team using anything other than magic are strictly forbidden. In order to split a monolith and read the code inside, a player needs to fire a special typeless magic sequence at it. Because of the exciting combat, it is the most popular event in the competition, always resulting in white-hot matches.

[8]

It was the fourth day of competition.

The main event would now take a backseat for five days, while the rookie competition got under way. It was the freshmen's turn to take the stage and battle it out.

The scoreboard saw First High in first place, with 320 points; Third High in second place, with 225 points; and all the other schools bunched together after them. With the 95-point margin between first and second place, First High had a wide lead—but not wide enough that the results of the rookie competition couldn't cause an upset; Third High had a good chance at a turnabout if they won the rookie competition by a large enough margin. On the other hand, First High simply had to keep the point differential from getting too big to keep their lead overall; they didn't *need* to win the rookie competition.

And overall victory was indeed the primary goal of every school here. The rookie competition would only grant half the points that the main one did, but those points would be added to the total score nonetheless. So for the competing freshmen, the real pride and honor of the Nine School Competition was their rookie events; things could get just as fired up as with the regular matches.

The events would play out in the same order as in the main competition: Today would feature the Speed Shooting qualifiers and finals and the Battle Board qualifiers. Unlike the main competition, however, Speed Shooting would host the girls in the morning and boys in the afternoon, with both divisions proceeding straight to the final tournaments. (The main competition's Speed Shooting directly followed the opening ceremonies, so it hadn't been possible to finish everything in one day.)

Like the other events, no CAD adjustments were permitted during matches. Still, the engineers would play a vital role *between* matches if the competitor wanted slight changes tailored to the situation. For that reason, while the competitors played their matches, the engineers generally stayed with them.

The tournament committee had structured the timetables so that, where possible, no two players from the same school would have a match at the same time. However, certain events, like Cloudball, would see many matches in a day, so most schools would have time-slot overlap at some point. Therefore, teams brought two engineers: a primary and a secondary. The overlapping could cross events as well, so naturally, a single engineer couldn't handle the entire competition.

But in the end, each team needed both engineers even if their match times never overlapped.

◇ ◇ ◇

"You're in the last race, Honoka?"

"Yes! It's in the afternoon, so it won't overlap with girls' Speed Shooting!"

Honoka Mitsui, smiling brightly, was piling on the pressure. Tatsuya found himself at a loss.

He was in charge of three events: girls' Speed Shooting, girls' Ice Pillars Break, and Mirage Bat. He wasn't handling only girls' events because he was a ladies' man, of course. It was mainly because many of the male freshmen on the team were firmly opposed to him...though that wasn't the only reason. A handful of certain freshmen girls had been very insistent he be assigned to them.

Miyuki, for example. And Honoka, and Miyuki, and Honoka, and Miyuki.

…Basically, it was all due to the vehement demands of these two.

Unfortunately, that created a problem. Of all the events, Miyuki's magical prowess was most suited for Ice Pillars Break. The student council and her classmates knew she was particularly effective with vibration- and deceleration-type magic. At the very least, they knew she sometimes triggered cooling magic unconsciously. With Miyuki in both Ice Pillars Break and Mirage Bat, the star event every school put their best girls into, the issue became what events Honoka would take part in.

First High's freshman final exam results from first semester featured Miyuki Shiba with the best scores, Shizuku Kitayama in second, Shun Morisaki in third, and Honoka Mitsui in fourth. That meant that, of the freshman girls, Honoka had the greatest practical magic ability after Miyuki and Shizuku. However, her abilities weren't very well suited to sporting events. She could use every type of magic flawlessly, and didn't have much trouble putting together intricate magic programs—but that meant she was more of a researcher than an athlete.

If there was one thing she excelled at above all others, it was illusion magic—a type of oscillation magic that manipulated light waves. Shizuku, however, specialized in both oscillation and acceleration magic. She could produce more power than Honoka in both categories, so she was more suited for Ice Pillars Break.

Tatsuya was going to be in charge of Miyuki for sure. That was a given. None of their upperclassmen were foolhardy enough to complain about *that*.

If Honoka had wanted Tatsuya to be assigned to her, however, then the easiest way would be to enter the same event as Miyuki.

Strategically speaking, though, putting your three top players in the same event wasn't a very good plan. In fact, it simply wouldn't be permitted.

That left events that *didn't* coincide with Ice Pillars Break, but in Speed Shooting, Shizuku would again be better off than Honoka. The event schedule was originally created to allow each player to compete in the events he or she excelled in, so from a certain point of view, this setup was inevitable.

With other strategic decisions also coming into play, Honoka ended up being put into Battle Board and Mirage Bat. (Their operation staff had initially suggested Battle Board and Cloudball, but Honoka insisted—with her friends' support—that she be in one of the same events as Miyuki.)

…With all that, and Honoka fervently insisting their match times wouldn't overlap, Tatsuya had a good guess at what she was really trying to say.

And it may have worked out when you looked at the timing. Unfortunately, swapping engineers like that would be bad for the team as a whole. And even if it worked out today, there was no proof that Ice Pillars Break and Battle Board *wouldn't* coincide on the sixth day—the third day of the rookie competition.

He knew Honoka understood all that. It was simple…

But today, for whatever reason, Miyuki wasn't giving him any help here. He sighed, both at Honoka and at his younger sister, and said what could be construed as the words of a two-timer. "…I would love to give your CAD a look, but I can't. I'll make sure to watch your races, though."

"Really? Okay, it's a promise!"

He heard someone stifle a giggle. He knew who it was, but his brain decided to pretend he didn't.

And perhaps, from an onlooker's point of view…he *was* the very image of a philanderer.

◇ ◇ ◇

Though he couldn't call the affair with Honoka minor, it *was* ultimately a side episode when it came to the main event. Now that the curtains were raised, he needed to focus on the matter at hand.

After finishing his final checks, Tatsuya handed the long, slender rifle for competitive Speed Shooting to Shizuku and instructed her to check how it felt. CADs absorbed psions from the magician, then sent them to activation programs, which were information bodies made up of even more psions. If there were any issues within this communication process, it wouldn't matter how well adjusted the other parts were—the device would be useless. Any hardware miscommunication issues would mean they'd need to replace the CAD with a spare; any software bugs would mean he'd have to work double time to fix them.

"Mm... It's perfect. Even better than mine."

Neither Shizuku's face nor voice were particularly expressive, so when he'd first been paired with her, there had been times when Tatsuya couldn't tell if she was being serious or lying. But by now, he'd gotten used to it. As a rule, she didn't lie. If something would be inconvenient for her to say, she'd just keep quiet.

"Again, Tatsuya, don't you want to come work for us?"

But *that* he still couldn't get used to, because the difference here was whether she was being serious or simply joking around.

"...If you can joke around, then I think you'll do fine in your match."

"I'm not joking."

Tatsuya frowned.

She was essentially asking him if he would form an official CAD maintenance contract with her. And she'd already asked him at least ten times. He was pretty sure, given her personality, that she wouldn't find the repetition of such a joke funny...but he also couldn't bring himself to take her seriously.

"It doesn't have to be exclusive..." she continued.

She had shown him her personal CAD earlier so he could come up with modifications to use in the competition, but it was so well tuned that there was nothing for him to do. It wasn't surprising; a famous magical engineer, said to be one of the top five in the nation, did her CAD's regular maintenance. And not just hers, either, but her entire family's.

When he first heard that Shizuku came from an extremely wealthy family, he couldn't help but be surprised. The Kitayama weren't famous for their magicians like the Ten Master Clans or the Hundred Families were. From what he'd heard, her mother was a top-tier magician who fell madly in love with the heir to a multimillionaire's fortune, and after a big fuss, got what she wanted in the end. Shizuku's father's line was bereft of magicians, and her much younger brother didn't have the kind of magical talents that let him use magic on a practical level. Apparently her father was a bit overzealous with his interest in her abilities, which made Tatsuya wonder if that wasn't the reason for the upgrades.

Shizuku's obsession with Monolith Code, however, was definitely the result of her father: namely, in the form of the magical competition skybox-ticket tours her father would take her on.

"...No matter how many times you say it, I'd still have to wait until I got a license."

The contract money and payment Shizuku had suggested the first time, when he'd been dumbfounded, was insane. It dwarfed even the vast sum paid to Taurus Silver. If he'd been just another student living off his parents' money, he probably would have passed out from the enormity of it.

However, doing free tuning work as part of a school event and actually doing it as a job for compensation were completely different. It wasn't technically illegal to operate without a license, but people would definitely see him as unqualified.

"Gotcha."

She nodded agreeably, just the same as always.

But how much she really understood, he was forced to wonder.

It might not have been at all memorable for Shizuku, but their conversation almost entirely cut down the pregame tension Tatsuya was feeling almost entirely.

Well, as long as it doesn't adversely affect the player, it's probably all right.

They had many meetings' worth of tactics behind them. Tatsuya had even given Shizuku's matches some thought and then put together a secret plan for her CAD. (It would only come into play when the players started facing off against one another in the tournament, of course.)

"Looks like you're on, Shizuku."

"Yeah."

There was only one thing left to say before her turn on the field:

"Good luck!"

"I'll do my best!"

Such was their last, simple tactic.

◇ ◇ ◇

"Is this seat open?"

"Oh, Miyuki! Yeah, you're good. Take a load off!"

This question had actually been posed to the girls numerous times since they had sat down in the stands. Unlike this instance, though, they had all been random guys with ulterior motives—even in spite of the fact that Leo and Mikihiko were sitting at either end. Each time, though, Erika had turned the smooth talkers away with a bloodthirsty lie and saved those seats.

The seating order was: Mikihiko, Mizuki, Honoka, an empty

seat, Erika, and Leo. They'd left Miyuki's seat in the middle, because if they didn't have walls on either side of her, then who knew how many reckless, fearless, cocky people would come along?

Erika hadn't been pleased at first that she was sitting next to Leo, but Mizuki had persuaded her. Leo and Honoka were in different classes, so they weren't very well acquainted; in light of that, Erika had reluctantly agreed. But despite all that, they didn't seem to be glaring at each other today.

Everyone except Honoka seemed to have been checking the day's competition schedule before Miyuki arrived; they all had spectator pamphlets in their hands. (Honoka didn't need to look anything up at this point, since she was actually competing.)

Miyuki looked back up to return their greetings, when Mizuki, who had looked back at her pamphlet, suddenly spoke. "...Oh, Honoka. Are you all set for your match?"

"It's all good! My race is in the afternoon," she insisted, giving Mizuki a slightly stiff smile.

Miyuki spoke next, her tone one of playful annoyance. "Honoka... if you're already nervous, you won't even last until your match."

"Argh...I know, but..."

"You'll be fine, Honoka. And my brother agrees, doesn't he?"

"Well, yes..."

"You came here to take your mind off the race, right? Let's just cheer for Shizuku."

"...Yeah, you're right." Honoka nodded firmly—a little *too* firmly. She clearly couldn't get her mind entirely off her worries. Perhaps it was pointless to tell her not to be concerned; she was highly serious and tended to think about things too much.

"...Umm, did I say something I shouldn't have?"

So when Mizuki, ignorant of what she was doing, delivered the final blow, Honoka grimaced a little.

◇ ◇ ◇

As the freshmen's little incident—innocent by some standards—played out, the two seniors of the student council plus the disciplinary committee chairwoman were sitting a little farther off.

"Mari, shouldn't you be sleeping?"

"Nah, it's not like I'm sick. I'll be fine as long as I don't push myself. And shouldn't you be in the tent, Mayumi?"

"It's not a problem; I'm not miles away or anything. If something happens, they'll tell me." Mayumi combed away the strands of hair on her cheek. The parting revealed a voice communication receiver worn on her ear.

"Maybe, but I feel like you and Ichihara *both* not being there is an issue…"

"It isn't. They basically forced me to take the day off."

"…Your jokes still don't make much sense to me, Ichihara."

Ichihara's answer came without even a smirk. For a moment, Mari wondered if she was grumpy. After all, her staff position had essentially been usurped.

Of course, Mari knew that couldn't be. Suzune oversaw the entire operation staff (which consisted of only four people, but still). Labor was divided among them so that they could work on individual strategies. The biggest separation was that the male staff members planned for the boys' matches and female members for the girls'. In today's events, Suzune was in charge of the girls' Speed Shooting.

…However, there wasn't much strategic planning that could be done for this event. It was mostly up to the players' own abilities. Calling it a pure contest of brawn over brains wouldn't be that far off the mark. If there was one role the officers had to play, it was selecting spells suited to each player and making broad settings to their CADs to match…but then that overlapped with the role of the technical staff.

And all the magic selection and CAD settings for the freshman girls' Speed Shooting had been done by Tatsuya himself, all the way from the planning stages through to execution. Suzune had agreed to the plan beforehand, of course, but she wasn't the type to get angry over something so petty.

"You know…now that I think about it, this is the first time he'll get to show off his real skills as an engineer."

Mari's words betrayed her curiosity. Mayumi nodded, too, also quite interested. "Yes. When he was with me, he just gave me a little help. I can't wait to see what the CADs he had complete control over turn out to be like!"

"The players all seem very favorable toward him. Especially Kitayama."

Suzune's words were no exaggeration. Excluding Miyuki, Honoka, and Shizuku, the freshman girls' squad, with its all–Course 1 lineup, as well as most other Course 2 girls, had a kind of allergy to letting other people handle their CADs. But after so many practice sessions using Tatsuya-adjusted CADs, any such negative emotions had vanished entirely. The change was sudden and drastic—enough to be called radical.

"Some of the players brought their own CADs today, too," Suzune remarked.

Mari sighed. "Wait a minute… That's not going to get in the way of his actual job, is it?"

"He seems to be managing his time well. He only does them favors once their matches are over."

By *favors*, she meant *CAD adjustments*. The players who used the competition CADs adjusted by Tatsuya had started to bring him their personal CADs, too. Not just one or two people, either—basically every single one of the female freshman athletes was doing it.

"Now that's a good, honest way to increase his fan base."

"He's 'good' in some strange ways, don't you think?"

Mayumi and Mari exchanged glances, then smirked.

◇ ◇ ◇

If Tatsuya had heard Mayumi's comment about him increasing his fan base, he would have groaned and denied it. In fact, up until the banquet, all the girls had been avoiding him (or at least, that's how it'd felt).

But of course, it went without saying that he didn't have extrasensory hearing powers. All his attention was on the shooting range where Shizuku stood.

He didn't have the kind of eyes Mizuki had, either. Instead, he had the ability to read and understand information structures. If he did a full adjustment on a CAD, he knew every single piece of information regarding it. And with a bit of effort, he could perceive the results, even if he couldn't perceive the processes that *led* to those results.

Beyond him, Shizuku readied herself.

The starting lights began to ignite, one by one.

Looks like it'll be fine this time, somehow…

Unlike in Mari's accident, there were no signs of Shizuku's CAD having been tampered with, but he still wasn't about to take his eyes off the action.

◇ ◇ ◇

The final light came on, and a moment later, a piece of clay shot into the sky.

Immediately after entering the scoring area, it exploded.

The next shot smashed apart in the middle of the area.

Then, on each end of the field, two pieces blew up at the same time.

Most of the audience gave gasps of admiration. Miyuki and the others, watching closely from the stands, couldn't help but sigh in relief at the smooth start.

Shizuku's eyes were razor-sharp. So sharp that it seemed like she wasn't even watching where the targets were coming from.

"Whoa. This is exciting," Erika mumbled in wonder.

"...Did she set up a magic region over the entire scoring area?" asked Mizuki, doubtful of her own analysis as she turned to Miyuki and Honoka.

"She did! She's using a spell that makes solid objects in the region vibrate, and that's what's breaking them. She mixes short waves with long waves, causing pieces of the objects to expand and contract, like she's weathering them. It's like how even the hardest boulders get weak and break when exposed to sudden heat and sudden cold."

"More precisely, she has several hypocenters—like for earthquakes—set up all over the scoring area, and she's creating virtual wave motion that causes the objects to oscillate. She's not using the spell to directly vibrate the targets themselves; instead, she's created a zone of event alteration that does the job for her. When a target comes into contact with the sphere of waves around one of the hypocenters, the virtual wave motion becomes *actual* wave motion inside the targets, causing them to break apart."

Honoka and Miyuki kept their eyes on the shooting range as they went through their paired explanation. Mizuki just kept nodding along.

◇ ◇ ◇

"...I see. So that's how it works."

By coincidence or inevitability, the same conversation was happening at the same time among the trio of seniors.

"As you know, the scoring area in Speed Shooting is a cube in the air, forty-nine feet long on each side. Shiba's activation program sets up a cube of thirty-three feet inside it, then defines nine hypocenters: one at the middle, and eight around it." Suzune was relegated to providing the explanation here, since she'd been privy to Tatsuya's adjustment plans. "Each point is handled with a number, and by inputting one of those numbers as a variable into the expanded activation program, it creates a sphere of virtual waves spreading out from the hypocenter. The waves reach out to twenty feet. So, she only has to activate a spell once to create a destructive sphere thirty-nine feet across, around whichever hypocenter she wants."

"...I feel like she's overusing her strength. Is Kitayama bad at coordinate settings?"

"She does seem to like using brute force over precision..." To Mari's question, Suzune maintained her poker face. It was basically her default expression, but in her eyes was a glimpse of a shadow of empathy mixed with wryness. "The purpose of the spell is not to compensate for precision but to gain speed at the expense of precision."

"...So then she could do pinpoint attacks if she wanted to?" Mari asked. "I don't get it."

"This spell is unique in how the coordinates are handled by values," Suzune explained, as she looked back to the freshman shooters in front of her. Perhaps the answers came so easily because she'd been asked them already. "In Speed Shooting, the distance from the player to the scoring area, the direction, and the size of the area are all constant. That means the hypocenters, which need to be part of the spell; the virtual cube they're positioned in; and its distance and viewing angle to the player are all constant, too.

"Because of that, she doesn't need to keep putting in the coordinate variables every time. Instead, there's an option in the activation program that allows her to just use a number from one to nine when she triggers it to determine where it goes off. With such rough aiming, she could also let the CAD automatically pick which point is most suitable to trigger with its aiming control system.

"There's also no need to change the power or duration of this spell. They're actually handled as constant values in the activation program. The player just has to use the CAD's assistance to pick the point, and then, without being conscious of many variables, pull the trigger and see her targets disappear."

The heat was reaching its end. Shizuku hadn't let a single target past yet.

"You don't need to concentrate on controlling it, so she can just activate the spell to take full advantage of the calculated area. She can cast continuously or multicast as she wishes."

The match timer hit zero.

A perfect score.

"The name for the spell is Active Air Mine. Apparently Shiba thought it up. I mean, with all the factors in there, it's a fairly large activation sequence, and only effective because of Kitayama's magical throughput."

"…The exact opposite of how Mayumi's magic works."

"…He thought of something like this?" Mayumi didn't sound so much impressed as irked.

"Still…it's really interesting." On the other hand, Mari sounded more interested than anything. "In actual combat, the relative position between you and your opponent is never the same, so from that standpoint, it isn't practical…but if you didn't set up a virtual cube in the air and instead made *yourself* the center, couldn't you make an active shield in all directions by putting the hypocenter on the circumference?"

"The issue, then, would be duration. If it's too short, it would be hard to time; too long and you could get caught in it yourself."

The problems Mayumi cited didn't serve to dampen Mari's enthusiasm. "Well, that depends on how good the caster is. Like you said, if you can time it properly, you can make it not last as long… Okay, I'm gonna grab him tonight and get him to install this on my CAD."

"…Just don't get in the way of the matches."

This time, Mayumi's response was 100 percent irked.

◇ ◇ ◇

"Good work," congratulated Tatsuya, giving Shizuku a towel as she came back from the shooting range. Engineers weren't managers, so handing out towels wasn't in the job description, but he didn't possess such petty pride.

"It was kind of anticlimactic." She wasn't being modest; she really thought that. She wiped a few beads of sweat from her brow, looking dissatisfied.

Shizuku also looked happy, though, and couldn't hide it—nor did she likely want to. The cutoff point for making it out of the qualifiers, for the rookie competition at least, was around 80 percent every year. You couldn't score better than perfect, though. Being so far over that cutoff would get her into the tournament for sure.

"I figured they wouldn't do anything to surprise you. No evil shots that went in strange directions."

The magic Shizuku had used hadn't covered the entire scoring area. There were definitely blind spots, which the targets could have exploited by skirting around the edges.

However, based on the shooting machines' specifications, Tatsuya had predicted that the committee wouldn't set them up to fire along grazing paths like that. If a piece of clay didn't pass through the scoring area, they'd need to restart the match to preserve fairness. The fault would lie with the tournament committee, so from a competition viewpoint it was an unneeded risk.

He'd thought it through far enough that he hadn't been too worried, but it was still a relief to see the plan go off without a hitch.

"You worry too much, Tatsuya. We're only rookies—nowhere near good enough for them to need to go for blind spots to thin the playing field."

She had brought up a reasonable point. "Well, so far, everything's gone as planned," Tatsuya replied, switching gears—then urging his athlete to do the same. "But you'll be up against human opponents in the quarterfinals. I made sure to adjust your CAD this morning, so could you check and see how it feels?"

"On it."

The finals would be formatted differently than the qualifier. In the qualifiers, athletes competed in speed and accuracy, seeing how many of the hundred clay pigeons they could destroy in five minutes.

The tournament, though, would have multiple players in one area, and the shooter who destroyed more pigeons would win the match. In addition to speed and accuracy, the game would now demand technique, such that one player's magic didn't get in the way of any others'.

Normally, athletes used different magic in accordance with different styles of play. When using specialized CADs for competition, people would generally switch to an entirely separate CAD when calling on a different type of magic.

Tatsuya would now get to work on the CAD for Shizuku's upcoming opponent—though there was still one more match before that.

And so Shizuku, by herself, headed to the tent where her other tournament CAD was being held.

◇ ◇ ◇

"All three made it through the qualifiers…"

Mayumi had returned to First High's main tent to find the Speed Shooting qualifier results waiting for her. Now she was looking them over and talking to herself.

"You wouldn't say the freshman girls this year are especially good or anything, would you?"

Eight of the twenty-four players in the qualifiers would advance to the tournament. One school having three of those players was pretty much unprecedented—both in the main *and* rookie competitions.

"Come on, drop the act, Mari," Mayumi called to her.

Mari shrugged silently. It was her *I guess you got me* pose. "How is Battle Board going?"

Suzune purposely took the effort to get out her terminal and check. (She didn't have to—she had it all memorized.) "Two boys' races ended with neither passing qualifiers, and for the girls, one got through."

"Only one of the boys is left, then…" Mayumi murmured. "I'm sure Mitsui will pull through the qualifiers for the girls… After all, we have Ah-chan over there doing her best."

"We may need to put a little more work into fostering our engineers," said Katsuto with a rather bitter look, viewing the same results on his own terminal.

◇ ◇ ◇

The Speed Shooting quarterfinals would be held on four shooting ranges.

If all eight athletes had come from different schools, the matches would have all been simultaneous. When multiple people from the same school were involved, though, they would change the times so their matches wouldn't overlap. (There would be no intraschool matches in the quarterfinals.)

Still, compared to the semifinals, which would be held on the same range one at a time, the time between each match was short. With three from First High's girls' squad advancing to the quarterfinals, the engineer would end up being very busy.

"...Are you all right, Tatsuya?"

Shizuku, who had been relegated to the final match, gave one look at Tatsuya when he ran into the waiting room (though not technically a "room," since they were in a tent). Somehow, it looked to her like Tatsuya was a little out of breath.

"I'm fine," he answered curtly, starting his final checks on her CAD.

As Shizuku looked on, or rather, stared at him, he quickly scrolled through the tuning device's monitor to make sure there weren't any abnormalities. Finally, he looked back at her.

"I know you know this already, but this one is completely different from the one you used in the qualifiers. We don't have much time left, but if something feels even a little off, I'll do what I can to fix it. So don't hesitate to tell me."

Shizuku took the CAD and positioned her shooting stance. After pressing her finger down on the trigger a few times, she lowered the rifle. "There's nothing wrong. It's so perfect it's scary."

"I see." Tatsuya didn't sigh outwardly, but the tension in his face definitely relaxed. Shizuku gave him a determined look.

"Both of them won."

"Yeah." She was referring to their teammates, who had played in previous matches. Both of them had gotten past the initial qualifiers like Shizuku had, and then had won their way through to the semifinals. "You'll be fine." Tatsuya used the same words, though for a slightly different reason this time. "Do it like you always do, and you'll win."

"Of course." She, too, gave her usual short answer, but with an unusually firm nod of her head. "You've already set everything up for me to win, so now I just have to go do it."

"That's the spirit." He saw her off with a grin, not bothering to correct her somewhat premature declaration of victory.

◇ ◇ ◇

"It's Shizuku's turn now..."

"Come on! Why are you the one getting nervous, Mizuki?"

"Isn't it exciting, Erika?" asked Mizuki, bouncy. "If Shizuku wins, all three of our students will be in the top four!"

"Try not to overheat from all the excitement, okay?" Honoka warned, then declared with full confidence: "Shizuku will win no matter what!"

"Just take a deep breath, Mizuki," teased Miyuki, though the other girl obediently began to do so.

"...I guess this is just me as usual, huh?" Mizuki asked, sheepish.

"...Mizuki, you can be a real joker sometimes," laughed Erika.

With effort, Mizuki finally regained her calm. It was less a result of her deep breathing and more realizing that Miyuki and Honoka weren't worried at all.

"I wonder what kind of trick we'll see this time," whispered

Mikihiko with just a hint of jubilation, prompting Erika to give him an interested look.

The one to actually answer him, though, was Leo. "Me, too. I can't even imagine what'll show up this time!"

"His brain is like a jack-in-the-box!"

"You got that right!"

It had been a long time since Erika had seen Mikihiko so clearly interested in magic. It didn't seem to her that the change was just from him getting to watch other people's matches, though. *Maybe something happened between him and Tatsuya at some point*, Erika thought.

"Huh? What's that…?"

Her thinking was interrupted by a discordant tone from the person she'd been thinking about. "What's wrong?" Erika asked.

"That CAD…"

Mikihiko had his eyes on the CAD Shizuku had slung under her arm, hanging from a strap on one of her kimono's sleeve ties.

At first, the rifle-shaped CAD didn't appear to be much different from the competition devices all the other players were using, save for the strap attached to it. However, the mechanism was quite a bit thicker than the others.

Mikihiko's school didn't see CADs as very important. They still mainly activated spells using amulets. But after the accident last year, he had stuck his nose in modern magic books and hadn't taken it out yet.

He was trying to make up for what he had lost, and the results of his efforts were visible in his regular exam grades. He could now proudly state that he'd become more knowledgeable than most modern magicians regarding CADs.

And if his eyes were correct, then… "Is that…a multipurpose one?"

"Wait, seriously?"

"Huh? But that would be…"

"I've never heard of a multipurpose broom shaped like a rifle! Is it even possible to put a targeting system on one in the first place?"

Leo, Mizuki, and Erika all voiced their obvious doubts in turn.

But Mikihiko, confident in his assessment, shook his head. "The main part of the device, right above the trigger—that has to be the Centaur series, FLT's multipurpose CAD that they put on vehicles. They don't actually have an interface. They connect to an external input device, which is why there's a grip and a targeting system connected to it."

"You have a very sharp eye," said Miyuki with a smirk, turning to him.

"Wait. Then it's..."

"That's right, Erika," Miyuki stated proudly. "My brother made it himself, specifically so that Shizuku could use a targeting system with a multipurpose CAD."

Erika was speechless for a moment. Her own unique-form CAD was made to order. She knew how much work went into something like that.

"I don't even feel like being surprised anymore..." muttered Leo. "But why?"

"For this match, of course," replied Honoka.

Her simple response wasn't nearly enough to answer Leo's question, nor those of the other three. But there was no time to elaborate. At that moment, they all turned back to watch with bated breath, as if they'd practiced the maneuver.

The starting lights began to tick on.

◇ ◇ ◇

Red and white pieces of clay flew through the air.

Shizuku's targets were the red ones.

Three of them arced through the air, gathered together at the center of the scoring area, and broke apart.

"Movement...? No, that's not it. Convergence magic?"

The tents used by the schools as bases of operations were fitted with large multipartitioned monitors showing how each of the events was progressing. Mayumi and Suzune were using almost an entire screen to watch Shizuku's match.

"That's correct."

This time, a red clay pigeon about to fly outside the scoring area found itself being sucked into the center, and then it shattered.

"And that was what she used in the qualifiers, right?"

"Yes. She's continually activating convergence and oscillation magic."

Meanwhile, pairs of the white clay pigeons were colliding with each other and breaking apart.

The strategy Shizuku's opponent from Second High used was fairly orthodox: She cast movement magic on the clay targets themselves, essentially turning them into bullets to ram into other targets. It was orthodox because its effectiveness had been proven many times in the past.

But since the beginning of her opponent's turn, the white targets frequently missed one another when they neared the center of the scoring area. The ones around the edges were mostly hitting, though, so it wasn't a lack of technical experience on the side of the player, but...

"I think I get it. She has a broad view of all the clay pigeons flying through the scoring area. The convergence magic increases the density of the red targets, which makes the white targets bounce away from the center..."

The basic principle behind convergence magic was that it selectively gathered targets with predetermined properties (within an area defined by the magic program), then sent them to coordinates also defined by the magic program. When used on physical objects, it increased the targets' physical density while lowering the physical density of all other objects in the area. This density change gave convergence magic its effect.

The dry-ice bullet spell Mayumi had used earlier contained a convergence formula as well. Hers would gather carbon dioxide at the beginning to acquire enough bullets. In her case, it *wasn't* that once the carbon dioxide was collected in one area it would push away all other gases and create an area with a high density of CO_2; rather, it made the CO_2 flow toward specified coordinates while at the same time making the other gases flow out.

Shizuku's magic was essentially the same, if the carbon dioxide particles happened to be red pieces of clay. Her convergence spell defined a region—in this case, the center of the scoring area—and overwrote the information inside that region with "a space where the red clay pigeons collect." In more concrete terms, the spell altered the approximately sixty-six-foot-square space covering most of the scoring area and made it into a space where the closer to the middle the red clay pigeons got, the higher its density.

The area was a very large one, while the number of clay targets flying into it was low. That lightened the load for the caster, since the alteration target wasn't the space itself but instead the distribution of the targets *within* that space. The red clay pigeons would be pulled toward the center via the information alteration brought about by the magic program, while the white clay pigeons would veer off course if it passed through the middle. The clay pigeons directly under the Second High player's influence weren't subject to this secondary interference, but the targets she was trying to ram them into weren't under the direct control of her magic. Shizuku's magic would change their flight paths, which was why the white shots were missing their marks.

The rules of the Speed Shooting tournament allowed interference like this, so long as it didn't directly affect the opposing player. However, the intervals between the clay pigeons being fired were irregular and very quick. Normally, it was quite difficult to get in the opponent's way while still shooting down your own targets. Many players ended up defeating themselves by not committing to either interference or shooting, but the convergence magic Shizuku was using was both an obstruction for her opponent and a means of destroying her own targets, making it a substantially effective tactic.

There were instances of such tactics in the past, albeit not many, and they'd been shown to be effective. It demanded strong event influence from the player, though, so not everyone could use it. There weren't many opportunities to see it in person, but Mayumi had researched tactics like these thoroughly.

Her doubts, though, weren't about the spell itself but about something else. "But why is the oscillation spell at the end triggering only some of the time?"

When multiple targets gathered, they would go on to collide in the middle and break apart. If there was only one red clay target flying through, Shizuku used an oscillation-type spell to crush it. If this was all included in a single spell, then that final process, where it would destroy the target with oscillation magic, should have been going off all the time, not only some of the time.

"Is it scheduling things so if there's more than one target, it makes them collide before the oscillation spell goes off?" Not even she could believe her own reasoning, and her voice made that obvious. There was no advantage to setting up timings like that.

"President, I believe I said she was continuously activating convergence and oscillation magic," Suzune corrected, with a slightly mean smile.

Immediately after those words were spoken, Mayumi understood. She reflexively cried out, "No way! Specialized CADs can only be loaded with activation sequences of one type!"

"I understand your doubts, but that isn't a specialized type. It's a multipurpose one."

Suzune's answer only caused more confusion. "But that's impossible!" Mayumi replied. "They're completely different, from their OS right down to their architecture. And targeting-aid subsystems are made to fit the architecture of specialized CADs. Isn't it technically impossible to attach one to the frame of a multipurpose CAD?"

Mayumi's tone steadily calmed throughout her talking, but the flush in her cheeks betrayed the fact that her agitation hadn't completely gone away.

Suzune's smile changed as well—into a gentle, mature one, made to calm others down. "That's what I thought as well. But it turns out it *is* possible. This isn't something Shiba came up with; I believe they announced it last year in Germany."

"...Last year? But that would make it brand-new technology!"

"I think you should contain your surprise, President. This isn't much. He told me to keep quiet about this, but Tatsuya has some even more amazing brand-new technology that you'll see later."

"I... Well, if it's a secret, then I'll leave it at that. I guess I'm just a little shocked he'd tell you, Rin, and not me."

"You're one of the players, President. I'm sure he didn't want to cause you any undue stress."

"I suppose you're right... If Tatsuya had told me beforehand that he had a spell like this, it definitely would have stressed me out."

Mayumi sighed and looked back to the corner of the monitor, which showed the remaining time and the players' scores. There wasn't much time left, and victory was all but assured.

◇ ◇ ◇

Thirty seconds left.

During the past two weeks, thanks to endless practice, Shizuku had taught herself to accurately measure the five-minute match time internally.

The moment a red clay pigeon flew into the blue sphere shown in her goggles, she pulled the CAD's trigger.

The target swiftly crumbled.

Using the safety goggles as an aiming device was allowed by the tournament rules. In fact, it was rarer to see a player not using a gimmick like that. (Leaving aside cases like Mayumi, who had her own means of targeting.)

But Shizuku was probably the only one using an HMD, or head-mounted display, to mark off the space in front of her rather than aim at her targets. Or perhaps it would be more accurate to say *Tatsuya* was the only one.

Tatsuya always came up with plans for everything that were completely removed from orthodox know-how. At first, it had bewildered her; but in the end, maybe it was a good thing that she had no prior sports experience, because it hadn't taken her long to get used to it. And once she had, it felt so right to her that she couldn't imagine using any other equipment or spell.

In any case, it was nice and easy. She felt almost none of the stress that came with magic usage.

Shizuku was aware that her lack of precise control was her weakness. Because of that, she had always requested that CAD engineers give her assistance functions so those precise settings could be done smoothly. She wanted a CAD that would let her aim properly and control her power properly, even at the expense of speed. She was confident enough that her own magical processing power would make up for her speed.

But the spell Tatsuya put together had made those precise settings completely unnecessary. It wasn't trying to make up for a weakness; it was simply emphasizing her strengths to the extreme. It maximized her magical throughput, which allowed high-speed continuous casting; and what's more, it maximized her magical *capacity*, which allowed her to build huge magic programs.

And the CAD in her hands...

She was surprised that he'd connected a targeting-assistance system to a multipurpose CAD, but she was even more surprised with the speed at which it processed activation programs. Multipurpose

CADs lost out to specialized ones in terms of processing speed. That was just common sense: It was a structural necessity. The two types differed in hardware, software, and architecture; their differences could be likened to dedicated processors versus normal ones, or super-computers and generalized ones.

Given equivalent units in their cores, multipurpose CADs would never outperform specialized ones in terms of processing speed. The margin was always big enough for humans to tell.

And yet...this CAD was putting out the kind of speed a specialized one would.

Five more seconds.

—A target flew in.

—She pulled the trigger.

—The magic activated.

—The target shattered.

Her processing speed was almost exactly the same as with the specialized type she'd used in the qualifiers. Tatsuya had said it was because he had restricted this CAD to only two types of activation magic—and also that it was only possible for this exact event.

It was a trick nobody could use in everyday life.

Shizuku didn't understand the detailed logic behind it, but she figured she didn't have to. Magic was a tool. CADs were tools. You just had to know how to use them. Everything else could be left up to the experts.

She didn't use the Active Air Mine for the final two shots; instead, she loop-cast the convergence spell to destroy them.

"Perfect," she said, confirming her score with a victorious smile.

◇ ◇ ◇

As the clock struck noon, First High's tent was filled with a giddy air.

"This is remarkable, Tatsuya! Amazing!"

Tatsuya winced a little as a hand slapped his back. As her petite appearance might suggest, Mayumi didn't have the arm strength to hurt him very much. She was persistent, though, which made it annoying.

"…President, please calm down."

After making eye contact with Suzune to signal for help, the young woman quickly remonstrated with Mayumi on his behalf. Ever the helpful upperclassman…but at the same time, she *had* left him out to dry until he asked. Tatsuya was starting to feel like the two were birds of a feather.

"Oh, sorry!" Mayumi immediately stopped hitting him. She was calm enough, at least, to realize she was being overexcited about it. However, she didn't appear to want to let him go just yet. "But it really was amazing! We clinched first, second, and third place!"

"I didn't win the finals and semifinals. It was the players…" Tatsuya insisted weakly.

"Well, yes! Kitayama, Akechi, and Takigawa were amazing, too! You all did so well!"

Rewarded with a broad smile from their student council president, the freshman girls' Speed Shooting team—which was hanging around, too—all thanked her at once, looking nervous but happy.

Though not as excited as Mayumi, Mari threw her own praise into the ring, her own expression cheerful. "Still, you have to admit you did something great, Tatsuya. It really *was* remarkable."

"Right… Well, thank you."

"Don't seem so discouraged!" she insisted. "Everyone here has the same opinion: Our players have all the top spots now, and that speaks volumes for your skill as an engineer."

Shizuku and the others gave firm nods.

"I still can't believe it myself!"

"It's like I suddenly got really good at magic."

Those comments came not from Shizuku but the other two. Shizuku simply nodded along as though this whole thing had been inevitable.

"We're even getting poked by the university. They're saying they might officially record the spell Kitayama used in the Index."

But at this follow-up explanation from Suzune, Mayumi's eyes widened, Mari seemed dumbstruck, and Shizuku froze.

The Index was the short form of *National Magic University's Encyclopedia of Magic and Spell Index*. As its name implied, it was an encyclopedia compiled by the National Magic University, wherein was listed the name of every spell. If they were going to record the spell itself, then that meant the magical establishment recognized it as a new type of spell that could stand on its own, rather than a variation of another spell. *That* was a major goal and honor to magic development researchers everywhere.

However…

"I see. If anyone asks who developed it, give them Kitayama's name, please."

"What?! You can't do that!" Shizuku hastily drew near at Tatsuya's uninterested reply. "You came up with that on your own, Tatsuya!"

"…But they use the first user's name as the developer of new spells all the time, you know," he pleaded tiredly, taking a step away from Shizuku and gesturing with his hands for her to calm down.

"Mm… Being too modest can annoy people, you know," chided Mari, eloquently defusing the tension.

But Tatsuya only shook his head, his reluctance evident. "I'm not being modest."

"Then what *are* you being?" she protested.

"I'd just rather not shame myself by putting my own name as the developer. I can't actually use it."

It was true. If people knew he was the spell's developer, a lot of people would come asking for a demonstration. If he had to say he couldn't use it, and turn them away, people would start to suspect he stole someone else's idea. Tatsuya's evasion wasn't without reason, but…

"…If you can't use it, then how did you make sure it worked?" Mari asked.

It was way outside the realm of logic to build a spell using only theory. If it were possible, though, that would make him a mad scientist ignoring the risks of other people operating it. That would be considered immoral.

"It's not that I can't use it at all. It just takes too much time for me to activate it, so it's more of a practical thing."

Mayumi saw Tatsuya's answers starting to come apart and intervened. "All right, Mari, Tatsuya. This isn't something to be arguing about right now. We just got off to a great start here. Keep at it for the next events, Tatsuya!"

Tatsuya watched as Mayumi smiled and patted his shoulder. He bowed humbly to her.

◇ ◇ ◇

The news of the success of First High's Speed Shooting team was rippling through the other schools, too.

Third High, in particular, had come into the competition this year hoping to wrest victory from the reigning champions. Now, after the unexpected accident in the girls' Battle Board, they were excited. Though the accident was unfortunate, it had given them a chance to get their foot in the door. The results were affecting them more than anyone else.

"Masaki, you're saying First High didn't win because of the players' individual skills?"

Masaki Ichijou, standing in a ring of twenty people—all of Third High's rookie competitors—nodded in response, all eyes on him. "Kitayama, who won the tournament, had amazing magical power. I can understand *her* winning it all. But the other two didn't seem like they were *that* amazing. If this were just about magic power, they wouldn't have been able to take second and third."

"Plus, we have the upper hand in Battle Board for now. I don't think the level of their freshmen this year is especially high."

Third High had entered two boys and two girls into Battle Board; both boys passed the qualifiers, as did one of the girls. As for First High, only one of their three boys made it out, with their only girl doing the same.

"George is right. Our players are no worse than theirs. That means there must be a different reason."

"Ichijou, Kichijouji…what do you think it is?" asked the girl who had lost in the Speed Shooting semifinals to First High students. Masaki and Kichijouji exchanged glances. They were thinking the same thing.

The answer came from Kichijouji. "Their engineer," he stated. "I think the engineer assigned to the girls' Speed Shooting is really good at their job."

"I agree, George. The winner's device… Did you notice it?"

"Yeah…it was a multipurpose type."

Kichijouji's answer sent a shockwave rippling through all the freshmen present.

"But that's… It had a targeting system on it!"

"That's right! I've never heard of a multipurpose device shaped like a rifle!"

"Neither have I," Kichijouji agreed. "I've gone through every manufacturer's catalog I could think of and can't find anything like it."

The simultaneous protests caused Masaki's face to cloud over even more. "…It's not something that's for sale…but people have combined a targeting system with a multipurpose device before."

A dumbfounded voice came from the circle: "Are you serious…?!"

The boy who said it didn't actually doubt Masaki was serious, but Kichijouji knew how to deal with this. "We're serious. It's some new tech they unveiled in Düsseldorf last summer."

"Last summer?! That would make it brand-new!"

"Yeah. I didn't know about it either until I looked it up."

"If you didn't know about it, then there's no way we could have…"

An awkward silence ensued among the circle of freshmen. Shock, unease, doubt…and shards of fear were all present.

"…I'm surprised George knew about it. There's a reason he's the brains of our operation!"

The girl's statement was meant to soften the serious mood…but Kichijouji couldn't go along with it. "Yeah…but the prototype they showed off in Düsseldorf didn't hold up to practical use. It was slow and imprecise. It was really just a proof of concept, to show that you could technically put the two things together."

Kichijouji was still frowning, his face dark. Masaki answered in a bitter tone: "But the device Kitayama from First High used had all the speed and precision of a specialized one, and also the strong point of multipurpose ones: having activation programs from different families. If all this is supposed to show us how good their engineer is…then that engineer is way above high school level. They'd be a monster."

"To hear Masaki say that, it must be really serious…"

"It's not physically possible for one engineer to be on all the events, but…"

"We'll be in for the ride of our lives in any event that person's in charge of. We should go in thinking we have a two- or three-generation handicap with our devices."

Kichijouji's suggestion, followed by Masaki's ominous prediction, invited a gloomy silence among the teammates.

◇ ◇ ◇

Tatsuya, being regarded as something other than human by the main players of a rival school (though not, of course, having any inkling of such mutterings), arrived at the girls' Battle Board course after finishing a slightly late lunch. The fourth through sixth races were scheduled for the afternoon. Honoka would be in the sixth race, so he didn't need to get there this early just to keep his promise.

"Oh, Shiba! Is something wrong?"

Upon seeing Tatsuya with Miyuki and Shizuku in tow, Azusa quirked her head to the side. The motion made him think of a squirrel with a berry in its hands, and in spite of his melancholic attitude, caused his face to soften. He pulled back as he felt his lips about to turn into a smile, and he tried to keep a straight face, but his tension was gone. His lips had already gone too far.

"...Were you just making fun of me in your head?" she asked.

"No, of course not. I was just admiring your concern for others."

"...You *were* making fun of me, weren't you?"

Her squinting glare also looked exactly like a little kid pouting, and Tatsuya had to turn his eyes away to keep himself from laughing.

"...Fine, I don't care," said Azusa after glaring at him for a while and finally sighing—and sort of telling *herself* that, rather than Tatsuya. She probably had to deal with reactions like his on a daily basis. Her posture gave off a weird, semi defeated air.

It was the kind of posture that made him feel guilty about leaving her be. "——I really wasn't thinking poorly of you."

"...Really?"

"Really."

"Really, really?"

"Yes, really."

She looked up at him suspiciously. Because of their height difference, even with her head raised, her eyes were upturned. Tatsuya nodded firmly.

Finally, his uselessly brazen attitude convinced (or perhaps deceived) Azusa, and she smiled again. "All right. I trust you, Shiba."

As soon as she said that and grinned at him, he felt a disturbance next to him. He didn't need to look over to know what it was. In his mind's eye, he could clearly see Miyuki's eyebrow twitching.

Sheesh, he sighed to himself. Now he'd have to cheer her up again tonight. But it wasn't like he particularly hated doing that. Maybe he *did* have a slight mental problem.

——But leaving all that aside…

"Anyway, is something wrong? There's still over two hours until Mitsui's race."

"I was getting uncomfortable, so I got them to let me leave."

Azusa, who had again cocked her head to the side, noticed Miyuki giving her a wry smile from next to Tatsuya.

She sent a questioning glance to the girl. "…My brother pays too much attention," Miyuki stated, implying there was nothing to be done about it.

On his other side, Shizuku offered consolation: "But now they're fired up, so I'm sure it'll be fine…"

"O-oh, I see how it is…"

Azusa was honestly pretty sharp, having figured it out just from that.

Shizuku and the others occupying the top positions had been the target of congratulations during lunch. People were coming around to sing their praises, and not just the staff members. Some of the upper-classmen who were off today and watched it came, too. On the other hand, not many of them mentioned Tatsuya's achievement, and when they did, it was generally only in passing.

And it had put an unusually bright flame of antagonism into the hearts of the *boys'* Speed Shooting team.

That in and of itself was actually desirable, like Shizuku had said. As long as they directed that newfound tenacity and desire for victory in the right direction, it would be a good thing for everyone. But some of them gave him these looks like he'd just killed their parents or something. Tatsuya wanted to tell them to give it a rest already. Of course, if he actually said that, a fight would break out. That was why he'd come to the stadium early: to avoid any pointless trouble.

The Nine School Competition's grounds were built on the south-east area of the National Defense Force's Mount Fuji maneuvering grounds. Though it was only on one area, the Fuji maneuvering grounds were vast, and walking between stadiums was a bit of a hike. But without such a big space, they couldn't set up the Battle Board course or the Monolith Code field.

The Battle Board racecourse was a twisting, two-mile-long, man-made water circuit. There was one course for the boys and one for the girls. Bleachers for the audience had to be constructed there as well, so just putting the course together needed a ton of space.

Out of convenience for those moving around the grounds, the courses were at the edge of the land set aside for the competition (so you could get to where you needed to be without having to go around the giant courses). Because of that, people almost never ran into players from other events nearby, such as the kids playing in Speed Shooting at the moment.

"I could have gone back to our lodging for a bit, but I decided my time would be better used here if there was something to do…"

"Really?!"

Azusa wasn't the one who cried out. All of a sudden, Honoka had burst out from the space set aside for the athletes. She must have overheard them.

"Then, please, can you take a look at my CAD, too?!" she asked.

Recently, Honoka had begun favoring the term *CAD* over *assistance* because of Tatsuya. That aside, the enthusiasm with which Honoka appeared made him want to smile. He fought against the impulse, though, and schooled his face, then gave her a light rebuke.

"Come on, Honoka. You're being rude to Azusa." It would have been natural to take Honoka's attention as showing dissatisfaction with Azusa's skill.

"Oh! Um, I'm sorry!" Honoka apologized hastily.

"Don't worry. I know you didn't mean it that way," said Azusa with a dry grin, shaking her head. Her tone of voice made her sound like an older sister. This time, Tatsuya found it a lot harder to suppress a grin.

* * *

On average, Battle Board races took fifteen minutes. The preparations, however, took over twice that. They had to get out the boards, inspect the raceway, and repair anything magically damaged. With some extra time worked into the schedule on top of that, each race was planned for a one-hour time slot.

The final race would begin at 3:30 PM exactly, and its racers were already at the starting line.

It was hard to settle your nerves with so much waiting time, and it was possible a racer would finish without having displayed their true ability. (In fact, every year, several of the boys and girls in both the main and rookie competitions ended up that way.) But amusing herself in idle conversation with Miyuki and Shizuku seemed to have benefited Honoka. Her concentration seemed to be at a peak as she stood on her board now.

What had really happened was that Miyuki, growing increasingly concerned with how Honoka seemed to cling to her brother, pulled the girl into a pointless conversation to get her away from him. Still, it looked like it had allowed Honoka to get into the right mind-set.

The wet suit that covered every inch of her, from wrist to ankle, along with thick swim shoes, was to protect her body from falls, friction, and impact. But it was also tight fitting on the body, so it made her curves appear more striking than they really were.

On her thigh sat the big outlined letters of an ICHIKO logo. With provocative proportions that one wouldn't think belonged to a high school freshman brought to the forefront by her colorful wet suit, Honoka waited at the starting line, one knee down on the board.

Her CAD covered her forearm. It was wide and thin, the increased surface area allowing for larger control buttons. Tatsuya hadn't done anything to it; he'd turned her request down right off the bat. He *did*, however, take a nominal look at its systems to make sure nothing was broken, but there was nothing amiss. Azusa and Honoka had eventually pressed him for advice, and in the end, he'd given her one thing:

The heavily tinted goggles Honoka wore were something Tatsuya had brought her. The midsummer sun just beginning to set was bright in the west, and enough to be an obstacle when facing it directly. However, most racers preferred not to wear goggles or sunglasses, since they didn't like it when water droplets stuck to the surface and blocked their view.

Azusa felt it could only be disadvantageous to narrow one's view, but Honoka didn't hesitate to put the goggles on.

"...Come to think of it, why did Honoka set up so many light-based activation programs?"

It was rare for an engineer to say anything about activation program types. Tatsuya, who determined everything including the activation program lineup, was an exception. Most engineers just installed the programs the player wanted onto their CAD. Azusa knew from the players' profiles that Honoka excelled in illusion magic that used oscillating light waves, but her frank opinion was that illusion magic had no place in this event.

"The Battle Board rules state no player is to magically interfere with another. They do not, however, prohibit hindering an opponent as a result of interfering with the surface of the water."

"What does that have to do with it...?"

Azusa's question brought a menacing grin to Tatsuya's face—and nothing more.

The sixth qualifier race of the girls' rookie Battle Board competition commenced.

And not a moment later...

Almost the whole audience had to reflexively look away from the course. The surface of the water had sparkled brilliantly, like a camera flash had just gone off.

One of the racers fell into the water. Another one lost her balance and stopped accelerating, while the final one dashed straight out in front.

As though she had predicted the situation—and, in fact, she had been the one to create it in the first place—the racer with the heavily tinted goggles, Honoka, leaped ahead.

Down below, Tatsuya cheered an "all right!" and Azusa looked up at him with a mildly astonished expression.

"…Was this your plan?" asked Miyuki as she took off her sunglasses. Her voice, too, was mildly astonished. (Incidentally, Tatsuya had given the three of them sunglasses before the race started. Miyuki and the others just put them on like he told them to.)

"Well, it's not *technically* against the rules…" Shizuku's voice was somewhat reproachful as well. She probably thought others would say this wasn't in the spirit of fair play.

But if it had been considerably unfair, they would have given the yellow flag. There was no race-suspending flag waving right now, though. And no red flag, of course, which would have suggested disqualification for the rule-breaking player. That meant the tournament committee had accepted Honoka's spell and Tatsuya's tactic as legal.

"…Using an optics spell on the water's surface? I never would have guessed," said Azusa with admiration—she was evidently honest about everything.

"When most people think about interfering with the water's surface, they tend to only think about how to make the water behave differently, like by making waves or whirlpools. But the rules specifically state that you can interfere with other racers by magically interfering with the water's surface. It would probably be too dangerous to boil it or freeze the entire thing, but I think it's very strange that nobody else has tried to use flashing."

Being blinded like that when completely unprepared meant the other racers wouldn't be able to see again right away. The racers, with their scrambled vision, wouldn't be able to go full speed down the meandering course, in spite of its mostly gentle curves…and Honoka had already gained a decisive lead on them.

"…And there we have it."

◇ ◇ ◇

"...I want to know whose plan that was."

Mayumi and the others watching via monitor didn't suffer the same blinding flash thanks to the screen's light adjustment, but it was still enough for them to calmly acknowledge the ingenuity of it, as well as their own surprise. (Though saying they were "calmly surprised" may have been a strange way of putting it.)

The one to answer Mari's mumble and Mayumi's demand was Suzune. "It was Shiba's, why?"

"What?" Mayumi tilted her head to the side, a little confused. "But Tatsuya's not even assigned to this event."

Suzune's reply may have been a little too polite: "Mitsui was the one who suggested the plan. However, Shiba informed me that he was the one who put it together, including the activation program lineup."

The fact that she went out of her way to say "including the activation program lineup" indicated that even Suzune herself thought it was exceptional.

"...It's one thing after another with that kid," Mari huffed, almost reproachful.

"What's wrong? You don't seem to be in a good mood."

Mari didn't answer. Her silence, though, spoke volumes about what she was thinking.

"...Tricks like that are important," remarked Mayumi. "The Old Master said so." From what Mayumi could see, Mari was mad she hadn't thought of such a strategy herself. She prided herself on having a rainbow of techniques at her disposal, so this wasn't funny to her.

"This is a tactic nobody for the past nine years has thought up, so I believe you should simply be impressed."

"...I *am* impressed. Doesn't that get to you, though?"

Suzune's swift comment had forced Mari to reluctantly admit her jealousy. Though, of course, Suzune had only said what she had because Mari was a tolerant enough person to admit her own faults.

"But isn't this a one-time-only thing? What will they do for the tournament?" asked Mayumi, even though it wasn't an answer to Mari's question.

However—

"I don't think you have to worry about that. The man isn't thinking that far ahead."

"You're right. This is just an opening move for the next match."

—Her concerns appeared to be unwarranted.

◇ ◇ ◇

"Hmm… Maybe this wasn't a good thing for Honoka…" Tatsuya muttered to Tatsuya himself as he watched the girl cross the finish line, having maintained her lead from the start. Next to him, Miyuki's features darkened as she looked up at him.

"…What's wrong?" asked Azusa in hushed tones, hesitant to be overheard given how the two of them were acting.

"Oh, no, I mean…" What she got back were short, stammered words of apology, though Tatsuya didn't simply ignore the question. "It seems like she could have won this race by pure speed, so…I was just thinking maybe she didn't need the light flash."

"Oh… Well, the blinding spell let her take the lead at the start, so wouldn't that make your plan a success?" Azusa didn't know what the two of them were getting at, and cocked her head to the side again.

"Standing out like that is going to make the other players wary of her…" Tatsuya said.

"The semifinals have three people in one race," added Miyuki, "so the next one might end up being two-on-one for her."

Azusa finally understood what they were worried about. "What, is that all?" she asked with an indifferent laugh.

"'Is that all'…? I think it's a pretty significant disadvantage." But Miyuki's reservations were met with a cheerful shake of Azusa's head.

"She didn't need to do that. All the other schools are *already* wary of us."

"I see…"

For a moment, Tatsuya mistook her bright declaration for boasting.

—Only for a moment, however.

He wasn't so dull that he didn't realize she meant it as praise for him.

◇ ◇ ◇

"I won! I won, Tatsuya!"

No sooner had she gotten off the course than Honoka ran straight to Tatsuya in her wet suit and announced her victory. She was practically jumping up and down in glee.

"Uh, yeah. I saw. Congratulations."

He felt the eyes of not only his teammates but also the staff members from other schools on him. While giving his congratulations, he put his hands up in a calming gesture.

It had the opposite effect.

Somehow, she had misinterpreted it. She tightly grabbed his proffered hands and gave him a look with moist eyes that looked about to cry. "Thank you so much!"

Miyuki never came to him with such a straight display of emotion. And so he stood there dumbly, his decisive lack of experience in this arena biting him in the rear, as Honoka actually started crying.

"I always choke up at the worst time… I've almost never won any kind of event like this in an athletic festival or meet or anything!"

That was the first he'd heard of this. If that was true, then they had potentially made a huge miscalculation in their initial assumptions for the rookie team.

But as Tatsuya's eyes wandered about, wondering what to do, he suddenly saw Shizuku behind Honoka, waving her hands, palms out, at him. She looked like she was trying to tell him that wasn't true.

With Honoka still holding his hands, Tatsuya looked over to Shizuku, who began moving her lips silently. *When she was in elementary school*, they read.

Oh, so she's talking about elementary school... Tatsuya sighed.

"It's all thanks to you I got through the qualifiers!"

It wasn't as though she was trying to lie to him, but...this was a bit much for a mental hang-up, in his opinion. He decided not to bring up the fact that Miyuki was staring icicles at him (though the projectiles she was flinging were much sharper than most icicles).

It took a little while before he could get Honoka calmed down again.

◇ ◇ ◇

Whether in physical competitions or board games, victory is uncertain without drive.

Magic competitions were the same. Watching a teammate perform and getting hyped up to go out there and do your best is a basic psychological system. Victory is a silver bullet for raising morale. However, sometimes drive gives way to excitement, and excitement is directly linked to a loss of direction. An example of this now lay before the girls' eyes.

"Morisaki finished in second..." Mayumi said, her disappointment implicit.

"...but the other two didn't make it out of qualifiers," Mari finished, her disappointment explicit.

The first day of the rookie competition had ended, and the senior officers of First High were gathered in the meeting room. Everyone gave a collective sigh at the boys' Speed Shooting rankings.

"The boys' and girls' results basically canceled each other out..."

"That isn't quite true," said Suzune, nullifying Mayumi's timid remark. She gave her calm analysis. "Third High got first place and fourth place, so the girls still built up a lead for us. And I don't think negativity is appropriate." Still, her explanation wasn't enough to wipe away the air of stagnation from the room.

"...You're right. We can't let ourselves be pessimistic. The girls did better than we expected them to. For today, let's just be content with taking the lead."

Mari sounded like she was trying to convince herself, but Katsuto disagreed, his face grim. "Shooting wasn't the only thing the boys did poorly in. Two of our girls made it out of the surfing qualifiers, and only one of the boys."

"If their slump drags on, we may have trouble next year even if we're all right this year."

"You mean they'll make a habit of losing?"

"It's possible."

Katsuto's remark made both Mari and Mayumi fall silent, their faces hard.

The First High officers, aware their institution topped the magic high schools, were tasked with winning every time. They couldn't content themselves with idleness, with just making sure this year went well.

"We may need to give the boys some extra support," remarked Katsuto gravely.

"But what can we even do at this point, Juumonji?" objected Mari.

As she said, it was a little too late. The rookie competition had already started. They couldn't change out any players or staff members.

Though she urged him for an answer with her eyes, he gave no objection in return. However, when she looked at him, it didn't seem like he was out of answers. It seemed more like he had his own plans and was opting to keep silent for now.

◇ ◇ ◇

At long last, tomorrow—actually, at this point, *today*—would be Miyuki's debut.

Since the incident with Mari, there had been no instances of sabotage related to the criminal organization Kazama had warned him about, but Tatsuya couldn't let his guard down. If his guess was correct, the "enemy" would plant their trap directly before the events. He considered the possibility of nighttime sabotage to be low, but there was no harm in staying on his toes. He was up against highly skilled people with plans unknown to him.

He put a tight lock on the systems of the CAD he'd just finished performing final adjustments on. After putting it back into the vault and setting three more locks, he finally left the work truck behind him.

There was nobody around. He couldn't feel anyone, human or not.

The enemy probably wouldn't expect this much caution from him. Kazama and his subordinates, the very best of the Independent Magic Battalion, were working with him in the background. Even if the enemy had schemes in mind, he suspected he himself wouldn't be the target of a direct attack.

Tatsuya didn't wander around idly, however; he went straight back to the hotel's side entrance (after a biometrics scan, of course) and to his own room.

Though, as he stood before his door, he noticed something: His only roommates were lifeless machines. So as he stood there in the hallway, this late at night, the long hand on the clock having made more than a full circuit after the previous day's change, he shouldn't have felt anything from inside—but he did. And yet, he didn't hesitate to unlock his door and enter anyway.

"Do you have any idea what time it is?"

Unlike one might expect, the first harsh scolding came from Tatsuya.

Unlike usual, the thing inside his room couldn't be laughed off.

And even more unusual still, the one on the receiving end of the tongue-lashing felt the same way.

Her shoulders jerked as she quickly rose from her sitting position on the bed. Slowly, timidly, she looked up at his face.

"If you don't get enough sleep, you won't be able to concentrate tomorrow. An unexpected mistake could still make you lose," he reprimanded.

"I'm very sorry!"

Tatsuya's face indicated his seriousness, and Miyuki burst out with an apology and a bow, sounding ready to cry. Hearing and seeing her this way, it was impossible for Tatsuya to keep up his disciplinarian streak.

"...It's fine as long as you understand. Come on, I'll bring you back to your room, all right?"

Perhaps emboldened by his change of tone, Miyuki looked up, resistance in her eyes.

"Miyuki?"

"Tatsuya, just... Do you just have a little time to spare?"

"...Just a little."

Being stubborn with her would be a waste of time. Tatsuya knew this from experience, so he prompted her to continue with a half-hearted affirmation.

"I heard from Shizuku. You refused the honor of having your name in the Index."

"Well, not officially."

"But if they officially asked you, you'd still turn them down."

"Yeah," agreed Tatsuya curtly. Miyuki gritted her teeth. She stood there for a few moments, contemplating something.

"...Is it in consideration for our aunt?"

"Yeah."

A terse and immediate response. Miyuki looked down, trying to stifle tears.

"The National Magic University is extremely effective in its investigations. Mass media runs gossip sites under the guise of news sites, but the university is entirely different. Their investigative levels rival the military's secret service. Developers of new magic use the university's data, and they receive special privileges for it. That's why they all get thoroughly investigated. They want to eliminate the possibility that they're spies from enemy nations or terrorist groups. It's nothing like the examination for entering high school. Silver is one thing the Yotsuba are meticulously blocking information on, but it's pretty likely me using the name Tatsuya Shiba would reveal my connection to the family."

His voice was a little too cold to serve as consolation for his almost-crying sister, but he explained his reasoning nonetheless. He couldn't compromise on this, even if it meant making her cry. At the same time, though, he needed to say it to convince himself.

Miyuki kept her head down and remained silent.

Tatsuya felt a mite of relief at not hearing any sobs. "And, I mean, just being in the Nine School Competition carries the risk of them finding out about me, but being named in the Encyclopedia of Magic and taking part in a high school event are completely different. The Yotsubas' guardian must remain in the shadows. Do you think our aunt would approve of a social outcast being in the limelight?"

Miyuki didn't say anything. She couldn't give him any peace of mind, either. That was her answer to his question.

"I don't have enough strength yet. Someday, one-on-one, defeating Maya Yotsuba, the Queen of the Night, is likely possible. My 'dismantling' has a good affinity with her 'night,' after all. But even if I managed to defeat our aunt now, I couldn't overturn the entire Yotsuba family. Military force and violence aren't enough. Even if we drive our aunt out, someone else with worse plans of manipulation will show up. We have no choice but to obey her for now."

His words were less to convince his sister and more to convince himself. And after he finished persuading himself of that fact…

Miyuki embraced him.

She buried her near-crying face in his chest; *cling* would have been the word to use for the situation.

"...I'm on your side."

"Miyuki..."

"I'll always be on your side, Tatsuya. The time will come one day. I know it will. Until then, and even after that, I'll always be on your side."

"..."

Judging by the hands on the clock, they had spent much more than "just a little" time.

But he decided, wrapping his hands around Miyuki's back...to let her do as she wanted for just a little bit longer.

[9]

It was morning. The fifth day of the Nine School Competition had begun, and it was to be the second day of the rookie competition. This morning, Tatsuya stood before the Ice Pillars Break stadium, where the freshman event would soon be held.

Vehicles specialized for field operations were busy using their giant mechanical arms to set up three-by-six-by-three-foot pillars of ice at regular intervals. Up close, it made him think that the mecha anime of ages past weren't too far away from becoming reality.

"...If you ignore how inefficient they'd be, anyway."

"Tatsuya, is something the matter?"

"Nothing, never mind." He hadn't realized the words had actually come out of his mouth, but his response garnered no further questions. "Why don't we get going?"

"All right."

They had stopped there for only a moment on their way to a match. After urging Miyuki onward, the siblings headed for the waiting room, which sat at the base of one of the scaffolds.

◇ ◇ ◇

Thirty minutes still remained before the first match of the day's events. Tatsuya made it to the stadium with plenty of time to spare.

"Good morning!"

Or at least, he thought he had—until he saw the athlete for the first match already present.

"Good morning… Sorry for making you wait."

"No, no!" insisted their first girls' Ice Pillars Break player, Eimi Akechi, with a smile and a shake of her head. She brushed her brilliant ruby hair out of her face with one hand. "I got here too early, that's all."

"Good morning, Amy. Any particular reason you're here so early?"

"Good morning, Miyuki. I woke up before my alarm went off. I think I'm still excited from yesterday."

Her other name was Amelia Goldie. Her full name was Amelia Eimi Akechi Goldie. She was a quarter English, and her nickname "Amy" actually came from the English name "Amelia," not her Japanese name "Eimi."

A magician's abilities varied greatly depending on genetic disposition. And because magic was tightly linked to national power, countries sheltered and cordoned off all those with magical blood and prohibited them, whether officially or unofficially, from marrying across borders. (For this nation, which advocated freedom of matrimony on the surface, the prohibition was "unofficial.")

Their grandparents' generation, though, wanted to "cross-breed" their "superior blood" to "develop" better magicians. In those days, international marriages of magicians with allied nations were encouraged. As a result, magic high schools had a higher proportion of enrolled students with Western or Indian blood than the national high school average. Leo was one example, and this female student named Eimi Akechi was another.

As one might imply from her statement, she had participated in yesterday's Speed Shooting, as well; this was the second day she'd be with Tatsuya. Aside from Miyuki, Honoka, and Shizuku, Eimi had been the first one of the girls' team to warm up to Tatsuya. Even he found her a cheerful, easy person to talk to.

As the two girls quickly began to make conversation, Tatsuya deftly removed a CAD from the case he'd brought. After giving it a once-over, he handed it to Eimi.

The unrefined, twenty-inch-long, shotgun-shaped specialized CAD was a poor match for her. Even though most of its materials had been made lighter than its real-life counterpart so she wouldn't have to worry about recoil, it still looked heavier than a basic handgun CAD.

Eimi twirled it around like a cowboy and swiftly leveled it, aiming out the window.

"...Amy, you're secretly American, aren't you? Not English?"

"Not you, too, Miyuki! I keep telling people I'm not American," she complained, though in a good-humored way. "My grandma comes from a family where every male since the Tudor dynasty had the right to be called *Lord*!"

Still in her pose, she fueled the CAD with psions. Tatsuya didn't see her release the safety; it had been a very swift and precise CAD motion. Brilliant, even, though in a different way from Morisaki's quick draw.

"How is it?"

"Hmm... Let's just say I totally know how Shizuku feels."

It seemed everyone on the freshman girls' team knew about the offers of employment from the heiress to the mega-rich Kitayama family. "No issues?" he asked quickly.

"None, it's perfect!" she replied with a grin, letting the gun down.

Aside from her ruby hair and moss-colored eyes, Eimi's appearance gave the impression of Japanese lineage. Still, she looked young for her age, and her innocent grin only made her face seem more youthful. "She doesn't realize it, huh...?" he muttered.

Eimi tilted her head in confusion. She kept smiling, though, mainly because she didn't know what he'd actually said about her.

"I-I'm going to adjust it a bit. Could you put on this headset for me?"

"Huh? Why?"

"Amy...it's not that you got up early, but that you couldn't sleep well last night, isn't it?"

Even Eimi couldn't keep smiling at *that* unexpected deduction. "...You could tell?"

Tatsuya nodded silently at her widened eyes before taking the CAD from her hands and placing it on the tuning machine.

"...I think you're even sharper than my parents," said Eimi in a resigned voice as she obediently put the measuring headset on and placed both hands on the sensor pad.

As the measured values scrolled by on the display, Tatsuya's expression grew distinctly grimmer. To Miyuki, it looked like Eimi was making herself smaller and smaller as Tatsuya's face changed.

"Umm, Tatsuya?" His sister didn't ask anything specific, but he suddenly brought his face up, forced a smile, and began to massage his temples.

"Amy, by any chance are you a person who doesn't use a sound-sleeper?"

"Wait, you too?" she asked him.

Tatsuya nodded, his expression now considerably softer.

"Wow. A buddy! Yeah, doesn't it just creep you out? With all those weird waves and stuff?"

"They've proven it has no adverse effects on health, but...I agree, they don't feel good. But if I *really* can't get to sleep for some reason, it's a different story. Especially if I had, say, a match the next day..."

"Okaaay, I get it," Eimi moaned good-naturedly, not unlike what might be elicited from a parental reprimand.

Tatsuya couldn't help but quirk a wry smile. "I'll up the feedback a little for you... It might feel a bit strong, but you'll have to deal with it. You don't want to lose because you didn't get enough sleep, do you?"

"Please and thank you! I'll deal with it! If I lose, I'll just end up being everyone else's plaything!"

The remark itself didn't mean much, but she blushed and placed her hands in odd spots on her riding pants. Tatsuya found himself completely motionless for a second.

"Not that I'm doubting you, Miyuki, but…what were you two doing in your room?"

"It-it's not like that at all!" his sister protested. "Tatsuya, I've done nothing to feel guilty about!"

"I get it… Your room is a safe zone, huh?"

"Amy! Stop giving my brother weird ideas!"

An uncomfortable silence settled on the room. *This is going to require a very sudden change in topic*, he thought to himself, though he was unsure just exactly for whose sake that excuse needed to be delivered. "…Thankfully, this is the first match of the morning. Once it's over, take a nap until your second one. Miyuki, sorry to bother you, but could you go get a capsule ready?"

"Yes, Tatsuya. I'll be back soon."

After sending Miyuki out to go through the process of borrowing a sensory-deprivation capsule (a closed bed that completely blocks sound, vibration, and light), Tatsuya started on the more delicate CAD adjustments.

◇ ◇ ◇

Eimi looked a little tired during the first match but managed to win with three of her own pillars left at the end. The backlash from playing the match while exhausted let her fall into a sound sleep without time to even grumble about how dark or cramped it was.

Now Tatsuya stood in the waiting room. The fifth match—the second one for the First High girls—was about to begin.

I feel like I've said something awfully similar to this not too long ago, he thought. But he couldn't resist asking anyway: "Shizuku…are you really going out in that?"

"Yes, why?" she said, her eyes clearly wondering if something about her outfit was amiss.

Tatsuya felt a headache coming on.

In Ice Pillars Break, you had to protect the twelve ice pillars standing on your forty-square-foot half of the field from a scaffolding that stood thirteen-feet high, while trying to knock over or destroy the pillars in your opponent's field. The players would use only pure long-distance magic. None of them would need to use their bodies.

Consequently, the clothing a player chose to wear for the event didn't matter at all. (Excepting clothing that would get in the way of using a CAD.) There was only one rule for how to dress: abide by public decency. As a result—and, though he didn't want to think about it this way, *inevitably*—the girls' Ice Pillars Break event had long since turned into a fashion show.

When Kanon was playing on the second and third day of the main competition, she was in sports gear that wasn't very different from regular clothing: short leggings, a dress-like shirt that covered them entirely, socks that went up to her thighs, and sneakers. Eimi had gone with a horse-riding style: a red riding jacket with a white high-necked shirt, slim white culottes, tall black boots, and a horse-riding cap that was also black.

But those were both costumes that showed up a lot, and they weren't particularly flashy. Shizuku's clothing, on the other hand...

"Hey, Shizuku..."

"What?"

"That *furisode*...isn't going to get in the way, is it?"

Yes, she was wearing a *furisode*—a long-sleeved kimono for eligible young women.

"I'll be fine. The sleeves are on the short side, and I'm tying them back," said Shizuku.

Tatsuya watched as she deftly used the cords on her *furisode* to tuck back the sleeves. The fluidity in her movements made it obvious she was used to wearing Japanese clothing. Still, he found himself having to make a mental retort. If she needed to tie her sleeves back, why did she bother wearing a *furisode* in the first place?

Without having much time before the match, Tatsuya gave up on persuasion before he began. Plus, if Shizuku had told him that this was how she dressed to get into the spirit of the match, then he would have been forced to withdraw his argument anyway.

Shizuku's chosen CAD—or rather, the one Tatsuya was making her use—was a multipurpose type. It would let her adopt tactics to balance her energy between offense and defense.

Even Tatsuya didn't use tricks and schemes every single time; in fact, he was unaware that the term *trick* would be applied to what he'd been doing in the first place. His job was purely to give the player the most suitable tools, while supplying a strategy that made full use of those tools. If a frontal attack was the most effective, then he'd use a frontal attack. And that was the case here.

When Shizuku appeared on the stage, the crowd stirred in response to her striking appearance.

She ignored it all with a nonchalant look, though, and raised her left arm in front of her, now exposed under the sleeve.

Her CAD was the same type she usually used: one with the console facing her from the inside of her arm. Though outward-facing consoles were more popular among female magicians, preferring to use the more "feminine" inward-facing ones could only be called an act befitting a proper lady. In this case, though, it did feel strange to see Shizuku with it, given her normal terseness, impassive expressions, and occasional merciless comments.

Such thoughts would have made her punch him without a word if she heard them. Relegating them to a corner of his mind, Tatsuya, like the others there, brought his monitor into focus.

From this moment on…

…it was Shizuku's job to focus on the field.

And it was Tatsuya's job to focus on her.

◇ ◇ ◇

"Miyuki…you're not staying with Tatsuya?" asked Honoka, who was sitting next to Miyuki, before the match. Miyuki was waiting, not in the grandstand, but in the seating reserved for players and staff.

She had left Tatsuya right before he went into the monitoring room for Eimi's first match. The two girls both played for the same school, so it would have been fine for her to cheer on her classmate from the monitor room as well, but…

"Ice Pillars Break is an individual sport. Shizuku and I will eventually face each other, so it would be unfair to steal a look at what she has in store, wouldn't it?"

Still, she would have had ample opportunity to see what Shizuku had in store during practice, since even First High didn't have more than one facility with which to practice for the event. But what Miyuki was really trying to say was something else: It was probably consideration for Tatsuya; she didn't want to distract him from supporting a player she would eventually face.

Shizuku, too, was probably offering her own considerations so that she wouldn't distract him, either. Honoka and Shizuku had been good friends and rivals since elementary school. Up until the end of middle school, Shizuku had been Honoka's most worthy opponent, and vice versa. None of the children in their community could stand shoulder to shoulder with them in magic talent. Upon entering high school and beginning their studies of magic in earnest, Honoka and Shizuku had both hoped to gain rivals aside from each other to encourage, in order to compete with them and improve.

At the same time, though, a thought always nagged at a corner of the two girls' minds: that they wouldn't meet anyone more talented than them. There were no other Ten Master Clans children in their school or cram schools, though they did meet youngsters of the Hundred Families, the Numbers. But even among them, there were no classmates they could call worthy opponents.

But they found their conceit utterly destroyed during the high school entrance exams.

It was done by this girl next to them—this girl who was simply too beautiful.

Honoka's practical grades on their regular exams ranked fourth behind Miyuki, Shizuku, and Morisaki, but, leaving Shizuku aside, Honoka didn't feel like she was any worse than Morisaki. The theme for their first exam had been simple ten-process spells. (Though calling a ten-process spell "simple" was something only Honoka's high level of talent allowed her to do.) Because of the lack of processing load, she had only lost to Morisaki because of his pure speed. Performing with more processes and more complex spells, Honoka believed she was clearly better than him.

But Miyuki was on another level. Her raw talent and actual skills were *both* so overwhelming that even feeling jealous of them seemed asinine. Honoka would have been able to accept it if she was directly related to one of the Ten Master Clans. In fact, that would be the obvious reason.

—At least, that's what Honoka had thought when she had first seen Miyuki in the enrollment testing room.

She'd unknowingly arrived at that conclusion because of just how shocking and overpowering Miyuki's magic was. For the four months after school started, that feeling didn't wane at all—in fact, it was getting stronger, more obvious. Honoka didn't think even Shizuku—despite her doing everything at her own impressive pace—could use regular magic if she felt Miyuki was nearby. After all, Miyuki was so good that when she'd been moved from the rookies' Mirage Bat to the main event because of her skill level, Honoka had sighed with relief in spite of herself, simply because they wouldn't be competing against each other.

After recalling the entrance exams, Honoka's thoughts naturally turned to the first time she had seen *him*.

The first time she'd noticed *him* actually hadn't been during that spat on orientation day. True, Tatsuya had saved her when the disciplinary committee chairwoman was about to grab her for using a magical attack against Erika and the others (which was against school regulations), but she'd actually met him once before that. On the day of the entrance exams, on top of the issue that was Miyuki, Tatsuya had coincidentally been in the same group as them.

Outwardly, the siblings didn't look much alike, and Honoka didn't have the free time to memorize everyone's name. So when she had first laid eyes on him, she hadn't seen him as Miyuki's brother. His practical exam results had been average. His speed, power, and scope were altogether not noteworthy—average, or even below average.

But his magic had been *beautiful*.

Honoka couldn't analyze magic programs like Tatsuya could. Nor did she possess specialized senses to detect psions or pushions like Mizuki did. Honoka was simply good at light wave–oscillation magic, which made her more sensitive than most other magicians to the noise created by light waves as a side effect of magic usage. Excess interference and pointless parts of magic programs caused the air to vibrate, and the photons in the air would react to that and give off a kind of noise like the fuzz in a garbled video.

She sensed absolutely none of that noise from his magic. That meant his magic programs were perfectly put together—and that he used every ounce of the magic power for the event alteration. His magic was delicate, born from the utmost calculation.

Honoka considered it beautiful. She'd never seen magic she felt was so mesmerizing before. And even though Miyuki's magic was so overwhelming, she couldn't forget his.

So when she saw Tatsuya without the eight-petal emblem on his left breast on that orientation day, she felt like she'd been betrayed. That was the reason she'd felt such unwarranted hostility toward him and his group.

—Why is he with them?!

—Why isn't he with us?!

*   *   *

Honoka had been seized with irrational anger.

It was true that his speed, power, and scope were pretty far below the passing line, for Course 1 students at least. But she had felt like he, able to construct such beautiful magic, had committed an unforgivable betrayal by being content as a substitute, as a Weed.

"...Honoka, what's wrong?"

She snapped out of it and looked over. Miyuki was peering at her, confused—and questioning. She must have thought it odd that Honoka had become preoccupied with her own thoughts in the middle of their conversation.

"I, um, sorry! Nothing's wrong."

If someone did that to her, she'd be suspicious, too. Her face flushed and she looked down for three reasons: what she'd just done, her unwarranted anger at the time, and how her anger had come from how much *he'd* been on her mind.

◇ ◇ ◇

"It's finally Kitayama's turn…"

"It looks like she's using a normal CAD this time."

After seeing the two female officers silently sitting in front of the main screen as if holding a meeting, Suzune, currently tasked with compiling the competition results coming in one after another from different events, sighed. But even that purposely-conspicuous demonstration of discontent did nothing to affect them.

"I wonder what kind of clever scheme we'll get to see this time."

"Who knows? Maybe he planned a straight fight just because he knew we'd be waiting for something."

Mayumi and Mari continued to stare at the big screen featuring the Ice Pillars Break stadium, like little kids clustering around their favorite TV show.

Suzune gave up, sighed again, and went back to her work, still with nobody to help her.

Neither Mayumi nor Mari batted an eyelash at Shizuku's clothing. This was their third time at the Nine School Competition, so her *furisode* wasn't all that striking. In fact, they were just a little surprised they'd seen so few of the long-sleeved kimonos this year so far. Well, that was probably the reason Shizuku had chosen it—so she wouldn't feel particularly embarrassed. She came to see the competition every year, so she was familiar with the attire.

"Oh, oh! It's starting!"

The two of them leaned in closer to the screen.

◇ ◇ ◇

On the poles standing on either side of the field, red lights blinked on. They changed color to yellow, and then to blue, and then a moment later...

Shizuku's fingers danced across her console.

On her half of the field were twelve pillars of ice. She targeted them all and projected a magic program on to them.

A split second later, her opponent's magic program came crashing into her field.

Using movement magic to topple the enemy's pillars was a popular tactic. Unfortunately, her opponent's spell couldn't even budge Shizuku's pillars.

◇ ◇ ◇

"Oh, so it's Information Boosting, is it?"

The screen in each school's main tent had an option to analyze activated spells. It displayed their types and strengths in color, much like a thermal image. The function told them, in detail, what the battle was like at any given moment.

Information Boost was an anti-magic technique that suppressed the variability of information bodies in an existing state by taking some or all of their eidos and copying it into a magic program. After those properties were copied, the program could prevent any magic-based alterations that would affect those properties.

The screen was now showing how the movement spell the enemy player used had been nullified by Shizuku's magic, which strengthened her pillars' positional information: in other words, the property of the ice pillars "being in that spot."

"I have to say, this is a pretty simple tactic."

"I guess you were right after all, Mari."

Suzune, listening to them, muttered, "It isn't like he was trying to think of plans just to outwit you two," but they were both too engrossed in the match to hear her.

"Of course, for a magician with as strong magical influence as Kitayama, the simplest tactic would be to use Area Interference, not Information Boost."

"As far as I could tell from yesterday, she has very high capacity, too. Copying eidos wouldn't bother her. And since she wants to block a specific type of spell like this, Information Boost is more effective."

On the screen, the player from the opposing school used a movement spell again, but it was nullified just like the first.

And in that one moment when the attacking magic misfired...

...three of the opponent's ice pillars broke apart in a row.

"...What was that? Mayumi, did you see what it was?" asked Mari, dubious.

Mayumi looked at her, seeming a little unsure of herself. "I can only guess from this side of the screen, but..." Though the analysis images were being done almost in real time, being there and feeling the magic directly was completely different. "I think it was an application of Resonance Disruption."

When magic was applied to a target indirectly, no magical effects would appear on it. She needed to deduce the spell that had been used from the surrounding images.

"I think she used an oscillation spell on the ground in the enemy's field that continuously changed wave frequencies. Then, when the spell created sound resonance with a pillar, it stabilized the frequency, and then amped up the power to create a state of physical resonance."

"I get it... She used the ground as a medium to indirectly get to the other player's pillars, avoiding any anti-magic. Kanon's Mine Origin forces it, but this spell is more technically sophisticated. I can't tell which of them is the upperclassman!"

"It takes time to find the points of resonance, which is probably why she stalled with Information Boost. I wonder if frequency manipulation is her thing."

"Yeah."

They were both remembering Tatsuya's typeless magic, with which he'd defeated Hattori by scrupulously controlling psi-wave frequencies and creating constructive interference. Neither of them had a doubt that the technique displayed on the screen was more a Tatsuya-esque arrangement than a personal technique of Shizuku's.

◇ ◇ ◇

That's Shizuku for you. She's using it perfectly.

Tatsuya nodded to himself, keeping watch on his athlete via monitor.

The enemy player was already down to four pillars. All twelve of Shizuku's were still there. Her biorhythm curve displayed on the monitor showed only light fatigue; it was holding steady at a level that wouldn't affect her magic usage at all. There were absolutely no signs of her condition dropping like Eimi's had, due to Eimi's lack of sleep. And so Shizuku was executing both Information Boost and Resonance Disruption just as smoothly as expected, if not more so.

In the end, Mayumi and Mari's conjecture had been half-right but half-wrong: Resonance Disruption was a spell Shizuku's mother specialized in. For a high school student, she was able to use it at a very high level of proficiency even before she teamed up with Tatsuya.

However, the original Resonance Disruption was a two-stage spell. First, it continuously increased the frequency of the target objects directly. Then, at the moment the frequencies of target and spell matched—which was when the target would have the least resistance to an event alteration trying to make it oscillate—the spell stabilized the frequency and basically vibrated the targets to death.

When directly casting the oscillation spell on a target, the caster could locate the points of sound resonance by feel, thanks to the eidos resisting the magic program's influence. However, when applied *indirectly* like this, the caster would have to estimate whether or not the resonance was happening on the target by other means.

Tatsuya was the one who put together the activation sequence to do that as a magical process rather than having to rely on a measurement device.

Shizuku was using this Resonance Disruption derivative spell, which added a new process to a spell she was already familiar with, wonderfully well. She displayed a level of mastery that spoke to the fact that she'd practiced quite a bit on her own, outside of the school's practice hours.

As the next enemy ice pillar crumbled, one of her own was knocked down.

It was very clear to Tatsuya, though, that it was her opponent's final shot at getting *something* done.

Her opponent fueled that attack with all the magic power at her disposal. She'd probably acknowledged that she would inevitably lose, and tried to, at the very least, avoid a complete shutout.

He turned away from the screen and gazed upon Shizuku's distant back with his own eyes.

Her psi-wave flow was absolutely stable.

She showed no sign of excitement or eagerness as she continued defending her pillars and attacking the enemy's.

She probably hadn't gone into this with the greedy goal of a perfect victory, so the way she was fighting gave him peace of mind.

And right after Shizuku's opponent launched her final, full-power attack, unable to put up any sort of meaningful resistance...

...the girl's last three ice pillars crumbled to the ground, like fragile towers of sand.

◇ ◇ ◇

Miyuki's match was the last one of the first round. It was a long waiting time from morning's start, but part of it was set aside for lunch, so she probably wouldn't feel like much time had gone by. This was Tatsuya's third match since the beginning of the day, though, so he had no time to wait.

Miyuki and Tatsuya were in the players' waiting room now. Honoka and Shizuku were nowhere in sight. They said at lunch that they'd cheer for her from the grandstand, so they'd likely already met up with Erika and the others by now.

As not-exactly replacements, Isori and Kanon, and even Mayumi and Mari, had come to root the siblings on.

This is a big group for it, though... he thought to himself, sighing a little. However, he chose to say something different, of course. "I'm happy you came to support us...but shouldn't you be sleeping, Chairwoman?"

The sabotage accident during the Battle Board semifinals that had led to Mari sustaining wounds that would take a full week to heal had happened only three days ago. Although the magical healing had been effective and she could go about her normal life as long as she wasn't reckless, it was clear that resting in bed would have been the better option.

"I keep telling everyone it's not serious. It's not like I'll be jumping or prancing around. What's the problem?"

"I suppose..." he said, thinking she pretty much *did* have a serious injury. Instead, he turned to speak to Mayumi. "Is it all right for you to be away from the main tent, President? Weren't the boys playing their matches, too?"

"They'll be fine. I left that to Hanzou. I'm retiring the month after next, anyway, so I can't be doing *everything* by myself."

Her reasoning was correct, but her motives, on the other hand... Still, she wouldn't be getting in the way of the event, so further questions would do him no good.

"Miyuki, we have a good cheering team, but don't let that make you too nervous."

He heard a snort of amusement but chose to ignore it. The others probably thought him overprotective, but his sister would (and should) always be his sister.

"I'll be fine," she replied. "You're with me, aren't you?"

Plus, as she looked up at him, her eyes filled with wholehearted trust, such noises would never have affected her anyway.

◇ ◇ ◇

When Miyuki got on stage, the audience stirred mightily.

"Well, it *is* pretty surprising..."

"But it looks good on her. Don't you think so, Kanon?"

"I mean, it *is* surprising how good it looks."

As Tatsuya listened to Kanon and Isori's conversation in the background, he continued making sure their screen was in order. He finished setting it up in the blink of an eye, then looked at Miyuki, suddenly wondering what was so surprising.

She had on a white, unlined, kimono-style shirt and scarlet women's *hakama*. She wore her long hair tied back in a white ribbon,

Yes—strictly speaking, her hairstyle wasn't quite right, but it was the exact outfit for which one might expect her to be holding an evergreen branch or a bell instead of a CAD. Her beauty was already more than anyone could imagine, but now with the clothing, she exuded a sublime air. Though, truly, it was beyond sublime—the adjective *divine* wouldn't have been an overstatement.

"That poor girl on the other side. I think she's overwhelmed now."

"She probably can't help it. Even I might have gotten a little nervous if I were in her shoes... Or was that the whole point?"

The voices of Mayumi and Mari he heard from behind him had definitely been meant for him, so he turned himself around and answered them.

Still, his reply took the form of another question. They weren't on the same page. "The 'point'?" repeated Tatsuya. "I don't believe her clothing is too unusual for magic rituals."

"...Tatsuya, is your family Shinto?"

The one who asked seemed to be more confused than him. Mayumi's question was asked with hesitation, while Tatsuya shook his head without any. "I wouldn't say that, but we're still certainly Japanese."

"That's certainly...true..."

After seeing Mayumi stammer and nod, Tatsuya turned to face the screen console again, effectively putting an end to the conversation.

Tatsuya's excuse made enough sense that they found it hard to object to on base principle. Still, if anyone else had seen everything that had taken place today, they would have doubtlessly noted a contradiction in his attitude.

He had been so resistant to Shizuku's *furisode* despite it being Japanese clothing. But now he had no misgivings whatsoever about his little sister's shrine maiden getup. Something was definitely strange about his sensitivities.

◇ ◇ ◇

Miyuki, who hadn't a thought in her mind regarding such skits playing out backstage (of course), waited for the match to start with a calm mind.

False starts were a major rule violation. She was well aware of her bad habit of triggering magic unconsciously when she got too into things. For her, the time she spent waiting before the match had to be used to keep herself in check, not to rally herself against the other player.

...Of course, that gave her an outward appearance of total tranquility.

Red lights shone on the poles on either side of the field. Miyuki opened her eyes and set them on the enemy field directly ahead.

A sigh came from the audience. Not just from one part, either, but from various places—no, the entire grandstand. Surprisingly, the young girls—more so than the boys—looked entranced by the strong light in Miyuki's eyes. The stadium was no longer here to see a match. Unfortunately for the other player, the crowd's eyes were glued to each and every movement Miyuki made.

The lights changed to yellow, and then the very moment they changed to green...

...an intense psionic light spread to cover both fields: her own and the enemy's.

And then—the field separated into two different seasons.

Miyuki's side, covered in intense cold.

The enemy's side, covered in the shimmer of hot air.

All the enemy's ice pillars had already begun to melt. With a look of desperation, she put together a cooling spell, but to no effect.

Miyuki's side had exceeded severe winter and become a frozen tundra...

...while the enemy's side had gone beyond the intensity of summer to become a scorching hell.

But even that was just part of the process.

Before much longer...

...an icy mist began to envelop Miyuki's side...

...and sublimating steam began to envelop the enemy's.

◇ ◇ ◇

"Is…is this…?" groaned Mari.

"Inferno…?" groaned Mayumi, both of whom Tatsuya heard from behind him.

He noted to himself how impressive it was that they recognized it, but he didn't turn around. His eyes were scanning the monitor and the image of Miyuki's back.

Inferno was a midrange area-of-effect oscillation spell. It parted a target area, decelerating the oscillation and kinetic energy of all objects in one zone while pulling all that leftover energy into the other area and heating it up, thus obeying the laws of thermodynamics: It was a spell that reversed heat entropy.

This spell sometimes appeared on the exams for A-rank magician licenses, and caused a lot of pain and suffering for most exam takers, as it was an extremely difficult spell. For Miyuki, though, it came naturally.

As it was an area-of-effect spell, there was no worry of it sticking out of the field and breaking the rules. There was nothing to be that nervous about, but no matter how simple the spell, you needed to be careful. Tatsuya kept a close eye on her, ready to use any means necessary to intervene should something happen, even if it meant she would be disqualified.

But that, too, seemed about to end as a pointless worry. The enemy's field had reached nearly four hundred degrees Fahrenheit. The ice pillars had been created through rapid cooling, and so the ice was rough, with many air bubbles inside. Those air pockets expanded and began to create cracks in the loosened pillars.

Suddenly, the temperature stopped rising. A moment later, there came a shock wave from the center of the enemy field.

Miyuki had switched to a different spell.

The spell compressed and released air. With the enemy's ice pillars already in a fragile state, each and every one of them easily crumbled to the ground.

◇ ◇ ◇

Three hundred sixty players. Seventy-two technical staffers. Though some schools didn't bring an operations staff, there were more than four hundred fifty participants from the nine schools combined. Though a party (or banquet) could have supported that many people, they obviously couldn't host one every night of the competition.

Breakfast was buffet-style, and people left when they were full. Lunch was delivered lunchbox-style with the intention that it be eaten in the schools' tents, work vehicles, or brought back to the hotel rooms. For dinner, each school was assigned one of three cafeterias for one of three available hours. (The schools were separated to prevent any strategies from leaking.)

Dinnertime was actually the one time each day all the members from each school could meet. Their one-hour time slot was also a time to share the joys and sorrows of their match results.

And tonight, at First High's dining table, there was a clear division of cheer and gloom. The gloom came from the corner of the table with the freshman boys. The cheer came from the corner of the table with the freshman girls.

And among those female players was a lone male—Tatsuya.

"That thing Miyuki did was amazing!"

"It's called Inferno, right? The upperclassmen were all surprised. They said even A-class magicians have trouble with it!"

"You were good as usual, Amy! The first round was a little exciting, though."

"Your riding clothes and gun moves were awesome!"

"Shizuku was awesome, too! Her *furisode* was beautiful, and she didn't let the other player do anything. It was so cool!"

The rookie Cloudball event had ended with a second-place finish, plus another person who placed (sixth or above), so those results were just okay. But the rookie Ice Pillars Break event had all three players advancing to the third round, and after their good results in Speed Shooting, the female players were all in a festive mood again.

The Ice Pillars Break tournament consisted of twenty-four players, with twelve matches in the first round and six in the second. Three people getting to the third round meant that they had taken half of the top six spots for their school.

It was difficult to tell them not to get complacent now that they could see the amazing feat in front of them: having a single school take all three spots in the round-robin if their players all won the third round. The upperclassmen didn't look ready to reprimand them, either, as they watched over the girls' delight.

"Shiba, that thing Shizuku used—it was a variation of Resonance Disruption, right?"

The girl who asked was one of the freshmen Tatsuya wasn't in charge of. He knew her face and name but wasn't particularly close with her. Suddenly feeling eyes on him as he continued to eat in awkward silence (he wanted to move to another seat, but Miyuki wouldn't let him), he somehow managed a normal reply.

"Correct." His answer was curt, but his voice was still softer than usual. They were all freshmen together, but she was a Course 1 girl, to whom he didn't normally have the chance to talk. He had enough presence of mind to actively try not to scare her away.

His considerations, though, served to amplify the clamor.

"Then were you the one who changed the activation program?"

"The spell she used in Speed Shooting was something you made yourself, wasn't it?"

"And Shiba was the one who could program Inferno, too."

"I heard Shiba was the one who thought up Honoka's light-flashing strategy!"

Addressed in rapid succession with no time to answer each question, Tatsuya winced internally, but the girls were in a kind of manic state. The festive atmosphere was a great change of pace from the tension of the events, and this over-the-top complimenting was, in a way, the girls singing their own praises, thus building their confidence and getting rid of their anxiety. He understood the psychology behind what was happening, so he listened to them, not intending to rain on the parade.

"Must be nice… Maybe if Shiba had been assigned to me I could have one."

Still, *that* was going a little too far, and he couldn't overlook it.

Nevertheless, him being the one to chide the girl for it would make things worse. He exchanged quiet glances with Miyuki, who sat next to him.

"Nanami, that's not a very nice thing to say."

Her gentle reproach made the female student realize what she'd said had been a criticism of the engineer assigned to her.

She hurriedly stood, both her countenance and mouth saying *oh no, no, no, no* as she looked around for her senior assigned engineer. After the engineer spotted her smiling and waving her hand, Nana quickly lowered her head in apology and sat back down, looking relieved.

"Ahhh, that was close!"

"Nana, you can't blame inexperience on your CAD."

"Hee-hee…I'm sorry."

The volume of the girls' conversation lowered, but it was still far from any kind of secret sharing.

"But I did still have more power than usual thanks to Shiba," said Takigawa, the girl who took third in Speed Shooting. Eimi nodded theatrically.

"And isn't CAD adjustment kind of like exposing everything inside you? I was a little unsure about a male engineer…but now I'm so glad Shiba was assigned to me! We should thank the boys for letting us have him."

To the massive misunderstanding she presented with her innocent smile, Tatsuya could only give a dry smile in return.

Unfortunately, there were those who couldn't let that go with just a dry smile.

"Huh? Hey!"

With a loud clatter and a bang, one of the male students got up.

Without turning back to the voice trying to stop him, Morisaki brought his plate to the serving window and left the cafeteria.

◇ ◇ ◇

Strangely enough, at the same time, in Yokohama Chinatown…

Melancholy, antsy faces surrounded a table with a full course of Chinese food—though not enough for the traditional three-day meal—the ingredients far more expensive than those at the high school students' table. The luxurious, colorful furnishings, predominantly red and gold, seemed to emphasize the dismay in the faces of those present.

"…Wasn't Third High supposed to have the advantage in the rookie competition?"

Their conversation was conducted in English.

"We even forced Watanabe to forfeit. And yet now First High is poised to be the victor, no?"

Ethnically speaking, however, they clearly bore the characteristics of mixed European and Asian heritage.

"If the favorite wins, we bookmakers will be the only losers."

"The casino has seen particularly many guests this year. The payout amounts aren't cheap, even for us. This could mean a huge loss for the business. If that happens…"

The men all looked at one another, faces grim.

"…Then everyone here will be purged by headquarters." One of the men looked up at a hanging scroll depicting a dragon twisting around in the air and roaring in gold embroidery, and then continued lowly, "Depending on how much we lose, the boss could even come personally to do it."

A heavy silence settled upon them all.

"If it's only death that comes, it'll be a mercy..." muttered some-one into the quiet.

His voice trembled in fear.

◇ ◇ ◇

Gender differences didn't matter as much in magical sports. Still, in consideration for the events where physical condition *did* play a role, such as Battle Board and Cloudball, they had split the boys and girls in the rookie competition this year, to match the main competition. From another perspective, it meant this was the first year they'd been separate.

It had been co-ed until last year. There was already compartmen-talization with the boys in Battle Board and Cloudball and the girls in the less physically intense Ice Pillars Break and Speed Shooting (certain schools had a bias toward having more male players, too), so previously, the audience would never have to be split between boys' and girls' events that were happening at the same time.

Still, between the boys' events and the girls' events—which were more popular?

Most years, in the main competition, the general attendees would gravitate toward the girls' events, while people in the military, police force, fire department, or universities tended to gather at the boys' events.

—As for this year's rookie competition...

"Look at all the people..."

"And I think there's still seats available over in the boys' events."

Two girls looked on with sympathy at the jam-packed grandstand from their entirely unjammed participants' seats.

The two were Mayumi and Mari.

"I feel like there's a lot of people from the university..." said Mayumi, this time glancing at the invitee seats.

"They probably couldn't settle for just the recordings of what happened yesterday," said Mari in agreement.

"Can you blame them?"

"I suppose not. We're here to see it, too, after all."

In order to maintain fairness of the players' conditions, the matches today would be played in the reverse of yesterday.

It was the sixth day of the tournament, and the third day of the rookie competition. The first match of the third round of Ice Pillars Break was about to begin.

Mayumi glanced at the clock, waiting for Miyuki Shiba to appear.

◇ ◇ ◇

Let's go back a little bit.

While Tatsuya and Miyuki were heading to the Ice Pillars Break waiting room, they found two students from Third High standing in their way. Both were boys. One had a physique very similar to Tatsuya's—their height and shoulder width seemed almost to match—of course, the other one was quite a bit better-looking. The other one was on the short side. However, he didn't leave a weak impression, perhaps because of his school's focus on combat training.

The two of them seemed to have noticed Tatsuya and Miyuki at the same time, and began to walk straight toward them.

The larger of the two got the ball rolling. "I'm Masaki Ichijou, a freshman at Third High." His tone was insolent, considering they were seeing each other for the first time, but Tatsuya didn't feel that it was strange or unpleasant in any way. Masaki Ichijou had a kind of style, brusque as it was. It seemed natural for him to take leadership over others and act accordingly, despite being a freshman just like Tatsuya.

And his eyes were gazing straight at him.

"I'm Shinkurou Kichijouji, also a freshman at Third High." The smaller of the two gave his old-fashioned name in a polite tone, though with a challenging look in his eyes.

"Tatsuya Shiba, freshman at First High. What would the Crimson Prince and Cardinal George want with me before the match?" There was no malice there; even *hostility* would have been the wrong word. However, Tatsuya's attitude was anything but friendly.

To put it simply, it sounded like barefaced fighting spirit. Tatsuya had replied in his normal, slightly rough way to this person he was meeting for the first time, just as Masaki had. Given the circumstances he was faced with, he felt it would be rude to show a pretense of courtesy to the pair.

"Well…I'm impressed you even knew about George."

"Tatsuya Shiba… I've never heard the name. But I won't forget it. Likely to be a genius engineer whose career began at this competition. I know it's rude to do this before a match, but we wanted to come and meet you."

"I'm very grateful that the boy genius who discovered one of the fundamental Cardinal Codes at the young age of thirteen believes I'm a genius…but it does seem absurd."

A selfish remark—he wasn't mincing words. But neither party flared up. Their intentions were clear as they took in the face of the enemy.

"Miyuki, you go get set up." Tatsuya didn't look away from the two. This was going to take a little longer.

"All right." Miyuki bowed once to Tatsuya, then went into the waiting room without so much as a glance at the other two, acting as though they weren't there. Her act of averting her eyes did not seem forced; her disregard was perfectly natural.

Masaki glanced after Miyuki for a moment but immediately looked back at Tatsuya.

Tatsuya, however, took that as an unmistakable moment of unrest and inexperience, and felt somewhat deflated. "…Don't you have your own match soon, *Prince*?"

While he didn't bother to hide his dismay, Masaki took a moment to form his reply. However, Kichijouji answered for him. "…We'll be playing in Monolith Code tomorrow."

This young man had won the rookie boys' Speed Shooting event, and Masaki was the most hopeful candidate to win Ice Pillars Break. Both of these aces being on their Monolith Code team together was, of course, something First High had expected.

"What about you?"

What do you mean "what about you"? he wanted to answer, but time was short. Giving a one-sidedly polite reply would have irritated him, though, so he gave an equally ambiguous answer. "Not assigned to it."

"I see… That's a shame. I do want to fight your players some time. And beat them, of course."

You picking a fight? wondered Tatsuya, but he quickly corrected himself: Picking a fight was exactly what they had come here to do.

"Sorry for taking your time. I look forward to seeing you again," said Masaki before Tatsuya had the time to reply to Kichijouji. The two of them quickly walked past him.

Self-important to the end, thought Tatsuya. But he didn't turn around. He simply headed to the waiting room to be with Miyuki.

"What did they want, anyway?" After coming out of the changing room, the first thing out of Miyuki's mouth was about the event a few minutes prior.

"Maybe they were scouting us out? There wouldn't be much point in that, but…" Tatsuya wondered aloud, choosing an inoffensive expression. He handed her the CAD he'd finished setting up while she was changing.

The match was soon. Being preoccupied with other things could only be a bad thing. Tatsuya wanted to be done with the conversation, but Miyuki giggled and failed to suppress a meaningful smile.

"I think they came to declare war on you, Tatsuya."

It wasn't that he didn't understand what she was getting at. He'd himself felt that they were picking a fight. But that seemed astounding to him.

"…You don't believe me, do you?"

Even with her upturned, pouting expression, he wasn't convinced. "Well, I mean…I'm not even a player. Those two are beyond magic high schools. The magical world already thinks highly of them. I wouldn't think they'd see me as an enemy."

When he said "see me as an enemy," he meant "see me as an equal adversary." Objectively speaking, he was quite a few levels below the two of them—so much so that, on the surface at least, even speaking of "levels" separating them seemed presumptuous. Nevertheless, they didn't appear to know his personal background. Thinking normally, it was insane that the Crimson Prince and Cardinal George would see him as a rival—at least, that was what Tatsuya thought.

When she saw that he honestly thought that and wasn't just being modest, his little sister heaved a sigh. "…Tatsuya, in this case, undervaluing yourself will lead to mistakes in seeing how the competition is going. I think you should try to look at how much attention you're being paid and how much antagonism people have toward you—or rather, toward your skills and tactics."

Unreserved remonstrance was unusual for Miyuki. Tatsuya found his eyes widening at the unexpected pressure and blame.

◇ ◇ ◇

Three times did Miyuki captivate the crowd with her mystical beauty, and overrun every enemy with overwhelming, almost divine strength.

Meanwhile, on the Battle Board watercourse, the first race of the girls' semifinals was about to begin.

The racers were already at the starting line. Honoka was among them.

"Umm…"

"……"

"This is, well…"

"……"

"I mean, you know…"

"……"

"What is going on with you two?" Leo asked in exasperation. As Erika tried to stammer something out, worried in the stands as she looked upon the three racers at the starting line, Mizuki just sat in the seat next to her, dumbfounded.

"I mean…isn't this weird? All the players are wearing those black glasses."

"Erika, just call them goggles, okay?"

Yes—as Erika and Mizuki had said, this time not only Honoka but also the other two were wearing heavily shaded goggles.

"Of course they are. It's the surest way of getting around Mitsui's blinding magic," returned Mikihiko. It was so sensible a guess that Erika gave a deflated laugh, almost as if she was disappointed.

"…What are you not happy with?" asked Mikihiko.

"Well, this is probably playing right into Tatsuya's hands, you know?" said Erika. "Players don't use goggles in Battle Board, because the splashing water can make it hard to see. They had a reason, but they grabbed their goggles just because she did that flash spell one time… There's plenty of other ways to deal with something like that…"

"You mean Honoka'll try to spray them this time?" asked Mizuki.

Erika nodded disinterestedly.

However…

"I don't know… I don't think Tatsuya would do something so simple," Mikihiko added.

"…You might be right," agreed Leo.

Erika's curiosity swelled.

There was no flash of light right at the start this time.

"Did she get a late start?!"

"No, she's right behind them!"

After passing through the gentle curves in front of the grandstand, Honoka went into the first sharp corner in second place.

"What?"

The racer in the lead took a clearly odd course around the turn. She decelerated heavily and turned through the *middle* of the track. Honoka, who had also decelerated, made her way tightly around the inside of the corner, passed the racer who took the *long way around*, and got into first place.

"What was that?"

Normally racers slowed way down and stuck to the inside, or kept some speed and wheeled around the outside. Slowing down so much and taking the corner with plenty of room left on the inside could only be called lazy.

"...I think I saw a shadow on the water."

At Leo's voice, Erika narrowed her eyes sharply and said, "There it is again!"

Now the racers were coming up to a big, gentle curve. The racer Honoka had passed slowed down more than usual with too much space left on the outside as she took the curve. As a result, her distance to Honoka widened.

"...Oh, so that's how it is," nodded Mikihiko.

"Huh? What?" asked Erika.

"I think Erika was right," he said in an excited voice, forgetting his usual emotional discord. "Tatsuya was trying to get the other racers to wear shaded goggles. But it wasn't so she could splash water in their eyes—it was to make it hard to see dark places."

"Oh! I didn't think illusion magic could be used like that!"

"Yeah. She can control how her opponents move just by making it brighter or darker. I guess magic really does all depend on how you use it..."

"...You two seem to have it figured out, but I haven't!" Leo complained sourly.

Mikihiko, lost in his own little world, snapped back to reality. "Oh, sorry, sorry! Basically, Tatsuya's plan was..."

◇ ◇ ◇

"Shiba's plan was very simple. She makes the water lighter or darker with light wave–oscillation magic. Their goggles are already dark, and now things get darker for them. They think they're seeing the end of the course where the light parts meet the dark parts, so they try not to go into the dark parts. Basically, she's making the course more narrow for them than it actually is."

In the main tent was Hattori, who was filling in for Katsuto. Katsuto had gone to watch the boys' Ice Pillars Break with Kirihara, who had tagged along. He listened intently to Suzune's explanation.

"They know for a fact that the track should be wider, but they get confused because their eyes' visual information says otherwise. And no athlete can go as fast on a narrow course as she can on a wider one. They can't use the full extent of their abilities. It's a basic tactic."

"...But wouldn't Mitsui be affected by that, too?"

"She's been practicing a lot for this."

The answer to Hattori's question was simple indeed.

"...Normally, I feel like the caster would just think it wouldn't affect them."

"She probably couldn't leave it at that. Shiba was telling her that the course is always the same width, and that she should learn with her body instead of relying on her eyes."

Kirihara groaned. "...So it looks like a trick, but it's actually straightforward... His personality isn't the only bad thing about him."

Suzune laughed aloud.

◇ ◇ ◇

Once the morning's events ended, First High's tent was in a state of complete jubilation. They had won all three matches of the rookie girls' Ice Pillars Break. All three of the spots for the afternoon's round-robin had been taken by First High players. Honoka was on to the finals in Battle Board as well. They were like an army on a steady, victorious advance.

The ten freshman boys, though, couldn't be as festive. Normally, the boys' accomplishments wouldn't have been so unfavorable compared to the girls'—but their misplaced impatience was causing them to make mistakes, and those mistakes cost them matches, causing them further impatience and haste. They were stuck in a vicious circle.

Meanwhile, the three girls' Ice Pillars Break players—Miyuki, Shizuku, and Eimi—and their engineer, Tatsuya, had been called to the hotel meeting room rather than to their main tent.

"We don't have a whole lot of time, so I'll be quick." Mayumi had been the one who called them, and she'd greeted them alone. "This is the first time one school has taken up the entire finals league. Shiba, Kitayama, Akechi, you all did extremely well."

The three were courteous, quiet, and flustered, respectively, but each bowed at the same time to thank Mayumi for her praise.

"The tournament committee has a suggestion for this unprecedented occasion. Since our school will receive the same number of points no matter what order the three of you come in, they were wondering if the three of you wanted to share the championship equally."

The three exchanged glances as Tatsuya's lips curled up cynically. He didn't care what the tournament committee's excuses were. They were very clearly just trying to make things easier for themselves.

"I'll let you all decide whether or not to accept the proposal. But I can't give you much time to decide, so please talk it over now."

Eimi's eyes began to wander restlessly at Mayumi's words. She was well aware that her strength wouldn't give her any chance of winning against either Miyuki or Shizuku. She'd thought third was good enough, but now, with the possibility of winning it all—even shared—it was harder from a psychological standpoint to let the opportunity pass.

Miyuki looked at Tatsuya.

And Shizuku looked at Miyuki.

"Tatsuya, what do you think about it? You'd probably have it hard if they fought each other."

I see. Mayumi would want to settle things with a shared victory, thought Tatsuya. It was probably the most desirable outcome for her as the team leader.

Still, Tatsuya didn't feel the need to consider such things very carefully. He'd just state the facts he knew. "Frankly speaking, with Akechi's current condition, I think she should avoid any more matches. All three of hers were hard fought. I'm pretty sure it will take more than one or two hours to recover from that."

"I see… Akechi, do you agree?"

"Er, well…I was already thinking I should probably forfeit before all of this anyway. He's right. I wouldn't be on my best game, so I figured I'd talk to him, then decide… Shiba knows what condition I'm in better than I do, after all."

There was a tinge of guilt in her voice. She probably thought taking the tournament committee up on its proposal would be unfair. That seemed to be the main reason for her current discomposure.

"All right." Mayumi smiled sympathetically and nodded, then looked at Miyuki and Shizuku.

"I…" Shizuku was the first one to speak. "I think I want to fight." She stared straight back into Mayumi's eyes, her own filled with strong determination. "I don't know how many more chances I'll have to seriously compete with Miyuki… I don't want to let this chance go."

"I see…" Mayumi looked at the floor and sighed. "What do you want to do, Miyuki?"

"If Kitayama wants to have a match with me, then I have no reason to refuse her."

Mayumi had been certain she would give that answer—Miyuki was extremely strong-willed.

"All right, then… I'll go tell the tournament committee that Akechi will forfeit and Shiba and Kitayama will have a match to decide first place. It will probably take place first thing in the afternoon, so you should probably get ready quickly."

The first one to bow to Mayumi's words was Tatsuya. As he turned to leave the meeting room, Miyuki and Shizuku immediately bowed and followed him, while Eimi, flustered, lowered her head and excused herself.

◇ ◇ ◇

The audience seats were overcrowded this time. Now that the signs said there would be a final battle for the rookie girls' Ice Pillars Break event instead of the normal tournament following the round-robin, the committee had decided the event would be the first of the afternoon, purposely scheduled at a different time than all the other events.

The seats for those participating in the general competition were just as jam-packed as the ones for the regular audience. Tatsuya was among them, with Mayumi and Mari on either side of him.

After finishing adjusting both Miyuki's and Shizuku's CADs, Tatsuya sat himself in the rearmost row of the seats reserved for competition participants. He wasn't siding with either girl. He'd told them that beforehand—along with a few words of encouragement for each.

It had been a nice story, but Mayumi destroyed it. "But you really would have rather been with Miyuki, right?" she asked with a leer. She seemed to get more impish around him.

"Yes." Part of it, of course, had to be how she got irritated when he gave no good reaction to things like this.

"…It didn't take much for you to admit it," sighed Mari. Her sighs were becoming commonplace. She put up a pretense of evil, but her true nature was more virtuous than Mayumi's…well, maybe. "Do you know what the term *sister complex* means?"

"I fail to understand how rooting for your own family in a match constitutes a sister complex." It was a sound argument but a transparent one. That, too, was starting to be customary.

But Mayumi and Mari seemed to be learning.

"Yikes, did you hear that, Mari? He got defensive."

"Yeah. He's got it bad. Maybe he'll never be cured of it."

This time, their usual underclassman-bullying pattern was different. They were fake whispering to each other with him right between them, obviously within earshot. Tatsuya sighed. Why did they need to do that?

Tatsuya's intermission skit in the stands was nothing more than a breather before the final curtain rose. As though to prove it, as soon as the two athletes ascended the main stage, the crowd quieted.

Two girls stood facing each other, a field in between. One in a white unlined kimono and scarlet *hakama*, clear to the eye. One in a light blue *furisode*, cool to gaze upon.

Miyuki didn't tie her hair back, nor Shizuku her sleeves. The long hair and *furisode* sleeves fluttered in the summer breeze.

They created a stifling silence.

Both were raring to go but calm and collected; their spirits were not battle crazed. After all, only magic would play a part in this game.

The starting light came on.

Then, the moment they changed color and became the beacons to start the battle—

—two spells fired off at the same time.

A heat wave assailed Shizuku's field.

Her ice pillars, though, were holding up.

It was Inferno, its heat wave bringing the entire area's temperature up. But it found itself repelled by her own Information Boost, which blocked temperature changes within the pillars.

A rumbling in the ground assailed Miyuki's field.

The vibrations, though, found themselves suppressed before they resonated.

Miyuki's own spell reached the enemy both on the surface and under it: an area-of-effect spell that suppressed oscillation and movement within her own field.

Each tried to reach the enemy's ice pillars with event alterations while simultaneously blocking the other's spell. It was a battle that would be praised by professionals and admired by experts; they were evenly matched—or so it seemed.

The two girls didn't seem to think so.

I can't reach…! She's so strong!

Shizuku's Resonance Disruption was being completely blocked. Miyuki's heat wave was still covering her field, though.

The Information Boost, an anti-magic spell, blocked magic-based information overwriting for target objects. Miyuki's spell was converting into physical energy; Information Boost couldn't eliminate those effects. Shizuku could block the magic-based heating of the ice pillars themselves, but it was only a matter of time before they began to melt just from the heat now in the air.

Then how about this?!

Shizuku's CAD-covered left arm dived into her right cuff.

When she pulled her hand out, it was holding a handgun-shaped specialized CAD.

This was the trump card Tatsuya had given her.

She pointed its muzzle at the front row of enemy pillars and pulled the trigger.

When she saw Shizuku's left hand holding a handgun CAD, alarm shot through Miyuki's mind. *Using two CADs at the same time?! You learned how to do that, Shizuku?*

Using multiple CADs was her brother's special technique—and it was advanced enough to be called *special* in every sense of the word. Tatsuya had encouraged Miyuki to learn how to control multiple CADs simultaneously, too, but she'd refused, saying she couldn't do it. She felt it was too soon to try the technique, since it required an absolute handle over her psions. Her magic tended to go out of control; trying to snatch her brother's special skill was too far above her station.

Now, though, right in front of her, Shizuku had a second CAD in her hands. As she finished booting it up, no psionic signal interference appeared.

For just a moment, Miyuki's magic paused. It was on a continuous loop, but now it was suspended.

That was when Shizuku's second spell came at her.

"Phonon Maser?!" cried Mayumi. Tatsuya found himself once again genuinely impressed she knew of the spell.

There was white vapor rising from the front line of Miyuki's pillars. In the three matches before this, she hadn't let an opponent touch any of them—in a magical sense—but now they had taken an actual attack, sustaining damage for the first time.

Phonon Maser was an advanced oscillation spell that boosted ultrasonic frequencies to the quantum level, thereby forcing them to become heat waves.

This was the tactic Tatsuya had given Shizuku to defeat Miyuki… but his expression was sullen. Not because Miyuki looked like she'd lose.

But because he realized that, in the end, this wouldn't be able to surpass her.

Miyuki's alarm lasted only a moment. After Shizuku sent out her new spell, she changed hers as well.

The steam stopped rising from Miyuki's ice pillars—it had stopped sublimating. She hadn't blocked the ultrasonic attack steadily transforming into heat waves, however. Instead, she began to use cooling magic to out-cool the heat applied by Phonon Maser.

Right there and then, a white mist covered Miyuki's field. It began to slowly press toward Shizuku's side. Miyuki could tell that the other girl had increased the interference on her Information Boost. But unfortunately...

I'm sorry, but that isn't enough, Shizuku.

The advancing mist was a cold wave. She was altering the air's temperature, and Shizuku's spell obstructed fusion. It would do nothing against Miyuki's attack.

Mari let out a moan. "...Is that...Niflheim...? What kind of fantasy world is this...?"

Tatsuya himself empathized with her quite a bit, but he didn't say anything.

The area-of-effect cooling spell Niflheim. The spell, by nature, homogeneously cooled targets in an area, regardless of the targets' specific heat or phase. It did have an applied usage, though: creating large areas of cool air such as diamond dust, dry ice particles, and sometimes even liquid nitrogen mist. Then you could ram that into a target.

And now its power had been pushed to its maximum level.

The cloud of liquid nitrogen passed into Shizuku's field and disappeared at its edge.

Then, liquid nitrogen droplets began to stick to one side of Shizuku's pillars—the side facing Miyuki. Puddles began to appear at their bases.

Miyuki released Niflheim and activated Inferno again.

Shizuku's Information Boost was applied to the pillars, but the pillars had been there all along. It wasn't applied to the *new* substances attached to them.

The extreme increase in temperature surpassed the cooling effects, causing the liquid nitrogen to instantly vaporize.

Then its rate of expansion increased by seven hundred fold.

* * *

With a loud roar, Shizuku's ice pillars all collapsed at once. Had the roar been from the pillars falling, their bases having been dug away, or from the vapor explosion itself?

The surface of the pillars shattered to pieces, the strength of the explosion telling the story.

Perhaps the sight struck the judge dumb—it took a moment for him to announce the end of the match.

◇ ◇ ◇

"Congratulations on winning, Honoka," said Shizuku as she headed back to her room to change out of her racing gear, having gone through her post-race medical checkup.

"Thanks... Sorry you didn't win, Shizuku."

"Yeah...it sucks."

Her voice was so monotonous that her remark might have made others doubt whether she really thought that, but Honoka had been her friend since elementary school. She couldn't mistake how Shizuku really felt.

"Shizuku..." Honoka took her friend's head, just slightly lower than her own, and held it to her chest.

Shizuku let her do it, her hands dangling at her sides. "I never thought I could win."

"Oh..."

"But I got completely shut out."

"......"

"This sucks, Honoka..."

"...I'm sorry."

Several moments passed like this.

"...Thanks. I'm fine now," said Shizuku eventually, pulling away. There was no trace of tears on her face.

"You're okay…? Do you want to go for some tea? I'm a little hungry."

"…Yeah."

"Okay. I'll go get changed. I'll only be a minute."

Honoka's cheerful behavior made Shizuku nod and smile, slightly embarrassed.

No sooner had they set foot in the tea lounge than Honoka stopped dead in her tracks. Someone had gotten here first. Her eyes locked with Miyuki's.

She couldn't just turn around and leave, but she also couldn't just sit down with her casually like she usually did. The timing was so bad she wanted to cry.

"Congratulations on winning, Honoka."

Miyuki's smiling face was brilliant like it always was, but it seemed somehow artificial this time. It looked like Honoka wasn't the only one who couldn't do something like she usually did, though it wasn't as big a deal in her case.

"Honoka, congratulations on the victory."

Without wasting a moment, Tatsuya cut into the unpleasant mood with his usual tone of voice. Letting Honoka stand there or making her force an unnatural smile would have made things worse, but he didn't give her the time. Of course, the act inadvertently cut off Honoka's escape route.

"Oh! Um, thank you…"

The mood in the room wasn't advancing, nor was it retreating. But the one to break it was Shizuku. "Tatsuya, can we sit with you?"

"Of course. Go ahead," he said, standing up and going around the back of an empty chair as Miyuki, cup and saucer in hand, moved from the seat across from him to the one next to him.

"Here you go."

"Thanks."

Without hesitation, Shizuku took her seat in the chair Tatsuya had vacated, which was now across from Miyuki. Similarly, Miyuki's old seat now housed a blushing Honoka. After calling over a passing waitress and ordering a cake set for Honoka and Shizuku, Tatsuya looked at the two of them again.

"Let's celebrate the one-two finish, shall we? My treat."

"What? Are you sure?"

"…That sounds good to me."

Honoka was hesitant, but Shizuku got the picture and nodded, without showing any unnecessary restraint. Tatsuya was trying to comfort her. Honoka breathed a sigh at seeing her friends make up faster than she thought, and then finally started thinking about herself again.

"Um, well…" she said.

"Yes?"

"Well, it was all thanks to you that I won! Thank you so much!"

Once she started thinking about it, she realized she still hadn't thanked Tatsuya for the victory. It had caused her more inner turmoil than before, but she managed not to trip over her words of gratitude.

Tatsuya smiled slightly and nodded. "I only did a little."

He didn't act modest and refuse her thanks; he didn't want to make a big deal out of it. And he knew Honoka wouldn't try to argue the "a little" point, because she knew what he meant by that smile.

Tatsuya turned his gaze to Shizuku, his smile disappearing. "I feel like I should apologize, Shizuku."

"Huh?" Shizuku looked back at Tatsuya with an expression saying she didn't understand what he was referring to.

"I mean, maybe the end result was inevitable, but that match should have been closer… It was a poor judgment on my part. I think mastering Phonon Maser in two weeks was too much to ask of you."

"Oh, that… No, it's not your fault at all," she said with a firm shake of her head. She didn't know why he was apologizing. "If I didn't have that, I wouldn't have even been able to counterattack. It's my fault for not mastering it. I should be apologizing to you. If I was really on top of it, it would have been a better match. And I'm sorry to you, too, Miyuki, for not being much of an opponent."

"That's not true. I was really surprised when you did that. First you had such a high-level spell, and then you started using multiple CADs at once."

After Miyuki smiled at Shizuku and shook her head, the former turned a joking glare on Tatsuya.

"Tatsuya, you didn't spare any effort in trying to defeat me, did you?"

It was quite a difficult question to answer, and it took Tatsuya a moment to find one. But in the end, all that came out was an excuse. "...I did everything I could for both of you."

Miyuki knew that was the truth, even though it *was* a cop-out. But given how she actually felt about the whole thing, the answer didn't satisfy her. "Geez...You'd think you could at least be biased toward your own sister."

"Oh, come on. If I had eased up on you, you would have been a lot angrier."

A girl complaining to her friends about her older brother would have been, in the rest of the world, a totally natural thing to do. However, it was extremely rare for Miyuki in particular to do it, and it invited smiles not only from the arguing Tatsuya but from Honoka and Shizuku as well.

◇ ◇ ◇

It was the seventh day of the tournament, and the fourth day of the rookie competition.

Today was the day the rookies' Monolith Code qualifying round-robin would be held. However, despite that being the main event, the audience's attention was drawn instead to the spectacle that was Mirage Bat.

Only girls played Mirage Bat. The costume consisted of a colorful unitard, a fluttering miniskirt, a sleeveless jacket, and a vest. It had become a fashion show (cosplay event?), just like Ice Pillars Break, though it had a different sense of dazzle to it.

After all, there *would* be young girls jumping around in mid-air wearing these costumes. If there were a magical sport ranking of "gorgeous," it would top the list. Naturally, because of this, it drew the interest (or rather, very close attention) of male fans.

Still…if Tatsuya wasn't imagining things, there seemed to be a little *too* much interest this time. The gazes weren't passion-ridden or sex-obsessed. No, they were pricked with thorns and full of hostility.

"…I guess you really are thickheaded when it comes to yourself," said a young woman to Tatsuya, teasingly. She was a player who'd just finished getting ready to go into the first match.

"I won't deny that I'm dull…but you could tell, Satomi?"

"Of course!"

Her name was Subaru Satomi, and she belonged to Class 1-D at First High. She was a Course 1 student, of course. Satomi was actually her surname, despite its commonness as a first name; Tatsuya and Subaru weren't close enough to be on a first-name basis.

"Everyone's watching you, Shiba."

She reminded him a little of Mari, specifically how she seemed more popular with the same gender than with the opposite one. Otherwise, they resembled each other only a little, and physically, they'd be quite different when placed next to each other.

Consider, for example, dressing them both in tuxedos. Mari would be the female beauty in men's clothing, but Subaru would play the "pretty boy" role in a theater production. That was probably where the impressions they made diverged. A lot of Subaru's speech and behavior was boyish, perhaps because she was aware of all that, though she wasn't rough or ill-mannered or anything. Also, she had very sharp insight, as she was showing now. "You got us into all the top spots in Speed Shooting *and* Ice Pillars Break. Smart people would know that optimized software was a big part of that, and they *have* to be wondering who the engineer who did the adjustments was."

"...It's not hard to look up which engineer was assigned to what..."

"Exactly. The other schools are starting to be afraid of you, Shiba."

If Subaru was right—and he didn't have the means to deny it—then the situation was not going in a good direction for him. Competition or not, he was being forced into literally everything in his life without ever being fully prepared. But that was how the world worked, he supposed.

Still, this time around, he was *far* too unprepared. By all rights, Tatsuya Shiba should not have been in the limelight until he graduated high school.

"All right... Maybe I'll grab the win with this little boon, too. I honestly don't think I can lose the qualifiers with a device like this."

They stopped in front of the doorway leading to the field. Subaru held her right arm up, and her bracelet sparkled in the morning sunlight. She gave a daring smile over her shoulder.

Tatsuya gave her a thumbs-up and saw her off. As she said herself, she'd probably get through the qualifiers—using the CAD he'd adjusted. He would have rather not stood out, but he also couldn't give less than his best. Maybe he could have, back when he'd just enrolled as a Course 2 student—a Weed—and only one specific person was actually expecting anything out of him, but not anymore.

Mayumi and Mari had specifically selected him for the Nine School Competition. Katsuto had supported their decision. Hattori had swallowed his pride and recommended him, and Kirihara had fearlessly made himself a test dummy. Honoka, Shizuku, and the other female players had their hopes riding on him. And what's more...Miyuki believed in him unconditionally and gave him all her help.

Human bonds, once forged, were hard for even him to dismantle.

◇ ◇ ◇

Mirage Bat would have six qualifying matches, each with four people. The six who won those would then have one final showdown.

The event had the least number of matches in the Nine School Competition, but that didn't mean the strain on the players was lessened.

The matches were each three sets of fifteen minutes, making it the longest play time in the competition. With a five-minute break between periods, the total match time could reach one hour. Even though Ice Pillars Break and Monolith Code had no time limit, they were orders of magnitude shorter than this.

To add to that, during the match, the players would all be constantly triggering movement magic to move through the air. Some likened the strain on the players to that of a full marathon.

And there were two matches per player per day, at that.

Stamina-wise, the actual play was said to be more rigorous than Cloudball and Monolith Code. Because of that, in consideration for the players getting exhausted, there was a large interval between the qualifiers and final, further setting apart the sport itself.

The first matches would begin at 8:00 AM. There were two separate fields, so the qualifiers would end at noon.

The final match would then start at 7:00 PM, making it the only night event in the competition.

Outwardly, because of the player strain, it seemed better to split the qualifiers and finals into two separate days, but there was one good reason for the one-day schedule.

Mirage Bat consisted of players using sticks to hit holographic spheres projected in the air. (Strictly speaking, the spheres were stereoscopic; modern midair imaging technology was strictly different from holography in how it created the images.) This meant that the fake images floating thirty feet in the air would need to be distinguishable or else the event wouldn't work, making it unfit for playing under the bright midsummer sunlight. On clear days, the third pair of matches, which was played close to noon, would see airships spreading a sun-blocking screen and things of that nature.

The sport's inherent characteristics lent themselves to the game being played at night.

Lest the light rays projecting the virtual images from the stereo-scopic image projectors be blocked by the players' bodies, they were positioned at the very top of the light poles surrounding the field in a circular fashion; those very light poles spoke to the fact that the event was designed with night play in mind.

◇ ◇ ◇

After the second matches ended—with Honoka and Subaru both making it out of the qualifiers, as planned—Tatsuya went back to his hotel room to take a nap. The two players would be going to their own rooms and using their sound-sleepers to get some good sleep, too, as it was imperative to recover one's stamina before the final in this event.

As an engineer, Tatsuya didn't need to rest his body, but it was definitely a good choice to rest his nerves. He'd really wanted to use a sensory-deprivation capsule, but those were prioritized toward the players, so he decided to just close up the opaque curtains in his room and lie down.

The third matches of Mirage Bat would be going on right now. He was lucky that he'd been assigned to the first and second. It was only one hour's difference, but one hour was more than enough to heavily influence how much of his stamina and mental power he restored.

He wanted Miyuki to have an early match in the main competition's qualifiers as well, but that wasn't something he had any control over. He decided there was no point thinking about it and ended that train of thought.

Truthfully, he wasn't physically tired. He couldn't force himself to sleep, so instead, he simply let his mind wander to whatever distractions it pleased.

As he lay in bed, eyes closed, his thoughts jumped to yesterday morning.

Masaki Ichijou and Shinkurou Kichijouji—they were the same age as him, but they were both geniuses who already had firm reputations in the magical world.

Masaki Ichijou... Three years ago, during the Invasion of Sado by the New Soviet Republic—conducted at the same time as the Great Asian Alliance's Okinawa Invasion—he had been part of the defensive line as a volunteer soldier at the young age of thirteen. As a magician, he was a combat veteran who had, along with his family's current head, Gouki Ichijou, buried many an enemy with his Burst.

Despite the battle itself being small-scale (the Soviets still denied any relation to the armed group that invaded Sado), his exploits earned him the title of Crimson Prince of the Ichijou. ("The Crimson" was a nickname of respect, for one who had emerged victorious despite being covered in the blood of enemy and ally alike—it referred to being bloodstained rather than bloodthirsty.)

Shinkurou Kichijouji... He was the genius magician who had discovered one of the theoretical Cardinal Codes, also at the young age of thirteen. His nickname, "Cardinal George," which combined his first name with the code he discovered, was so famous that every researcher studying magic-program theory knew of it.

That the two had enrolled at the same school in the same year was a coincidence verging on unfair. With the two of them on the same Monolith Code team, they would be invincible, at least among the rookies. *Unfortunately for Morisaki's team*, thought Tatsuya sympathetically, though it was not his problem at all.

If there was one upside... *it was that Burst is ranked A in lethality.*

The Ichijou's trump card, Burst, was divergence magic that vaporized fluids inside a targeted container. If used on a living being, it would vaporize its bodily fluids and rupture its physical body. If used on a machine powered by an internal combustion engine, it would vaporize the fuel and cause an outburst. Ones with fuel cells would end up the same. Even if there was no combustible fuel on board, there would still be battery fluid, oil pressure fluid, coolant, lubricant... There was no machine that used absolutely no fluid, so one execution of Burst would stop and destroy any machine.

A combat spell that sent soldiers and machines alike to their graves, Burst had been developed with pure military usage in mind. It would be, of course, caught in Monolith Code's anti-harm regulations.

Still, an heir to one of the Ten Master Clans and nicknamed the Crimson Prince would have more than just Burst in his pocket...and now that I think of it...

His unbridled thoughts left behind Monolith Code and the two who had declared war on him, moving on to the Monolith matches themselves. But he hadn't come to analyze combat strengths or plan anti–Third High measures—he just idly remembered that First High's second match would be starting soon.

We won the first match just fine, and our second is against the lowest-seeded Fourth High. Pretty sure there won't be any upsets...

With his eyes closed, he lent himself to the sleep calmly advancing upon him.

◇ ◇ ◇

After waking up from his afternoon nap and returning to the event area, Tatsuya felt a disturbance rippling through the place. The air covering the grounds where the school tents were set up felt one step away from sheer panic.

And the air was centered on First High's tent.

"Tatsuya!"

No sooner had he set foot into their tent than Miyuki came rushing straight for him. Shizuku was there, too, beside her.

"Miyuki? And Shizuku…? Weren't you with Erika and the others?"

He thought Miyuki and Shizuku had planned on watching Monolith Code with Erika's group until Honoka woke up—she would be getting ready at five for the final match.

But they were here instead, which meant…

"What happened?" he asked. Then, without waiting for an answer, he continued, "Was there an accident in Monolith Code?" He didn't ask *if* something had happened. It was pretty clear from the general mood that something *had* happened.

But then Tatsuya felt that things were actually worse than he might have imagined.

"Yes, an accident, I suppose…" Miyuki stammered.

"That wasn't an accident, Miyuki." Standing beside her, Shizuku broke in with a firm tone of voice. Her words were still controlled, but there was an unmistakable wrath burning in her eyes. "It was an intentional over-attack. It clearly broke the rules."

"Shizuku…we shouldn't jump to such hasty conclusions yet. There's no proof that it was intentional on *Fourth High's* part."

"That's right, Kitayama." This time, it was Mayumi who'd interrupted, having come up behind them. "It's hard to think this was just an accident, but we have to be sure before we do anything. The more rumors you start, the more they'll get out of control, and suddenly it turns into the truth."

It was probably rude for Tatsuya to think this, but he noted that was a very logical, *upperclassman-like* explanation. As he gave a glance to Shizuku, who apologized after being gently reproached, he thought to himself, *I guess there is a reason she's student president.*

…And then Mayumi gave him a squinting glare.

"…What is it?"

"…You were just thinking something really rude, weren't you?"

H-how does she do that?! Tatsuya couldn't help his confusion. But just the same as her, he had more life experience than his age would suggest. "No, I was simply reflecting on how conscientious our student president is…?" Topping off his mask of sincerity with the standard, fake confusion at having been falsely accused, he answered her, his voice inquisitive.

"…Really?" Mayumi's eyes turned even more suspicious, but then the brunt of it softened for the moment. It wasn't that she failed to find a hole in his act; it was probably because they didn't have time for this right now.

"How bad were the injuries?"

"You can tell just from our conversation that Morisaki's team's been hurt, huh?" Mayumi sighed, the fact that she found him hard to deal with evident on her face. "…Well, it's bad. They were playing on the urban stage and took a Battering Ram inside an abandoned building. The rubble fell on top of them."

"…If the spell was used with people inside, Battering Ram gets elevated to rank A lethality. This isn't some out-of-control spree in Battle Board—it sounds like a painfully clear violation of tournament regulations," Tatsuya muttered.

The Battering Ram spell they were referring to was a spell developed as part of research on a psychokinetic technique called Thoughtbomb. It applied heaviness to a single section of a target object, then overwrote the eidos of the entire target. It needed to work on an area that could be conceptualized as a single surface—one wall in a building, one part of the ceiling, or at least a section marked off by pillars or something. It required a high magical capacity and strong magical influence.

It was a difficult spell, and if you just wanted to destroy a building, it would be simpler to just crash a hammer into it with movement magic. You couldn't just trigger it by mistake, unless perhaps you were a magician who specialized in the ability.

"It is… They were wearing military-grade protective suits, but it doesn't mean much when thick chunks of concrete fall on you.

Thankfully, their helmets and an observer immediately casting weight-reduction magic saved them from anything worse…but the three of them will take two weeks in magical care to fully heal. They need undisturbed rest for three days, too."

Mayumi still seemed to want to avoid judgment on whether it was intentional or accidental, and she diverted the topic slightly.

"…That's worse than I could have imagined."

He fully understood that Mayumi couldn't make any careless remarks given her position, so he refrained from pursuing the topic any further.

"Yes," Mayumi added, grim. "It may sound indiscreet, but looking at their treatment made me feel sick."

She was right—that was a problematic statement toward those who had been hurt. Still, maybe that just spoke to how disturbed she was, and how much she was opening up to him.

"I don't really understand what happened. Were the three of them all grouped up in the same building?"

Tatsuya didn't really have to be the one worrying about this, but the established tactics in Monolith Code were either to have one person on offense and two on defense or vice versa. All three team members being knocked out by the same attack made it a little hard to understand what kind of situation they'd faced.

It was Shizuku who answered him, unable to clear the anger from her voice: "It was a surprise attack right after the match started. They would have needed to scout before the starting signal. Battering Ram aside, the false start must have been intentional."

"I see… The tournament committee must be panicking," said Tatsuya with a mean smile.

"Because they couldn't prevent the false start…?" asked Miyuki, clearly confused. She was too straightforward and honest to consider things as rebelliously as Tatsuya could.

"That's not a big issue. It's more that the unstable empty building they were placed in at the start was an indirect cause of the accident—which I'll call it for now. They might want to stop the rookie Monolith Code event entirely."

"...I suppose that's one way of looking at it," nodded Miyuki seriously to Tatsuya's reasoning. Not a moment later, Mayumi interrupted.

"Some people did call for a suspension of the event...but they decided to keep going with the qualifiers, just without us or Fourth High. In the worst case, we'll have to forfeit the second qualifying round."

Mayumi's words made Tatsuya frown in confusion this time. "In the worst case? Our team can't possibly play another match, so we don't really have a choice, do we?"

"Well, Juumonji is negotiating with the tournament committee now to figure out what to do."

"Right..."

The Nine School Competition didn't allow player substitution after the start of the qualifiers, but maybe he was trying to get them to acknowledge a special case here because of the unfair play. Unfortunately, their Monolith Code team was the cream of the crop—the freshman boys with the highest practical exam grades. Even if they did substitute others in, it would be difficult to win. *Would it be better to take the Monolith Code points out of the whole thing because the rules were broken?* he thought to himself.

Mayumi didn't, of course, know that he was doing such scheming calculations in his mind. "...Hey, Tatsuya. There's something I wanted to talk to you about."

The tinge of fawning in her voice was doubtlessly because of the succession of accidents making her feel insecure and unconsciously wanting to find someone to rely on. That's what Tatsuya thought to himself as he tried to ignore his little sister's real-time glare... He'd have preferred she directed it toward Mayumi, but he couldn't say that.

"Could you come with me for a bit?"

She must have been hesitant to let others hear about this.

Now there was a duet of stern stares on him, but Tatsuya pretended not to notice, and followed her.

◇ ◇ ◇

They went to the back of the tent, past the divider. Because it was a tent, the divider was just a piece of cloth, which normally had no soundproofing qualities. But overturning natural laws was what magic was for. Restlessly, Mayumi immediately created a field that blocked sound from getting outside.

"This is an excellent soundproofing wall."

"You think so?" She chuckled. "Thanks." Mayumi sat down with a nervous smile and gestured for Tatsuya to take the other chair. "Anyway, getting right down to it…"

"Yes?"

Silence.

She said she'd "get right down to it," but now she seemed to be having difficulty actually broaching the topic. He didn't like the idea of staying here alone with her for very long, for multiple reasons, so he decided to get things rolling himself.

"Let me guess—you want to know if this could have been sabotage, too?"

"…Yes. I wanted to hear your opinion on that. With Mari, you pointed out that CADs could have been tampered with, right?"

Tatsuya nodded.

"If they did the same thing this time, it would explain Fourth High's violence, but…how would someone prove it?" she asked.

"The only way would be to catch them in the act."

"Even if someone borrowed the CADs from Fourth High…?"

"*If* there were still traces of their activation programs being swapped out… Considering how silent Seventh High has been after their disqualification, though, I don't think we can hope for much."

"Oh…" Mayumi lowered her gaze to her hands, which were folded upon the tabletop.

That must have been what she was hoping for, thought Tatsuya as he looked at that display.

Without looking up, the young woman asked another question. "…If someone is trying to sabotage our school like you believe, Tatsuya…what do you think they're doing it for? A grudge? Or is it revenge for what happened this spring?"

Oh, so that's *what Mayumi was worried about*, thought Tatsuya. She was afraid this was retribution for them having ridden into the main base of the terrorists, who had infiltrated the school. Tatsuya possessed information to deny that. He knew this incident hadn't been orchestrated by the remnants of the broken terrorist group Blanche, or by anyone cooperating with them. If he told her what he knew, he could assuage her fears for her.

But for a moment, he didn't know whether it was okay to reveal it to her.

In the end, though, he decided to discard one of the cards from his hand. "…It's not related to that incident."

"Huh?" said Mayumi, looking up suddenly. "How do you know that?" Her return question was a reflection of her desire to know his grounds for saying that.

Tatsuya could fulfill that desire. At the same time, though, he couldn't reveal *everything*. "The night before the opening ceremonies… Well, it was already daytime at that point, I think. Anyway, in the middle of the night, there were thieves trying to sneak into the hotel. Three of them, and each of them had handguns."

"…That's the first I've heard of this."

"They forbade me from talking about it. I just happened to be there at the time, and ended up helping apprehend them… I don't know much about who they are, but it seems like the people meddling with this year's competition are part of a crime syndicate based in Hong Kong."

He substituted for the parts he couldn't reveal with a fabrication of events that sounded reasonable. Luckily, Mayumi didn't seem to doubt any of it. "It might have just been a coincidence...but don't do anything too dangerous."

"It feels like less of a coincidence and more of me just getting caught up in everything." Tatsuya sighed and shrugged, but Mayumi gave him an intent, suspicious look. She came to her senses before long, though, knowing this wasn't the time.

"Oh... They forbade you from speaking of it, right? Well, then, thank you for telling me."

"In exchange, I ask that you don't tell others."

"All right. I promise." Mayumi raised her right hand and pretended to swear an oath.

The natural and playful gesture almost made Tatsuya laugh out loud.

"...Again, this might sound indiscreet, but I feel a little better."

"...I just wouldn't let anyone else hear that."

"It's okay. I only say stuff like this when you're around, anyway."

Oh, dear. How am I supposed to interpret that? thought Tatsuya, a little worried. Was she still going on with the whole "friendly little brother" remark from the other day? As always, her mind was full of mysteries he couldn't solve.

◇ ◇ ◇

"How did it go?"

"As planned. First High will have to forfeit Monolith Code."

Yokohama Chinatown, on the top floor of a certain hotel. With reds and golds dominating the loud, gaudy furniture in the large room, five men sat at a round table, tea in front of them.

On the wall was a hanging scroll with the undulating, twisting body of a dragon in midair, embroidered with gold thread.

"Monolith Code has the most points out of every event. The rookie competition may only give half, but it's nothing to sneeze at."

Each of the men smiled and nodded. However, their faces did not look well, and their smiles were shows of courage, a brave expression—at least on the outside.

◇ ◇ ◇

After that, Mayumi told him to help her rein in the disturbance among the freshman girls, so he stayed put in the tent…but he had absolutely no idea what he was actually supposed to be doing. He was pretty sure it was the role of their female seniors to care for the female players' mentality. Inwardly cursing his stupidity for having nodded so easily, he got to work adjusting the CADs that would be used for the finals, acting like nothing had happened.

But before he knew it, that simple act found him surrounded by the freshman girls. Tatsuya personally wanted to think it was because they were flocking to their leader, Miyuki, who had already been next to him. Unfortunately, he wasn't dull enough to blindly believe that. Their eyes were all on him, that was for sure.

Not in an excited or passionate way. He couldn't mistake that, of course; he was no narcissist. Nor was he so mature that he didn't notice any of their gazes at all.

At the same time, though, he *was* dull enough not to understand what they meant.

He found it extremely difficult to work, given all the silent stares, but he couldn't threaten them in order to drive them away, either. They weren't trying to make pointless conversation with him or get in his way, either. Without much else he could do, he decided not to pay attention to them, and continued his work in silence, the same as he always did.

He looked the same as always.

His working looked the same as always.

It was just that Tatsuya didn't know how valuable that was.

His abilities forced him to keep staring directly at the truth: that everything in the world was always changing. Nothing was ever permanent for him.

So instead, as Miyuki watched the girls calm down a little after watching him act the same as he always did, she smiled and nodded in his place.

His presence of mind—or at least the outward appearance of such—had the biggest mental-stabilizing effect on Honoka. Her face had gone completely white when she first heard Morisaki's team had been in an accident, but with Tatsuya starting his briefing now as if nothing had happened, she was very quickly calming down. The speed of her change was actually enough to make Tatsuya start worrying instead.

"Our strategy won't be any different from the qualifiers. Mirage Bat is all about endurance, after all." Of course, he couldn't do anything right now about the worry he felt; the final match was soon. He didn't have time for that. He put his worry to the side and focused on the tactics in his mind. "Going all-out is strictly forbidden. What you need is to be calm and pace yourself."

Tatsuya's eyes went to Subaru; she made a point of flinching away.

"No silly tricks this time either, Honoka. Making fake orbs with illusion magic like you did in practice is only going to deplete your stamina."

This time, his warning made Honoka flinch.

"I just want both of you to focus on your strengths. If you do that, you'll be fine, and you'll get the one-two finish."

Though Tatsuya's bold declaration that they would take first and second did give them a little bit of anxiety, it gave them much more confidence. Together, they nodded resolutely.

◇ ◇ ◇

It was still midsummer, but the longest day of the year was already behind them. When seven o'clock came around, the sun had already gone down and the blue sky had changed into a starry one. The surface of the lake glittered with the reflection of heavenly light.

In the middle of the lake, standing on foothold columns, were six girls. Their costumes were thin and exposed their bodylines but, strangely, were not provocative. Instead, in the wavering light of the water's surface, they engendered the feel of a fairyland—it was clear indeed why the event had so many male fans.

In Mirage Bat, players competed to see who could strike and erase the most stereoscopic spheres, projected thirty-three feet above the ground, with a special stick. There was no impact upon hitting the spheres, though, and you wouldn't see them splitting or smashing apart. A processor analyzed the position of the players' sticks and the projection positions of the spheres. If both were located in the same place, the projector would stop projecting that sphere, and a point would be added to the player based on the signal from their stick.

There were two skills that determined victory in this event. One was how quickly one could leap up to where the spheres were being projected. The other was how quickly one could determine *where* they were being projected. Of these two factors, the second, surprisingly, tended to be overlooked. Nothing was faster than light, so people generally figured that you just had to be the fastest in order to perceive the light from the stereoscopic image and then move at it—but there were exceptions.

There was a time lag of less than a tenth of a second before the stereoscopic image formed in midair. If one could sense the wavering of the light waves as the image was forming, she could determine the location of the sphere before even seeing the light.

Honoka's senses were keenly attuned to light waves—or, more accurately, the changes in eidos that signaled the occurrence of light waves—so this had given her a large advantage in the qualifiers, and would do so again here.

A moment before a red sphere formed overhead, Honoka triggered her spell. The other players watched her do so with resignation. The next sphere formed. It was blue. Blue spheres stayed lit the longest, and were the easiest to rack up points with. The five players all began expanding an activation sequence at once. The first to leap into the air was Subaru. The two girls from First High were always the first ones to begin activation processing and the first ones to end it.

Competing, even more so than the players on the field, were the technical staff, watching from outside, either gritting their teeth in anger or biting their lips in anxiety. With such a large, stable difference in points, no one could discount how much of a difference there was in the ability of the CADs. But every school had chosen devices that came right up to the regulation limit, so their hardware specs were the same...

That left the software capabilities as the differentiator. And that pointed to how much better the *engineer* was.

"Damn it! How can they get such complex movements from such small activation programs?!" came a voice from somewhere. The person was probably filming Honoka's and Subaru's activation processing (the activation program's expansion until it was read) using a camera with a Kirlian filter (a filter for visualizing the density and activity levels of psions).

The First High girls jumped toward the stereoscopic images in a straight line—ignoring the effects of gravitational acceleration—then stopped in front of the shining orbs, scored, made a parabolic path back to a foothold, and canceled their momentum to land.

Neither Honoka nor Subaru had to do anything to their CAD at all for this sequence of movements. That meant that the entire activation program they were calling upon when they jumped contained every part of the process until they landed. The smaller the activation program, the faster the activation processing. And the fewer times one cast a spell, the less stress on the magician. In other words, it was optimizing the fastest event alteration with the least amount of magic power.

"It's like they have Taurus Silver over there or something!" grumbled someone else, with an angry click of their tongue.

"Ah-chan, what's wrong...?"

Azusa suddenly snapped out of her wide-eyed, frozen state and turned around to see Mayumi looking at her mysteriously. "Oh...it's nothing..." she said, looking down and making herself smaller.

"Okay," responded Mayumi, looking back at the match. Azusa reacted to things like that all the time, so she probably wasn't concerned.

But this time, Azusa's mind was filled with something other than embarrassment.

It was *like* Taurus Silver...? Someone had just grumbled that before, but this time, it was both glad and distressed. For some reason, it rang in her ears.

The completely manual arrangement of that activation sequence... The usage of latest technology to connect a specialized CAD subsystem to a multipurpose CAD main system... The technical skill needed to implement loop casting on a multipurpose CAD... Inferno...Phonon Maser... Niflheim... All of them high-level spells whose activation sequences aren't even public domain...

As someone who also wanted to be a magic engineer, all the stunts that had taken her by surprise in this tournament spun around in her brain.

"Like"? It's "like" they have Taurus Silver?

No, this... Wouldn't this be impossible if it wasn't Taurus Silver himself...?

Suddenly, she heard a voice in her memories:

—Perhaps he's actually a Japanese man, and young like us, too—

"...Are you sure nothing's wrong? If you're not feeling well, then you can go get some rest..."

"No, really, it's nothing..."

Mayumi stared at her, her eyes a mixture of puzzlement and worry. Azusa had jumped a little out of nowhere, but Azusa didn't have the focus to make excuses.

That voice came back to her in her memories. What if that wasn't just speculation, or a crazy guess?

Really? For real, real? For really, really real?

That one word was all Azusa could think of.

Outside, in the now-distant reality, the first period ended with her two underclassmen having taken an overwhelming lead.

◇ ◇ ◇

In the end, as Tatsuya predicted, the rookie Mirage Bat event ended with Honoka and Subaru taking a one-two finish. Right after the match ended, without time to share in their joy of victory, he was called back to the meeting room.

There, in contrast to his completely manic and unrestrained (female) classmates, his upperclassmen were hiding their emotions beneath careful expressions.

Mayumi, Mari, Katsuto, Suzune, Hattori, Azusa. The officers of First High were arrayed before him. He saw Kirihara and Isori there, too.

They'd just had people fall to major wounds, so nobody could show outward happiness, but nevertheless, their expressions looked a little too stiff. Hattori, in particular, had on an enigmatic stare, like he'd had no idea what expression to make and just decided to make his face into a mask instead.

Tatsuya steeled himself. This wasn't going to be good news.

"You did good work today. Thank you for helping us get better results than we anticipated." Mayumi came at him with considerably formal and ceremonious words.

His keen eyes did, however, pick up on Mayumi very quickly

glancing at Katsuto before she spoke. "Not at all. The players all did excellently." Tatsuya, too, came back with a safe, formal answer. He hadn't felt this level of tension since right after enrolling.

"Yes, of course. This is a result of Mitsui, Satomi, and everyone else all doing extremely well, too. But everyone here acknowledges that your achievements have been huge. Practically undefeated in all three events you were assigned to... We've secured at least second in the rookie competition at this stage, and I think it's thanks to you."

"...Thank you," said Tatsuya after a pause, lowering his head slightly in humility. He kept his eyes away from hers as he waited for her next words, but moments passed without her broaching the main topic.

Tatsuya slowly brought his gaze up to see Mayumi giving Katsuto a stern look. Apparently Katsuto had tried to begin this seemingly difficult conversation instead. What on earth had them hesitating this much?

Upon realizing Tatsuya was looking at her, Mayumi blinked slowly and thoughtfully. "As I told you before, we've secured at least second place in the rookie competition, even if we were to forfeit Monolith Code. Second right now is Third High, and in the rookie competition there are just fifty points between us. If Third High places first or second in Monolith Code, they will win the rookie competition, and if they place third or lower, we will win."

That meant that their strategic goal of not letting the point differential grow too large in the rookie competition in order to win the entire thing had been met. If that was true, then what in blazes were they this nervous about? And why did they call *him* here, anyway?

He finally started to get impatient with them. "I was under the impression from before the rookie competition began that this would be enough."

Mayumi seemed to understand that his mood was turning foul. A tinge of dismay crept into her otherwise blank expression. With clear urgency, she said, "Now that we're here..."

Still, she didn't try starting fresh; she appeared to be trying to get everything out all at once this time.

That was when Tatsuya finally realized what they all wanted from him.

"We all want to win first place in the rookie competition." At some point, her tone of voice reverted to its usual cadence. "Did you know Masaki Ichijou and Shinkurou Kichijouji are on Third High's Monolith Code team?" asked Mayumi.

Tatsuya replied with a simple yes.

"I see… Ichijou aside, you personally might know more about Kichijouji. With them on the same team, their prospects of losing the tournament are slim. If we forfeit Monolith Code, they will pretty much inevitably win the rookie competition."

So they wanted him to…

"So, Tatsuya…will you enter Monolith Code instead of Morisaki's team?"

…And that was the "business" Mayumi told him. Tatsuya had surmised that midway through.

"…May I ask two questions?" he said.

"Yes, what is it?"

He was 90 percent sure of the answer, but he wanted to make this clear. "The two remaining qualifying matches are being delayed until tomorrow, right?"

"Yes, they are. Given the circumstances, we had them change tomorrow's match schedule."

"Isn't it prohibited to change players even if they're injured during play and can't go on?"

"Again, with the situation, we had them make a special exception."

He'd expected both answers. Accepting them, though, was another story. "…Why was I selected instead of anyone else?" This wasn't so much a question as a roundabout refusal. He just couldn't outright say no to his upperclassmen and still be courteous.

Probably, Mayumi had so much trouble discussing this because she kind of knew Tatsuya would be like this, and hadn't thought of a way to convince him. Even as she smiled amicably, she had a look of worry to her. "Because we thought you'd be the most appropriate substitute…"

Mari, who until now had left it to Mayumi to say everything, saw her friend stammering and added herself to their group persuasion. "Leaving your practical exam grades aside, you're probably number one among the freshmen in actual combat skills."

It still wasn't enough to silence Tatsuya, though. "Monolith Code isn't 'actual combat.' It's a magical sport where physical attacks are forbidden. I'm sure you know that without me pointing it out."

"I still think you're a cut above the rest, though, even in pure magical combat," said Mari, shooting a glance at Hattori. He scowled bitterly.

It was a very callous and, thus, effective means of persuasion. Even Tatsuya now couldn't keep using his "lack of power" as an excuse. That wasn't the only card in his hand, though. "I'm not actually a player. If you need a replacement, there are several people left who are entered in only one event."

This time, Mari didn't have a response.

"Even if we don't account for how proud Course 1 students are, I would think choosing a member of the staff as a replacement player is bound to have mental repercussions in the future."

That was probably what they were *most* worried about, and the part they least wanted to talk about. People considered the rookie competition to be a way of training the new students. Even if they won this year, if it had a negative effect on their main competition results next year and the year after that, it would be putting the cart before the horse, in a way. If they elected a staff member to replace someone in a main event—and a Course 2 student at that—it wouldn't be just the leftover players; the pride of the entire Course 1 freshman class could be completely torn to shreds.

Mayumi and the others had nothing to say to that. Deciding that the conversation seemed to be over, Tatsuya opened his mouth to clearly decline.

That was when Katsuto's heavy, serious voice came out.

"Do not hide from this, Shiba."

Tatsuya found himself unable to immediately reply. He didn't understand what he'd just been told.

He knew he'd been giving excuses dressed in a sound argument. It *had* still been a sound argument, hadn't it? If he entered the event, then they might still get second even if he couldn't beat Third High. Forty points separated first and second place in Monolith Code. If they came in second, they could still win the rookie competition.

But in that case, no matter how anyone looked at it, Tatsuya would be the driving force behind their victory. The Blooms, steeped in their cheap elitism, would never be able to accept that. Even if he lost in the qualifiers anyway, the very fact that a Weed stepped in as a substitute for Monolith Code would be intolerable.

"You're already a member of our school's team." Katsuto's indication, however, shoved itself right into the little air pockets in Tatsuya's thoughts. "This isn't about whether you're a player or part of the staff. You are one of the twenty-one people chosen from among two hundred freshmen."

Between the lines, he said this: Tatsuya's very existence had already caused a lot of mental distress and chaos among the Course 1 students.

"And now, with an emergency in front of us, our team leader, Mayumi, has chosen you as a replacement. You are a member of this team, and now that you understand the job placed before you, you will fulfill your duty as such."

"But I..." He still had to say *something*. If he did this, then he...

"You are a member of this team, so we will not allow you to go against our leader's decision. If you believe there is a problem with her decision, then we, her supporters, will deal with that. You are not allowed to object to anyone but us. Not to her, not to anyone else related to this…not to anyone."

Tatsuya's eyes widened as he broke off. He finally understood what Katsuto was saying. They didn't care who didn't like this or the final result. They were the ones responsible for this, and they would bear all that responsibility.

"Don't run away, Shiba. You may be a substitute, but now you've been chosen, and you will do your duty."

His words didn't just apply to the Nine School Competition. There was no "substitute" system in the Nine School Competition in the first place.

Don't use your status as a Course 2 student to run away.

Stop making excuses.

Don't hide behind your position as one of the weak.

That was what he meant by "you may be a substitute." The word *substitute* also meant "Weed."

All of his escape routes had been blocked off.

But how could he run away after hearing all that?

"…All right. I'll do my duty."

Mayumi's and Mari's faces relaxed.

Katsuto nodded firmly.

"Who will the other members of my team be?" he asked, aware that he was speaking in a slightly more familiar tone. Of course, up until now, he'd been speaking in a more formal tone than he usually did to his seniors.

"Your choice."

"What…?" Tatsuya wasn't trying to play dumb. Once again, he didn't understand what Katsuto had just told him.

"You can choose the other two members of your team." Katsuto rephrased it as though he'd just remembered that he needed to give

Tatsuya by-the-book permission. "I'd prefer it if you could decide now, but if you need time, you can take an hour and then come back."

Upon hearing those words, Tatsuya reflexively thought, *Same as usual.* It was the same when they stormed Blanche's hideout in April. He didn't seem to mind giving decision-making power to an underclassman at all. If this had been Katsuto *pushing* the responsibility on him, it would have just been an underhanded way of protecting himself. But responsibility was the one thing Katsuto wouldn't let go of. *It's less like he was raised to be a leader and more like he's just that way,* Tatsuya thought. Then, he shook off his unchecked thoughts and returned his focus to the question at hand.

"No, I don't need any time to decide who to choose, but..." Two candidates had already come to the top of the list in his mind. "I don't know if they'll accept."

"We'll be present to convince them, as well."

...Meaning they won't let them refuse. For the first time, Tatsuya realized that the next leader of the Juumonji actually had a very pushy personality. "Is anyone all right? Even people not already team members?" For some reason, Tatsuya had started to feel more at ease with this. He felt himself getting pretty carried away here.

"Huh? Well, that's—"

"I don't care. Just more exceptions to add to the list. What's one or two more?"

"Juumonji..." Mayumi looked at him in shock and a little bit of reproach, but not a muscle on Katsuto's face budged.

"Then I'll take Mikihiko Yoshida from 1-E, and Leonhard Saijou, also from 1-E."

"What?! Shiba!" Hattori quickly tried to interrupt, but Suzune waved her hand and stopped him.

"That's fine. Nakajou?"

"Wh-what?!" Azusa's oversensitive reaction didn't get a blink out of Katsuto, either.

"Call Mikihiko Yoshida and Leonhard Saijou here. I believe they're staying in the hotel apart from our support members."

Despite Katsuto seeming so frank and audacious—and actually being that way—Tatsuya was surprised he knew so much. Still, he supposed students who weren't official members or ones who came to cheer for them staying in this hotel were fairly exceptional. Anyone who knew the reasons behind it would have their eyes on them. He guessed it wasn't that strange that Katsuto knew. Still, Tatsuya found himself completely impressed.

"…Tatsuya, may I ask your reason for choosing them?"

Mari had left the persuasion to Katsuto, and probably didn't want to object to Tatsuya's choice at this point. Still, she had a clear expression—not of being unable to accept it but more a degree of suspicion.

"Of course. The main reason is that I haven't seen much of the boys' matches or practice sessions." Tatsuya had been working maintenance for the girls this whole time, so he hadn't actually seen *any* of the male freshmen's matches *or* practice. "I don't know anything about what magic they're good at or what their capabilities are. The match is tomorrow. If I tried to learn about them from square one, neither our strategy nor CAD adjustments would make it in time."

"…But you're familiar with those two—is that it?"

"Yes. Not only are Yoshida and Saijou in my class, but I know them well."

"Hmm… You have a point. Even with another engineer helping with adjustments, teamwork is difficult when you don't know the others on the team."

Mari nodded thoughtfully, and then suddenly gave him an evil grin.

"But that's not the main reason, is it?"

Tatsuya didn't hesitate for a moment at Mari's question and gave a blunt response: "They're strong."

"Are they, now?" she asked.

The confidence in his voice caused not only Mari but also Mayumi, Katsuto, and Suzune to give him very interested looks.

◇ ◇ ◇

"Wait, Tatsuya... You serious?"

Leo kept asking that same question, not out of doubt so much as a complete loss of what to do.

"Look, President Saegusa is one thing, but do you think Chairman Juumonji would tell such an intricate lie?" Tatsuya's answers were getting more and more dismissive.

"I don't know anything about the student president..." Leo sighed. He looked like he was about to pinch himself to make sure he wasn't dreaming.

"I guess you're serious..." Next to him, Mikihiko's eyes wandered around restlessly, not knowing where to land.

"Miki, why don't you calm down a little?" Erika asked.

"My *name* is Mikihiko!"

Still, Erika's typical jab seemed to distract him a bit. He flumped down onto an empty bed and sat.

This was the twin-single room Tatsuya used. After the officers had unanimously agreed to the two substitutes—though it seemed pretty much compulsory—he had dragged the two of them here to explain how they were going to do things.

Erika and Mizuki coming along for the ride was pretty typical. Furthermore, outside the room, Miyuki, Honoka, and Shizuku had been grabbed by Eimi, Subaru, and some other team members not able to extricate themselves from this ring of wild excitement.

"Yeah, but...Mikihiko and I haven't prepared for this at all."

"Right... We don't have CADs. We don't even have anything to wear."

Mikihiko's face looked a little pale. His sudden promotion, this unexpected event of his Course 2 self being selected as a player for the rookie competition, was confusing and intimidating for him. He wouldn't ever admit he was acting cowardly, of course.

Leo seemed the same as always, but his usual tough expression was hiding in the shadows now. At a glance, he didn't seem to be on board with this.

Tatsuya hadn't expected Leo to seem so timid about it—Mikihiko was another story—but he certainly wasn't about to stop himself from getting them involved. He'd be damned if he was the only one working hard here.

"Relax. I don't have any gear for the match, either."

"How is that supposed to make me relax?" retorted Leo, without skipping a beat. Tatsuya waved his hand dismissively.

"Relax. And if you can't relax, then stop worrying."

"Wait, isn't that the same thing?" That immediate retort came from Erika.

Once again, he reflected on how much they were on the same track. "I suppose you're right. Well…I guess I can only say the same thing, but you'll be fine. Nakajou is handling our protective clothing and inner wear. She may not look like it, but she's always on top of things. She'll get us things that fit perfectly, with no problems."

The "she may not look like it" garnered no argument. None seemed to object to the evaluation of her having a good head on her shoulders despite her appearance.

"I'll get the CADs ready. I can get them done in an hour per person."

Normally, it was said that in order to tune a CAD from a blank slate to something usable and suitable for the magician using it, you needed three times that amount.

But neither Leo nor Mikihiko seemed very surprised. One of them probably didn't understand how amazing the one-hour turnaround was, but Tatsuya had been a veritable jack-in-the-box of surprises these past four days. They felt like Tatsuya could probably do anything.

"Is that enough? It's already nine. You need to do your own, too, right?" Erika, who out of the four of them knew the most about how much work CAD adjusting took, was the only person with a worried look on her face.

"I'll be fine. I can do my own in ten minutes."

Her fears seemed to be groundless. Reminded again of how outside the norm he was, Erika gave a grand old sigh. "In ten minutes? Huh, ten minutes...? Remind me again why I even bother worrying about this stuff."

"Unfortunately, that really *isn't* much time to work with."

"Huh?" Tatsuya's out-of-character complaint changed Erika's partially affected listlessness so quickly that he could almost hear it.

"This was all so sudden that I don't have anything resembling a good plan. We don't have any time to practice either, of course, so we'll be going in without it. With only a rough plan behind us when we step out there, it'll basically be a slugfest. I can't work under conditions like this."

The things spilling from Tatsuya's mouth were more like idle grumblings than complaints.

Erika's stiff expression loosened up and she nodded in an exaggerated way. "...You're right. Cunning is how you operate, huh?"

"Gee, you didn't have to put it that way..." Erika's purposely mean expression caused Tatsuya's shoulders to slump and his facial muscles to finally relax. "Anyway...nothing will get done if I keep complaining about something set in stone. While Ichihara and Nakajou are getting the necessary things together, let's go over our strategy."

"But you just said there wasn't time to make one." Erika wasted no time in tripping him up, but Mizuki stood in her way—well, actually, she just stepped in front of her—her expression low-spirited.

"Erika...let's not get in Tatsuya's way, okay?"

"Hey! Mizuki, I was just trying to do something about the gloom and doom in the air—"

"Okay, but before you start goofing around to get rid of the gloom and doom, quiet down a little. You're the one who said they don't have time."

Recently, Mizuki had finally gotten the knack of how to deal with her friend. She wasn't letting people pull her around and fluster her as much as she used to.

Meanwhile, Erika groaned and puffed out her cheeks at being treated so lightly. Still, she didn't keep teasing him; whatever she said, however she acted, she was ultimately here because she was worried about Tatsuya, Leo, and Mikihiko.

"First, our formation…" Tatsuya continued, as though the disruption never happened. "I want to be on offense, Leo to be on defense, and Mikihiko to be flexible."

"All right, then. But what do I do on defense?"

"I have a question, too: 'Flexible'?"

Maybe Leo and Mikihiko had both resigned themselves at this point. Or maybe they'd been roused to action. Maybe they'd just gotten serious (actually, that was the most probable option), but whatever the reason, now that they'd switched over to a positive stance, Tatsuya found himself easily explaining:

"On defense, you'll be protecting our monolith from enemy attacks. You know how to win Monolith Code, right?"

Leo answered the question a little bit shakily. "Make the enemy team unable to keep fighting, or download the code in the monolith to a terminal, right?"

"Yeah. To read the hidden code, you need to fire a special type-less magic program into the monolith. The magic program is like a key, and it'll split the monolith in two. You're not allowed to put the monolith back together once it's been split, but you *are* allowed to block the spell that splits it. Also, the maximum range for the magic program is set at thirty-three feet. It's programmed not to unlock the monolith if it's triggered from farther away."

"…Which means the defender has to keep the enemy team from

getting within thirty-three feet of his monolith, to hold back the key magic program from getting to the monolith if someone fires one, and to get in the enemy's way so that they can't read the code if they do split it, right?"

"You get an A." Tatsuya nodded, satisfied at Leo's answer. "Normally, you can use anti-magic to block the key from being triggered, but you can stop the monolith from splitting with hardening magic, too, if you use it how you normally do. To be more precise, even if the monolith is split, you can keep it from opening up. That way, you don't break the rule of *not putting it back together after it's split.*"

Leo looked at him incredulously, and then dubiously. "I don't wanna say this, Tatsuya, but that's pretty much the *definition* of *cunning...*"

But it would take a stronger nasty remark (well, a joke between friends) to disconcert Tatsuya. "You say the same things as Erika, you know."

Leo was the one to cry out in dismay: "Would you drop it?!"

"What is that supposed to mean?!" Erika wasted no time following on Leo's heels.

"Okay, okay, Erika! Let's stop, all right? Leo, you calm down, too." With Mizuki's arbitration, the two immediately averted their glares at each other.

"...All right, I get what the key is for," said Leo, pulling himself together. Then he asked, "What do we do to beat the enemy? We can't punch or kick them, right? Not to brag, but I'm terrible at long-range attack magic."

"We'll use this," said Tatsuya, pulling out the "sword" he'd gotten Leo to test out.

"...But aren't physical blows against the rules?" asked Leo.

Tatsuya held out a thin booklet. "A pamphlet?" Before Leo could ask what it was for, he noticed a note stuck to a page corner. He flipped to that page instead of asking. "The Monolith Code rules...?" The page contained a simple explanation of rules for those with no background knowledge in the event, and a printed photograph of what the matches looked like.

"Like it says there, using magic to propel physical objects into opponents doesn't constitute breaking the rules."

"Propelling physical objects with magic… Oh. I get it."

The sword's blade was disconnected in the middle, and it would move around in midair in accordance with the movements of the hilt. In magic system terms, the blade was being extended without a middle, but to the eyes it looked like a disembodied sword blade jumping around in the air. Since they weren't physically connected, it met the requirement of "using magic to propel physical objects."

"Wait, Tatsuya, is that why you made this in the first place?"

Leo's question was actually serious. Tatsuya smiled drily and shook his head. "I'm really starting to feel like you think too highly of me… This was just something I made on a whim. I'm not *completely* obsessed with evil plans."

He could tell that neither Leo nor Erika really believed him on that point, but time was short, so he ignored it.

"This armament CAD, the Mini-Communicator, is already set up for Leo," he explained. "I also changed it so the separation distance and connection time are variables, so don't mess up with it."

"Yikes, going in without practice, huh?"

"All of tomorrow is basically going to be unpracticed." He paused, then smirked suggestively. "Besides, I can guarantee it'll be easier to use than last time."

"Well, I guess that's fine, then." Leo responded to Tatsuya's villainous smile with a confident grin as he took the Mini-Communicator.

"Next up is Mikihiko's role in all this…"

"Yeah, Tatsuya, what am I supposed to do?" Mikihiko leaned forward on the bed. He'd been clearly lost at first, but now he started looking ahead—or at least had found his fighting spirit. Having a little bit of pep in his step would be beneficial in this situation, so he passed over it and began to explain.

"When I say 'flexible,' it means I want you to support both the attacker and the defender as needed." After answering simply, he then turned to a question: "You have other kinds of long-range magic besides the lightning spell you used before, right?"

"Well, I guess..." stammered Mikihiko in reply.

Most families that passed down old magic tried to keep the magic abilities they possessed a secret. With how much magic had been categorized and systematized under the name of modern magic studies, magic had been formalized, save for a few special cases. However, those types of ingrained values would likely continue to be heavily reflected in their unconscious actions. But Mikihiko was going to be on the same team as the rest tomorrow, so him not being up-front about his abilities would constitute a serious issue.

"That lightning spell is rank C lethality, right?"

"...All it does is paralyze the targets, so a rank C would make sense. It's not on the rank list, though, since it's not public."

"So it's a private spell... Does that mean you'd have problems using it tomorrow?"

"No...it should be fine. The casting process is what we're keeping a secret, not the theory behind the spell itself. If I use a CAD instead of amulets to trigger it, there won't be a problem...but, Tatsuya?"

"What?"

"Didn't you...say this before? About how... Well, the Yoshida family spells have a lot of unnecessary parts, and that's why I can't use magic the way I want to."

"Yeah."

Erika's eyes widened as she listened, but Tatsuya unflinchingly—or perhaps unreservedly—nodded. Mizuki covered her mouth with her hands. Even Leo couldn't say anything. Labeling techniques that had been polished and refined over many years by famous old magic families as defective required a ton of confidence. Or an impudent, insolent narcissist—a frog in the well, so to speak—who was convinced that his way was the best way. But Tatsuya didn't seem like the latter.

"...Then can you teach me more effective techniques?"

"Not teach new ones—but I can rearrange the ones you already have."

"...Sorry, but I don't understand the difference." Upon closer inspection, Mikihiko's hands were tightly folded, and very slightly trembling.

"For example, I think that lightning spell is derived from Thunder Child. All I can do is eliminate the unnecessary bits in the technique and rebuild it into a magic program that will give you the same event-altering effects with less calculation. The spell you use will be the same as the one you already know."

"...I guess it's really true you can understand spells just by seeing them. You're right—it's derived from Thunder Child. The technique itself is disguised to make it difficult to figure out its weak point. But that probably has to do with the unneeded parts you're talking about."

"Back when we needed long incantations for spells, having a safeguard against the possibility of something interrupting you was probably effective. But now that CADs have sped everything up in modern magic, countermeasures that take advantage of a spell's individual properties—as long as one can't determine the type of spell from the activation program—don't mean very much. If you first noticed the spell after it changed into a magic program, the caster would activate it while the person was trying to choose a countermeasure. The really effective anti-magic spells in modern magic are the ones that nullify the effects of all spells, regardless of their type."

Mikihiko chuckled once. Strangely enough, the laugh didn't seem self-deprecating. "Ha-ha, I get it... Old magic was supposed to have more power behind it, but it can't stand up to modern magic, huh?"

"That's not correct, Mikihiko."

"Huh?"

"Neither old magic nor modern magic is better than the other. Each has its strengths and weaknesses. A straightforward clash would give an advantage to modern magic due to how overwhelmingly faster it is. That's all. If you were doing a surprise attack from where they couldn't sense you, the power and secrecy of old magic would win out. Remember what Old Master Kudou said? What matters is how you use it. And I recommended you because I believe the surprise factor your magic has will be an important weapon."

"The surprise factor...? That's the first time anyone's ever said that to me," said Mikihiko seriously, closing his eyes. After a moment, he opened them again decisively, as if to drive away his hesitation.

"All right. The magic I can use is programmed in my CAD, not just my amulets, so please, arrange them as you see fit. I'll trust you on this one."

"Thanks, Mikihiko. And since we trust each other, there's one more thing I want you to tell me."

"That's fine. We need it, right? I'm not going to hide anything. My father is the one who sent me here, so even if one or two secrets get out, he can't complain."

"You don't need to worry. I'm a tight-lipped guy."

"Err, me too. Tight-lipped. I promise not to tell anything about what I hear."

"Me too."

"You already know I'm tight-lipped!"

The others in the room, who had been staying quiet until then, spoke up as if competing for the award of most secretive. Mikihiko directed a suspicious gaze to the last of them, but he overrode his emotion with reason and nodded at Tatsuya.

"Then I'll be short. Can you use Vision Synchronization?"

There was a pause before answering—not out of hesitation but pure surprise. "...You even know *that*? Kokonoe tells you everything, doesn't he?"

"Kind of."

"...You really are full of surprises, Tatsuya. Um, the answer to your question is yes. I still can't use Fivesense Synchronization, but I can use Sense Synchronization once or twice."

"Just vision is fine, Mikihiko. Now, about our strategy..."

Tatsuya wasn't speaking particularly quietly, but Mikihiko naturally leaned forward and turned an ear toward him.

As Tatsuya previously asserted, he finished tuning Leo's CAD in less than an hour.

With his retuned device in hand, Leo headed for the outdoor practice ground with Erika. She'd volunteered to be his practice partner so that he could get used to the Mini-Communicator.

It was already pretty late, but Tatsuya had given in; since Erika was with him, there would be no mistakes from either one of them.

And now, as he pushed madly along tuning Mikihiko's CAD, Azusa, who was next to him, watched him in a daze. Mikihiko, the CAD's user, was wide-eyed at Tatsuya's unique adjustment style and typing speed, but such surface details weren't what shocked Azusa.

Right now, Tatsuya was working on arranging activation sequences, rebuilding techniques activated by traditional casting tools from old magic into spells usable by modern magic. That process was not smart by any standard—there were redundancies and slight errors here and there, as though it was an awkward machine.

Azusa personally wouldn't find fixing those errors to be very difficult. But the arrangements expanding before her eyes were complete, fundamental rewrites. Tatsuya clearly understood operational theory, from activation to magic, and he was currently rewriting before her very eyes the entire activation program—into something that wouldn't harm the magic programs' base functionality.

Activation programs were like the blueprints for magic programs. Rewriting an activation program also meant rewriting a magic program. If you went beyond slight fixes to make one more suitable for the magician and reached a level where you could eliminate needless parts of the magic program's process and optimize it, that was no longer "fixing" or "arranging" the magic program—it was essentially improving it, to the point of improving the spell itself.

When Tatsuya had told her, before even starting, that that was what he'd been going for, Azusa had honestly doubted it was even possible. But now, before her eyes, without any experimental verification—no, without even observing how the spell actually worked in reality—he extracted the essence of the spell directly from the activation sequence, got rid of the unnecessary parts, and rebuilt it into a brand-new activation sequence, all in a *text editor*.

Azusa had originally volunteered to help Tatsuya for the rookies' Monolith Code once he was switched to a playing position, but she couldn't possibly touch such crazy work. As she went over the newly written activation programs, checking for syntax errors—since that was about all she could do—the suspicions she'd been having crept ever closer to conviction.

This boy, Tatsuya Shiba, is nowhere near a high school–level magic engineer…

He's even beyond being a simple magic engineer…

He has to be…

As Azusa sat there, her mind in chaos, Tatsuya finished the work of rewriting Mikihiko's activation sequences in exactly one hour.

[10]

The fifth day of the rookie competition began under a veil of confusion.

There had been an unprecedented rule violation during Monolith Code the day before. First High, which had been rendered unable to continue the match due to injury, normally would have forfeited their remaining two matches, but the competition committee decided to allow the matches to be postponed to let First High enter a substitute team.

Monolith Code used an irregular round-robin system where each school would play four matches in the qualifiers, with the top four teams advancing to the finals tournament. If two teams tied, any victories by forfeit or default due to disqualification would be subtracted from the number of total wins and their results then compared. If there were none of those, whichever had a head-to-head victory would advance to the tournament. Failing that, whichever team had won a match the quickest would advance.

Currently, Third High had four victories, Eighth High had three, while First, Second, and Ninth had two a piece. Ninth High won out over Second High for having a shorter total match time in their two victories, whereas First High had one win by default, meaning their two victories wouldn't get them into the tournament.

If First High won the special matches today against both Second and Eighth Highs, the ones to advance would be First, Third, Eighth, and Ninth. If they beat Second High and lost to Eighth, it would still be First, Third, Eighth, and Ninth Highs in the tournament. If they lost to Second High and won against Eighth, then First, *Second*, Third, and Ninth Highs would advance. If they lost to both Second and Eighth Highs, the tournament would contain Second, Third, Eighth, and Ninth Highs.

All in all, the score tally was a little bit strange. The important thing was that if First High beat Second High, then Second High wouldn't make it out of the qualifiers even though they currently had a lead due to First High's one default victory. It was only natural that Second High would be very unhappy with the exception being made. Plus, if they won the first match and then didn't try on the second, Ninth High would probably make a lot of noise about match fixing.

"...So in order to settle everything in a friendly way, we can't lose either of our two matches..."

"If we're going out there, we're going out there to win. No questions asked. If we lost, there would have been no point in having this exception made in the first place."

"I guess I shouldn't have been worried."

That was a conversation between Tatsuya and Mayumi.

All three members of First High's substitute team being non-registered players was a source of confusion as well. Instead of choosing substitutes from their players representing their top ten in abilities, they had picked one from the technical staff and two complete newcomers. Some speculated First High had Monolith Code specialists up their sleeve, but if they had, they would have just entered them in the one event. Thus, the other schools were having a hard time figuring out what they were planning.

And when the three of them appeared on the field, it only heightened the bewilderment.

"…We stick out like a sore thumb…" mumbled Mikihiko, not quite able to calm down.

Tatsuya understood but put a quick end to that thought. "Any player who comes on the field is bound to draw attention," he said, feigning ignorance.

"No, not that…" replied Mikihiko, shaking his head and looking over to Leo. "It's, well, *that's* what stands out…"

Leo looked down at his waist, knowing exactly what Mikihiko's glance meant.

The voices from the seats lent credence to Leo's guess (though they couldn't hear them, of course). Their protective suits and helmets were the same as the other schools' teams.

"A sword? Aren't direct strikes against the rules?"

However, the presence of the Mini-Communicator did encourage the crowd to start muttering. Less than 10 percent of those in the audience realized the "sword" hanging at his waist was an integrated armament CAD. Even among the players and technical staff, only a few people knew that they even existed. The crowd's muttering was inevitable.

Plus, the normal way to use an integrated armament CAD was to elevate an actual weapon—the integrated armament—using magic. More slicing power for katanas, more stabbing power for spears, more pure force for blunt weapons, more defense for shields…

Examples of the magic used included High-Frequency Blade, Acceleration, Momentum Increase, Hardening, and Reflector, but each of those was meant to raise one of the weapon's natural abilities— that's what made it an integrated armament CAD.

It was a sword, so it should have had a spell to bolster its direct physical attack power, like its slicing or stabbing power. And those familiar with CADs knew that would be against the rules of Monolith Code.

However, Leo wasn't the only one drawing stares.

* * *

"There he is…"

"Yeah. I didn't think he'd be showing up as a player."

"Double handgun–style, with a bracelet on his right arm on top of that… Can *anyone* use three devices to their full potential at the same time?"

"It's *him* we're talking about, though. I doubt it's a show of force or a bluff. Those specialized types in his left and right leg holsters are long-barreled handguns…"

"So he won't be using it as a trump card. He's going to be using both specialized devices at once right from the start. If he just wanted to use magic of different families, he could have just gone with a multi-purpose type…"

"Why don't you show us why you're using multiple devices at once, Shiba?"

The eyes of all the schools' players and staff, symbolizing this conversation between Masaki and Kichijouji, were locked upon Tatsuya—the super-engineer they hated so much for capturing all the top positions in every event he was assigned to. That was what the other school members thought of him; they didn't know he was a Course 2 student. Tatsuya was drawing caution from the opposing school's team, too, with his irregular style open for all to see. Nobody was able to laugh at him.

The only exception was none other than the few seats up in the grandstand reserved for First High.

The female freshman athletes were giving passionate cheers, while in contrast, the male freshman athletes stared at him coldly.

There were also cheers for the opposing team…

…and boundless curiosity that dominated all those things.

That was how the match between First High and Eighth High began.

◇ ◇ ◇

"The forest stage? Against Eighth High?" muttered Mari, her eyes on the monitor display.

"We'd be at a disadvantage…normally, anyway," answered Mayumi, also watching the screen.

Monolith Code took place on various outdoor stages following certain rules. The Nine School Competition used five stages: forest, crag, grasslands, canyon, and city.

Of all the nine magic high schools, Eighth High put the most effort into outdoor practice. The forest stage was like home turf to them. The stages were *supposedly* selected by a program that generated random numbers, but now, for this special match, the team that would have gotten away with a default victory had been given an advantageous stage. It was hard not to have doubts about it being deliberate.

…Still, Mayumi, Mari, and the other officers gathered in their tent weren't very worried. The First High execs were all well aware that Tatsuya received private training from Yakumo Kokonoe the *ninjutsu* user. An environment with a lot of obstacles, like the forest stage, was essentially the best place to use *ninjutsu*. That was common sense for them.

Still, for the other schools that didn't know the truth, it was a huge miscalculation. Between the two start positions, where the monoliths were set up, was a distance of half a mile. They would need to run that distance, weaving between trees and brush, with their protection suits, helmets, and CADs equipped. It would take five minutes at the very least. Not to mention that they'd probably advance while being cautious of the enemy. Even if there were no battles on the way, it could easily take twice as long.

…But on the contrary, a battle broke out near Eighth High's monolith before five minutes had even passed.

Cameras to detect rule violations were always on all the players, and their video feeds were up on the big displays in front of the grandstand. With all the things getting in the way on this stage, the audience had to rely on them.

Right now, one big display hanging in the air showed Tatsuya from behind, having just leaped out in front of an Eighth High defender.

"So fast…!" muttered Kichijouji.

"Self-acceleration?" answered Masaki in the form of a question, his eyes fixed on the display.

The figure was only in the image for a moment; in the next, he was outside the frame.

Now in the picture was the defender on one knee.

The picture changed angles to show Tatsuya running around the right side of the defender and sprinting toward the monolith.

"No, it doesn't look like he's using magic to move… Wait!"

The defender pointed his CAD's muzzle at Tatsuya. Tatsuya's previous attack seemed to do no more than cause the enemy to break posture.

The handgun-shaped specialized CAD with a shortened barrel section expanded an activation program. A moment later, the screens doing the psion visualization processing showed the Eighth High player's expanded activation program being blown away by a quickly expanding nonphysical shock wave—a psionic explosion.

A moment ago, Tatsuya had been holding a CAD in his left hand. From what people could see from behind him, his right hand had been empty. But now, in the image, he was running while pointing the CAD muzzle in his right hand at the defender.

"When did he…?!" asked Masaki, unable to manage the *pull it out* part of the sentence.

Kichijouji replied, though it didn't answer the question. "Could that have been…Program Demolition?"

"Program Demolition?!"

With only a cursory glance to the defender, who was now standing in a daze after his activation program was destroyed, Tatsuya went in front of the monolith and pulled the trigger in his right hand.

After seeing the key Tatsuya fired activating, and the enemy's monolith splitting in two, Honoka clapped and jumped up. "He did it! The monolith opened!"

But Shizuku, next to her, frowned in puzzlement. "...That's strange."

"What is, Shizuku?" asked Eimi from among the cluster of freshman girls there.

"The monolith is open, so why is he retreating?"

She was right. Tatsuya didn't approach the monolith to read its code. Instead, he switched direction and ran into the shadows of the trees.

"You're right," replied Eimi. "Miyuki, what do you think?"

"Even my brother would have trouble entering five hundred twelve characters with the enemy pestering him."

Victory in Monolith Code was achieved by either knocking out all the enemies or by transmitting the 512 characters hidden inside the monolith to the referee's seat. The clamshell-shaped wearable keyboard on his left arm was a terminal for entering in that code and transmitting it. Tatsuya may have been a quick typist, but putting in 512 characters on a hard-to-use setup would still take some time.

"Oh... I guess this is the first time I've seen someone use the key before the defense was disabled."

As Shizuku mumbled out what sounded like an excuse, the Eighth High defender ran after Tatsuya, into the brush.

"Wait... Was that...?"

Mari might have been the most shocked at the anti-magic Tatsuya used.

As she croaked out words as if out of breath, Mayumi, next to her, spoke in an oddly unemotional voice. "Program Demolition... I had a hunch, but I guess he *can* use it..."

"Mayumi, you know what he just did?!" demanded Mari, almost about to grab hold of her.

Mayumi glanced at her, then looked back at the screen. "Program Demolition rams a cluster of compressed psionic particles directly into a target without going through the Idea, and thereby explodes the particles. It blasts away any psion information bodies *it attaches itself to* that contain magical information, like activation programs or magic programs. It's called Program Demolition because it does just that: it demolishes magical programs.

"I say magic, but it's just a cannonball of psions that don't have any event-altering effects like magic programs do, so Information Boost and Area Interference won't affect it. Plus, the pressure applied by the cannonball itself repels the effects of Cast Jamming. It has no physical effect at all, so it just goes straight through any obstacles. And then it blows up any magic being triggered at the target coordinates. You can eventually nullify it by meeting it with a very strong psionic flow or by creating a defense with many layers of psionic walls.

"But other than its short range, it has no flaws. It's a typeless spell, said to be the strongest anti-magic out of anything practical... but almost nobody can use it. I know I can't. You're not *messing up* the spell; you're *blasting it away*. I can't create that kind of pressure with my psionic retention capacity. It's a superhuman feat."

"...So it's like a big muscle-head swinging around a hammer and wrecking buildings with it?"

Mayumi had to laugh at the roundabout analogy. "I see you're still calm enough to say such mean things, Mari. But you're basically right. After his bout with Hanzou, I decided that Tatsuya was one of those magicians who liked to stay very technical and delicate with his skills...but I guess he's actually more like a really powerful warrior."

"Then that accident we ran into on the way here...?"

"That's probably it. I didn't see it, but you did, right? Someone blew away at least ten overlapping magic programs while it was happening in one attack... How high *is* his psionic retention capacity, anyway?"

*   *   *

For their formation, Eighth High had gone with one defender and two attackers. The two attackers had split to the left and right to advance. One of them finally made it to First High's main base.

"Oh, no, Tatsuya! You need to hurry!"

"You can do it, Leo!"

First High's main base—where their monolith was set up—was placed in direct view of the cheering seats. As Erika and Mizuki watched, Leo, stationed in front of the monolith, pulled out the sword at his waist.

The attacker came out of the shadows of the trees. In his hand was the same specialized CAD as his teammates—he was clearly aiming to take down Leo, the defender, before going to open the monolith.

Then, two things happened at once:

The attacker pointed his CAD at Leo, and Leo swung his armament device, the Mini-Communicator, in a horizontal slash.

"He got him!"

"He's good!"

Mizuki and Erika both cheered.

The metal sheet flying in a horizontal arc, straight through the cluster of trees, struck the Eighth High player with force and sent him toppling to the ground. Leo, who had been standing in the perfect position to attack past those trees, had found the attacker in the exact spot he wanted, then slammed him with the detached blade.

The blade came hurtling back, recombining with the sword and returning it to normal. Leo looked up at the sky, then fired the blade in his hands straight overhead and stopped it high in the air.

"Warriooooooor!"

With a shout, he swung the blade down. It traveled with appropriate angular velocity and delivered the finishing blow to the fallen Eighth High player.

* * *

"What was *that*?" asked Suzune. She hadn't raised her voice, but it sounded like there was a nick in the blade of her usual coolness.

The one to answer was Azusa, who had been up last night helping him adjust it, and thus knew about it. "That's the Mini-Communicator, an armament device and original spell that Shiba developed," she explained. "An armament device and an original spell of the same name... How on earth does it work?"

Suzune nodded. "I see. That's a novel idea. The system seems a bit slipshod for something Shiba made, though."

"Slipshod?" repeated Azusa, seemingly confused.

Suzune answered as if carefully giving instructions. "Yes. This spell is extremely limited by the user's physical characteristics and the environment it can be used in."

The third Eighth High player was wandering through the woods. This was called the forest stage, but they obviously weren't using the forests at Mount Fuji. It was an artificial hilly area constructed on part of the maneuvering grounds that they'd moved trees into—a training field, and nothing more. In the half century since transplanting them here, they'd become native to the area. Still, a half-mile-long forest wasn't something one could get lost in.

But right now, he really had lost track of where he was.

"Damn it, where the hell am I?! Stop sneaking around! Show yourself!" he hollered, his irritation on clear display as he activated a spell that would erase ultrasonic waves. By themselves, they weren't that powerful; at most, they would give you a minor ringing in your ears.

But this ringing was really bothering him for some reason. His helmet was general-purpose gear used in the army, but it mainly protected one's head from impact and pressure. It didn't keep gas or sound out at all. It left his face out in the open, too, with several small holes at each ear for him to hear out of.

If he came under sonic attack, he'd have to protect himself with his own magic power. He returned the CAD, which matched his teammates', to his holster, then took a spare terminal-shaped, portable multipurpose CAD out of his pouch. His plan had been to fight the ultrasonic waves intermittently assailing him while making his way toward the enemy monolith.

But no matter how far he went, he never came across the enemy base.

There was something he hadn't realized. A super-low frequency sound was mixed in with the super-high frequency sound. While he was preoccupied solely with the latter, the former was disturbing his semicircular canals. With limited vision, he had to keep turning left and right to see around him. And because the organs that allowed him to keep track of his direction were disturbed, he was in a state where he couldn't get an accurate handle on what direction he was going.

If he'd known he had lost his sense of direction, he could have chosen to look at a compass. But he hadn't realized how his senses had been thrown off—plus, he was in an artificial environment he couldn't imagine getting lost in, making it hard for him to correct himself.

He had been caught in a snare created by his own opinion.

The one who'd created the trap was Mikihiko.

The spirit magic: Echoing Labyrinth.

The target wouldn't be able to locate the caster, even if they wanted to counterattack, because their sense of direction was screwed up. Actually, he probably couldn't have found Mikihiko even if his sense of direction had been working fine.

Mikihiko was using spirits—information bodies separate from physical forms—as a medium to conduct this sonic attack. Even if the player figured out the magic's source, he would find only spirits wandering there.

It was a stealth technique that kept the caster from being discovered. This was exactly what Tatsuya valued in spirit magic: the element of surprise.

As he tailed the Eighth High player, who was trying to advance but was actually retreating, he decided it was time to move to the next phase of the plan.

Now that he'd pulled the defender away from his monolith and lured him into the woods, Tatsuya considered which plan to take: take him out or coordinate with the others? Taking the defender out would get him out of the picture long enough for Tatsuya himself to input the code. But if he wanted to coordinate, he would continue stringing the defender along by running around, and then Mikihiko would input the code.

He thought for only a moment before deciding to eliminate him. He pulled out his left CAD, pointed it at the ground, and pulled the trigger. The motion activated a weight-decreasing spell, and he lightly jumped off the ground over the trees. Now that he'd used magic, his opponent should have figured out where he was. The usage of magic created an unavoidable reaction in the nearby eidos. Following the ripple of that effect allowed a magician to locate where the caster had been at the time they'd activated the spell. Experienced magicians could even tell what type of magic had been used, but would the Eighth High player be able to figure out he'd used a weak weight-decreasing spell? Even if he could figure out the type, could he predict that Tatsuya had used it to jump above the tree cover?

—That would actually be better for Tatsuya.

He was jumping from tree branch to tree branch *without using magic*. Furthermore, he was almost perfectly preventing the recoil from showing on the trees when his legs sprung off them, too.

Sure enough, the Eighth High defender stopped at the point Tatsuya had jumped from. He looked up.

His back now turned, Tatsuya pulled the trigger in his right hand.

The big displays doing the psion visualization processing showed a typeless magic psi-wave overtaking the Eighth High defender. He wobbled a bit, then crumpled to the ground.

"...I bet that was Resonance. The typeless one."

"He resonated the psi-wave with his biological wave motion and took him down."

Kichijouji nodded at Masaki's words. "It looks like his right-hand device is for typeless magic, and his left-hand device is for weight magic."

"George...doesn't his typeless magic seem strangely like old magic?"

"You think so, too, Masaki? *Shugendo*...or maybe *ninjutsu*. Biological wave motion—I think old magic calls that *ki*. It looks like a magic system that specializes in controlling it."

"I don't think even people who do old magic call it *ki* anymore. That sounds too phony."

"Huh? It's not like you to berate people on taste, Masaki."

The Eighth High defender hadn't completely lost his ability to move, though. He was at least conscious. But right now, he didn't have the leg strength to chase Tatsuya.

Tatsuya leaned down on a branch and used it like a spring to take a big leap. He faced down, pulled the trigger in his left hand, and then hit the ground running without even seeming to land first. In the blink of an eye, he made it to the monolith.

The screens in the tents displayed Tatsuya opening the clamshell cover and smoothly typing in the code.

Mayumi heard cries from afar, coming from Eighth High's cheer squad, and for some reason glanced at Mari.

Mari was looking at her, too. "...They won."

"...They did."

This meant they'd be advancing to the finals tournament. For some reason, though, they didn't feel like waving both hands in the air and celebrating.

After the code was sent, the match-ending siren went off. Before the First High flag got all the way in the air, those in the school's cheer squad were going crazy.

"They won! They won!!"

"That was amazing! Totally amazing! It was flawless, a flawless victory!"

"Congratulations, Miyuki!"

"Your brother did it!"

The high-pitched, excited voices were all coming from the freshman girls.

They acted like they'd already won the championship.

In the general attendance seats there was a slightly more subdued mood of celebration.

"Phew... This is bad for my heart."

"Why? Tatsuya and Leo and Yoshida are all unhurt."

"Well, I was just worried about everyone but Tatsuya..."

"Huh? What were you worried about?"

"I mean... Well, a few things," replied Erika, tripping over her words for some reason.

Mizuki cocked her head to the side. "You're being weird, Erika."

Erika had ten or twenty things to say to Mizuki calling *her* weird, but she didn't make a point of making her friends distressed for no reason, so she decided to let Mizuki treat her like a weirdo for now.

◇ ◇ ◇

The next match would be in thirty minutes and it would pit First High against Second. The interval felt short, but for Masaki and Kichijouji, who would be playing First High later today (or at least, were convinced of such), it was nothing to worry about. First High's players getting worn out was actually something to be happy about, but such a thought was of the corrupting sort. Masaki consciously drove it from his mind.

They hadn't announced yet what the next stage would be. Still in the stands after the previous match, Masaki spoke to Kichijouji sitting in the seat next to him. "What did you think of that match?"

"You're not asking about the match in general, are you? You're talking about *him*."

"Yeah. How would you attack him, George?"

"I get the feeling he's *really* used to fighting. The way he moves, the way he predicts what others will do, his positioning... I think we should be more worried about his combat technique than his magic abilities."

"Well, what about his magic abilities, then?"

"I mean...Program Demolition did surprise me, but...he got a free shot with Resonance at the player's back, but it still didn't knock him unconscious. Maybe there's something about that we can exploit."

"Hmm..."

"Come to think of it," Kichijouji continued, "at the beginning, I think he used a weight spell to ruin that other player's sense of balance. He probably wanted to knock him down entirely, but then he only went down on one knee. Even the gravity-decreasing spell the First High guy used to jump into the trees wasn't strong enough to actually push him to the top. Maybe he can't actually use very strong magic? Maybe he's used to using really advanced devices and can't use his full power with low-spec ones."

"That could be it. He has so much skill at arranging programs, he's probably always used hardware tuned up to match. It's very possible that he hasn't gotten used to the low-spec devices in the competition, since his substitution was so sudden."

"Well, we don't know why, but do we need to? Just looking at his magical power, I don't think we need to be afraid of anything but Program Demolition. What we really need to be on guard for is his tricks, like what he did to the Eighth High defender at the end."

"...You mean there's nothing to fear from a totally frontal fight?" Masaki asked.

"I don't think so. The question is *how* we force him into a straight fight... If we can do that, you'll win a hundred percent of the time. For example, if we get the grasslands stage, there's every probability that we'll win."

◇ ◇ ◇

Mikihiko, in the First High waiting room waiting for the next match, was fidgeting, standing up and sitting down restlessly.

"Mikihiko...why don't you relax a little?" Leo asked, lightly swinging around the Mini-Communicator to get a better handle on its weight now that Tatsuya had adjusted it post-match.

"Leo...you're so energetic. I mean...we don't see the people in these classes regularly."

Leo looked him over, wondering what he was on about. But Mikihiko's desperate answer caused Miyuki to giggle charmingly.

"Yoshida, you're more shy around strangers than I thought," she said, as she stood behind Tatsuya. He was sitting in a chair, leaning over its back as she gave him a shoulder massage. She turned her amused, radiant smile on Mikihiko.

"I actually think his attitude is normal," offered Tatsuya. "Boys our age are the shy sort, Miyuki."

"Oh, Tatsuya. You've never once shown me any shyness."

Tatsuya opened his closed eyes slightly, bent his head back, and looked up at her from below. She gave a high-pitched giggle, all the while gently massaging her brother's shoulders with her long, pale, delicate fingers.

Sure, I may be a little shy around strangers!
But looking at the two of you is more embarrassing than that!

...Mikihiko couldn't say that, though. He was worldly-wise enough not to.

It was then that the partition in the tent's canvas (which wasn't actually made from hemp but rather a twenty-first-century, high-tech cloth) folded over and Mayumi and Azusa entered. As soon as they saw the siblings, they froze, and Azusa's face went beet red. Mayumi's didn't, but she looked at Tatsuya like he was a slightly dirty stray dog.

"...I feel like I'm being badly criticized right now. Or mocked," said Tatsuya bluntly, sitting up straight.

"Just your imagination," replied Mayumi, before looking away and clearing her throat. For his part, Tatsuya had already stood up by the time she looked back at him.

He...really seems like a soldier, she found herself thinking.

He had assumed a pose with his legs slightly apart, his back straight, and his hands clasped behind his back—and it seemed very natural. She felt there was nothing out of place about it on him: no nervousness, no stiffness, no attempt to act cool.

Thanks to that, her own behavior began to strike her as quite childish. "...Really, it's nothing." As a result, even that unnecessary assertion made her hate herself a little just for saying it. She needed to get to the point. "I just wanted to tell you that they decided what stage the next match will be on."

"You came all this way to tell us? Thank you very much," said Tatsuya, bowing a little in gratitude, while inquiring with his eyes.

"You'll be in the city stage."

The answer was so unexpected that it took Tatsuya a few seconds to reply. "...After what just happened yesterday?"

"The stages are randomly selected. It won't take things like that into account."

"I see..." It was actually impressive, how far they were going with this, given how obvious it was. Tatsuya didn't mention it, however. "I'm finished adjusting our CADs, so we'll go over there right away."

"Good work," said Mayumi, nodding.

Leo and Mikihiko had already finished getting ready. They had their protective suits back on—they'd only shirked the upper portion previously—and still had their helmets; it was all they needed. Meanwhile, Tatsuya slid his arms through his jacket sleeves and made sure the zipper and clasp were done up firmly.

Just as he finished buckling his holsters and placing the CADs in them, Azusa spoke up: "Umm, Shiba...?"

"What is it?"

"Saijou's device... What will you do with it?"

"What do you mean?"

"Well...with being inside rooms, and having staircases that stick out of buildings, won't it be hard to use the Mini-Communicator? The spell just makes the blade float in the air—doesn't its power depend on how strong the person swinging it is? The blade is stretched out, so he can swing it at the same speed as the base, which is good...but without the space to swing it, he can't build up enough energy to take someone down, so..."

"Ichihara said that, didn't she?" With the rest of her story brilliantly seen through, Azusa turned red again, this time for a different reason. "Just the sort of accurate analysis I've come to expect from her...but you don't need to worry. Even inside rooms, there's enough space to swing a long sword. He may not be able to use a thirty-foot sword, but he can use a three-foot one."

Tatsuya glanced at Leo, who nodded confidently back.

◇ ◇ ◇

First High versus Second High: In the face of the accident yesterday, each team's monolith was positioned in a room on the third floor of a five-floor building. The sheer audacity of not taking responsibility for or admitting to past mistakes once again reminded Tatsuya that, from a business viewpoint, Magic University was a bureaucratic organization, too.

—Of course, certain parts of yesterday's "accident" didn't seem like a mistake or the responsibility of the tournament committee.

Besides, Tatsuya personally found it more convenient to have the monolith hidden away like this rather than it being placed way out in the open, so he certainly wasn't about to complain.

Right now, he was hiding out on the top floor of the building that housed Second High's monolith. He'd overtaken them with his technique, slipped past their detection, rounded the buildings, and then jumped from rooftop to rooftop *without using magic*. He'd gotten this close without the defender even realizing it.

Slipping from building shadow to building shadow while staying hidden meant that it had taken a decent amount of time to get here. Even though they'd advance to the finals tournament if they lost, the tournament would have first place in the qualifiers face fourth place, and second face third. Facing Third High in the semifinals versus facing them in the finals held completely different meanings. He'd left Mikihiko behind to give Leo backup this time, but Tatsuya decided he didn't have much time left. "Mikihiko, can you hear me?"

"I hear you, Tatsuya."

The usage of communication devices was not prohibited in Monolith Code matches, but not many schools used them. It was easy with today's technology to figure out where the electric signals were coming from even if you couldn't decode their contents.

And with only three members to a team, if they got so far apart that they needed to use a communicator, it would be mostly impossible to do any meaningful coordination. So normally, there was no need to use one.

However, there was a good reason Tatsuya was using one now. "I'm going. Figure out where the monolith is."

"Can't go much longer here. Hurry!"

"Got it." That meant they were already in combat. Tatsuya tapped the bracelet on his right wrist and activated a summoning spell.

With a shout, Leo slashed his Mini-Communicator horizontally. The small metal piece sixteen inches long and eight inches wide—the other part of the blade—flew in an arc toward the Second High player. Using physical strength to make up for the blade's lack of weight, Leo swept out the attacker's legs.

The player toppled to the ground. If this had been actual combat, Leo's next move would be to run to him, step on him, and deliver the finishing blow, but Monolith Code rules prohibited hand-to-hand combat.

"Mikihiko!"

Leo, knowing his classmate couldn't physically hear him, sent him a signal through the spirit Mikihiko had "watching" them somewhere in this room.

The reply came in the form of ball lightning materializing in the air. The electric attack struck the downed Second High player.

But Leo didn't have the time to revel in having taken down a single person. He detected a movement spell being cast on his body by someone else, and quickly shouted, "Halt!"

Using the microphone affixed to his helmet, he triggered the voice recognition switch on his left-arm CAD. He was using two CADs at the same time—parallel casting—but the spells were of the same type, so there was no interference to prevent it from activating.

Fortunately—at least, in this case—his personal CAD was made with sturdiness and mechanical reliability in mind, and was a pre–second-generation device in terms of activation program expansion abilities. That meant it fell within the restrictions for the Nine School Competition. Tatsuya didn't particularly like the ambiguity and lag time that came with a voice-recognition function, but given the situation, it was better he use something he was familiar with. Thus he'd simply (heavily) modified the activation programs already installed on it; Leo's personal CAD still worked the same way as always.

And just as intended, despite his CAD being completely behind the times, Leo's spell to block the enemy's movement magic attack made it in time.

Using the place he was standing—the connection between the bottoms of his shoes and the floor—as a reference point, his spell stabilized the relative coordinates between his body and that point. You could call it an application of the spell Mari had used in Battle Board, but it was more like a downgrade. Unlike her spell, which was set up to allow freedom of movement while remaining relatively fixed to the board, the "stabilization" magic Leo had just used made the unmovable floor the reference point and stopped his entire body from moving. The spell lasted for only a moment.

But despite it being such a massive downgrade, he made it in time to cancel it out, and it held, even when the enemy's spell was active.

This building had probably been designed to be a school.

Gazing into the hallway through broken interior windows, he could see the second enemy player going past.

Leo pulled his right hand back like he was going to thrust, but by the time he was ready, the enemy was already gone.

Carefully approaching the remaining attacker—the previously downed one, who was occasionally twitching—Leo removed his adversary's helmet. According to the tournament rules, a player whose helmet was taken by an enemy was forbidden from continuing in the event.

Well, that's one down, he thought to himself, knowing nobody would hear it. *I'm counting on you, Tatsuya. I can't hold out much longer here.*

Tatsuya's summoning spell energized the spirit *that was already attached to him.* He couldn't use spirit magic; he could only sense the energized independent information bodies, not control them. Modern magic used false information created by a magician to overwrite the information bodies accompanying events; it wasn't meant to control the information bodies themselves. He could, however, activate a summoning spell, the foundation of spirit magic.

His artificially created, virtual magic calculation region had been constructed in the conscious regions of his brain. Because of that, if he had a magic program described by an activation program, it didn't matter what kind of magic it was—he could *consciously* decipher the activation program that was the blueprint for that magic program. That was why he was able to do it: All he was doing was building a magic program with that information and projecting it.

It wasn't on the same level as actually *using* magic. He was simply imitating the magical activation process and nothing more. But if the necessary information was recorded in it, it didn't matter whether it was an imitation; the effects would manifest throughout the recorded scope.

The unenergized spirit Mikihiko had attached to Tatsuya had now been reenergized by Tatsuya's spell. This immediately created a link between it and its "master," Mikihiko. Tatsuya couldn't control spirits, but in this case, he didn't need to. Because, in a sense, his job had been to bring this spirit linked to Mikihiko into the enemy's base.

The spell had probably tipped off the defender to his presence. Tatsuya wanted him to leave the monolith and come running up to this floor.

He moved, stepping quietly.

Mikihiko knew that Tatsuya had successfully performed the summoning after having been called by the spirit "contracted" to him. *Seriously, why are you a Course 2 student, Tatsuya...?* he thought, in the back of his mind, while focusing on the distant spirit.

In actuality, physical distance didn't mean very much for magic. The Idea, the giant magic platform, didn't contain a concept of physical distance at all. Normally, the only thing that would be influenced by distance was typeless magic, the sort that fired psions directly, without going through the Idea first.

Humans, however, are restricted by their five senses and by their experience. When something is physically far away, a human will think of it as far away. That *consciousness of the distance* was what magical "distance" really was. The more distant the caster was aware of something being, the more difficult it was to successfully cast a spell there. So the secret to casting spell at a distance was to *feel* that the target was close by.

In that respect, spirit magic could use communication with spirits—a transmission of intent—to make one's spirit feel as though it were near something the caster was not. Spirit magic could be called magic that easily overcame physical distance.

—As it was doing now.

I see it.

Vision Synchronization.

Instead of drawing spirits near to read the information recorded within them, he used a link through the Idea from a spirit *already under* his influence to garner real-time information; that was known as spirit magic's Sense Synchronization. By restricting that information to only the visual sort, he could get a clearer image: That would be Vision Synchronization.

By manipulating independent information bodies of current atmospheric phenomena—spirits from the wind family—Mikihiko easily discovered the position of the enemy monolith.

But now was where things really started. As he maintained two links, one to the enemy base and one he attached to Leo, he said to Tatsuya, "I found it."

That was fast... He found it already? As Tatsuya leisurely reflected on how convenient spirit magic was, he kept his muscles as tense as he possibly could.

After all, he was currently hanging from a ceiling.

This building imitated a structure being either taken down or put up, because the air-conditioning pipes were wide-open across the ceilings. Tatsuya had grabbed hold of one of them and looked down at the Second High defender passing by, treading carefully as he checked left and right.

He'd probably heard Mikihiko's voice over the radio, but it didn't seem to make him think he should look *up*.

No, thought Tatsuya. As far as he could tell, the defender was suffering from tension-induced tunnel vision right now. His breathing was a little ragged, too, like he'd dashed up the staircase.

He didn't seem like he was very fit to be on defense, but any positional mistakes by the enemy were a good thing for Tatsuya and his team. Empathizing would be hypocrisy here.

Tatsuya considered letting him pass, but instead, he let go of his support with both hands, and pulled out the CAD on his right hip in midair. As he touched down, he pulled the trigger.

His opponent didn't even get the chance to look behind him.

The spell he'd just used was a simple psionic shock wave. It would induce the *illusion* of a concussion for just a few seconds, rendering the player unable to fight for that time. Those few seconds would be a decisive advantage in actual combat, but this was a sporting event in which direct attacks were against the rules. Confirming out of the corner of his eye that the enemy player had fallen over, he began to run to directly above the point Mikihiko had given him.

It was only two rooms away; it didn't even take him ten seconds. He felt the defender finally beginning to move as he pointed his CAD straight down. Each floor in this building was about ten feet from floor to ceiling. From the fifth floor to the third floor was within thirty-three feet.

He pulled the trigger.

Tatsuya felt the slight recoil from the eidos alteration. Just to be sure, he went down the opposite staircase from where he'd come.

His senses attuned to the spirits, Mikihiko looked at the code written inside the monolith. He moved his viewpoint. Leo still hadn't engaged the enemy yet.

Praying for just a little bit of luck, in accordance with the visual information being sent to him by the spirit, Mikihiko began typing in the code to his wearable keyboard.

As the match-ending siren wailed, Tatsuya continued to run from the defender's Windcut spell while Leo was about to launch an all-or-nothing assault with the monolith at his back.

"Phew," sighed Mayumi in satisfaction. "That was a positively thrilling match."

"This guy..." replied Mari disagreeably. "He was just fooling around at the end, wasn't he?"

"Huh? He was?"

"He could have dodged that attack easily," Mari rebuked, scowling. "Why didn't he just go take the guy down?"

"I don't think he could have even if he wanted to," Mayumi replied calmly.

"Why not? He used Resonance in the last match. It even took Hattori down."

"That's because the competition CAD's hardware isn't good enough to process that spell. Even in the last match, it didn't completely take the player out of the running, remember? We pushed this role on Tatsuya *yesterday*. He only had one night to prepare for this, and in that one night, he adjusted Saijou's CAD, he adjusted Yoshida's CAD, and thought of a plan to bring out the best in both of them. I know it's irritating because you have a high opinion of him, but don't you think you're being a little irresponsible by having such high hopes for him without giving him the proper time to prepare?"

"I...I guess so," said Mari apologetically, shaking her head firmly. But suddenly she stopped. "By the way, Mayumi..."

"Hmm? What is it?" Mayumi steeled herself, sensing a potentially spiteful retaliation coming her way.

But that probably played right into Mari's hands. "You know, you sure do make a point of defending him."

"Huh? N-no, I…"

"And now you're blushing, too. Well…even *you're* gonna have a tough uphill battle ahead of you with that sister complex…"

"That isn't it at all!"

Mari's doubts were left unsettled thanks to that quintessential teenage-girl derailment (though calling it that might be misleading), but elsewhere in the stands, another person was expressing the same kind of dissatisfaction, though with different grounds for the complaint.

"In the end, the only spells he used were Program Demolition, Resonance, Phantom Blow, and weighting magic… I understand why he didn't use Dismantle, but no flash casting or Elemental Sight? Seems like cutting corners to me…"

"He has reasons he needs to keep secret. You know that, Doctor."

"Still, Fujibayashi… I suppose flash casting is one thing, but random nearby magicians wouldn't be able to tell what he'd done if he used Elemental Sight."

Medical Major Yamanaka and Second Lieutenant Fujibayashi of the Independent Magic Battalion were currently having a fairly meddling conversation. If anyone had known who they were, they would have jumped in surprise to hear it, because the two were wearing inconspicuous summer clothing to blend in. At first glance they seemed like a couple—or perhaps, a doctor and his nurse (they'd accepted whatever misunderstandings her calling him "doctor" might create)—and any fragmentary, unfamiliar terms anyone nearby heard were assumed to be psychology terminology and promptly ignored.

"Even still, if his movements gave away that he could see things he shouldn't be able to, it would raise suspicion with anyone attentive. Elemental Sight is less a perception-type spell and more a strange ability. Depending on how he used it, it might garner even more attention than Dismantle would."

The Elemental Sight they were discussing was an ability Tatsuya had to perceive the Idea "background."

Modern magic, with its four families and eight types, projected a magic sequence on to various information bodies via the Idea, the dimension information bodies lived in.

This meant that a magician who used modern magic had the ability to access the dimension via code, so, at the end of the day, Tatsuya's ability to consciously *sense* that dimension's very existence could be seen as a simple expansion of the regular ability.

However...the effects brought about by that "expansion" were massive.

Because as long as something existed with a physical form, it would create an information body footprint in our dimension.

Information brought by support systems like the five senses or clairvoyance—which itself was no more than an expansion of one's perception of the physical—didn't designate coordinates for the excited information bodies that made magic. But with this ability, one could be conscious of an information body group and aim directly.

The only things that could escape Elemental Sight's aim *were things that didn't exist.*

In passing, the Japanese name assigned for the spell was actually a mistranslation. It stuck, though, and led to the name becoming expert terminology whose original meaning had been lost.

Elemental Sight originally referred to the power to see the elements—in this case, the four symbolic elements represented by classical theory.

However, the scholar who originally translated this term mistook the meaning of the word *elemental* for that of an elemental *spirit*. Because of that, the Japanese name for *Elemental Sight* ended up being *spirit sight*. Of course, there were many people who noticed the mistake, but it ended up being left alone because it sounded more *magical* in nuance than its correct alternative.

This sort of mistranslation was just another obstacle that served to further separate experts from everyone else…but the fact that nobody wanted to correct it was worrying at best and reprehensible at worst.

But getting back to the main subject…

Yamanaka already understood what Fujibayashi was telling him. Elemental Sight was another of the sort of skill that you'd expect to be confidential, like Mist Dispersion was.

Still, it would take more than that to convince him. "I suppose we may be just as guilty for telling him not to display his skill, but…"

They hadn't simply—or rather, purely—come to cheer for Tatsuya. The boy was more than strong enough mentally not to reveal techniques that should never be seen, even under duress. Yamanaka, Fujibayashi, Kazama, Sanada, and Yanagi were all confident about that. Still, there was always a chance. A one-in-a-thousand accident—a confidential spell being used in a public environment—would demand immediate action. That was why they were watching Tatsuya's match.

So Yamanaka was right—they weren't in a position to criticize the Yotsuba, who were secretive to begin with. Even if he *would* have liked to see Tatsuya get serious and show off even a little bit of his true skill.

"But I do think he'll end up having to use flash casting. He may be strong, but he'll need more than just a low-spec CAD to go up against the likes of the Prince and the Cardinal," concluded Fujibayashi, as if to soothe the doctor's mental discord.

But not everyone watching had their eyes solely on Tatsuya. In fact, most of the audience was watching Leo, who had shown off a never-before-seen armament, and in a flashy battle to boot.

And though they were few, some in the crowd were paying attention to Mikihiko as well, as he accurately used Clairvoyance to see the 512-character code from a distance. Not all of them were ignorant of the mechanism behind Clairvoyance; one of them, in fact, was a childhood friend who knew all about it.

"Come on, Miki... You're doing it just like you used to!"

"Huh? What's he doing 'just like he used to'?" Mizuki asked Erika. She'd been muttering something to herself intently.

Erika gave her a vague answer as her mind sunk deeper into her own world. She understood what Mikihiko had just done. Her relationship with him was deeper than she let on, and frankly, deeper than she told herself it was.

Sense Synchronization was by no means a simple technique, but back before the accident, the "boy genius" Mikihiko could do it as easily as breathing. But ever since the accident, he'd never been able to use magic this smoothly.

Huh... His scars have already healed. Sometimes she would hear sentimental lines like "Physical wounds heal, but mental ones never do," but in real life there were physical wounds that would heal and ones that wouldn't. So in the same way, there should be some mental scars that didn't heal and some that did.

Miki...do you see it? You're using magic today the same way you used to.

Erika didn't have the ability to distinguish spirits. Her eyes couldn't see them. So she couldn't be completely sure if spirit magic worked or not, but she was a daughter of the Chiba, so she had very well-polished personal combat skills instead.

To a certain extent, she could tell just from a person's tiny gestures, eye movements, and changes in expression when a person used magic, what they used it on, and whether it succeeded or failed.

Her eyes as a daughter of the Chiba, the "eyes of the swordsman," perceived that Mikihiko's magic had gone off the way he'd wanted it to.

Seriously, this is getting on my nerves... Why don't you see it? You're already back on your feet.

Right now, Mikihiko's strength had returned, but his confidence hadn't. His casual expression was something she understood, and she understood it because of all the experiences they had shared since they were children, when they were forced together and followed each other around.

Now, all he had to do was get his confidence back. He just had to believe in himself…

"…Erika? What's wrong? Erika!"

"Huh? What?"

"Don't 'huh, what' me. What's wrong? You suddenly got lost in thought. Are you worried about something?"

"Huh? Oh, well, yeah, I guess I am a little. That match was really close just now, you know? I was wondering if they'll be okay in the next one," she said, giving a spur-of-the-moment excuse.

Mizuki meekly let herself be fooled, saying things like "now that you mention it" and "I'm sure they'll be fine" and "We just have to cheer them on." Erika wasn't really listening, though, as she sunk back into her thoughts.

◇ ◇ ◇

The finals tournament matches were announced.

The first match of the semifinals would be Third High versus Eighth High. The second match would be First versus Ninth. The qualifier results were Third High in first, First High in second, Eighth High in third, and Ninth High in fourth. Normally, the competition rules would pit Third High against Ninth and First against Eighth, but First and Eighth had just finished playing a match against each other, so yet another special exception was applied.

The tournament would start at noon. Tatsuya's team would be in the second match, but they couldn't miss Third High's game. It would be a slightly early lunch, but Tatsuya, with lunch box in hand, took Miyuki back to the hotel.

The state of the tent right now was not conducive to a relaxing meal.

Leo and Mikihiko had evacuated to their own rooms a few moments ago. Honoka looked like she wanted to come with them, but that would incite all her classmates to follow her, which would make leaving the tent pointless. Shizuku had been the one to whisper that in her ear and stop her.

The siblings, after shaking off all sorts of gazes in their direction—mostly impassioned looks toward Miyuki—quickly left the event area. But when they arrived at the hotel lobby, they were greeted with an unfamiliar sight.

"Hmm?"

"Oh my…"

In a corner of the lobby stood Mari, a hint of embarrassment coloring her face. In front of her was a slightly older man, but still young. He couldn't be mistaken for a teenager. He was probably around twenty. Both of them had heard she had an older boyfriend; could this be him?

He was relatively tall—he stood a little higher than Tatsuya. The siblings had been around enough specialists in the field to know at a glance that his lean, firm body didn't belong to an athlete but to someone well trained in combat and martial arts. Most people would probably describe his features as handsome. Mari's looks were slightly androgynous but brought no shame to the description of "pretty." The two were a good fit for each other.

Suddenly, Tatsuya slowed his pace.

"Tatsuya?" said Miyuki from a step ahead of him, turning back and tilting her head.

No, Tatsuya wasn't plotting anything rude, like making fun of them or peeping on them. He knew the young man's face from somewhere, and taking a moment to search his memories had caused him to pause in his tracks. "…That's the Nine School Competition for you. You run into celebrities all over the place." The desire to talk to the man crossed his mind, but he was well aware that he should be more discreet, given the situation.

"Do you know him?"

"He's world famous in certain circles." He stepped up to Miyuki and urged her on; he would explain himself as they were walking.

However, just as he abandoned the idea of butting into the little rendezvous, someone *else* ventured to do just that. Her high-pitched voice caused both Tatsuya and Miyuki to stop.

"Brother Tsugu! Whatever might you be doing in a place like this?" demanded a familiar voice using *much* more formal language than they were used to.

As Erika strode closer to the young man, Miyuki checked back at Tatsuya. "'Brother'? Is he Erika's...?"

"If my memories serve, he's her second older brother. Naotsugu Chiba, the child prodigy of the Chiba. He still goes to a National Defense university, but some count him a genius at close-quarters magical combat—among the top ten in the world."

"I had no idea he was so amazing...but wouldn't Erika be proud of an older brother like that? Her standoffishness seems strange."

"I feel the same way. I hear the Chiba view Mr. Naotsugu as a heretic...though I don't think Erika would care much about orthodox concepts like that."

"I don't think so, either..."

As the siblings conversed, Erika flared up at her older brother—without even giving a glance to Mari, who was standing right next to them. "I had thought you were on an official trip to Thailand for sword instruction! What might you be doing here?!"

Erika seemed to have blown her top. She always gave the impression of looking at others and the world around her with a certain cynicism, so this passion and care was highly unusual.

"Erika...calm down a little?"

Though the young man—Naotsugu Chiba—tried to soothe her, Erika's excitement didn't wane at all. "How do you suggest I calm down?! Brother Kazu is one thing, but there was once a time when I couldn't even *imagine* you abandoning your duties!"

"Okay, but just calm down... I didn't abandon my job or anything..."

Naotsugu Chiba seemed to have a gentle, mild attitude in contrast to his military fame. With his younger sister showing no signs of "calming down" in the presence of others, he couldn't rebuke her. He could only explain himself.

"Oh, is that so? Then you're suggesting that *I'm* mistaken in your cooperation with the Thai royal family magicians for sword instruction?"

"Well, no, you're right about that…but I didn't come back home without permission—I got approval, so…"

"I see. If you needed to suspend an important job relating to Japan-Thailand diplomatic relations, it must have been for something very important. Oh, so important. An emergency. So why might my older brother be present at a high school competition?"

Her tone had calmed down, but Tatsuya could tell that her mood was growing all the more foul for it.

Naotsugu could probably see it, too—he was starting to grimace very slightly. "Diplomatic relations? No, it's nothing like that… It's really just part of my university club activities, a friendly exchange of military cadets before they're appointed…"

"Brother!"

"Yes?!"

"It might be goodwill between students or club activities, but this was a mission you were *officially appointed* to! It is certainly not the sort of thing you should be neglecting!"

"Yes! Yes, you're right!"

At the unexpected sight of one of the top ten warriors in the world, Tatsuya couldn't help but be surprised. "I've heard the term *henpecked husband* before, but I don't think I ever remember hearing of a *henpecked brother*…"

It was getting hard to watch, so he averted his eyes, only to find Mizuki fidgeting a short distance away. He gestured her over. She looked relieved and trotted to them.

"Tatsuya…what's going on with Erika?"

"I really don't know, either..." She could ask, but all he could do was cock his head in puzzlement.

Next to them, Miyuki piped up, clearly suppressing a giggle. "Tatsuya, I believe Erika is venting her anger," she said.

Tatsuya didn't know what she meant by that. "Venting? About what?"

"I think you'll find out soon."

As Tatsuya and Mizuki looked on, now even more confused, the "siblings' quarrel" entered a new phase.

"Brother, do not tell me you abandoned your duty to see this woman?"

"Like I said, I didn't abandon—"

"That wasn't what I asked!" Erika snapped, flat-out refusing the explanation. She slung a look to Mari, whom she had ignored until now (likely on purpose), before turning her stare back to Naotsugu. "How disgraceful... The child prodigy of the Chiba, my own brother, shirking his duties for a woman like this..."

"...Erika," interrupted Mari at last, finally unable to maintain—or rather, endure—her silence. "You know, I *am* still your upperclassman at school. I don't remember telling you it was okay to refer to me like that."

Erika, however, completely ignored her. "You've been corrupted ever since you started dating this woman. Imagine that, someone with full mastery over the Thousand Blade style of swordsmanship so infatuated with cheap magic that he forgets to improve his own skills..."

"Erika!" That was probably off limits for Naotsugu. His timid attitude vanished as though it never existed, and his spirited rebuke made Erika's shoulders jump in surprise. "Improving your skills demands that you always incorporate new techniques. That's what I think, and that's what I did. Mari doesn't have anything to do with it. I heard she'd been injured, and I couldn't just stay put over there. She told me I didn't have to come. And even if she hadn't, *you* are the one disgracing the family name with all your discourteous behavior."

Erika bit her lip and fell silent but didn't take her glower off him.

"Now apologize to Mari, Erika."

"...I refuse."

"Erika!"

"I refuse! You abandoned an official mission to be here! That's the undeniable truth! And it's also true that it's this woman's fault!" But once again, the situation seemed to turn around. "My opinion will not change! Brother Tsugu, going out with this woman has corrupted you!"

She spun around and very quickly walked away from her brother.

◇ ◇ ◇

"Erika! Erika, wait!"

As Erika left the lobby and went to the elevator bank—where the lobby was completely out of sight—she heard Mizuki's voice and finally turned around.

She opened her mouth a little, clearly surprised. "...Tatsuya. And Miyuki...did you overhear that?" Her tone and expression had returned to that of the typical Erika.

But to Tatsuya, it looked like she was holding back tears. "Sorry... we didn't intend to eavesdrop."

"Tatsuya, next time we eat, it's your treat."

"Hey! Oh, fine. Nothing too expensive, please."

"Negotiations successful!" said Erika with her usual whimsical, carefree expression. She was back to her normal attitude, so Tatsuya didn't want to make a fuss about it and then have her worry about him.

"Erika, have you eaten lunch yet?" asked Miyuki.

"Huh? It's still a little early... Oh. No, well, I'm not going to eat yet, but maybe I'll come with you anyway," she responded, half refusing and half accepting.

"Tatsuya?"

"Well, we were going to eat in our room. If you don't mind us eating, do you want to come?"

"Yeah, sure! Mizuki's coming, too, right?"

"Yes! Umm, if I'm not intruding."

"There's nothing for you to intrude on…" said Tatsuya.

"Huh? No, that's not what I meant!"

"Geez…Tatsuya, you're so mean. Stop teasing me."

After being used to change the mood, Mizuki, even after taking a seat on the bed, was still fuming. Even so, she knew she wasn't really being attacked or anything, so Tatsuya gave a dry smile and bit into his sandwich. For their part, Mizuki and Tatsuya both planned to ignore what had just happened.

But then the person herself, Erika, brought up the earlier scene. "All right, then… Don't you all have something you want to ask me?"

Miyuki was the only one to take her up on the topic with a composed face. "I didn't know the one dating Watanabe was your older brother."

"Oh. He's so dumb. He lets that woman seduce him. It's pathetic, and aggravating…"

"He's a world-class *kenjutsu* expert, right? You shouldn't be calling him dumb," Tatsuya said.

"Huh? …Oh, I get it. I should have figured you'd know who Naotsugu was."

"Erika," said Miyuki, pronouncing each of the syllables slowly. "You don't need to call him something different just because we're here. Brother Naotsugu, right?"

"Ahh, just forget you heard that! It's just a thing I have to do!" Erika suddenly grabbed her head and dove into the bed. Such "well-bred" word usage must have been embarrassing for her.

...Tatsuya was a little confused, though. He'd rather her be embarrassed for falling face-first onto a man's pillow and then pressing her face into it.

"Now, now. It's easy to tell that you love Naotsugu," Miyuki stated plainly.

"..."

Erika was *not* the only one who locked up. Miyuki had just dropped a bomb of pure cold, and it froze Tatsuya and Mizuki for a moment, too.

"...That's not it!" shouted Erika, shooting back up. Half of that had been spoken into the pillow, so all they heard was "not it," but it still felt like an appropriate reaction in this case.

Her attitude was like a cornered monster roaring—in other words, *transparent.* Miyuki let herself giggle, and then dropped another bombshell: "I didn't know you had a brother complex, Erika."

"I..." Erika was speechless.

And then the critical point passed and the explosion came.

"You're one to talk, you stupid brother-obsessed idiot!"

—Neither Tatsuya nor Mizuki would ever tell anyone what happened after that.

◇ ◇ ◇

"...Hey, Tatsuya, you don't look so good. Are you okay?"

"You look really tired..."

Tatsuya had joined Leo and Mikihiko in the general audience seats, but they both came straight at him with the comments. "I'm a little fatigued, that's all. More emotionally than mentally. I'll be fine once this match gets my spirit up."

On the other side of Tatsuya, who was waving his hand dismissively, were Miyuki and Erika, sitting down as though nothing had happened. Behind them was Mizuki, who was behaving just a little suspiciously. Leo and Mikihiko didn't notice; their attention seemed to be on the match that was starting.

"…Sorry. I feel like we let you bear the full brunt of everything."

Mikihiko seemed to have misunderstood, albeit in a favorable (and slightly convenient) way. "No, that's not true. I'm fine. Don't worry." When Tatsuya said "that's not true," he really meant it, but his purposely-vague way of saying it showed good character.

"Well, if you say so," said Leo. "You've been doing a ton already, so don't force yourself to do any more."

"Thanks. I know." *He really is an excellent friend, and so wasted on me*, thought Tatsuya. "I'm fine in that regard, too." He certainly didn't want to make such a rare friend worry, so he did his best to give him a firm nod of his head.

But then, as soon as the match started, Tatsuya's not looking so good was too trivial to care about. Their interest—including his, of course—was drawn to the match between Third High and Eighth High, currently unfolding on the crag stage.

It had developed into something much more one-sided than they'd thought it would. It might be more appropriate to say that one person had the stage all to himself.

The crag stage was modeled after a karst topography and was the stage with the second-fewest obstacles after the grasslands. Large boulders protruded from the ground in several places to provide cover, but there wasn't much height difference between them, and no groves of trees to block vision.

Between those crags came one player out of Third High's camp, walking calmly. Masaki Ichijou had confidently exposed himself and was now on the march.

Eighth High wouldn't let that go. They fired off spell after spell at him. Even the attacker who had used the crag shadows to move toward Third High's base was contributing to the concentrated fire.

However…

Masaki didn't stop walking.

The stones and boulder fragments flung with movement magic were all shot down by an even more powerful movement magic. The weighting and oscillation spells being directly applied to him were being nullified by Area Interference, which stretched three feet from his body. As if to scorn the futile effort, Masaki didn't even bother walking any faster.

As Leo and Mikihiko stared agape at the overwhelming skill, Tatsuya openly praised the ability. "Interference Armor…and here I thought movement-type area interference was the Juumonji's forte," he remarked. "He's not out of breath after using the spell for so long, which means it's more than his capacity for calculation that's big. He must be very good at breathing. The only thing I can say about it is that he has good magical sense."

In this case, when spells of the same type were used one after another, "breathing" referred to the exchange of spells: one ending and the other being triggered. The smaller the overlap time between the first and second spells, the less burden it carried for the magician. People described magicians who had a small overlap time as "good at breathing."

Miyuki was extremely good at breathing as well, but from what Tatsuya could tell, Masaki's senses rivaled hers.

The unending, powerful defense forced the Eighth High attacker to stop his assault. He started to run for Third High's camp, hurriedly trying to hide himself. He'd given up on taking Masaki down and noticed he could keep his team in the running if he attacked the opponents' monolith first.

But unfortunately, his act was careless. It might have been spurred by panic. He'd turned his back on defense and his thoughts ahead—literally. Masaki wasn't going to let him get away with it. A close-range explosion blast sent the Eighth High attacker flying face-first into the ground.

"The convergence spell Deviation Release? He could have just used Compression Release… He likes doing things big."

"Deviation Release?" Miyuki asked from beside him. "I don't know that spell…"

Tatsuya answered without taking his eyes off the field. "That's because it's a little obscure, and not effective given the amount of work it takes.

"You could think of it as stuffing air into a cylinder, closing it up, and then turning the other end at a target and taking off that lid. Highly compressed air fires out of the open end. Its advantages are that it normally generates more power than Compression Release, and that you can change the explosion's direction. But if you just want more power, you could increase the amount of air you compress. And if you wanted it to go in a certain direction, then you can just ram a Compression Release into them.

"…Or maybe he's trying to lower its lethality rank by using a spell in a gray area. In cases like these, it's a pain to be too powerful," he noted, smiling cynically.

Miyuki looked at him as though she wanted to say he was the same way, but he pretended not to notice. While Tatsuya was drawing upon his vast stores of knowledge, Masaki was steadily approaching Eighth High's base.

Seeing that the situation was getting worse and worse, the two Eighth High players left on defense rushed Masaki at once. A boulder broke apart, and its fragment sailed toward Masaki. Tiny sparks began scattering on the ground at Masaki's feet as well—probably a forced release of electricity from the minerals within, thanks to an emission spell from one of the Eighth High players. Both spells had to be called advanced level: the first for its scope, and the second for its alteration difficulty.

The only reason Tatsuya's team seemed to easily win against Eighth High had been because they couldn't use their full power. In a face-to-face matchup, they would have had a harder time.

But the two-pronged frontal attack was easily nullified by Masaki. The stones being fired at him were bounced away by a movement-vector-reversing force field deployed around Masaki in a sphere, and the electrical discharge was held back without going off.

A hammer made of air slammed into the Eighth High players. As soon as it made contact, the compressed air easily removed any combat strength the two of them had.

A siren blared, signaling the end of the match.

Neither Kichijouji nor the other player had taken one step out of Third High's base from start to finish, and in the end, had done precisely nothing.

"The Ichijou's 'prince' is more than we expected..." said Mayumi to Katsuto, looking away from the screen.

Her usual buddy Mari was absent. Right now, she was busy with something that would invite any who intruded on her to be kicked by a horse. She was still severely wounded and needed bed rest, but Mayumi and the other officers hadn't been hard on her.

"It kind of seems similar to your style, Juumonji."

Katsuto found it difficult to respond to that. Sure enough, before he could reply, Suzune came into the conversation. "He probably knows it. Ichijou's combat style was always mid-range, preemptive, saturated bombardment. In the qualifiers, in fact, he *did* render the defenders helpless from a distance. I don't have any proof...but I think this might be Ichijou provoking us."

"Provoking us?" repeated Mayumi, tilting her head.

"I don't know if he knows my style or not, but he's probably provoking Shiba, telling him to face him in a straight match of blows," answered Katsuto.

"Oh... Well, I guess I understand, but..." Mayumi's expression said more than enough—she thought that was childish. Tatsuya's weapons were his mobility and perception, and the unpredictability guided by those things. From the previous two matches, it was clear that he excelled more in combat skills than magic power. *Tatsuya would never be lured in by something so obvious,* she thought.

But Katsuto didn't agree with her silent message. "It *will* provoke Shiba."

"Huh? But it's Tatsuya..."

"There's a wide gap between them already. He has very few chances of winning. This happens to be one of those chances."

"They have me there..."

Tatsuya, in the general audience, was obviously too far away from their main tent to hear Katsuto's remark. But he completely understood what it was Katsuto meant. And he knew that Third High's true objective—probably Shinkurou Kichijouji's goal—was to drag him out into a frontal fight by purposely showing an opportunity. Even more ironically, taking them up on it would give First High the highest chance at victory, too. *Though Cardinal George isn't one to be underestimated...*

"Seriously! That's a hell of a defense he put up."

"And we didn't get to see anyone but Ichijou do anything, either. We can't think of a plan like this."

Fortunately, Leo and Mikihiko seemed to have misunderstood Tatsuya's grumble for something else. They'd been taken in by Masaki's strength, but it didn't do as much mental damage as knowing they were ants drawn into an inescapable ant lion's pit.

"We can make some assumptions about Kichijouji. I don't know about the other player, though."

"Wait, you can?"

Tatsuya opted to control the conversation by letting it run in the other direction. "The Cardinal Code that Shinkurou Kichijouji discovered was the weighting plus code. He entered Speed Shooting, too. So his specialty is probably Invisible Bullet, which directly adds weight to what it affects."

"Cardinal Code?"

"You mean you can apply weight to a part of something instead of altering its information bodies?"

"Right... This will take a little while. Are you listening?"

Leo hesitated at Tatsuya's reminder, but Mikihiko unflinchingly nodded.

"There's a concept in magic program research called the Cardinal Code hypothesis. It's pretty widely supported. Basically, it says that for each of the eight types of magic—acceleration, weighting, movement, oscillation, convergence, divergence, absorption, and emission—there exists one fundamental magic code each for increasing or decreasing their power level, also called plus and minus. So, sixteen formulas in all. But then, the theory goes that if you put all sixteen of them together, you can construct spells of all families at once.

"These fundamental magic programs are called Cardinal Codes. As for the conclusion it states... Well, the hypothesis is wrong about being able to construct spells of all families through a master formula, but the Cardinal Codes do exist."

"...It's wrong, but they still exist?"

"...I'm sorry. I'm confused already."

Mikihiko and Leo voiced their objections, and Tatsuya put his hand up to calm them down. "Relax, I'll explain.

"There are spells among the four families of magic that you can't construct *only* using the Cardinal Codes. So the Cardinal Code hypothesis is incorrect. However, there *are* magic programs with features that can be called *fundamental*. In modern magic, you create various effects by defining the state of alteration to be created by the spell. The things that actually *cause* the alteration to occur are also defined within the spell—the magic program, the code. But without defining the spell's ideal *end result*, it won't come to pass. It won't stick, so to speak.

"Meanwhile, Cardinal Codes can *directly* cause an end result. In other words, they're magic formulas that *define* the eight types of magic *themselves*. With that, a caster can use a spell to apply energy directly to a single point on an object *instead* of affecting all the object's eidos.

"Currently, the weighting plus code is the only one discovered. And the one who discovered it is Third High's Shinkurou Kichijouji, or Cardinal George."

Mikihiko faltered at hearing those final words. "Shinkurou Kichijouji...? I knew I'd heard that name before... So he's Cardinal George?"

Tatsuya looked at his expression and thought for a moment that he'd bungled things. He couldn't take back what he already said, though. "That's right. So Masaki isn't the only one we need to be cautious of. Outstanding scientists don't necessarily make outstanding performers, but the Cardinal Codes are annoying enough in their own right."

Spells using Cardinal Codes defined their effects directly, so they didn't need to define the results of its event alteration. Normal spells, however, did. Battering Ram, the spell that had directly caused Tatsuya to be placed in the Monolith Code event, and Invisible Bullet had similar effects: Both brought about a situation in which pressure was applied to one point on a surface. Battering Ram, though, needed to alter the entire surface to which pressure would be applied into a state where all that pressure would be applied to a single point. In contrast, Invisible Bullet didn't need to overwrite the state of the surface to which pressure would be applied. And the surface could be a wall, a floor, the surface of a human body—anything. Invisible Bullet overwrote the pressure *itself*.

Therefore, the magic program, which described the information needed to overwrite all its targets' information, became much, much smaller. It wouldn't alter the information of the target itself, which also made it necessarily unable to be blocked by Information Boost, which prevented event-information alteration on a target.

The smaller magic programs and the ability to use spells that weren't affected by the event-alteration target's information intensity gave the caster a very large advantage.

"Thankfully, Invisible Bullet has one fault: The person needs to be able to see the point of action. Which is rather ironic. It's precisely because the Cardinal Code allows the spell to work directly on the target rather than the eidos. Physical obstacles can block an Invisible Bullet attack. You can guard against it with Area Interference as well, but Information Boost won't do anything, so be careful."

"All right," said Mikihiko, nodding. "I'll be careful."

Leo nodded after him, until he reservedly said, "Hey...I've got a question."

"What is it, Leo?"

"This might not have anything to do with the match...but you said there were spells you can't construct with only the sixteen Cardinal Codes, right? Wouldn't that mean you knew all sixteen of them?"

Attitudes, words, and actions could sometimes fool Leo, but he was certainly no fool. His breadth of knowledge aside, he actually had pretty high intelligence. Tatsuya thought he knew that, but the perceptive question surprised him. "...Shinkurou Kichijouji is the only one who has ever discovered a Cardinal Code. I just know about spells in the four families you theoretically wouldn't be able to create based on the Cardinal Code hypothesis."

Just as Leo opened his mouth, about to ask another question, Miyuki interrupted them. "Tatsuya, shouldn't we get going soon?"

"You're right. They'll decide the next stage soon. Let's go to our tent."

Tatsuya stood up and turned away, summarily rejecting any further questioning.

◇ ◇ ◇

Their match with Ninth High would be fought on the canyon stage.

The canyon stage was an artificial ravine with a bend in the middle. Because flowing water would give various advantages and disadvantages based on whether you were upstream or downstream, it was less of a canyon and more of a long, bent lake surrounded by cliffs. And even then, the water wasn't deep (about twenty inches at its deepest point), so it was more like a long, bent *puddle*.

Mikihiko would be unchallenged here.

He summoned a white fog to cover the long, narrow field that was bounded on either side by cliffs. The audience, who now had no way of seeing the match, began to boo. Soon, though, they quieted down—they'd all come to see a magic competition. The audience understood just how difficult it was to maintain a cover over such a large volume of space with magic, and knew it equated to a skill-level difference. Plus, the fog was thinner around the First High competitors and clung more thickly to the Ninth High players.

With the fog in their way, the Ninth High team couldn't get close to First High's monolith. They attempted several times to clear the fog, but virtually every time they dispersed it, the veil of whiteness would immediately return, stealing away their vision and mocking their efforts. Blowing the fog away by creating wind was pointless, since the air that replaced it was full of fog, too. Raising the temperature and dragging up the saturation point also only served to spur the water in the lake to evaporate faster, thus uselessly increasing the discomfort index in the area.

This old-style spell was a bounded field that created fog. It froze the air's water vapor regardless of the saturation point, which meant that raising the temperature would just end up increasing the amount of water vapor the spell supplied and thus thicken the fog. Also, bounded field magic included the concept of closing things in, so causing air currents would do nothing but circulate the fog-filled air.

By its nature, modern magic did a poor job at continuously applying effects to a vague target. In order for similarly modern magic to wipe out this fog spell, a caster would need to be aware of the bounded field—the area Mikihiko was magically affecting—or else they wouldn't be able to take any effective countermeasures. Unfortunately for them, the Ninth High rookies didn't seem to know much about old-style magic.

Though, aside from the fact that the fog was *not* artificially uniform, it had no special effects. It had no glamour effects, didn't cause weakness, and didn't prevent anyone from leaving. But just the fact that you couldn't see through it was enough to limit a person's actions.

Keeping an eye on the Ninth High attacker trepidatiously edging along the cliff face, Tatsuya blended into the fog and easily reached Ninth High's base. The fog was purposely thinner around him, and gave him at least enough vision to trot over there. Even if he had zero vision, though, it wouldn't have hindered him. Because in a situation like this, when he was sure the audience wasn't looking, he could freely use his natural-born eyesight.

He looped behind the Ninth High defenders without them noticing and fired the key. The roaring caused by the cover falling off the monolith and revealing the code made the defenders hastily turn around, but Tatsuya had already left. This time, he wouldn't need to summon any spirits. Spirits under Mikihiko's control were the ones maintaining the field of fog, and Mikihiko had eyes in every last speck of it.

The match between First High and Ninth High ended in victory for First High, without a single skirmish.

◇ ◇ ◇

The final match would take place after the match to determine third place. No matter how long a Monolith Code match needed, it didn't take more than thirty minutes. Still, they allowed for a break before the finals began—it would be two hours from now, at 3:30 PM.

Tatsuya, who was also assigned to CAD adjustments, spent the free two hours in the competition area, but Mikihiko and Leo decided to leave and relax for the time being—though it wasn't certain if they did so because they just couldn't stand watching another display of affection between the siblings.

In the end, the boys decided to meet up again one hour before the match started, and in the meantime, each would go wherever they liked. Leo said he was going to grab a light meal in the cafeteria, then take a rest in his room. Mikihiko, not the glutton Leo was, went up to the observation floor at the top of the hotel.

The hotel had been constructed on maneuvering grounds at the foot of Mount Fuji, and the observation room let people get a close-up view of the mountain. The Yoshida's deity magic was old magic of the Shinto family and, if categorized even further, would fall under earthly deity Shinto-type (the kind of Shinto that worshipped the gods of the land).

Mount Fuji held special meaning for a user of old Shinto magic. The deity enshrined at Mount Fuji was one of those "gods of the land," who had married one of the heavenly deities (or the descendants thereof). The Fuji faith wasn't restricted to either earthly or heavenly deities.

And even without such dogmatic connotations, the so-called sacred Mount Fuji was a site of many major magic-related powers. If you went out onto the balcony of the observation room, you could feel the breath of the sacred mountain on your skin—such were Mikihiko's thoughts as, after ascending to the top floor, he met someone he hadn't expected to see there.

Wearing a straw hat to block the sunlight was Erika, leaning with her elbows on the balcony railing and staring out at Mount Fuji. She turned her head to look at him. "Huh...? What's wrong? What are you doing here?"

"I came to see Mount Fuji... What are you doing here by yourself?"

As he said, nobody else was in the observation room—or the entire top floor, including the balcony—except Erika. Though, now that he was here, it was just the two of them. Obviously, it was no exaggeration to say everyone present was watching the Nine School Competition. They both had free time, but the third-place match would be starting shortly. Coming all the way back to the hotel and going up to the observation room, from which you could see nothing but Mount Fuji, was something only real weirdoes or those with a special goal in mind, like Mikihiko, did.

"I, well, I guess I wanted to be alone," said Erika, looking back at the scenery, her expression seeming somehow lonely.

Mikihiko felt a little dismayed. Still, he couldn't just walk out and leave, and standing in the doorway would be strange. Without a choice—at least, that's what he told himself—he took up a position next to Erika.

"Mikihiko..." Erika began, her eyes still fixed on Japan's highest mountain.

"Huh? What?" Something felt out of place here.

"Can you feel it?"

"Huh?"

"You came to feel the breath, right? Can you?" Her choice of words was natural, but the tone of her voice was different. She expressed herself in the same way as always, yet differently at the same time. As she straightened up, off the railing, her expression was one of sincerity he'd not seen for these last four months, perhaps longer. The last time he'd seen it had been before she cut her hair, after she'd started growing it out that spring. It was two years ago, when he never saw her without a katana in her hands...

"...Mikihiko?"

"Er, sorry. Yes, that's right," he responded, flustered, finally realizing what was out of place.

Erika was calling him "Mikihiko"...

"I came to feel the breath," he replied.

"Not that."

"Huh?"

"That's not what I'm asking... *Can* you feel the mountain's breath?" she asked, turning an unexpectedly serious stare on him.

A bit daunted by that stare, Mikihiko stood up straighter and took a breath. He exhaled everything, then breathed in. It was important to maintain rhythm, but more important was the mental image. With his exhalation he created a vessel, and with his inhalation he took that vessel in.

He wasn't inhaling and exhaling—he was exhaling and inhaling.

After a few of these breaths, vitality began to fill his body. It wasn't particles like psions or pushions but waves closer to energy itself, a power sometimes called *prana*. Mikihiko was taking in the breath from the sacred mountain. When Erika's eyes saw that, her face turned into an uncharacteristically reserved smile.

—One that looked a little lonely.

"Erika...?"

"What? See, you *can* do it."

"...Sorry, but what are you talking about?" Her self-centric abridgments were always thick in her speech, but this time, Mikihiko felt like he was the one at fault for not understanding her.

"Have you noticed, Mikihiko? You've been using magic like you used to—like before the accident. Back when people called you the wonder child of the Yoshida."

"Huh?"

"No, wait. Not like before—maybe even better. The sharpness of your senses, the way you created the fog barrier, the way you took in the breath... It's all coming as naturally to you as breathing."

He didn't respond with a "no it doesn't." He didn't say "What gave you that impression?" There was no way he wouldn't know what her eyes were saying at this point. She was the swordswoman of the Chiba.

"That's great!" Suddenly, she gave him a clap on the back, sending

Mikihiko stumbling half a step forward. "Miki, at this rate, you've got nothing to fear from Third High! You'd better do your best in the finals!" Suddenly her usual self again, she left without waiting for a response.

"My *name* is Mikihiko!" he retorted to Erika's back. But at the same time, he breathed a sigh of relief.

He wasn't sure what he was relieved about, though, or why...

◇ ◇ ◇

Tatsuya, who should have been having another moment with his little sister (or so their teammates had taken to expect), had been called to the venue gate right after his two teammates left.

"Excellent work, Ms. Ono."

Haruka had been the one to call him there. "Hey! You're not supposed to tell your superiors 'excellent work'... You did that on purpose, didn't you?" Tatsuya gave her a wry smile, and her shoulders drooped. "...I guess this is all I have anymore... Now that my secret's out, I'm just a minor character. I'm fated to be buried under an ever-expanding list titled 'The Rest of the Cast'..."

"You're getting a little too meta for me, ma'am. I don't even understand what you're saying."

"That's all right. Every woman needs an air of mystery, after all."

"...Would you mind giving me the thing I kept with you? I don't have very much time, and I know you don't, either, ma'am." Tatsuya held out his hand, prompting an ostentatious sigh from Haruka.

Slinging him an expression that said she thought he was a killjoy, but simultaneously knowing he was right, she obediently handed over the electric bag (a suitcase with an electrically assisted caster attached) she'd brought for him.

"Sheesh... A little more appreciation would be nice. I'm your counselor, not your errand girl."

"I wasn't the one who asked you to bring this, ma'am. It was Master. Still…you're right. If you're unhappy with odd jobs, can I interest you in an *actual* one?"

"I didn't mean you needed to find something for me to do."

"Incidental income you won't need to report on your taxes… Does that pique your interest?"

A visible shock registered in Haruka's eyes. Tatsuya watched her with an unconcerned expression. How did someone with such an agreeable disposition (not personality) work as an intelligence operative?

He didn't have to wait very long. "…I suppose you have me there," she said. "It *is* my job to help students with their anxieties. This is no time to be saying it isn't my job or that I'm not being paid overtime."

I see, thought Tatsuya. *So that's the pretext she'll use to agree with me. But…* "Unfortunately, it *isn't* your job that I'm referring to, ma'am—it's something else."

That immediately sent Haruka's guard up. "…What are you going to make me do?"

This time he actually started to worry. She was so easy to read. How did she get by? Though, he figured he wouldn't mind one bit if someone caught her in a blunder and twisted her arm… "The Hong Kong–based international crime syndicate No-Head Dragon. I'd like you to figure out where their hideout is, ma'am."

Haruka looked left and right, panicked, and then quickly stepped close enough to embrace him. "Why do you know about the No-Head Dragon?!"

Her tone was one of agitation, but at least she still remembered to lower her voice. Unfortunately, even if she asked, it was a question he couldn't answer. His connection to Kazama and the Independent Magic Battalion needed to stay a secret. That was a direct order from his aunt, the current leader of the Yotsuba. Even if he were to say something vague like "I happened to hear about it," there was no telling where it could lead.

Instead, Tatsuya responded abstractly, in a way that could be interpreted various ways. "I would think it natural to investigate an enemy attempting to cause us harm, ma'am."

Still, Haruka realized he was referring to the sabotage taking place at the Nine School Competition. "...What are you planning? Public Safety and the COIA are already on the move. You don't need to get involved," Haruka whispered, in a way that could get them in trouble if someone saw them. Miyuki was one thing, but he also hoped Honoka and Shizuku and the rest of them didn't see.

"I don't plan on doing anything at the moment, ma'am. I'm just uneasy about not knowing where they are when the time comes to counterattack." Tatsuya paused. "By the way, people will misunderstand us if you do that."

Haruka forcefully pulled away from him. Her pride as his senior worked hard to hide her embarrassment in a smile. Tatsuya was really beginning to consider recommending that she wash her hands of the whole intelligence business... Nevertheless, he was sure she'd accept his request.

"...Insurance, is it?" she asked with a searching stare.

"You may take it that way if you wish, ma'am," he said, immediately nodding.

"...All right. Give me one day."

"One day? That would be fantastic."

That was unrestrained, no-strings-attached praise.

Haruka, looking somewhat unsatisfied, gave an embarrassed grin.

◇ ◇ ◇

After lugging the electric bag back to the tent, he ignored the intrigued stares coming from all the remaining staff members and took the bag's contents out.

With a remarkably unreserved attitude, Mayumi came wandering over to get a peek at what he had, then asked, "...A coat?"

"No, it's a mantle." Tatsuya held up the black cloth and spread it out. It was a long, Western-style mantle. Even with his height it looked like it would drag on the ground.

"That too?"

"This one is a robe." He placed the black mantle on a desk and spread out the gray cloth for her to see this time. It was a hooded robe, and it, too, was long enough for its hem to drag.

"What on earth are you...*using* them for?" Mayumi asked.

As question marks flew splendidly about the tent, Miyuki alone had to stifle a know-it-all smile.

"We'll be using them for the finals. Boy, am I glad they got here in time."

"Tatsuya, won't those be against the rules?" asked Miyuki with a slightly serious face, leaving aside Mayumi, who couldn't keep up with the conversation.

"I think they'll be fine, but I'll submit them to the device check before the match. It doesn't say anywhere in the rule book that you can't wear clothing with magic circles woven in."

Upon hearing his answer to Miyuki, a few more question marks popped up over Mayumi's head. She asked, "Magic circles woven in?"

"Yes. Magic circles are a medium for old-style techniques, and operate under the same principles as seal magic. This mantle and robe bestow on their wearers an effect that makes magic easier to use."

"So it's for support... I suppose it's not a problem as long as specific techniques aren't used for it..."

Mayumi looked over at Suzune, and she nodded. "There won't be any problem with the rules. It seems to me, though, that they simply hadn't envisioned a case like this."

Mayumi frowned a little and turned back to Tatsuya. "Hey, Tatsuya?" Her voice was less anxious and more worried. "We're refraining from celebrating at the moment, since there are still matches going on, but as soon as we got to the finals, we clinched the rookie competition championship. You don't need to force yourself too hard on this."

"I understand."

She didn't need to mention that—Tatsuya had already half given up on this match.

…At least, at this point.

After asking Isori to do a check on the mantle and robe (the Isori family was known as an authority on seal magic, and Isori himself hadn't bothered to hide his own interest), Tatsuya stretched and left the tent.

Mayumi had given him a mission by appointing him as a substitute: to lead First High to a rookie championship. As soon as they reached the Monolith Code finals—in other words, *now*—he considered that mission complete.

His careful stretching was so to avoid injury later. Scratches and bruises were one thing, but if he broke a bone or severed an artery, an ability of his that he needed to keep secret would automatically activate. He could consciously stop it, but he wasn't sure he could stop it quickly enough. His self-restoration ability would heal his physical body in an instant, even before he realized that the damage had been severe enough to set it off. The Nine School Competition was being recorded on video. Even if it was a momentary thing that human minds couldn't perceive, they could always analyze the tapes afterward.

As he reminded himself of all that, he continued his stretching, which was really more like a yoga routine. Meanwhile, he noticed Miyuki coming out of the tent, but she didn't seem to be in any particular hurry. He kept on with his pre-match warm-up exercises until he finished.

"Here is a towel, Tatsuya." Right after he straightened himself, Miyuki held out a well-cooled wet towel. Miyuki had spent more than a little time under the midsummer heat, but the towel felt as cold as if she'd just taken it out of a refrigerator…which wasn't unusual considering the type of magic she specialized in. With all the things she did so casually like this, he was reminded that she really was too good a little sister for him.

If the times hadn't changed, she would probably have a whole flock of men willing to give up their lives for her. No, even in this world, his sister might be able to say one word to have a man risk his life. Putting himself aside, he who would risk his life in a heartbeat, he was stricken by a chill and a shudder at what her future held.

"Tatsuya, is there something on my face?" She probably didn't actually think anything was on her face, but the difficult-to-read expression on her brother's face left her with no other way to ask.

Tatsuya didn't have much of a way to answer, either, so he gave an evasive reply.

"Tatsuya…" Miyuki's response was to…*not* pursue the fact that he'd dodge the question. "The final match is coming up. I believe your next opponents are quite strong…"

"…Me too." There was no point trying to act tough. If this were a real battlefield and not a match, if they were to come to blows without any limitations, then if those two came at him together—no, even if it was just Masaki Ichijou—he didn't currently have the confidence to assert that he could win.

"With your strength and skill restricted like this… And it may be misplaced for someone belonging to those who restricted them to be saying this, and it might be unpleasant, but…"

Her head down a little, she paused for a moment there. But her face soon came back up. Embarrassed, she declared: "…I still believe that you wouldn't lose to anyone, Tatsuya."

Without giving him the time to reply, she turned away, light and quick as a swallow, and went back into the tent. Tatsuya watched her leave, standing stock-still for a moment.

I really can't win…

Like Miyuki said, she fulfilled an important role in the system restricting his strength. There was no doubt that one of the reasons he couldn't use his true abilities was Miyuki herself.

But Tatsuya…he didn't consider his sister to be selfish. She believed he wouldn't lose to anyone. That was basically a wish, her desire for him. Mentally speaking, Tatsuya wasn't mature enough to completely understand those sorts of subtleties.

On an intuitive level, however, he understood it. Perhaps he understood precisely *because* Miyuki was the one to express that wish.

And Tatsuya couldn't ignore his little sister's wishes.

This wasn't something someone had ordered or otherwise arranged for him to do. That was just a predisposition—the way he was put together. That was what he meant by not being able to win.

Apparently, he wasn't going to be able to lose the next match. But that was easier said than done. He sighed. No matter how he crunched the numbers, his prospects for victory were slim.

◇ ◇ ◇

After the third-place match ended, they announced that the finals would be played on the grasslands stage. The two schools had completely opposite reactions upon hearing that. Some in Third High's tent were even cheering.

"It's just like you said it would be, George!"

"We got lucky, Masaki."

Although they had the self-control not to raise their voices in joy, the two of them couldn't hide smiles.

"Now we just need to see if he'll take the bait…"

"He'll definitely take it. With no obstacles on the grasslands stage, answering our straight one-on-one fight is the only way he has a chance of winning."

"I suppose he needs to try to survive that way, because he has Program Demolition."

"That's right, Masaki. His tactics seem to be deliberately strange, but they're actually the results of extremely precise calculations. If he had no countermeasures, he might tend toward clever schemes, knowing the odds weren't in his favor. But since he has Program Demolition, he should choose a straight fight, since it has the highest chance of winning."

"And then you just have to suppress their defender and supporter."

"I don't think the defender will be a problem. I think he's pretty skilled at hardening magic, but he doesn't seem to have many strong points besides that. As for their supporter...he seems to specialize in old magic. Given his name, he's probably from the Yoshida family. It's scary to go in without knowing what he'll do, but modern magic has a speed advantage over old magic. The lack of obstacles on the grasslands stage works in our favor in that regard, too."

"And in your case, you have the advantage of being able to use the Cardinal Code."

"Unfortunately, the rookie championship got taken away from us... We have to at least win Monolith Code."

"Yeah." Masaki nodded forcefully. "We can do it."

"The grasslands stage, a stage without obstacles... This will be a hard battle, Tatsuya." Miyuki's words represented the opinion of everyone who came to encourage him.

"No, this is better than the canyon stage or the city stage. But we can't ask for everything."

Those words caused not only Miyuki but also his teammates, Leo and Mikihiko, to cock their heads in confusion.

Tatsuya elucidated. "The Ichijou family's Burst spell converts liquids into gases and uses the expansion as destructive power. Anyone in the family is probably great at attacking with water vapor explosions. The canyon stage basically has tons of gunpowder all over the field. In the city stage, there are water pipes that have water in them. Compared to those, there's no 'liquid gunpowder' on the grasslands stage. Even the Prince probably can't scoop water out of the ground and use *that* as blasting powder. Of course, the forest stage or the crag stage would have been easier...but we'll have to be happy with it not being the canyon stage, since that was the worst option."

The freshmen all seemed to be convinced by that, but the upperclassmen's faces remained clouded.

"...But that doesn't mean your disadvantages go away," remarked Mayumi. "Without obstacles on the field, you have to fight magicians specializing in long-range combat."

"Do you have a plan, Shiba?" followed up Hattori. It was extremely rare for him to address Tatsuya directly.

Tatsuya was honestly surprised, and he couldn't hide it. It took a moment to respond. "In a normal fight, I honestly wouldn't have any options...but Ichijou seems to be paying too much attention to me. If I can bring him into close range, I might be able to do something."

"But hand-to-hand combat is forbidden," said Kirihara.

Tatsuya gave a slightly unsure smile. "It's okay if you don't understand right now. I do have a plan, though."

◇ ◇ ◇

The final Monolith Code rookie match.

It would have been nice to be able to say the audience roared at the players' appearance. Unfortunately, far more in the stands were murmuring in confusion.

Exposed to the curious, rubbernecking eyes, Mikihiko pulled his hood farther over his head. On the other hand, Leo, who had nothing to cover his head with, tucked his face into his mantle's high collar, trying to hide as much of it as he could. "Hey...I told you these clothes would be weird..."

"But I already explained how to use them," replied Tatsuya, not so subtly advising Leo to drop the subject.

"...Why just us?" grumbled Mikihiko in complaint; Tatsuya was the only one not wearing a costume.

"Why would I wear something that made it that hard to run? I'm our vanguard," Tatsuya replied, slapping down Mikihiko's objection in the name of strategy.

"Shit...I bet she's laughing at us..."

Leo left out *who* he was talking about, but the other two didn't need him to specify.

"Aha-ha-ha-ha-ha... That's...that's hilarious! What *are* those?! Aha-ha-ha-ha-ha..."

In line with their prediction, Erika was laughing uproariously in the stands.

"Erika, you shouldn't..." Mizuki, embarrassed, tried many times to reprove her. Eventually, Mizuki got her down to the level of snickering.

"Ahh, that was a good laugh!" Erika cried with glee. "That's why you can't blink when Tatsuya's doing something!"

"...But now even more people are looking at *you!*" hissed Mizuki, curling herself up a little.

"Sorry, sorry! It was just so funny to me for some reason. I'll stop being so loud, so cheer up, Mizuki!"

"Geez... For goodness' sake!"

Feeling the stares on them turn back to the field (she wasn't brave enough to look directly), Mizuki finally brought her face up.

"But what could they be?"

There were no obstacles on the grasslands stage, so the audience had a clear view of the entire field. Still, they were too far away to make out tiny details, so the big screens were showing the faces of the players, like they did for the other stages.

Erika's gaze fixed on Mikihiko and Leo, displayed on the screen depicting First High's base.

After staring at them for a few moments, she shook her head in resignation. "I got nothing. I don't know why they're wearing that. And Tatsuya wouldn't be bluffing."

"...Look at all the spirits around Yoshida's robe..." muttered Mizuki to herself.

"Huh?" responded Erika, surprised, turning to look. Mizuki had taken off her glasses, and her eyes were tinged with a strange hue. Erika sucked in her breath.

Much of the crowd was in a fuss over Leo's and Mikihiko's clothing, which was somehow anachronistic, out of place. Not many could be seen scoffing or laughing at it, though. The minds of the audience were curious about what the robe and mantle would be used for.

The team they were playing, though, needed a little more than curiosity.

"Couldn't it just be a bluff?"

Masaki and Kichijouji shook their heads in unison at their teammate's guess. "He knew who George was..." said Masaki. "Is it to deal with Invisible Bullet?"

"The spell might not have any penetration...but it would take more than a single piece of cloth to stop it. He seems too smart to come up with a plan as naive as that."

"Maybe he's just trying to get us to think that way?"

"That's certainly possible, but..." Masaki struggled to find words.

"...I just don't know," said Kichijouji. "I didn't think he'd *still* have something up his sleeve..." He bit his lip. For someone who prided himself on his ingenuity, this was especially frustrating.

"We can't go in completely unguarded, but we can't stand here thinking about things we don't understand," said Masaki, a little more firmly than necessary, in an attempt to clear Kichijouji's doubts. "The brute-force approach is bound to have some risks anyway." Nevertheless, even *he* found himself a little lost.

The point of curiosity for the audience was a point of caution for the opposing team.

There was no way the players, nor those cheering for them in the stands, could have known the *second* reason the crowds were in a fuss, though. The stands near the main office were murmuring about something else.

An unexpected guest had arrived nearby.

"Mr. Kudou! Whatever might you be doing in a place like this?!"

Usually, the old Kudou would spectate the events from his screen in the tournament headquarters VIP room. But now, all of a sudden, here he was in the visitors' seats.

"I just thought I'd watch from here for once."

Retsu Kudou nodded placidly at the tournament committee members standing at attention in greeting, then took a seat in a leather chair hurriedly prepared for him.

"Well, you certainly do honor us with your presence, but…"

Why all of a sudden? was the implication, to which Kudou answered casually, "What? I happened to spot an interesting young man is all."

The time right before a match was probably the moment the players' minds were full of the most doubt. However much confidence they had, however sure their victory may have been, they wouldn't really know the outcome until they actually went out and fought for it. This wasn't a seasonal league, where they played the same opponent several times. In this event, they would only ever play each team once. That meant there was much more uncertainty about how strong the enemy was.

But those doubts only lasted until the starting whistle.

Once the flames of battle were lit, none could be allowed such doubt.

With the signal to start the match, each base began firing at the other.

Magic-based artillery attacks.

They were met with great joy from the audience, while those in First High's cheering section were struck dumb with surprise.

There were about three hundred thirty yards between the two bases. A short distance compared to the forest or canyon stages, but if this were a live firing range, assault rifles would have a tough time of it; this would call for sniper rifles.

As each team fired, their CADs thrust out before them looking like automatic pistols, they walked toward one another.

Tatsuya sported his double handgun–style like he did in the qualifiers and semifinal. He shot down the enemy's attacks with the CAD in his right hand while he fired his own attacks with his left. On the other side, Masaki had consciously abandoned any defense and was now devoting himself to attack.

As a result…the already-wide margin in attack power was getting bigger and bigger.

Each one of Masaki's ranged attacks had enough impact to finish the job, while Tatsuya's ranged attacks were no more than a screen. His shots were *reaching* the enemy, but that was about it. The oscillation spells were too weak for Masaki to need to focus on defense; the Information Boosting wall that magicians unconsciously emitted was enough to block them. Tatsuya was also firing far less.

He had plenty of dirty tricks up his sleeve, but his magical abilities were undeniably inferior. *In the normal sense*, anyway. Just the fact that his attacks were hitting at all from this range, while his own body was exposed and it was hard to actually see, was surprising.

"Now that's what I call grit…" groaned a male senior.

"Is he actually in Course 2?" said one female player to her teammate.

Rather than the strength of the magic itself, the mental capacity required to use magic the right way under the pressure of all those attacks had the upperclassmen raising their voices in surprise.

But Mayumi, Katsuto, Suzune, Azusa, Hattori… None of their faces looked well. This was just an exchange of greetings. It was clear to them that Tatsuya was being forced to play more defensively with every step closer they got—and attack less because of it.

At Third High's base, Kichijouji was surprised—but for a different reason than the First High cadre.

The spells Tatsuya was using right now were of the oscillation family. But in the three matches before this, he had only been using typeless magic and weighting spells. *Did he reorganize his activation programs in less than two hours...?*

Kichijouji shook his head to rid himself of such idle thoughts. However amazing his method of CAD adjustment, they wouldn't affect this match. Only the results of those adjustments would influence the outcome. This wasn't the time to be impressed by Tatsuya's adjustment speed. That was just another doubt—one that could lead to an upset...

"Just as planned. I'll get going, too."

"Sure, you take care of the rest!"

Without realizing that, at some point, he had started to look down at his opponents as lower than himself and his team, Kichijouji began to run in a roundabout path, avoiding Masaki, toward First High's base.

When Kichijouji left their base, the match entered a new phase. Most of the spectators' eyes, however, were glued to the battle between Tatsuya and Masaki.

Some were breathing sighs of admiration toward Masaki, who continued to fire powerful magic without end, never missing. Yet even more were sitting in admiration of Tatsuya's Program Demolition, which was shooting down all of Masaki's spells.

Not many of the spectators knew about Program Demolition, advanced-level anti-magic that it was. It required an abnormal amount of retained psions, so even researchers in the field wouldn't have had many opportunities to see it before now.

But even without that knowledge, the big screens equipped with psion visualization processing capabilities were showing fiercely radiant psionic bullets materializing in midair, shooting through the compressed air spells of Masaki's and blowing them to a million pieces.

It was a marvelous, fantastic spectacle, worthy of excitement. The magicians in the audience—and those with the makings of such—who could visually perceive psions were looking straight at the field rather than the screens, overawed by the madly dancing storm of psions in the air. The mind-boggling, emotionally moving, completely absurd sight had captivated them.

Right now, Tatsuya was focusing his mind on shooting down Masaki's attacks. He did still see Kichijouji jumping out of Third High's base, though.

As if that were his cue—actually, it was *exactly* his cue—Tatsuya switched from his current careful stride to an all-out run.

Masaki didn't panic at the sudden dash. He took careful aim and fired compressed-air bullet spells at Tatsuya again and again.

One option would have been to run in a zigzag to avoid those shots, but Tatsuya didn't take that course. Masaki wasn't aiming manually, so such trivial evasive maneuvers would mean nothing. Instead, as he ran he strained his senses to spot the event alterations appearing in the air, ramming psionic bullets—his Program Demolition—into them, crushing Masaki's attacks before they even manifested. All the while, he tried to sprint through the three hundred thirty yards between them.

But the closer they got to each other, the easier it was for Masaki to aim. Physical distance might not have directly affected anything, but cognitively, the real proximity made it easier to feel the distance as if it were close.

The closer the target, the easier it was to aim. Especially when you were aiming at something you couldn't see, like the air. In this case, Tatsuya was the target of attack. Once he got within one hundred sixty feet, he was unable to keep parrying Masaki's attacks.

A stray compressed-air bullet flew straight at him. He used all his senses to detect it and all his martial arts abilities to avoid it, then continued toward his target. Tatsuya couldn't go straight for him anymore. The last several dozen feet were like a huge wall towering over him.

"Looks like he finally can't dodge the issue anymore," said Yamanaka in the stands, apparently amused at seeing Tatsuya being driven back.

"Don't be indiscreet, Doctor. Perceiving both the signs of the spell's activation and the bullets themselves with just his regular senses would be impossible even for Tatsuya. And in this situation, even without Elemental Sight, it can be chalked up to a sixth sense."

Fujibayashi's defense put a mean grin on Yamanaka's face. "Is that right? I suppose he could deceive the eyes of the masses…but I don't think he would fool our esteemed guest's eyes."

Yamanaka looked toward the main visitor's seats, his eyes pointing out the Kudou patriarch, who was watching the match with great interest. Fujibayashi shot only a brief glance in that direction before looking back at Tatsuya.

On his way around the field, toward the side of First High's monolith, Kichijouji found himself blocked off about a hundred yards away by Leo. Though confused at their defender advancing this far up, Kichijouji fired an Invisible Bullet at him.

Or at least, he tried to.

"What?"

A black wall stood before his eyes now. Leo had taken off his mantle and, after fluttering in the wind, it had stiffened into place, turning into a wall in front of him.

Then, from the side, a piece of metal slashed through the air toward Kichijouji. He dodged the armament's projectile by instantly activating a movement spell, one that sent him flying backward.

Then a sudden gust of wind was upon him. He used a weighting spell to reduce his inertia, then mitigated the damage from the wind attack by allowing himself to be blown away.

What a pain! Kichijouji cursed to himself, now aiming an Invisible Bullet at Mikihiko, who had appeared about thirty feet behind Leo. Kichijouji had decided to crush the nuisance on support fire first.

But as soon as he focused on the gray robe, he suddenly couldn't tell near from far. The shimmering of air blurred Mikihiko into a gray shadow, like he was looking at an out-of-focus analog photograph.

An illusion technique?!

As soon as he realized they'd taken advantage of the fact that he needed to visually aim the Invisible Bullet spell, he noticed the Mini-Communicator's blade coming down at him from overhead. It would be impossible to dodge at this point. He shut his eyes.

"Gah!"

But the one grunting the air out of his lungs was actually Leo.

Not even a second before his descending blade hit Kichijouji, it had veered off course and slammed into the ground. An explosion of air had then hit Leo's body from the side, knocking him to the ground.

"Masaki!" cried Kichijouji to his savior, omitting the thanks.

Kichijouji had fallen right into the enemy's trap, but Masaki had saved him with support fire even as he continued to attack Tatsuya.

Kichijouji's fingers danced across his CAD console and he activated a spell of the weighting family. The direction of gravity suddenly changed, and Mikihiko "fell" sideways without any idea of what happened. After he went down, Kichijouji, who had abandoned his hang-up on his own magic of choice, sent a weighting-increase spell at him.

He heard a grunt squeezed out of Mikihiko's mouth as he was pressed to the ground.

Tatsuya, though, hadn't been silently watching that happen, either. In the moment Masaki had diverted his attention toward

Kichijouji, Tatsuya had closed to within sixteen feet of him. With his martial arts abilities, Masaki was now within striking range.

Closing the distance required only a single leap.

A look of unmistakable discomposure crossed Masaki's face. It was much like panic—perhaps his instincts warned him of the threat, given the experienced soldier that he was. Then he let loose a barrage of sixteen compressed-air bullets—and each one of them went over the regulation for magic strength.

The anti-magic spell Program Demolition was a technique that blew apart a magic program with a bullet of compressed psions. Because it did so by force, it was extremely inefficient.

Though it wasn't widely known, magic programs *did* have a strength to them. Magic programs with powerful influence would, in turn, have strong psionic information bodies composing them. In order to use force to blow away a magic program from a caster of Masaki's level instead of technically analyzing it, even Tatsuya needed to compress a huge amount of psions—more than a normal magician would be able to wring out in an entire *day*.

And there were sixteen of them now, in this one moment.

Immediately, he knew Program Demolition wouldn't make it in time. But he didn't choose to use Dismantle. Stubbornly, he refused to use the confidential spell. He would keep his Program Dispersion spell, which dismantled the bodies composing information, hidden. Instead, he intercepted the shots with Program Demolition.

As a result, and perhaps inevitably…

…his interception only got to fourteen shots, and the last two slammed into him.

As he saw Tatsuya sink to the ground at his feet, Masaki suddenly very much regretted doing that. He had allowed himself to succumb to his sense of self-preservation and had fired a spell with much more power than the rules allowed. He knew as much immediately after triggering the magic.

It had been a momentary thing. Maybe the judges hadn't noticed. There was no red flag out…but he still knew he had committed a violation that would have constituted a forfeit.

He had to spend time considering all that.

And that created a blank moment he wouldn't be able to take back.

Ribs fractured. Liver veins damaged. Excessive bleeding predicted.

Combat power lowered beyond allowable levels.

Self-repair technique starting automatically…

Loading magic programs…

Reloading core eidos data from backup…

Starting repair… Complete.

—It happened faster that Tatsuya could think and was rectified just as quickly. The unconscious region of his mind's information processing speed far surpassed that of his conscious region's. By the time he was aware that he'd fallen, his body had already finished repairing itself.

There were feet in front of him, standing still, within arm's reach. Tatsuya didn't know why Masaki had frozen in place like that, leaving himself wide-open. Right now he didn't need to know. He didn't need to think about it, so instead he leaped up.

His right foot hit the ground, and with Masaki's tense face of surprise in front of him, stuck his right arm out. His right hand flew by Masaki's reflexively bent head, though at a farther distance. The thrust had not been aimed to strike him in the head. The moment it flew past Masaki's ear…

…a ripping sound rivaling that of a flash bang came from Tatsuya's right hand.

The roar made the stands completely quiet. Even Kichijouji, who was in the middle of combat, turned around and stopped.

Tatsuya's right thumb was pressed to the end of his right index finger, with his middle finger across his thumb. The players, the judges, the audience, those in the cheering section—everyone present looked on as Masaki crumpled to the ground and Tatsuya fell limp to his knees.

"What? What on earth was that?" asked Mayumi, looking left and right, her voice and face both completely confused.

But no answer came. Neither Suzune nor Azusa could give her one.

Instead, the answer came from the other side of Suzune, where Katsuto was sitting. "...I think he snapped his fingers to amplify the sound."

"...You're right," continued Suzune. "A simple amplification of sound waves. The loud noise ruptured his eardrum and damaged his semicircular canal, incapacitating Ichijou. It wasn't against the rules.

"His technique, despite it increasing the volume so much, is simple in construction. It requires only a single spell in the oscillation family. That's why Tatsuya could activate it in an instant even though he has trouble casting magic quickly."

Mayumi's reaction to the explanation, though, was an outburst bordering on hysterical. "I knew that to begin with! That was obvious just from looking at his right hand! How did he stand back up after being knocked down by Ichijou's attack?! Didn't that take him down?! He tried to intercept it with Program Demolition, and he didn't make it! He should have taken at least two of those shots! Tatsuya should be badly hurt by that attack! It was against the rules! How did he get back up and keep fighting?!"

"Saegusa, calm down," soothed Katsuto in a heavy, calm voice. Mayumi's face was white with the shock of Tatsuya having been badly hurt. "That's how it looked like to me, too. But the reality is that he got back up and took down the enemy with movements that would be impossible if he was that injured. Right now it just seems like he took damage from his own sonic attack. He's not hurt any worse."

"But..."

"I hear Shiba is skilled in old-style martial arts. I also hear that the old styles have skills to make their physical bodies stronger and to ward off impacts within their bodies. It was probably one of those."

"..." Mayumi didn't seem convinced by Katsuto's words, but for now, she managed to regain her calm.

"We don't know everything there is to know in this world. Magic alone is no miracle. And the match isn't over yet, either."

"...You're right. I'm sorry, Juumonji. And Rin."

Even while Mayumi and Suzune were reconciling, the battle had entered a new phase.

"His self-repair never fails to amaze me!" cheered Yamanaka—though in a low-enough voice so that others wouldn't hear him.

Fujibayashi turned an incredulous stare on him. "...Was that really the self-repair technique? I didn't even see the psions for when it activated."

"I couldn't see them, either. I bet not even Old Master Kudou could see them. His self-repair speed exceeds the speed of human consciousness, after all." Yamanaka finally noticed the grim look on Fujibayashi's face as she stared at him. "Oh, well...I definitely didn't see it. I never saw *Tatsuya Shiba using a self-repair technique he shouldn't be able to use*, I promise. Boy, he must be way stronger than most humans. Yes, truly interesting..." said Yamanaka, forced to suppress a manic laugh.

Fujibayashi gave him a stunned warning. "Even so, you don't want him becoming a test subject, do you? Our country has only two of them, and the world has only fifty. They would be extremely valuable for war."

"Well, I don't think he's weak enough to break from a few little experiments."

"That doesn't make it all right!"

The flat-out berating made Yamanaka flinch. "Well, you're right...and he did use it, like you said."

"Yes. It looks like the regulation low-spec CADs were too little for him to go up against Ichijou. I don't think he had much choice but to use flash casting, don't you?"

"A single flash-cast oscillation spell... Well, at least *our* secrets are safe."

The Yotsuba were the ones who wanted to keep flash casting a secret, not the Independent Magic Battalion. There were too many humane issues with the technology, so the regular military couldn't use it.

What the Independent Magic Battalion needed to keep secret was the *original* magic Tatsuya possessed. Despite the overwhelming disadvantage he'd faced, he hadn't used Dismantle. And he used his self-repair technique so quickly that nobody would have been able to see it. This would probably only result in a bit more regular attention heaped onto Tatsuya. If it had gone differently, the military might have been forced to *secure* Tatsuya so that he didn't fall into enemy hands—he was valuable as both a specimen and as combat potential.

That would, at the same time, equate to stealing even more of his freedom. If that had happened, it wouldn't be unthinkable to have to confront him—or even fight against him. Despite the things Yamanaka said, the doctor was very much relieved at this outcome.

"Having his left-hand CAD installed with oscillation spells was probably to camouflage it. He was thoroughly prepared as usual."

"If you're telling me *that's* a high school kid, then the world's gone wrong. Still, flash casting... Enemies would find that speed a serious threat."

Fujibayashi nodded slowly. "Yes...applying brainwashing technology to imprint an activation program on his memory region as image memory... Not reading activation programs from a CAD but rather from his memory region, thus shortening the time he needs to expand and read in the programs...

"The technology was developed even further with the singularity of his calculation region being in his conscious mind, so it shortens even the time he needs to construct magic programs by storing them in his memory region as image memory… That all completely makes up for any lack of speed his calculation region might have."

"Makes up for it with some to spare, I'd say. Is there anyone in our unit who can activate magic faster than him? Yanagi uses techniques in the same family as him, and even *he* would barely be able to rival him, I'd think."

"…You're right. I can't think of anyone else."

The two of them weren't watching the match anymore.

They just watched, worried, over Tatsuya as he remained on his knees.

Kichijouji was about to fall into complete panic. He couldn't believe what his eyes were telling him.

Masaki was lying on the ground. His opponent, Tatsuya, was on his knees, but there was still light in his eyes. Which meant…

Masaki…lost…?

What he was seeing was impossible. This should never have happened. Maybe they could have lost as a team, but Masaki should have had zero chance of being defeated.

"Kichijouji, get out of the way!"

Upon hearing the voice of their defender, whom he'd thought he left at the base, Kichijouji snapped out of it and reflexively used the Lightning Rod spell.

The short grass on the ground, now with improved electrical resistance, drew in the loosed lightning attack and the bolt dispersed into the ground.

Kichijouji finally realized that the enemy player he'd held down with a weighting spell before had unsteadily risen to his feet with ragged breath and his fluttering gray robe, and was now staring at him.

Mikihiko heard the roar but didn't understand what had happened.

He didn't have the time to look around to check, either. All he knew was that the pressure holding him to the ground had disappeared. So he had hurried to roll over, distance himself, and stand up. It was a reflexive evasive motion.

And then he finally understood. Leo had gone down. Tatsuya was on his knees. He wasn't out of the fight, but he didn't look very fit to keep going.

And in front of him, Masaki Ichijou had gone down.

You did it, Tatsuya!

He knew Tatsuya would be able to do something, but he still had reservations—it seemed like too much even for Tatsuya. But now he felt cheered by the reality before him.

Mikihiko's own condition couldn't be called favorable. In fact, it could be said that he was in *really bad* shape. His chest wheezed every time he took a breath. His bones might not have been fractured, but there definitely could have been a few cracks. He was slightly oxygen deprived from being held down for so long, and his back hurt; he had hit it hard when he fell. Quietly, he cursed his fate to himself—for all the grass on the ground, it certainly wasn't soft at all.

But he couldn't call it quits now—

Even if he was in terrible shape, and even if it was two-on-one.

Not *even if*—he *was* in that exact situation. But he still couldn't lose.

Tatsuya had defeated the Crimson Prince in a fair fight. Then Mikihiko would at least take down Cardinal George. That desire was the only thing holding up his trembling legs.

He used his CAD to fire a lightning attack. At the same time, he passed mana—signal psions—through his gray robe. The spirits of shadow inside his robe should have blurred his appearance.

Shadows weren't the same thing as darkness. You could see the outline of objects thanks to their shadows. The spirits of shadow were independent information bodies (isolates) based on the concept of shadows. By confusing the outline between light and dark, it would interfere with his opponent's sense of vision and make him unable to aim accurately.

This technique was originally the Yoshida family's, but Tatsuya had been the one to think up this scheme of activating the vision sense interference spell with this technique-enhancing robe and a CAD with thoroughly optimized software.

His senses had gotten close to how they'd been before—or even more so, according to Erika—in how well he could use magic. If so, that was thanks to Tatsuya. The reason they'd gotten to the final match was thanks to Tatsuya as well, without a doubt. And that meant that everything until now had all been thanks to him. The thought made Mikihiko bite his lip to encourage his body to stay upright.

Everything is thanks to him?
My pride won't allow that.
No matter what, I will put up one last act of resistance.
Shinkurou Kichijouji, you put me down in the dirt on my hands and knees.
This time, I'll drag you down to the ground!

With the triumvirate of pride, arrogance, and haughtiness, Mikihiko spoke to himself.

Tatsuya had said something, taught something, to him: Mikihiko's faults weren't coming from his strength. They were coming from his technique. If that was true...

Tatsuya, I'll prove what you said is right!

He ignored the magic brushing past him. Thanks to the shadow magic, he would appear blurred to his enemy's eyes. Believing in the strength of his own spell, Mikihiko reached into his robe and typed a long command into his large, two-handed, portable terminal-shaped CAD.

And after his right hand left the device, he slammed it into the ground beneath him!

* * *

Normal multipurpose CADs used two number keys and one selection key; using those three keys would expand an activation program. Some high-end equipment, especially high-end portable terminal devices, were equipped with shortcut keys that allowed the caster to use a frequent spell with a single motion.

Mikihiko had just hit fifteen keys. That was five times the length of the magic-activating process of normal multipurpose CADs. And yet the time required for that process was far less than if he was to cast it as old magic.

Because the device stored the same number of activation programs, Mikihiko would never have to hit any extra keys. Instead of compiling one spell from five smaller ones, he had specified five separate spells to be triggered in sequence.

The technique was based on the same idea as sequential expansion. Rather than putting together one magic program that included five spells, he constructed each magic program as the previous was firing. The usual process in spirit magic was to verify the effects of each individual spell while completing the technique with a voice interface. With one chain of sequential actions, he didn't have to check each spell on its own; he processed them all at once.

That was the solution Tatsuya had given to Mikihiko.

The ground trembled under his hand.

Not because the old-fashioned robed caster had slammed his hand to it—Kichijouji knew as well as Mikihiko did that it was the effect of a spell, one that oscillated the surface of the ground. And yet his appearance, action, and effect were so very *magician*-like that it gave off the illusion that the ground was swaying because Mikihiko had hit it with his palm.

As Kichijouji lost his balance, a fissure appeared, beginning at his opponent's hand and traveling toward his own feet. The earth was not splitting open; it was being pushed apart by pressure. Kichijouji understood this logically as well, but for some reason, his logical mind had lost all sense of reality. Quickly, he cast a compound spell of both weight reduction and movement in an attempt to flee into the sky.

But his feet never left the ground. The grass had entwined around his ankles.

——He didn't know of any magic that could control plants as if they were living creatures. The unknown spell shook his very soul. Logically, Mikihiko had probably made the grass coil by adjusting the air currents near to the ground. But modern magic was all Kichijouji knew. Such an ambiguous manipulation of air currents—not changing the wind direction to a certain angle but creating the vague effect of it getting tangled up—didn't seem possible to him.

The fissure reached his feet...

...and Kichijouji felt as though the grass dragged his legs into it.

Everything was an illusion. But to get away from it, Kichijouji poured every ounce of magical energy he had into his jumping spell—despite there having been absolutely no need to do so.

He tore off the grass coiling around him and flew much higher than he needed to. He was filled with relief at having escaped the unnatural green jaws—and he temporarily forgot about Mikihiko. He had, at that moment, lost his focus on the enemy he was fighting.

And that created a final opening. Mikihiko had activated five spells in succession. Rumbling, Fissure, Disheveled Hair, Ant Lion Pit—those were the four techniques that had already been activated.

And the final one, the lightning strikes from Thunder Child, shot Kichijouji out of the air.

"Damn you!" As Mikihiko watched the outcome, his hand still on the ground, the final remaining Third High player attacked him with magic.

It was the movement spell Earth Tsunami, which rent the ground, sending a mass of earth and sand at the enemy. Compared to how the spell was originally envisioned, this wave of land was actually quite small. Maybe he was weak with this type of magic, or maybe he had reduced its power to be in compliance with the rules.

Whichever the case, Mikihiko had already taken plenty of damage from Kichijouji. The attack had more than enough punch behind it to take him down. He thought about ordering the spirits under his influence to repel the earth—and immediately discarded the idea. Unfortunately, he didn't have that much power left.

In spirit magic, the spirits themselves didn't actually possess any strength. They were purely information bodies—no more than mediums through which to pass one's power of influence to alter the world.

I guess I lost in the end... he thought, watching the approaching wave of earth without even blinking—when suddenly, his vision was blocked off by blackness. There was a heavy, dull sound, like the earth had bounced off an iron wall, and it returned to the unmoving ground from whence it came.

Mikihiko looked toward where the black wall had come from.

There he saw his teammate, roaring and swinging his arm. His armament device flew in a wide arc, dealt a horizontal blow to the last Third High player, and knocked him down.

"...They...won?" muttered Mayumi under her breath.

"...They did," answered Suzune, also under her breath.

That was the signal.

Someone gave a cheer.

Two cheers responded to that single voice, and then four, and then eight, spreading outward in a chain.

Then the cheering exploded.

The unruly screaming from the First High students, joined together, made the ground rumble and the stands shake. It was an innocent, exceedingly pure display of emotion. It was at once giving praise to the victors and the sound of a hammer of judgment upon the defeated.

But for some reason, the ruthless uproar quieted quickly.

Because in the front row of First High's cheering section—

There was one girl there, looking at the field, hands over her mouth, tears of joy falling from her eyes. She stood up unsteadily, unable to find her voice, simply watching her brother wave his hand to her.

And as though to encourage her, applause began near her and steadily spread. Eventually the applause exceeded First High's cheering stands, transforming into congratulations from friend and foe alike, praising all the players who had just finished their fierce battle.

The entire grandstand was showering the players with a warm applause.

Tatsuya's team couldn't help but feel awkward at the unexpected wave of applause. Tatsuya took off his helmet and walked over to Leo and Mikihiko. All three purposely chose to avoid looking at the grandstand.

"…You really did steal the best part," said Mikihiko to Leo. "Was that your plan all along?" The snide comment, asked as soon as their eyes met, was to hide Mikihiko's embarrassment; that was clearly evident to both parties.

"Nah, course not. I really couldn't move for a while. I haven't been rocked that hard since that big motorcycle hit me two years ago."

"What? You got hit by a motorcycle?" Mikihiko gave him a *you must be joking* expression, but Leo nodded seriously.

"Yeah, it really hit me hard. There was some little kid behind me, and he couldn't get out of the way. So I prepared myself, and *bam!* …I got hurt, of course. Cracked three of my ribs. Well, it was better than that was, at least. Didn't hurt as much."

"Er…Leo? I just want to make sure. You were blocking those compressed-air bullets before with hardening magic, right…?"

"Aha, actually, I was too preoccupied with attacking… You guessed it. I couldn't put up a defense in time. That's a blow to my pride."

Mikihiko's face filled with question marks. To put it bluntly, the expression looked idiotic. Thankfully for him, nobody here was going to laugh at it, and the screens had switched over to a bird's-eye view of the field, so nobody could make out their exact expressions. "Then you...you were repelling Ichijou's attack magic with nothing but your body?"

"I didn't repel them! That's why it took so long for me to stand up. Huh? Mikihiko, your lip is bleeding. You okay?"

"Uhh...yeah, I'm, uh...fine." The conversation wasn't making any sense, and Leo's confession was even harder to believe. Mikihiko's eyes were wide with surprise, but Leo was in such a good mood that he didn't notice his friend's bewilderment. "By the way, Tatsuya, are you all right?"

"Hmm? Sorry, could you say that again?"

"I said, *Tatsuya, are you all right?*"

"Yeah... One of my eardrums ruptured. I can't hear that well right now. Anyway, Mikihiko, what's wrong? You look like you saw some kind of UMA [unconfirmed mysterious animal]."

Mikihiko indeed felt just like that—well, almost—but he was also arguing with himself. Maybe *he* was the one lacking common sense. But no, that was impossible. "Wait, so you didn't...hear any of what we were just talking about?"

"Sorry. I'm just now figuring it out from reading your lips. I did see that Leo got hit by a big motorcycle once, though."

"...You didn't *doubt* that at all?" asked Mikihiko slowly, trying to settle his internal argument and defend what he believed to be common sense.

"Doubt? Doubt what?"

Tatsuya's answer filled Mikihiko with despair. He looked up to the sky.

"Mikihiko, what the heck's wrong with you? You look depressed all of a sudden. In case you didn't notice, we *won*. The championship!"

"You're right..." Mikihiko suddenly turned an exhausted look to Leo.

Leo seemed to decide that he was really tired, and Tatsuya followed suit. Mikihiko watched them, lamenting. *In the end, it wasn't magic power or technique that had the last say—it was this guy's hard head.*

The applause showed no signs of stopping. Leo and Tatsuya, appearing to finally accept it, put their arms around each other's shoulders and waved awkwardly back at the cheering.

Mikihiko watched them, seriously starting to consider a new training regimen.

[11]

Everyone decided to leave the rookie championship party until the overall victory party.

One reason for this was that their three substitutes, who had entered Monolith Code and won both the event and the rookie competition, had sustained major physical damage and weren't able to join in the hijinks. The main reason, though, was because they were too busy preparing for Mirage Bat tomorrow, the event on which their overall victory rode.

First High's victory in the rookie competition had opened an even wider gap in total points between First and Third Highs. The difference was now four hundred points. Tomorrow's Mirage Bat would distribute fifty points to first place, thirty to second, twenty to third, and ten to fourth. Monolith Code, which would have its qualifiers tomorrow and its finals on the last day, would give one hundred points to first place, sixty to second, and forty to third. Depending on their results in Mirage Bat tomorrow, First High could clinch the victory without having to wait for the final day.

The players and engineers were all completely devoted to putting the finishing touches on the costumes (or protective clothing, in Monolith Code's case) and CAD adjustments. The members without anything to do were helping out in various ways.

Tatsuya purposely hadn't repaired his right eardrum rupture and went to the infirmary to seek conventional medical treatment. Then he used his self-repair magic to completely heal it, and covered his ears with medical-use earmuffs before going to do some preparations for Miyuki for tomorrow.

He felt a little sorry for deceiving his team members—in particular his upperclassmen—who were worried about his right ear without knowing it had already healed. Unfortunately, there were things he needed to keep a secret. He decided to keep them unaware of his lack of a conscience by enduring having to wear hot, sticky earmuffs in the middle of summer—though he knew the price should have been much steeper.

Of course, even with the words *complete devotion* used, there was almost nothing they needed to struggle over the day before. Actually, perhaps it would be better to say that there was *absolutely* nothing.

Last night, suddenly having to wipe clean two people's CADs—well, three people's, if you included his own—and then adjust them from scratch had been an extremely rare, unprecedented event. Although the business had changed from the rookie competition to the main one, Miyuki *was* planned to enter the Mirage Bat event. Preparations for that had been proceeding without any oversights. Just because he got caught up with other, more unexpected happenings for the day didn't mean that would affect this much.

"You shouldn't push yourself, Tatsuya. Get some sleep, all right? You've been working like crazy ever since yesterday."

"Miyuki, you should go to sleep as well. With you working so hard, this injured person will just keep pushing himself."

Tatsuya, having efficiently completed a full check on Miyuki's CAD, and Miyuki were half chased out of the place by Mayumi and Suzune, putting an end to the siblings' activities for the day.

◇ ◇ ◇

Meanwhile, however, there were others, driven against the wall, who couldn't get a wink of sleep.

"First High's victory is all but assured…"

"This is absurd! Are you telling us to give up? We would just be sitting here waiting to die!"

"If First High goes on to win, we'll lose over one hundred million U.S. dollars."

"With a loss like that, our deaths won't be easy! HQ was already balking at how much money we'd lose if this plan failed and they lost. We were the ones who convinced them. We'll be exploited by the organization even after we die—either as half-dead Generators if we're lucky, and as Boosters if we don't have the aptitude!"

The men around the table looked with disgusted eyes at the four men standing idly in the four corners of the room.

"We wouldn't have been able to meet this term's quota if not for this plan…but maybe we were too coercive."

"This isn't the time to be talking about that! …This has gone too far. We need to use any means necessary."

"That's right! We've been giving them all kinds of trouble since the beginning so that they'd lose the main event. There's no reason to be hesitating *now*, even if it means being a bit violent. Even if the guests start having doubts, if we don't leave any evidence, we can make any excuse we need. We have to be proactive *now*."

"Send a message to our supporters. Order them to have all First High players forfeit in the middle of Mirage Bat tomorrow— by force."

"They won't die if they're lucky. If they do…then it just means their luck ran out."

Suppressed laughter and smiles filled with madness were traded among them, the symbols of their agreement.

◇ ◇ ◇

In stark contrast to the good weather they'd been having, the ninth day of the competition was darkened by thick clouds that looked ready to unleash rain at any moment.

However, low sunlight well after sunrise was one of Mirage Bat's few favorable conditions. For Miyuki and the others who would be in the event, this was actually *good* weather.

"A fine day for a Mirage Bat match…" said Tatsuya to himself, looking up at the sky, "but it also looks like a portent of trouble."

Miyuki's features clouded. "Is something else going to happen…?"

"I don't know what they're after, so… There's no proof something will happen, but also no proof something won't. Still, you needn't worry, Miyuki. You alone I will protect, no matter what happens."

There was no ulterior motive in Tatsuya's words. For him, as long as he protected Miyuki, things were okay. At the core of his intentions, Tatsuya figured that even if other athletes were sacrificed, it was their own fault and no business of his.

But…perhaps he should have thanked the heavens that nobody was listening to their conversation. Had a third party been witness…if someone had seen Tatsuya looking up to the sky again—with Miyuki beside him, outside his vision, leaning in close, her face shyly downcast but smiling blissfully—the siblings might have given the surreal impression that one was attempting to destroy the other by means of self recrimination.

◇ ◇ ◇

Miyuki was set for the second match of the day.

In reality, the first match would have been better to compete in because it would have given plenty of time to rest, but Tatsuya hadn't expected *everything* to go their way. He decided to simply be thankful that she hadn't been in the third match. The pair decided to watch the first match from the staff seats close to the event field. There would be forty-five minutes between the end of the first match and the start of the second, but it would be a waste of time to move down from the guest seating to the field.

He looked at the players from the other schools—they were all next to the field, too.

"Kobayakawa looks like she's raring to go," said Miyuki of her upperclassman, one of the players waiting for the start of the match atop a column sticking out of the lake's surface.

Tatsuya agreed with her assessment. Mari had said Kobayakawa was moody, but faced with the possibility of assuring overall victory herself, letting her mind wander would certainly be the more difficult option. Whether she won or lost would depend on her opponents, but he thought that, at this rate, she'd be fine.

As the audience, their staff, and their teammates looked on, the starting signal sounded.

The rankings during the first period were hectic, a close battle with everyone constantly swapping spots, but when it ended, Kobayakawa was in the lead by a tiny amount.

Erika, who had been holding her breath without realizing it, sighed and relaxed, then she went to say something to Mizuki sitting next to her—when she blinked in surprise at her friend's unusual appearance. "Mizuki…are you okay not wearing your glasses?"

Magicians with pushion-radiation sensitivity wore glasses with aura-cutting effects to prevent them from being caught up in the violent emotions that inhabited a place like this, due to the influence of energized pushions. In this situation, with the entire audience excited for one thing or another, her taking them off would have put a huge burden on her mind.

"To be honest…it's a little hard, I guess." Erika noticed that Mizuki's hands, in her lap and holding her glasses, were shaking a little from time to time. "But I don't think I should keep running away from my power."

"I don't think you're running away…"

Erika had asked her a few times why she'd gone to a magic high school. Of course, Mizuki had said it was mainly to foster her magical qualities, which were rare. Specifically, she wanted to go to Magic University and become a magic engineer.

But at the same time, her goal was to study techniques to control her eyes, which saw too much. She had been getting the most instruction she could, at least as far as being a Course 2 student would allow her.

She was inexperienced, but she was always confronting her own power, so she wasn't running away. And Erika thought that borrowing help from tools was the natural thing to do while one was still inexperienced.

Maybe that was why...

"Nothing good's gonna come out of forcing yourself. I'm not gonna say nobody ever learns a skill in a single bound, but most who try hurt themselves. In your case, there's a chance you could do something you can't take back, isn't there?"

...she started talking a little more strictly to her.

Still, Mizuki left her glasses on her lap. "Yeah...but I don't think it's right to ignore something I can see when I really need to see it... If I had been looking properly when Watanabe got hurt, maybe I would have been more of a help to Tatsuya and the others."

"...So now you're keeping watch in case something happens?"

"Yes, and...I think Miyuki will be fine. I mean, Tatsuya would never let anything happen to her. But I don't think he has enough energy to go around for the other players today. He did so much work yesterday. And if—"

"—another player *is* a victim, Tatsuya wouldn't pretend not to see. Well, I guess not... He seems coldhearted and unfeeling, but he's actually a big softie."

"Tatsuya is really nice, and he cares about his friends!"

"Yeah, yeah, I got it." *But sometimes I feel like if someone isn't his friend, he would stay ruthless to the end.* She kept that thought to herself while attempting to calm Mikuki, who was gesturing with her hands to display her irritation.

Then Mikihiko, who had overheard their conversation from Mizuki's opposite side, interrupted them. "I understand you're worried about Shibata, Erika, but if Tatsuya's right and they *are* using spirit magic to sabotage, then her eyes would be the most useful thing to have. For now, I've constructed a barrier around us that mitigates some of the stimulation from the pushion radiation, so I don't think she'll suffer from any aftereffects."

Mikihiko's words, which were a little more passionate than they needed to be (at least, when speaking to Erika) made the redhead give him a teasing grin. "Is that right? You'll protect her, huh? Then if something happens to her, you'll have to take responsibility, got that? You know, the kind of responsibility a boy has to a girl, all right?"

"Wh-what?! This isn't the time for stuff like that!" Mikihiko argued, blushing and even forgetting his usual objection at her nickname for him.

Meanwhile, Mizuki's face was completely flushed. She was in no state to argue.

"...You're a really evil woman, you know that?"

And Erika, for her part, was unconcerned, refusing to comment on the sigh-mixed criticism coming from the second young man occupying the seat next to her.

As Leo, ignored, and Erika, feigning ignorance, conducted their usual lively dialogue, they heard the siren for the second period to begin. They both made faces that said they weren't done yet but still clammed up so that they wouldn't bother the players or the rest of the audience.

And then, not long after the second period began, it happened.

A green ball of light appeared in midair; Kobayakawa and one other player jumped for it at the same time. Unfortunately, her opponent was slightly faster in reaching the three-foot range of priority on the ball. Kobayakawa used a spell to cut her jumping momentum. Her body stopped mid-leap.

Then, just as she was putting together a spell to return herself to her original footing, she noticed another player was already there. Without panicking, she switched her magic program to land on the nearest open foothold. The movement spell would slowly glide her through the air diagonally, straight toward the foothold, without a care for gravity.

However, when her body should have descended diagonally... gravity took hold, and she began plunging straight down.

The entire audience could see her contorted expression as she realized that she was falling.

Shock.

Panic.

Fear.

The spell that should have supported her body wouldn't activate.

Magic had supported her for her entire life, and now it had suddenly betrayed her. The fact made her forget to even struggle as she plummeted toward the lake's surface. It was water, but she was still about thirty feet in the air. If she didn't land properly, it could be fatal. And Kobayakawa didn't show any signs of trying to break her fall.

But fortunately, this sporting event was designed with several safety measures in mind. When it became clear she had lost control and fallen, countermeasures were, of course, taken. A tournament committee member rose and fired a deceleration spell. It was likely less than a second between the time she started falling and the committee member's spell stopping her.

Even so, she had already crossed half the distance to the water's surface.

It had been enough time—and enough of a journey—to crush her spirit.

* * *

The clock was stopped, and Tatsuya watched with a pained expression as his upperclassman was carried off on a stretcher.

The dominant reason that boys and girls who study magic lose their ability is perilous experience caused by a magical failure and the subsequent distrust in the art. Magic was the power to trick the world. Magic itself was a false power that lay beyond the world's logic. Even so, if you could see the magic with your eyes, like Tatsuya himself could, it didn't matter if it was a false power—you could believe that it was right there.

But most magicians (in training) couldn't see magic. It was a vague, cloudy power. Even if they could see psions, they couldn't see how the magic worked on the inside. They could only know of it in theory.

Is the magic I'm using really coming from inside me?

This question was the problem—no, the doubt—that nearly all magicians faced during the course of their magical studies. And when directly confronted with the absence of magical effects when a spell failed to activate, or with a dangerous situation they thought they'd avoided with magic, that doubt could sometimes turn into belief:

I guess magic really doesn't exist.

Magicians possessed by this belief could never use magic again.

Magic was built on that frail, insecure, delicate mental balance.

…Kobayakawa might be all done for, Tatsuya said to himself, bringing the white-faced Miyuki's shoulder toward him to encourage her. The moment she was caught by gravity, the moment she became aware of that, Kobayakawa's face had been painted over with terror. He could easily say she was a stranger, but losing such a precious talent was still a lonely thing to think about.

Then, as if to cut off his emotions, the communication terminal in his breast pocket vibrated. Miyuki, who was pressed right up against him, looked up with questioning eyes. Tatsuya flipped open the fold-up voice communication unit and put it to his ear.

"Tatsuya, this is Mikihiko. Can you talk right now?"

"…Yeah, I'm fine."

He made sure that the unit's sound wave interference muffler was on via the light on it but still lowered his voice to reply.

"About the accident—unfortunately, I didn't see any signs of a spell."

"I see…"

"I'm sorry. You were counting on me, and I couldn't do anything…"

"It's all right. I didn't catch anything, either."

"But Shibata says she has something to tell you."

"Mizuki? Did she have her glasses off?" Tatsuya's voice was mixed with surprise—and not the fake kind.

But Mikihiko didn't answer the question directly. "Tatsuya, it's Mizuki."

"Mizuki, did you see something?" *And are you all right?* were the next words waiting in his throat, but he decided saying that would be rude to Mizuki, considering the spirit of her actions. She used her own magical sight of her own volition, and as someone who lived in that same world of magic, he decided the proper answer was to ask what the results were.

"Yes, well…Kobayakawa's right arm… I think I saw some lights inside it—or spirits—suddenly kind of burst out of it."

"I see… So you did see something. Those spirits that burst out, they dispersed?"

"Umm…yes, that's what it looked like. It was kind of like how old electrical appliances make a few sparks and then stop…"

"I get it. I see, I see… So that's how it is." Tatsuya now felt like he'd seen the inner workings of what the enemy had done, if only indistinctly.

She must have known over the voice communication that he had nodded. "Umm, Tatsuya…?" came the voice from the receiver, hesitant but also with a little bit of anticipation.

"You did great, Mizuki. That bit of info helped a lot."

"Thank you!"

Tatsuya's answer had preempted what Mizuki had wanted to ask and what she'd wanted to hear; she responded with a springing voice.

◇ ◇ ◇

Unfortunately, First High was forced to forfeit the match midway through.

After coming out of First High's tent, rank with an air of depression, Tatsuya headed for the tournament committee tent, where they did the checks on the CADs. He had left Miyuki in the players' waiting room—it was part of the tent but still a room, he supposed—to come here.

Judging by their actions thus far, he didn't think the enemy would interfere two matches in a row; they wouldn't use any directly violent approaches on the players. But on the other hand, the players needed to concentrate before the match began; it wasn't time meant for being bothered by miscellaneous matters like device checks. That was what he explained to Miyuki to stop her from coming with him.

The CAD regulation checking was a process that had been repeated many times over in the last few days; they were supposed to begin and end without incident. However, that optimistic belief had all but vanished from his mind the moment the CAD was placed on the inspection equipment.

It had been an entirely impulsive act. The official had taken the CAD from his hands and set it on the inspection device. And then, at the very same moment he began to work the controls…

…by the time he was aware of having detected something strange…

…his hands…

…had already dragged the man from the other side of the table and slammed him into the ground.

There was a scream.

And then, an angry roar came running at him—or more accurately, the roaring member from one of the security personnel.

Though the sounds reached his ears, they didn't reach his mind. An intent to kill radiated from him, entirely absent of any mercy. The footsteps stopped, and the clamor gave way to quiet.

This was the only "real" expression left to him.

"...You've been underestimating me."

There was a cry of pain, probably a physiological reaction to increased pressure on the man's pinned-down chest from Tatsuya's knee.

As the committee member Tatsuya had slammed down moaned in anguish, his mouth and cheeks began spasming at the terrible air of ferocity radiating off Tatsuya—his teeth unable to chatter, his mouth unable even to close.

"Did you think I wouldn't notice you *altering* something Miyuki would be carrying?"

The third parties here wouldn't have known about his family affairs. Still, though they knew nothing about that, they definitely understood one thing.

That sinister smile.

The committee member on the receiving end of the one-sided act of violence knew he'd touched something he never should have. He'd incurred the wrath of a dragon.

Without looking at any of the people around him, Tatsuya coldly asked a question of the inspector he was holding down. "What did you slip into Miyuki's CAD with the inspection device? I'm sure it wasn't just a virus."

The committee member's face stiffened even further. The fear and despair on it didn't belong to a person who had merely seen Death himself. It was the look of a criminal whose sins had been exposed to an agent of Hell.

"I see. You could modify the software end of a CAD like this, too. CADs following tournament regulations can't refuse a request for access from the inspection device, after all."

The closest of the group of security personnel that had run up to him to subdue him heard his lowly spoken words and gasped. The man's expression toward the CAD inspector Tatsuya was holding down changed; he was no longer looking at a victim but at a perpetrator.

"But I'm sure not *all* the accidents in this tournament were your doing, were they?"

The eyes of the man under Tatsuya's knee began to well up with tears, and he weakly shook his head several times.

"I see. Don't want to talk?"

As if showing off to the man, Tatsuya put his right fingers in a straight line and tensed his hand. He pointed his fingertips at the man like the crooked neck of a snake. Then, his right hand slowly approached the pinned man's throat.

None of those watching could take their eyes off him, and all were thinking the same thing. All imagining the same thing. This boy's fingers would easily pierce the pitiful criminal's neck skin, gouge out his throat, and hold a ceremony of merciless judgment for him in a pool of blood...

"What seems to be the problem?"

But the unavoidable cataclysm was, in fact, avoided—by the gentle voice of an old man. Not an intimidating or severe one. It was like a spring wind. It was like a calm, soft wave sweeping through the murder in the room.

"...Your Excellency Kudou." His ferocity settling as though an evil spirit was leaving his body, Tatsuya took his hand away, moved his knee, and stood up to greet the old man. "I truly apologize for showing such an unsightly display, sir."

"You're...Shiba, from First High. You did splendidly in yesterday's match. Anyway, what seems to be the problem here?"

Feeling Tatsuya's ferocity quelled, some began to move to subdue him for his violent outburst, but those in front who heard his next words stopped their colleagues.

"The CAD from a player belonging to my school had been illegally sabotaged, sir, so I subdued the offender and was about to question him as to who is backing him."

"I see."

Everyone present, everyone who had been frozen by Tatsuya's bloodlust, knew instinctively those words were a lie. Tatsuya would not have stopped at a simple questioning.

But the old Kudou didn't press Tatsuya on his intent. Instead, he only nodded. "Is this the CAD that was illegally sabotaged?"

"Yes, sir."

The old magician, once renowned as the highest and trickiest of them all, took the CAD from the inspection device, brought it up to his eyes, looked at it closely, and nodded again. "...You're right—it has been contaminated. I've seen this before. This is Electron Goldworm, one used by a magician from Guangdong in the East China Sea Island Theater."

After speaking, he shot a cold glare at the man who was still on the floor. The man squealed and crawled backward, unable to stand.

"Electron Goldworm is an SB spell that invades electronic devices through their physical wires. It's used to nullify high-end weapons."

SB spell referred to the nickname for magic that used autonomous non-physical beings (spiritual beings) such as spirits. In a somehow nostalgic tone, digging deep into his memory, Kudou began explaining the workings of the spell.

"Rather than altering the program itself, it interferes with output electrical signals. That means that, regardless of the operating system or the presence of anti-virus programs, it can cause electrical devices to malfunction for a long period of time. Our forces struggled quite a lot until we learned of the nature of Electron Goldworm... Did you know what it was already?"

"No, sir," answered Tatsuya without gesturing, maintaining an at-ease posture and behavior. "I've never heard of the term *Electron Goldworm* before, sir. However, I knew immediately that something like a virus had gotten into the system space I created."

"I see," said the old man, smiling pleasantly. But by the time his eyes moved to the prosecuted inspector, his smile had become the kind a hardened veteran magician gave when looking down upon an enemy. "So, just where on earth did you acquire the Electron Goldworm spell?"

The agent gave a cry and tried to flee the area on all fours, but the security officers who had assembled to subdue Tatsuya now restrained him instead.

"In any case, Shiba, you may get back to the stadium now. And use a spare CAD. With the circumstances, you don't need to have it checked again... Correct, Chairman?"

The old official—though years younger than Kudou—standing nearby quickly nodded.

"Someone committing illegal sabotage operations slipped into the administration committee. Such a scandal is unprecedented. I'm going to have a long talk with you after this."

The tournament committee chairman looked like he was about to faint but croaked out an affirmation. Kudou looked away from him and his followers, then gave Tatsuya another cheerful expression. "Tatsuya Shiba, I would like to hear your story sometime as well."

"Yes, sir. When the opportunity presents itself..."

"Hmm, yes. I will look forward to the *opportunity*, then."

Such was the first direct meeting between Tatsuya and Kudou.

◇ ◇ ◇

Upon returning to First High's tent, Tatsuya sensed that the stares on him and the emotions behind them had changed subtly but certainly.

Perhaps he could say that they were *back to normal.*

It was subtle because they were trying to hide it. But they were guilty of changing the way they looked at him; these were wavering minds, he could see it in their eyes.

Tatsuya was, by all means, still a dull person. He simply had certain emotional inclinations. It was just that those emotions to which he was more inclined were actually ones he felt extremely sharply.

He was dull when it came to goodwill.

But he was sharp and sensitive to malice.

The eyes directed at him right now were ones he was well acquainted with. They were things people felt toward strange, unknown, *different* beings: confusion, fear, and avoidance.

"Tatsuya..."

And the one girl not trying to avoid him greeted him with a dark expression and even darker voice.

That one pair of eyes, though, gave his heart great pain. "Sorry for worrying you," he murmured.

"Don't be sorry!" she cried, shaking her head firmly, her tied hair coming slightly undone. "You got mad at someone over me, didn't you?"

"That was fast. You've already heard what happened?"

He reached out with a hand to brush back the hair in her face. Miyuki, ashamed and downcast, still steadily answered her brother's question. "No. But whenever you get really mad, it's...always over me..." Despite her steady reply, she was slowly starting to tear up.

Tatsuya put his hand to her cheek and gently lifted her face. "...You're right. You're the only thing I can get seriously mad about. But, Miyuki, all older brothers get mad over their little sisters. It's the only *normal thing* still left inside me. You don't have to feel sad about it." He used his free right hand to take out a handkerchief, then used it to gently wipe the tears around his sister's eyes. "Besides...if you start crying now, you'll ruin all the lovely makeup. This is your big moment in the spotlight, you know."

"Oh, come on, Tatsuya...I'm not the only one in this match! That's called being biased," said Miyuki, giving a wry smile—but still a smile, and it outshone anyone else's. At least, that was how Tatsuya felt about it.

He also felt relief and satisfaction at seeing her smile again. He moved his hand from her cheek to her shoulder and then, when he looked up toward the tent they were about to enter, he once again noticed a change in the stares—and this time it was not a strange difference.

They were no longer hesitant, scared eyes peeking out of the shadows. Now they were just awkward stares, clearly fed up with this whole act and yet unable to look away.

"Oh my, Tatsuya." Mayumi greeted him with a conspicuously halfhearted gaze and a somewhat cold voice, as though saying that even at times like these, the student president had to represent the students. "When the tournament HQ told me a student had suddenly gotten violent with them, I had absolutely no clue what was going on...but I suppose it was just the sister complex in you throwing a fit over someone trying to make a move on your oh-so-precious sibling."

He felt extremely reluctant toward that expression, but as a damp, lukewarm wind—the kind right before a typhoon—blew in, Tatsuya understood that he was at an overwhelming disadvantage in terms of army strength.

So he snuck away to the workroom set aside for the engineers. This way, Tatsuya avoided the other members from First High hating him and isolating him. But whether or not that was really what he wanted... Well, if you had asked him, he wouldn't have been able to tell you.

◇ ◇ ◇

The sky had been cloudy since before dawn. Now, as 9:30 and the start of the second match neared, it showed no signs of recovery.

"Good weather today... I hope it continues until tonight."

"Apparently it's supposed to clear up this evening."

"The starlight could get in the way a lot, too...but I suppose it's better than rain."

Azusa, listening to the siblings speak as though victory in the qualifiers was assured, somehow didn't feel the conversation to be a careless one.

In general, the power gap between freshmen and juniors was larger than the one between juniors and seniors. That was because professional education in magic only really got under way starting with high school. So even if there was no rookie competition, there would be few cases of freshmen entering the main competition. Normally, if someone was reassigned from the rookie competition to the main one during the events, they would have trouble even making it out of the qualifiers, to say nothing of placing high up.

However... *Common sense doesn't apply to Miyuki, does it?* she thought. *Especially since Tatsuya's with her.*

Azusa's timidity aside, everyone knew she was a magician (in training) ranked at the top of her grade. Just the fact that someone so shy would be chosen for First High's student council was a sort of paradoxical proof of her ability.

As far as Azusa could tell, Miyuki had the skills to seriously aim for first place. Alone, her strength towered above the rest. But she had her brother giving her his full support, too. Even if Mari, the one initially picked as the favorite to win, was in peak condition and entering with her, Azusa wasn't sure even *she* could beat her.

She kept her onlooker's criticism to herself. She'd been assigned as an engineer for the third match, so she was currently doing the final checks on her player's CAD a little bit early.

The main competition's Monolith Code and Mirage Bat were the final events for the boys and girls, respectively, in the Nine School Competition, and the staff of every school was currently fully engaged. First High had come up to the event with one engineer for every player. So during this event only, the Shiba siblings were rivals to Azusa. Perhaps more accurately, as another engineer, *Tatsuya* was her rival.

But...even before starting, she couldn't think about winning or losing. It had stopped even feeling like a competition to her.

What happened before... When she was informed by tournament HQ that Tatsuya had assaulted a committee member, she was less shocked than *scared*.

She didn't find it surprising. Somewhere in her mind, she could see him doing it. She hadn't known him for very long or very personally, but she thought he wasn't the sort of guy to resort to violence for no reason. At the same time, though, she felt that if he *did* have a reason, he wouldn't hesitate at all.

Someone with no hesitation when it came to violence—that scared her.

Of course, Azusa wasn't naive. She knew magic had been developed for military purposes, and that a large percentage of magic's practical application still lay in war strength and as a deterring force. But whether it was military power or police force, it was still violence inherent in the administration. Responsibility as to its usage was split among many: those who determined it, those who ordered it, those who executed it, and those who oversaw it.

But she was sure he had decided it and executed it on his own, and bore the responsibility for it. That probably would have held true even if the other party had died. Even if it turned him into a killer.

His mind was cold and hard as steel, and it terrified her.

Upon hearing the details from him, her fear changed to surprise. He explained that he'd caught someone red-handed, illegally modifying a CAD and arrested him. The tearful, crumpled look on Hirakawa's face, the senior who had been assigned to Kobayakawa, was burned into Azusa's eyelids. It was easy to imagine how hard it must have been, and even easier to empathize: She hadn't realized the CAD had been tampered with. Because of that, her player was involved in an accident. And now, one of her most brilliant classmates might never be the same. But compared to that, he had... If Azusa had been in Hirakawa's place, she probably would have run away crying.

It was the undeniable truth that Tatsuya was a Course 2 student—the opposite of an honor student. An irregular. His practical exam grades were just barely keeping him afloat. There were never more than five students who failed a practical skills exam right after enrolling, so it was only natural people thought of his grades as "bad" as opposed to just "not very good."

But in reality, if you looked at his ability to respond to the kinds of situations magicians would actually find themselves in—instead of some measure of situational "true strength" measured by tests—you would think exactly the opposite.

For development, for analysis, and for adjustment work...and last but not least, for combat...

...his power level was above what most would consider first class.

If magic wasn't graded on pure ability and instead by the circumstances in which it was put to practical use, then he'd probably be the highest-honor student you could find. Which meant...

All these grades we're getting... What are they for? What does it mean to be in Course 1? Is there even a reason to separate Course 1 and Course 2?

That was how Azusa had started to think after seeing Tatsuya up close during the Nine School Competition. And it confused her. It made her anxious. She'd taken her values, her worldview, for granted, never doubting them. Suddenly they were uncertain and unreliable.

Azusa didn't possess the sort of ostentatious elitism others had in being proud of being a Bloom and looking down on the Course 2 Weeds. At least, not consciously. That wasn't to say she had no pride in the fact that her magical abilities were excellent, thus making her a great magic student at the school.

True, her future as a magician and as a magic engineer was still deeply shrouded in fog, but her confidence in her abilities gave her the courage to find that future. It was a precious partner to her. Even if she didn't realize it, the fact was this: Her confidence as a magician was pushing her forward.

Magic wasn't the only thing this applied to, either. Young people had big hopes and dreams—and big doubts to match. Their pride and confidence made up for their lack of experience and past accomplishments.

For Azusa, and for other honor students at magic high schools like her, magic was what created that pride, what produced that confidence. More specifically, it was her grades in magic that produced her confidence. But whenever she saw Tatsuya, her pride and her confidence started seeming unfounded.

Her test results when she was a freshman were undoubtedly higher than his, but she didn't think she could ever beat him. Not as a combat magician, not as a magic engineer, and not as a magic scholar. Even that particular rare magical skill she possessed, one she secretly thought was the only thing that Mayumi and Mari *couldn't* match... when she came up against Tatsuya, even that lost all meaning.

But still, Azusa never thought herself the type to worry so much over a sense of inferiority. And she was already over 90 percent certain that Tatsuya was *him*.

If he is, then of course I can't match him.

If he is, then the very act of feeling inferior is presumptuous of me.

That was what Azusa told herself.

But nobody else knows yet... Others didn't know, so they would be thinking about this issue more. They would be feeling it more—especially the other freshmen. They would ask themselves what their grades even *meant*, if it came to be that a Course 2 student fared better than them.

"Ah-chan, don't torment yourself too much, okay?"

Suddenly a voice addressed her from behind. Surprised, Azusa sprang up and turned around to find Mayumi directing a dry smile toward her.

"The boy's special." Despite her choice of words, her tone of voice was warm. "I'm sure other kids can't accept it…but one of the things you have to learn in high school is to accept things even if you don't like them. It's a fact that Course 2 students lag behind Course 1 students in magical ability. And it's also a fact that Tatsuya is at a higher level than us."

"What? But…"

Azusa was dumbstruck at the surprising words. She knew Tatsuya was several levels higher than her—even if he was *him*, she couldn't deny being personally disappointed by it. But Mayumi was at a really high level, and that was the standard. Azusa didn't think she was that much worse than Tatsuya.

"I don't lose in *every* respect, though," said Mayumi, taking a guess at her confusion and giving another wry grin. "In terms of overall magic ability, I'm better. In a magic firefight, as long as I have distance, I'd have the advantage, too."

But then she paused, sighing. Thinking of his strength seemed to exhaust her. "But there are definitely areas he beats me in. It may not mean much, but I can't even come near him in terms of anything CAD related. And it hurts me to say this, but he just knows more about magic than I do. He's making all the upperclassmen look bad, though," she added airily. "Everyone has things they're good and bad at. Nobody can beat someone else in absolutely *everything*. When I say Tatsuya's at a higher level, I mean that I can't even come *near* him in terms of magic engineering knowledge and skill."

Mayumi turned a firm, steady stare on Azusa, as if peering deep into her eyes. "But in exchange, both of our results in practical magic are way higher than his. So you don't need to be so pessimistic about it. It isn't like practical magic exams are meaningless. Test grades by themselves may not fully determine someone's worth, but they *are* still a part of it."

Azusa, still speechless, digested her words.

"And by the way…" This time, she heaved a *real* sigh. "Thinking that you're better than others makes it hard to bear not winning at everything. You'll forget that the distinction between Course 1 and Course 2 students is really just for convenience in putting together practical magic classes, which just happens to be based on your grades on the practical magic exams."

Azusa unwittingly opened her eyes wide. The unexpected truth in her words was such a shock that her mind was going blank. She wasn't *forgetting* anything. This was *actually* the first she'd ever heard of the course separation being just for practicum purposes.

"I suppose the uniforms aren't helping... At first it was all just because, when we increased the student count, they didn't have time to embroider them all..."

"What? Is that true?"

"Wait, you didn't know that?"

No, she'd never heard the inside story. Now she was speechless for another reason. A different kind of shock.

"Right, well, I suppose it's not well-known..." murmured Mayumi while Azusa just continued shaking her head no. "Did you know that a long time ago, First High had only one hundred students per class? They said we needed more magicians to rank with other countries, so First High's student body was the first one they increased. But the government jumped the gun. Instead of just putting more students here at the start of the following year, they accepted applications midway through it.

"But they couldn't suddenly increase the number of teachers midway through the year. We had even fewer magic teachers at the time than we do now. As a last resort, they decided to have the newly admitted freshmen focus solely on learning theory, then start them on practical application in their second year. That's where the Course 2 system came from.

"Unfortunately, thanks to the sudden influx of Course 2 students, the school made a mistake ordering the uniforms. The freshmen who entered that year had to make do with uniforms without the First High emblem on it, but that led to some misunderstandings nobody saw coming... The Course 2 system was just a temporary measure until they advanced to their second year. They were just extra students they'd let enroll to bring the numbers up. But then people decided they were substitutes. And in the end, they couldn't get enough teachers to match the unreasonable increase. Which brings us to the current system, where that little misunderstanding is now the official stance.

"And the truth is, they just left the uniforms alone after that, like it was the plan all along. Like they were covering up for their hastiness. When you think about it, it seems like it would be harder to make two different kinds of uniforms... The sewing is all done by an automated factory, so even though you still need different sizes, it would be cheaper just to make *one design*."

Azusa's mouth was hanging open. Mayumi's explanation truly had been jaw dropping. She couldn't believe that the whole Blooms and Weeds business, which had fostered such frequent, malicious, serious antagonism, had originated from something so stupid.

We can't let Miyuki know about this, she thought—she was too afraid of what might happen if they did.

Mayumi must have been thinking the same thing. "...Keep this a secret from Miyuki, all right?"

Azusa immediately nodded in agreement.

◇ ◇ ◇

Not knowing that she'd been labeled a dangerous individual by two of her upperclassmen in the student council, Miyuki stood on the Mirage Bat field in high spirits, waiting for the match to begin. She was in a good mood because this was the first time since the Nine School Competition had begun that her brother had allotted time just for her, and looked after her alone.

Normally, when they went home, they were the only two living there; she had plenty of time to spend with him alone. But that couldn't happen with their competition lodging. She certainly wasn't living in frustration (or at least, that's how she felt), but the length of time since this had happened contributed to her current happiness.

Her brother was watching her from the booth where the staff waited in the wings. Looking only at her. She felt like she could fly into the sky even without borrowing magic's power.

For now, she didn't care about the lecherous eyes on her costume, which accentuated her body's lines. She didn't have to try very hard to filter out all the stares except for Tatsuya's, tossing the rest in the trash. There's an expression about imagining the audience as potatoes—or onions or carrots—that's fundamental advice given to people who struggle with social anxiety, though it's largely ineffective. (People with the mental wherewithal to replace a crowd with potatoes don't have anxiety in the first place.) But right now, for Miyuki, everyone aside from Tatsuya *was* just a potato.

She knew her brother appreciated people with good posture, so the way she stood there was perfect as well. She looked the very definition of a beauty, standing like a dancer waiting for the music to start. Her pose caused the young men in the stands to feel short of breath, and made their hearts throb so much that they might have needed to be carried out on stretchers before the match even began.

Though probably not because of the electricity in the crowd urging them on, the siren to signal the match's start went off a few seconds earlier than planned.

Miyuki's body floated lightly into the air.

Each Mirage Bat player had two different costumes prepared. One was a midday costume, vividly colored so that they wouldn't get lost in the strong sunlight. The other was a nighttime costume, brightly colored so they would reflect light. Both were worn so that players wouldn't collide with one another—an unwritten rule based on prior experience.

The main color on Miyuki's clothing was a deep magenta. With one wrong step, it could have looked like a crude, unrefined color scheme. But when Miyuki wore it, it lent her an air of nobility. Her thick makeup, which also blocked ultraviolet rays, did nothing to damage that dignity. Her delicate body was still in the middle of its development, but her long, thin, straight limbs and the contrasting elegant curves of her chest and waist, rather than inspire some sort of basic sexual feeling, instead radiated the allure of a flowering tree in bloom.

She was truly as beautiful as a flower.

Though she leaped up toward the targets as fiercely as the others, she was the only one to whom the adjective *light* could be applied.

The audience's eyes were glued to her. If this event were graded on the beauty of one's performance, no one would have complained about her coming in first.

But this was the main competition, and the main event at that. The Nine School Competition wouldn't be so easy.

"Miyuki's trailing behind...?" muttered Mizuki in disbelief as the first period ended, letting out a held breath.

"The Second High player at the top...she might not be an IS [innately specialized] magician, but she must be extremely good at jumping techniques..."

"That's not all! She was planning out where she jumped so that she could block where Miyuki was going. Maybe she's not only good at jumping, but she's actually a Mirage Bat specialist?"

Mikihiko and Erika, sharing Mizuki's surprise, each offered their own thoughts.

"The Second High player was the other favorite to win, like Watanabe was..."

"With how much Miyuki stood out, it's no wonder they're keeping an eye on her. The seniors' pride is on the line, too."

Honoka and Shizuku expressed their agreement from a different viewpoint; they were in the general seats today, cheering them on.

"I don't think she's finished just yet," said Leo at the end, his cheerfulness blowing away the pessimistic air.

* * *

Miyuki recovered in the next period, and by the end of it, she stood atop the rankings. But the point differential was tiny. She still had energy left, but the others would have been pacing themselves as well in preparation for the third period. Nobody knew yet how the match would turn out.

Though she was being limited in terms of how many magic variations she could use, Tatsuya was still surprised that there were magicians at a high school level who could compete equally with Miyuki.

"This country is so small, yet so large…" he said to nobody in particular as he stood in front of Miyuki, who had taken a seat to catch her breath. His eyes weren't on her—they were on Second High's booth.

…But then, he felt a sudden tug at his sleeve. He looked down to see Miyuki stand up from her chair, and look him in the eyes with a strong light in her own.

"——Tatsuya, would you allow me to use it?"

Her eyes, her voice, and the fingers holding his sleeve all radiated her desire to win. She wasn't just a doll that people looked at because she was pretty or cute. Her face was now filled with a fierce determination, which Tatsuya liked seeing more than all the other expressions she had in her arsenal.

His lips naturally parted, and his eyes narrowed with warmth. "…Sure. Everything will be as you desire."

Originally, this was going to be their ultimate weapon for the final match.

But Tatsuya smiled and nodded, forgetting every calculation they had done.

"Huh? Miyuki's using a different broom."

Erika immediately noticed the change as Miyuki stood on the field for the last period. She had been using her regular, portable, terminal-shaped CAD before, but now she had a bracelet one on her right arm.

"But it looks like she's holding a CAD in her left hand, too..." indicated Mikihiko, looking closely.

Everyone tilted their heads in confusion at him, except for Honoka, who nodded in admiration. "Yeah...I guess she's using it early..."

"It?" asked Shizuku.

Honoka's face was a mixture of aspiration and bitterness as she answered. "Tatsuya made something secret just for Miyuki to use. A secret weapon, and Miyuki's the only one who can master it. Every single person here, and not one fewer, is going to be surprised... I'm sure of it."

Before Shizuku could ask what it was, the third period siren rang.

The bracelet on Miyuki's right wrist was a spare. The real thing was the specialized, portable, terminal-shaped CAD she gripped in her left hand. Its controls were simple: just an On/Off switch. Her finger hovered above the switch, and when the period began, she quickly pressed it.

An extremely small activation program expanded. It booted up, and continued to boot up over and over without pause. And then her body floated lightly into the air.

The Second High player moved to block her path. She was going to intersect with her from below and to the left. Miyuki's opponent was faster at ascending. At this rate, Miyuki would run into her, rather than the other way around. Miyuki accelerated her own flight speed and avoided it.

After seeing Miyuki bat away one of the light orbs, turn around, and stop in midair, the audience stirred.

Her magic power had accelerated her even further—in the middle of the jump.

The audience's surprised praise was for the amount of power she would have needed to do such a thing, within the bounds of common sense.

But after Miyuki stopped again in midair, she didn't descend to a foothold. Instead, she continued her elegant glide down the sylphic ice rink built in the sky. When the crowd saw her find the next target and move toward it, their cheers fell dead silent.

Two, three, four…

The other athletes needed to keep going up and down those thirty feet of height. Miyuki only had to move horizontally. It was never a competition.

After collecting her fifth point in a row, the frozen voices in the crowd began to thaw, little by little.

"Flight magic…?" murmured someone.

Even the other players were standing there, looking overhead, stunned. The murmur had been naught more than a whisper. But without the sounds of the players taking off and landing, they echoed eerily in the silent stadium.

Miyuki, swinging her stick, looked just as gallant as a Valkyrie—and just as elegant.

"Taurus Silver's…?"

The whispers continued.

"That's not possible…"

"That just got announced last month…"

The wave began to ripple through the stands.

"But that's…"

"That has to be the flight magic…"

All eyes present there, without a single exception, were on the girl dancing through the sky.

It was the dance of an angel, unfolding in the sky above the lake.

Her arms went out to her sides to keep her balance. Her legs spread out to change her posture. It looked like she was dancing hand in hand with the wind.

This revolution of modern magic, this miraculous performance of what some called impossible, were most befitting of this beautiful girl… Everyone, no matter their age, no matter their gender, whether friend or enemy, looked up to the sky dancer, entranced.

Everyone there had been taken—not by modern magic, not by old magic, but by the magic of astonishment and emotion.

The signal came to end the match, and until she returned to the ground, their spell of rapture continued.

—In the Mirage Bat qualifiers, on field one, in the second match, Miyuki had won her way into the finals by a large margin.

◇ ◇ ◇

It wasn't until the players left the field that the audience finally snapped out of their trance.

There was no order in which they needed to leave the field. They began to file out in order of whoever was closest to the gate when the match ended. Miyuki, who had landed near the middle of the lake, was the third of the four to exit. After curtsying toward First High's cheering section, she fluttered upward and glided toward the gate with the smoothness of skating on ice.

The graceful act caused the audience to erupt into applause.

One could see various guests frantically using their communication terminals. Some were practically frothing into their microphones, shouting, even sounding angry because of the excitement. Some were so unstrung that they were repeating the same thing into them and annoying whomever they were talking to. Some were frenetically typing on virtual keyboards, scratching their heads from time to time. Some were single-mindedly wielding pen devices on optical recognition panels… Everyone, in all kinds of ways, was trying to communicate the surprise they felt to those who hadn't been around to feel it.

Among them was one man, oddly expressionless as he looked at a message being displayed on his HMD. But basically nobody paid any attention to him.

◇ ◇ ◇

"We got a message from Number Seventeen. The target in the second match advanced out of the qualifiers."

"...Whoever it was, they saw through the Electron Goldworm. This was the proper result...but this is bad."

"That's not all. The target apparently used flight magic."

"Impossible!"

"It would be absolutely wonderful if she'd used up all her energy with that...but that's asking for too much."

"I don't think we have the leeway to be picky about how we do this anymore. What do you think?"

"I agree. A hundred deaths should suffice. We need to stop the competition itself."

"If we do, we'll only get our bets back. We won't lose anything, but it's still within tolerable limits."

"Won't the guests know something's up? Even leaving our business aside, those weapons brokers are a pain in the ass, since they have thick lines into a lot of countries."

"We can say whatever we want to the guests. Right now, we need to be more worried about sanctions against our organization than merchants of death."

"You're right... Is Number Seventeen enough to carry it out?"

"It would take more than a decent amount of skill to match a Generator. We couldn't get any weapons in with it, but Seventeen is tailored for high speeds. If we disable its limiters and have it go berserk, it could slaughter one or two hundred with its bare hands."

"No objections, I presume...? All right, disable its limiters."

◇ ◇ ◇

The wave of excitement eventually subsided, and as the audience, clustered in the grandstand in groups of two or three, waited for the next match, *he* sluggishly rose.

His exposed eyes reinforced an impression of impassivity. It wasn't that he was expressionless, though. That would imply a capacity to emote. He seemed lacking in the very *concept* of expression—he had an entirely, completely inorganic facade.

Suddenly, the man's body shook—an instantly activated self-acceleration spell. Before the magicians nearby noticed the spell, the man attacked another man who happened to be passing by. He brought his fingers, curved like claws, down toward his defenseless back.

—And then, unbeknownst to everyone, the incident was brought outside the stands.

By the time the man, Generator Number Seventeen, assessed the situation, he was already ten feet off the ground.

The first person he'd attacked after receiving his directive of slaughter had actually dodged his attack, despite his back being turned. This was even though he did it so fast that human perception wouldn't have been able to keep up, even if he'd attacked head-on.

The magician was able to move with speed beyond the possible limits of his physical strength by using a self-acceleration spell. But the only thing the spell accelerated was his movement—it didn't boost his sense organs' biochemical reaction speed, or his sensory nerves' transmission speed, or his cerebrum's information processing speed.

Human bodies were made to have much higher perception speed than movement speed. Because of that, one could still control speed that surpassed one's physical limits. But on the other hand, one couldn't control their physical movement when it exceeded the limits of their speed of perception. That meant even magicians had their limits. There was no limit to how much one could accelerate oneself in terms of magic, but there was a usage restriction on how fast one's brain could keep up with it.

Consequently, his speed, boosted by chemically strengthened perception speed, was not something a normal human—a *physically* normal human, regardless of magical talent—should have been able to keep up with.

And yet, in actuality, his descending arms had been stopped. And then, with them as a fulcrum, the force of his own falling arms had sent Number Seventeen's body hurtling into the sky. The moment his body, spinning like he'd been struck with an iron bar, spun and turned upside down, a fierce impact assailed Seventeen and he was blown over the grandstand fence and out of the stadium.

A movement spell with its acceleration process purposely omitted. The impact made him lose consciousness partway through, and when he came to, he was just about to slam into the ground from a parabolic arc sixty-five feet in the sky.

Normally, this situation would cause a man to freeze in terror or panic, unable to do anything about his fall. But this man was a Generator. A specimen whose will and emotion had been stolen through brain surgery and the administration of magically created drugs. His thought processes were controlled and pushed in a specific direction, so he had none of the various mental operations that would disturb the activation of magic—commonly referred to as *idle thoughts*.

He was a biological weapon built to use magic in a stable way in the middle of combat. A magician remodeled as a tool to generate magic. And a tool knew neither fear nor panic.

Calmly, or more accurately, *emotionlessly*, Number Seventeen triggered an inertia-canceling spell. Decelerating at this point would make damage unavoidable—it would be like suddenly slamming on the brakes. Decreasing his inertia instead was the result of calculations performed in the span of a moment; it would lessen the damage from impact.

The magical drugs weren't just to regulate his will, emotion, and perception. They were also for the purpose of heightening his physical faculties. Using his legs as springs, and even using his abdominal muscles, dorsal muscles, and arms to assist, he absorbed all the damage from the fall.

"Impressive that you made it in time from that stage."

Number Seventeen, both arms and both legs on the ground, looked up. And there he saw the man who had launched him here.

"Who are you? …No, you don't need to answer that. I'm sure you can't anyway."

Muraji Yanagi, captain in the Independent Magic Battalion, twisted his lips into a disdainful smile as he watched Number Seventeen on all fours like some kind of beast.

"Your physical abilities can't be purely magical. Are you an enhanced human?" asked Yanagi, his voice a blend of scorn and admiration. His opponent had flown over the grandstand fence, launched as high as a medium-size building, and fallen—and yet had still kept his combat stance.

"Yanagi, you're the one who said he didn't need to answer. And I think you're insulting him. You're also the one who jumped down from the same height, and your hands aren't even on the ground."

Number Seventeen moved like a four-legged beast to check behind him. Unbeknownst to him, another captain in the Independent Magic Battalion, Shigeru Sanada, had positioned himself there to block his escape route. If he still wanted to flee, it might have been possible. In terms of pure acceleration, Generator Number Seventeen was better than the two Independent Magic Battalion members.

But the directive he'd been given was to massacre the guests. Without any will or emotion, the only input on his movement decisions came from orders from the organization. In deference to those orders, Number Seventeen once again attacked Yanagi—one of the guests.

Before he could launch into an attack, Yanagi thrust his right hand out. Despite his clearly superior speed, Number Seventeen couldn't escape that hand—he was already charging, his posture low. As if being sucked in, his head rammed into Yanagi's palm.

Yanagi and Number Seventeen clashed.

The Generator bounced off without touching Yanagi's body and was slammed back into his starting position.

"It was a rhetorical question anyway," said Yanagi nonchalantly. "I was talking to myself."

"I'll let you off the hook, then. Still, I'm impressed every time I see that. Was that an application of Capsize?"

Predicting the enemy's movement vector, then using martial arts and magic in unison to draw that vector in, amplify it, or reverse it—that was the combat style Yanagi excelled in, and the skill that had thrown and repelled Number Seventeen.

"How many times do I need to tell you it's not Capsize? It was Turnaround. Capsize is the official technique, and Turnaround is the hidden one. And it wasn't quite an application, either. I just copy the stuff. The real Turnaround doesn't need magic."

"That goes against the very meaning of our existence. I'm going to tell on you to our CO."

"…Would you cut the nonsense and help me capture this guy?"

"Hmm…I suppose so. But Fujibayashi already has Lightning Rod nice and ready."

As Sanada spoke, there was a clicking of heels as Kyouko Fujibayashi, second lieutenant in the Independent Magic Battalion, showed herself. "…You two really get along, don't you?"

Her rear staff uniform included a tight skirt, and was not at all meant for fighting in. Normally that would present the perfect prey: an ideal opportunity to turn the situation.

But Number Seventeen just twitched and jerked. He wasn't in much of a state to oppose her—a whole bunch of slender, hair like needles were stabbing into him, sending electrical currents into his body. Of course, both the thrown needles and the unleashed lightning were Fujibayashi's spells.

"Fujibayashi, I thought you had better eyes than that."

"Maybe it's more of a sensitivity problem than an eyesight one. Do you want me to introduce you to a good counselor?"

"See? You're practically finishing each other's sentences."

With Number Seventeen in the middle, Yanagi and Sanada exchanged glances—and grimaces.

◇ ◇ ◇

Unaware of the dangerous act playing out behind the scenes, Tatsuya was having a leisurely early lunch in his hotel room.

After the match, while Miyuki was taking a shower, the tournament committee told him rather forcefully that they needed to inspect the CAD used for the flight magic. But he was guilty of nothing. He had a brief, mischievous thought about dropping Kudou's name to press their buttons, but it passed. Amusing himself by bullying weaklings from the safety of another's influence would be disgraceful, so he obediently handed over the CAD.

Other than that, he hadn't been caught up in any particularly strange uproar. He felt a lot of rather distant stares on him and his sister, but as long as onlookers didn't caused them direct harm, leaving them alone was the best option. Tatsuya had decided to leave the CAD with the committee and retreat to a private space.

Of course, even if he'd been aware that Sanada and Yanagi were acting in secret to prevent a mass slaughter, he would have done the same. Bluntly speaking, Tatsuya didn't care how many guests—about whom he knew nothing—could have died.

And even if upperclassmen from his own school became victims, it would have inspired in him little more feeling than that it was unfortunate. Because of that, he had opted against assertive action.

Miyuki would look sad hearing that, though, so he wasn't saying any of it or even giving the appearance of thinking it. Of course, that meant right now: Though it probably didn't need to be said again, Miyuki was standing in front of him, gallantly being too helpful.

"One of your virtues is that you always have your personal life in perfect order, but sometimes I feel like if you were a little messier, it would be more worth it for me to look after you."

Miyuki was in a good mood today. She was smiling, almost humming, as she seemed to enjoy wiping off the table. It was probably the recoil from not looking after him for the week.

"Miyuki, is there anything you want me to do?"

So when he had asked that at the end of their meal, the words were just a way to fill the silence, and didn't mean anything in particular.

"Something I want you to do, Tatsuya?"

However, Miyuki's reaction was unexpectedly strong. Her eyes widened and she smiled broadly as she thought about it. Tatsuya suddenly knew something was up but felt like he'd already gone too far to retreat.

His little sister made various gestures as she thought, like putting a finger to her chin and tilting her head, but suddenly she flushed as though she'd thought of something. She looked up at his face from the seat next to him.

"...All right, say it," he said with a somewhat wry smile, but gently.

Nervously, Miyuki began. "Earlier, you instructed me to rest a little after lunch, before the finals..."

"Right. You don't have to go to sleep right now, but you should make sure to get some sleep. And if not, you can just lie in bed. And don't tell me you don't want to—you have to rest your body."

"No, I will do what you told me to, of course, but...well..."

"Hmm?"

"Well...I was wondering if you could...be with me..."

She must have been embarrassed to say that; her face went red and she looked down.

"...You sure are spoiled, Miyuki."

"...Is that a no? I want you to spoil me."

"...No, it's fine. I can't sing you any lullabies, though."

Mayumi stared at Tatsuya with upturned eyes, then hit him with both hands in the chest.

Her white skin, all the way to her ears visible beneath her black hair, flushed crimson.

Despite being siblings, they were also young adults, so they obviously didn't want to use the same bed. Thankfully, though he was using this room as a single, it was actually a twin. Most of the equipment taking up the space had been brought over to the grounds at this point. He quickly brought the bed out of the wall and set it up so that Miyuki could use it to sleep. It was an almost entirely automatic process, so they didn't need to call for room service. (This wasn't a normal hotel, so they might not have even come anyway.)

He brought over a chair and sat down next to the bed she'd nestled into. He returned Miyuki's smile—which was an embarrassed one even by his measure—and gently stroked her hair.

Within a minute, she had departed for the land of Hypnos.

Four hours passed after Miyuki fell asleep, but Tatsuya remained at her bedside.

He was being faithful in granting her request that he be there. Being alone as he did this didn't trouble him.

The young woman slept soundly. Her face was completely peaceful. When he considered that it was a sign of trust, he began to feel a little tickled and proud.

They were siblings, but they'd only really started living together three years ago. Those three years were the only ones during which they lived like actual brother and sister. Before that, before that summer three years earlier, they almost never exchanged words, even though they lived in the same house. His bond with her was something their mother never would have allowed; she had forbidden even a sibling-like relationship between them. The decision had probably come from the Yotsuba as a whole.

Tatsuya wasn't about to start complaining about that or anything. His mind no longer possessed such faculties. He did feel inconvenienced, though, by the lack of any memory of being close to blood relatives at a young age. If he was unhappy about anything, it was that.

He had no memories of being very little and crying, or having a tantrum, or falling down, or wetting his pants—nothing that would have embarrassed him in front of an immediate family member. To him, Miyuki was always just a pretty girl who was one year younger. He couldn't see it any other way except in an objective light. That's why he always knew just how good-looking she was.

At the same time, the feelings swelling from the deepest parts of his mind recognized her as his little sister. His one and only true emotion left was ordering his *consciousness* to shower her with brotherly love. No memories, only feelings. Sometimes he thought that this is what it would be like to have amnesia. He knew, though, that he certainly didn't have that condition.

His feelings were unconditional precisely *because* his memories didn't present them with any conditions. That was why he was so blindly, intensely, and severely devoted to her. For all his other emotions, like anger and hatred, they failed to reach the surface; meanwhile, his love for Miyuki was entirely without hesitation, and that manifested itself as strange acts.

Tatsuya hadn't realized that. He couldn't step on the brakes, because he did things as a result of cold, hard calculation, not out of impulse. If he calculated that something was necessary, he didn't determine if it was *worth doing*, which was normally the next thing one would consider. He could think in terms of benefits and drawbacks, but not in terms of humanity.

He picked up the portable terminal on the nightstand. He called up the long encrypted message Fujibayashi had sent him again. There she'd revealed the truth behind the Mirage Bat sabotage, as well as the details of the attempted mass murder of guests that happened after the second match of the qualifiers.

He found that altogether impossible to forgive. *Plotting to drag Miyuki down to the ground* deserved certain death.

After placing the terminal in his pocket, he stood from the chair and leaned over the bed. He gently stroked Miyuki's hair and placed his hand on hers.

"Miyuki?"

No answer. She didn't seem to be awake. Yet in her sleep, Miyuki turned to the side and brought his hand to her cheek.

Tatsuya's lips parted into a smile at how happy her face looked. Behind that smile, Tatsuya decided he needed to protect that peaceful face. He didn't resolve himself to attempt it—*he decided it would be so.*

◇ ◇ ◇

The final match, unlike the afternoon ones, would be held under a full starry sky. The waxing moon was overpowering the starlight. Distinguishing the glowing spheres from below wouldn't be very easy under these conditions.

"How do you feel?"

"Perfect, Tatsuya. I'm fully ready to go, so I'd like to use the flight magic from the start…"

"That's fine. Fly to your heart's content."

"Yes!"

Miyuki leaped energetically onto the field as Tatsuya saw her off with a thumbs-up.

"Miyuki seemed like she was in a good mood," said Azusa to Tatsuya as they stood in the support staff's booth. They were watching Miyuki assume her starting position atop a foothold above the lake. Unfortunately, the player Azusa had been assigned to had lost her qualifier.

The finals would feature one student each from First, Second,

Third, Fifth, Sixth, and Ninth Highs. No school had been able to send more than one player here. This being the final girls' event, it became a stage for each school to show their pride.

Right now, the prominent female members were all here, save for Mari, who was recuperating in the hospital under strict watch. Since Third High sent only one player to the final match as well, Miyuki would assure First High's overall victory if she placed third or higher. This was the time to do their best cheering.

"I'm glad she's going into the match happy," said Mayumi with a smile from the other side of Azusa. "Tatsuya must have given her some good care and attention." She probably didn't mean anything about that, but her smile still looked like it meant *something*. Maybe there was something she didn't want Tatsuya to know.

"By the way, I don't believe Miyuki used a capsule," mentioned Suzune. "Did she get enough rest?"

The casual question *almost* made Tatsuya's poker face dissolve. "She slept for five hours, so I believe she got enough."

"I see. She must have slept very well. Did she sleep in a hotel bed?"

Tatsuya couldn't find the next words to say. He had to start being suspicious now. Were they asking because they knew how much of a bull's-eye these questions were?

"Oh, it's starting!"

Fortunately for him, everyone's attention turned to the field before the silence got weird.

This time, he was truly thankful for that innocent personality of Azusa's.

The stadium light reflected off the surface of the lake and the players' pale costumes alike, making the girls clearly visible high above the water. Among them, Miyuki and her pink costume drew more stares—and it wasn't only because she'd unveiled her marvelous feat of flight magic in the qualifiers.

Amid the wavering, flickering lights, she looked so ephemeral that the audience couldn't take their eyes off her; if they looked away for a moment, she might have simply disappeared.

Mirage Bat was also known as the Faerie Dance. Comparing girls to faerie creatures was overused, standard rhetoric, but right now, nobody would complain of any cliché if someone described Miyuki as being faerie-like.

The crowd's murmuring quieted like a receding wave. The event committee didn't need to persist in waving their silencing message boards.

With the people holding their breaths in anticipation, the final Mirage Bat match began.

As soon as the signal went off, the six girls all took off into the sky at once.

They hadn't jumped up. None of the six came back down to a foothold.

"Flight magic?! The other schools now, too?!" cried Azusa, her voice cracking.

"The Nine School Competition never ceases to amaze," said Tatsuya, impressed. "They've made the flight magic activation program their own in a mere six or seven hours."

He wasn't really surprised. The tournament committee had probably leaked the program to the other schools—probably under the guise of responding to suspicions that it wasn't fair play. He *had* left the CAD with them knowing that this was a possibility.

"The schools are all using the exact program Taurus Silver unveiled, with no changes," said Suzune, looking into the sky and frowning.

"…This is crazy," muttered Mayumi, annoyed. "You can't master this technique without practicing it first. I can't believe they'd place victory over the safety of their players…"

Tatsuya's voice, though, was relaxed, as though he was eager to see what the other schools could show them. "I think they'll be fine.

If they're using the exact technique, then the safety function will kick in if worse comes to worst."

The six girls danced through the air.

It was, by all accounts, a dance of faeries.

The fluttering dance in the night sky captivated the audience with fascination.

But as they slowly regained their calm, they were quickly surprised by how the match was progressing—it was unexpected.

They were all flying in the air. In terms of their level of using the flight magic, there wasn't much of a difference between any of them. But only the First High player was actually racking up points. The other players just couldn't keep up with her.

She was nimble, smooth, and elegant...

...as she turned, slid, rose, and fell through the air...

...and her free and lovely dance caused some to join her and others to yield the way.

At some point, the faeries dancing had turned into a ballet with one prima ballerina and five in a corps de ballet.

When the first girl shook and lost her balance in midair, there were screams from the audience. But when they saw her descend slowly and gently, they breathed a collective sigh of relief. Since there had just been a falling accident in the qualifiers, the tournament committee might have been even more relieved than the crowd, actually.

This was all thanks to the safety function in the flight magic. If the rate of psions being supplied from the caster fell below half, the variables included in the activation program beforehand would automatically switch into a 1-G soft-landing mode.

In First High's booth, Tatsuya sighed in relief as well. It looked like they hadn't done anything strange to the program. Oddly enough, with all the attention on the Nine School Competition stage, it had proven to the public that it was actually safe.

He grinned cruelly (evilly, perhaps) to himself. He'd have to take full advantage of that. As he looked on, he saw another girl drop out of the faeries' stage.

Those two were the only ones to drop out of the first period. They forfeited the match afterward. In the second period, another dropped out. By the final period, there were only three left.

Now, as long as Miyuki didn't forfeit the match, First High would win the overall championship. The most surefire tactic at this point would be for her to wait on one of the footholds and do nothing.

But nobody in First High's booth suggested such a *surefire* strategy.

First place had a huge lead right now. And it was, of course, Miyuki who held the spot. The overall victory was certainly important, but not a single person from First High believed she should sacrifice a personal victory for it.

With cheers of encouragement and trust at her back, Miyuki flew into the sky again in the last period. She didn't need to look to know that her brother saw her clearly through it all. She knew her wings would never break as long as she had that.

In the air, she spread her unbreakable, translucent wings as she frolicked among the multicolored lights.

Eventually...

...the other two players went down to a foothold and dropped to their knees, trying to catch their breaths.

The night sky was now the stage for a solo performance, and Miyuki danced her faerie dance.

The final orb of light vanished before her outstretched arms.

There was a moment of silence.

A single stop-motion frame.

The siren to signal the end of the match was drowned out by thunderous applause.

[12]

First High had clinched the overall victory before the last day even came around, but the celebration party was postponed until after tomorrow. ("Again?" complained one voice, which was then ignored.)

Tomorrow would feature the Monolith Code finals tournament, which would bring the Nine School Competition to a close.

First High's team had made it out of the qualifiers in first place for the tournament, as expected. Therefore, their players and staff weren't currently able to party.

Still, it was the only event left. Over half of their members were currently idle. So they borrowed the meeting room to have a pre-celebratory tea party centered on Miyuki, who had clinched First High's overall victory with her win in Mirage Bat.

Mayumi and Suzune facilitated the party, and the participants were mostly female players and staff. There wasn't a complete absence of male students, though, as the male freshmen, save for those injured, were in one corner of the room holding their cups awkwardly. (The junior and senior boys had their hands full getting ready for tomorrow's match.)

Not only Leo and Mikihiko, but also even Erika and Mizuki were here. That probably meant Mayumi's plan was for this to be more than a simple congratulations. (Erika had firmly refused, but Miyuki had dragged her here anyway.)

But for some reason, Tatsuya was nowhere to be found.

"...He said not to wake him up until morning?"

"Yes."

"That's understandable."

"He was going full drive this whole time..."

As the freshman girls traded rumors about a certain male student (in an order that was Erika, Miyuki, Shizuku, and Honoka), a junior couple approached them.

"Really? Your brother went to sleep already?"

It was Kanon and Isori.

"Yes," said Miyuki. "He said it was too tiring even for him."

"Well...that makes sense. He did get hurt, after all." Isori nodded deeply. Then he looked next to her and his eyes widened a little. "Hmm? Erika?"

"Kei, are you done doing tomorrow's adjustments?" asked Erika in a slightly teasing voice.

Isori gave a pained grin. "No, I'm taking a little break... Well, actually, Kanon dragged me here." Kanon looked a little irritated at that, but it probably wasn't just because she didn't like how he said it. There must have been something else that had happened.

"...Oh, Erika, you're acquainted with Isori?"

"They're friends of the family," said Erika, not noticing Kanon's pouting at all—or at least not paying any mind to it—and turning her whole body to Miyuki. "The Isori family is always helping the Chiba family out."

"It's not that much," said Isori, quickly shaking his head.

"No, no! It's the objective truth," joked Erika. "My broom is something we got Kei's family to make for me. Wait, actually, didn't you personally make it?" Erika produced her retracting baton CAD from thin air like a magician.

"Well, yes… The seal parts, at least."

"You built the sealing spells yourself? That's amazing…" Mizuki breathed in admiration.

"Kei's a genius, you know!" said Kanon, sticking out her chest, forgetting that she was supposed to be grumpy. Isori started blushing more and said "no, no" again.

◇ ◇ ◇

As conversation about his absence started to wane, Tatsuya slipped out of the hotel and headed to the parking lot used by the officers on base. The person he went there to meet had already arrived.

"I can't believe you made a woman wait. Don't you have any manners?"

"I'm sorry, ma'am."

They were both ignoring common courtesy, but she had a point—not about the woman thing but about being later than he promised—so Tatsuya gave a sincere apology.

Seeming let down by his lack of an excuse, Haruka didn't complain anymore, either. She gestured for Tatsuya to get into the car she was leaning against. He did as she wished, climbing into the passenger seat, and then Haruka got into the driver's seat.

Both the inside and outside of the car were dark. Without so much as a glance toward the ignition switch, Haruka took a portable terminal out of the door's pocket. Seeing her do so, Tatsuya extracted his own terminal from his pocket. He wasn't in the staff uniform but a black jacket gathered at the waist. It made his sides stick out a little, but Haruka pretended not to notice.

"You just need the map data, right?"

"If you know the members, I'd like that as well, ma'am."

Haruka sighed and looked at her terminal as Tatsuya sent her data first. When she looked at it, her eyes went wide.

"Is it not enough?"

"No, it's plenty," she said, erasing her surprise and using her own terminal.

Tatsuya briefly skimmed the data she'd sent and nodded once. "Thank you very much, ma'am," he said, bowing a little and moving to open the door.

"Insurance, right?" asked Haruka firmly.

"Yes, ma'am. Insurance," he answered curtly. By the time the words reached her ears, his back had already turned.

Tatsuya watched until Haruka drove the electric coupe beyond the gate and out of sight, then peeled off the gauze covering his right ear and walked over to another car. The passenger-side door opened without him having to knock on the window. Sitting in the driver's seat was a woman about the same age as Haruka.

"Who was that?"

"A public safety operative," he said, not hesitating to reveal her identity as he grinned at Fujibayashi. "She says her main job is a counselor, though."

Fujibayashi couldn't help but giggle. "So she's a part-time operative?"

"I don't think she has any issues with ability. Entry-level semi-professionals are more likely than seasoned veterans to follow confidentiality rules to the letter, so I can ask her to do side jobs. Well...taking a side job in the first place is a violation of professional ethics, but money makes the world go round, right?"

Fujibayashi narrowed her eyes at the dark words, which he spoke as though they weren't. And the words between them stayed cold and sober: "You know, I end up thinking this a lot... You're not ten years older and committing age fraud, are you?"

"I believe it's an issue of experience rather than age, ma'am. After all, I have *all sorts* of experiences on a daily basis."

Tatsuya's emphasis on *all sorts* made Fujibayashi casually look away. He wasn't particularly expecting a response. He took a data cable out of the glove compartment, and then, with practiced fluidity, manipulated the panel in front of the passenger's seat, sending the map data he'd received from Haruka to the navigation system.

"...Maybe I should ask for part-time payment, too."

"I believe you should demand an overtime allowance, ma'am."

"Labor laws don't apply to us, you know."

Even in modern times, where flexible hours were a mainstream part of how people worked, some laws had overstayed their welcome. With Tatsuya unable to manage even a forced smile at the dry office joke, Fujibayashi pushed the palm rest's one-handed controller up.

The car, one of the most popular models these days, rolled off into the darkness in a perfect silence impossible to encapsulate in any manufacturer's catalog.

◇ ◇ ◇

The very man who had ordered Fujibayashi to work "overtime" was also welcoming a guest off the clock.

"Please come in, Your Excellency."

The person Kazama had been personally showing in, without relying on an orderly, was Kudou.

Back in the senior's day, there was no rule that the Ten Master Clans weren't allowed to be in the public eye, or have high official positions. It had been essentially created because of Kudou himself, and what he experienced in the face of all kinds of strife and discord.

Kudou held the rank of major general when he retired from military service. Kazama was being formal with the elder of the Ten Master Clans not out of a personal reason, but in accordance with the discipline he was supposed to show in public.

Kazama was a B-rank licensed magician, and a member of a community of magicians headed up by the Ten Master Clans. However, he was an old-style magician classified as a *ninjutsu* user, so his feelings toward the clans, who symbolized modern magic, were some-what distant, if he had to say it. (Of course, as the leader of a team, his feelings toward his subordinates were different.)

Therefore—but that might not be the right word—*though* Kaza-ma's attitude was polite, it didn't exceed the bounds of formality.

"Leave us."

"Yes, sir!"

After having the orderly who brought them drinks withdraw out-side the room, Kazama once again looked at Kudou. "For what pur-pose have you visited us today? If you were looking for Fujibayashi, I'm afraid she is out right now on an errand…"

"I don't feel the need to go through senior officers to see my granddaughter… Why are you so upset about it? I just heard you got out of Tsuchiura for once, so I decided to pay you a visit."

"It's an honor," said Kazama, though he showed no sign of reverence.

Kudou cracked a dry grin. "I see your dislike of the clans is alive and well."

"As I stated previously, you misunderstand me."

"And as I stated previously, you don't have to feel like you need to lie to me. We were created as weapons to begin with, but you old-style magicians are simply *people* who inherited ancient knowledge. It's only natural you would feel discontent toward how we are."

He pronounced the word *people* one syllable at a time as if on purpose. Kazama found himself frowning. "…Old casters are the same—we make our bodies into weapons. There isn't much differ-ence between you and us, sir. If I feel any discontent, it's in how you emphasize to children and young people to think of us as something inhuman."

Kazama's comment could have been called vitriolic depending on whom you asked. But Kudou countered, his tone calm and collected. "Hmm…is that why you look after *him*?"

"…Him, sir?"

"Tatsuya Shiba. Miya's son. You pulled him out of the Yotsuba, right?"

Kazama's ensuing silence was less because he couldn't find anything to say and more a pause to glower at the man.

"Well, it isn't strange that I would know about it. At the time, I was the chairman at the Master Clans Conference, and now I'm a magic adviser to the National Defense Force. And I was a tutor to Miya and Maya, if only temporarily."

"...Then you must know that the Yotsuba gave up all rights to Tatsuya. Our agreement with them was that he remains a guardian of the Yotsuba, and that as long as he can fulfill that duty without hindrance, he would submit to the military. And that other than him being a guardian, they would not claim any other right of priority over him."

"Do you ever think it was unfortunate?" asked Kudou, leaning forward meaningfully.

"Unfortunate, sir?" repeated Kazama, at a loss.

Kudou smiled slightly, not appearing offended by this. "Yesterday's match was splendid. I'd heard he was the only successful case, but I hadn't imagined he would be that powerful." Former Major General Kudou peered into Kazama's eyes, as if searching for something. "In the future, he could stand side by side with the son of the Ichijou to form the center of our country's magic military power. Don't you think it wasteful that such a talented person would be stuck in one place as a personal bodyguard?"

"...Do you wish for the Yotsuba to weaken, Your Excellency?"

Kudou smiled thinly and nodded. "You certainly do put things bluntly. Part of the Ten Master Clans system is that each family holds the others in check, preventing any renegade magicians from appearing."

Kazama's silence indicated to Kudou that this was already something he was aware of.

"But at our current rate, the Yotsuba will grow *too* strong. Not long in the future, if Tatsuya Shiba and his younger sister continue to grow, and if Miyuki Shiba becomes Miyuki Yotsuba while Maya still lives, with Tatsuya as her instrument, then the Yotsuba could ascend to a higher level than all of us. No..." He paused, shaking his head. "Even now, the Yotsuba possess special skills the other families don't, as well as very powerful magicians, though few of them. They already stand out among the Ten Master Clans."

Kazama gave Kudou's words a sardonic grin. "That family has upheld the tradition you mentioned of *magicians developed to be weapons* the most. In terms of combat strength, I would think it only natural that they stand out."

"And that's just the problem. Major Kazama, you're right. Originally, we were developed as weapons—but it's different now. If weapons are all we are, then we will be driven out of the human world."

"Your Excellency." Kazama's words interrupted Kudou's reminiscent remark. "Just as you know of our affairs, we know about some of your own, your grace. We *are* aware of the real reason you think so much about Tatsuya."

This time, Kudou was the one to fall silent.

"In addition, I ask your permission to offer one piece of advice and one correction."

"...Go ahead."

"I don't believe Tatsuya requires pity. He is not a simple test animal meant to be lavished with pity. In fact, I believe he would find it undesirable."

"That was your advice, then?"

"Yes, sir. As for the correction... You spoke of the future, but Tatsuya is *presently* an important part of our forces. And this may sound like favoritism to you, sir, but Tatsuya and Masaki Ichijou are on entirely different levels of combat potential.

"Masaki Ichijou, when defending a point, would alone have strength rivaling that of a mechanized regiment. But Tatsuya has strength rivaling that of a strategic guided missile. His magic is a tactical weapon, which obviously requires layers of safeties. I believe that making him bear all the responsibility for managing everything would be the crueler option."

◇ ◇ ◇

Tatsuya did not sneeze several times in a row as the car headed east, as folk tradition would dictate.

The car Fujibayashi was driving—or more accurately, the car being guided by the traffic control system—was going east on the highway and would enter Yokohama City before night fell. To the east was the Port of Yokohama, and to the north (despite numerous direct daytime military conflicts in the area) was the Yokohama Chinatown, which had retained its prosperity even now that the twenty-first century was about to end. They parked on a hill overlooking the district.

"…They know foreign agents are swarming around here. Why don't they lock it down or do inspections? What are those politicians thinking?"

Tatsuya stood next to Fujibayashi as she looked down at the shopping district, bitter remarks on her lips. He shrugged. "Well, the story is that this city is the main base of resistance for the Chinese who fled from their tyrannical government."

"That's obviously a lie!"

"As I said, that's the story, ma'am."

"But there are limits. We may have won, but we haven't entered into a peace treaty with them yet. Japan and the GAA haven't fired any shots for three years, but we're still at war. Everyone knows they're using the city as a base for spy activity, but nobody takes any drastic measures."

Fujibayashi looked about ready to spit, but Tatsuya answered her in an aloof tone. "Maybe there are a lot of people who think the same way you do, Lieutenant."

The implication—or at least, the one she thought she heard—made

Fujibayashi's eyes go wide. She stared at him. "...Do you know something?"

"No. It's just a wish," he replied, turning his back to put an end to the conversation.

In front of him he now saw the highest building in the city. High in price as well but physically the tallest building. In the place of what was once simply called the Park Overlooking the Port until the middle of the century, was now a three-piece, super-tall structure that looked out over both the Port of Yokohama and the shoreline.

It was called the Yokohama Bay Hills Tower: a multiuse building containing a hotel, a shopping mall, private offices, and television stations affectionately nicknamed "Bay Hills" by the city residents. The goodwill magic organization, the Magic Association of Japan, had its Kanto branch office here as well, rather than in Tokyo. (Their main office was in Kyoto.)

Of course, the fact that this building was a purely private establishment was a well-known fact among non-civilians. The National Maritime Force and Maritime Police had offices here disguised as private companies for the purpose of monitoring the entry and exit of vessels into and out of the Tokyo Bay.

Everyone also said that the Magic Association of Japan's branch being here was a defensive precaution in case of emergencies. Tatsuya and Fujibayashi, though, knew that it was no mere rumor—it was entirely factual.

"Lieutenant, if you please."

"I really might ask for overtime pay after this."

The time was already close to midnight.

Fujibayashi pressed a small information terminal to the side of the emergency exit—a door that could only be opened from the inside. In her other hand, she used a CAD.

The door had no outdoor keypad, and no capability for being opened over a wireless connection. But the wall's electrical conductivity distribution had been altered, and thanks to a hacking program using the wall as a medium, the door opened up for them to enter. Fujibayashi hacked into the interior surveillance system, too, and had it make an exception for the two of them.

◇ ◇ ◇

The Yokohama Grand Hotel: a high-rise hotel built in Chinatown in the first half of the century with funds from Hong Kong. It had no relation to the New Grand Hotel, its predecessor, despite the similar name. One set of stairs up from the highest marked floor, in a place not known to the guests, was the *true* top floor. One of its rooms contained frantic moving preparations.

This room was the Eastern Japan HQ of the Hong Kong–based international crime syndicate No-Head Dragon. It was, so to speak, the control room for the syndicate's operation in the entire eastern section of the country.

Though, since the Hong Kong funds that operated this hotel had been taken over by No-Head itself quite some time ago, it was perhaps more accurate to call this the control room for *criminal* operations.

Though it was being prepared for a move, the people inside weren't taking any furniture. Their luggage consisted mainly of top-secret documents not recorded in any computer system. The paperwork was of such secrecy that it couldn't be entered into a system, even one outfitted with the strictest of security, so they *especially* couldn't be packed away by underlings. These men in the prime of life (albeit bordering on middle-aged), clad in brand-name suits, wiped the sweat from their brows with silk handkerchiefs, and their fingers, sparkling with gold, silver, and jeweled rings, awkwardly packed their things. Honestly, the very sight would have been amusing, if one were to watch.

Of course, for those involved, this was no laughing matter.

One of them abruptly stopped to curse. "Bastards… They won't get away with this!"

You could almost hear his teeth grinding.

272 THE IRREGULAR AT MAGIC HIGH SCHOOL ④

"I still can't believe a Generator was subdued before getting any combat results…"

"That was unexpected. I had no idea the Imperial Special Forces would just come waltzing into the picture!"

"And now we all have to run away under the cover of night. Ridiculous!"

"One win is all it takes for them to puff up with pride…"

Now that everyone here had expressed their true feelings on the matter, all the welled-up complaints their exhaustion had prevented were now coming out.

"We'll have our revenge on the Imperial Army. But dealing with that brat should be the first thing on our list."

"The impudent child who completely undermined our plans?"

"Tatsuya Shiba, was it? Where's he come from?"

"We…don't know the details. We could only find his name, residence, school affiliation, and appearance. We don't know of any dependents or his family makeup. We don't know anything beside the fact that his parents are office workers. We couldn't find a single bit of personal data on him except for things related to his daily life."

"What the hell? The whole world knows this country has been putting all personal data into a database. Shouldn't there be more than that in the private database?"

"We should probably assume the data wasn't locked—that an organization deleted all data regarding him. There's no other possibility."

The officers of No-Head Dragon's eastern Japan branch scrutinized their colleague's face intently, then looked to one another in silence.

"…Isn't he just a high school student?"

"You would need extremely high privileges to be able to completely overwrite a civilian database, even *with* national influence. Or enough influence to freely intervene with the highest authority in the nation…"

"Then who the hell was it…?"

Suddenly—while the men all paused their packing—they heard a muffled cry.

There were four figures standing idly in the corners of the room. They were Generators, given to the eastern Japan branch officers as protection tools. One of the four magic-generating devices, each assigned to one of four magic types and acting to prevent attacks from the outside—the Generator who had an active Information Boost up on the outside wall—had been the source of the cry.

It didn't take long for them to realize why. They were *made* to understand:

There was a gaping hole in the south wall of the room.

It hadn't been broken through, cut through, or destroyed: It had turned into concrete, sand, and powdered cement, leaving the steel frame, rebar, and pipes intact.

And the cry—it had been a cry of pain, from the recoil of the Information Boost spell being broken.

But the pained voice continued for only a brief moment. But it didn't matter, anyway: The officers abruptly comprehended its reason for existence, with only a few moments of thought.

No-Head Dragon wasn't a simple crime syndicate. It was a criminal organization that abused magic. To be appointed as an officer, you needed to be a magician. So of course, all the officers of the eastern Japan branch were magicians. They used magic, and could perceive it. And they could perceive what was happening right now.

The Generator's body-information eidos skin—the defensive wall of boosted information every magician expanded unconsciously to protect them from other magicians—had been torn from the Generator's person. That was why he'd cried out.

Though—it might be more visually faithful to describe it as armor dissolving and evaporating.

And a moment later, static appeared over the Generator's body like it was a stereoscopic image, even though it possessed a physical body—and then its outline disappeared, along with the clothes it was wearing.

In the empty space where the Generator had been, a weak flame popped into existence. It was blue, purple, and orange. Without any time for the sprinklers to go off, it disappeared with a flash.

Tiny ashes fell to the carpet. They were the only remains of the Generator's body.

The officers, scared out of their wits, couldn't shout or scream. They simply exchanged gaping glances, terrified.

And then, all of a sudden, the phone rang.

It was the sound of a call from the secret line, which was only used within their organization.

One of the officers very slowly picked up the receiver. The panel indicated that there was no video feed. There was only audio for this conversation.

"Hello, east Japan branch of No-Head Dragon."

What they heard from the speaker was the voice of a young man—of a boy.

◇ ◇ ◇

Tatsuya and Fujibayashi had come to the rooftop of Yokohama Bay Hills's north tower. There were television broadcast antennas and a radio communication relay up here. Fujibayashi pushed the same terminal as before against the relay and began pressing things on its touchscreen panel.

"…All right, hacking complete. I overwrote the radio communication to link everything here."

"As I've come to expect from the Electron Sorceress. This is one thing I couldn't imitate, no matter how I used my skills."

"Thanks. I'd be out of a job if someone could imitate me so easily, though." She smiled lightly, but deep down, the comment hadn't seemed completely in jest.

"You cut the wired communication, right?"

"Captain Sanada already took care of that."

Tatsuya picked up the voice communication unit attached to the information terminal in his left hand. After punching in the code Fujibayashi gave him, he set it up to talk and held it there, ready to go with a single push of a button.

He took his wind-breaking biker shades out of his chest pocket and put them on. Then he removed his long-barreled CAD out from its spot in his left shoulder holster. It was a specialized CAD, silver and shaped like an automatic pistol.

He stood before the fence at the edge of the roof and pointed his right hand down at an angle. His CAD's "muzzle" was now aiming at the distant Yokohama Grand Hotel, down the hill.

"...So this is a Generator?"

"Yes, without a doubt. This is the first time I've captured one, but its features match the intelligence department's reports perfectly."

There was easily more than a half mile directly between the roof of Bay Hills and the top floor of the Grand Hotel. The pistol-shaped CAD Tatsuya held had no scope on it, of course. But even so, Fujibayashi didn't ask him if he could see. She was fully aware that he could see just fine.

Fujibayashi herself saw in a different way than Tatsuya, but she could still see how many magicians and Generators were in that room.

"Magic-generating devices robbed of their humanity. The miserable end of magicians developed as weapons..."

Fujibayashi's lips pursed.

"...I apologize, ma'am. I've said too much."

She gave him a cold, silent stare, and Tatsuya offered an awkward apology.

Not all magicians consented to being weapons, of course; it was certainly an inappropriate remark, so he apologized. Though, he couldn't deny the fact that he felt empathetic toward them.

Generators were similar to the way he was.

Consequently, within the bounds of his remaining emotion, he felt the greatest hatred. They were unpleasant and harmful beings. His mind wouldn't falter when faced with destroying such *devices*.

The Silver Horn Custom, Trident... Tatsuya pulled the trigger of his favorite magically optimized weapon. It activated his original magic, Dismantle, which was designated a military secret.

The technique had dismantled the building's outer concrete wall into a fine powder of its constituent parts.

While that physical hole opened in the wall, another hole opened conceptually, for the purpose of closing off any interfering magic, allowing Tatsuya's "vision" to reflect the inside of the room more clearly.

The Generator was in shock at its active spell being broken apart. Normally, a magician wouldn't take this much damage from his or her spell being broken; was this a negative effect of not being able to pause or suspend its magic under its own volition...?

Tatsuya's analysis of the event may have been calm, but his will to attack—to *kill*—was alive and well. He discerned the Area Interference coming from the broken Generator, as well as the five officers and their other three magical guards.

Tatsuya pulled Trident's trigger. He'd already input the information he'd collected on the damaged Generator—notably its Area Interference field, its eidos skin, and its physical body—as variables.

Three magic processes fired one after another with not even a fraction of a moment between them. The first process dismantled the Area Interference protecting the target. The second process dismantled the Information Boost protecting the target, while the third dismantled the target's entire body, deconstructing it down to atoms.

It was no longer acknowledged as organic matter, and didn't even leave behind a trace of the fact that it had once been a living creature. Everything broke apart into single elements and their ions: Proteins split into hydrogen, oxygen, carbon, nitrogen, and sulfur; bones broke into phosphorous, oxygen, calcium, and other trace elements; and even blood, nerves, stored nutrients, and excretions fell apart—*everything.*

The light elements, represented by hydrogen, traveled along the ceiling and left the room by way of the hole in the wall.

The gas from the combustible elements linked with the released oxygen and spontaneously combusted.

The way it happened might have looked like a human body catching fire.

But the truth behind it was not that it was *destroyed by fire*—it was that it *disappeared.*

"Dismantle" consisted of three processes combined into one magic program: It took the magician's body, which should have been protected by magic power, and wiped it out of existence, without allowing any opposition at all.

"Trident... I guess this is what it means when your hair stands on end..."

The specialized CAD had been tuned up to fire three spells simultaneously.

The Index had given the name *Trident* to a different kind of spell. But the Independent Magic Battalion knew that Trident was a ruthless, three-stage dismantling spell, and it was also the name of the CAD optimized for such a spell.

Fujibayashi couldn't conceal a shudder and a murmur. Unconcerned, Tatsuya booted up the voice function on the information terminal he had standing by.

The relay hacking had stolen all meaning from the private line's authentication system.

"Hello, east Japan branch of No-Head Dragon," greeted Tatsuya, in an unnaturally cheerful tone.

◇ ◇ ◇

The officer who picked up the phone turned back to his colleagues, unable to hide the wonder on his face. This line was for the officers to communicate among themselves; it was even private from the one they used to contact international HQ. Without being a branch leader or a member of the main council, you couldn't use it, even if you *were* a member of the organization. In fact, you wouldn't even *know* about this line. Furthermore, No-Head Dragon had no officers in their twenties, much less in their teens.

"…Who is it?"

Perhaps the only reason his tone of voice *wasn't* imperious was because of the fear struck into his heart from the human disappearing act he'd just witnessed a moment ago.

"I'm much obliged for what happened at Fuji."

The voice sounded like it belonged to a boy in his teens, but the way he expressed himself was far more mature than that.

"Such being the case, I've come to return the favor."

As he spoke, the Area Interference field surrounding each of the officers suddenly vanished.

It wasn't just the one on the phone. Everyone, save for the magical equipment that lacked volition, looked reflexively to one corner of the room.

Before their eyes, a weak blue flame flared up and disappeared. The sprinklers then reacted to the heat source and sprayed a high-pressure mist from the ceiling. The Generator, who had just been standing there, had evaporated without leaving a trace.

"Where is he?! Number Fourteen, where's he coming from?!" shouted one officer, harried.

All magicians could detect what a spell had been cast on and from where it had been cast, based on the reaction from the event alteration. If someone had used a spell strong enough to disassemble a human body to the atomic level from such close range, then normally, there was no way they *wouldn't* know where the spell had come from.

Even if they couldn't detect the exact location, they should have been able to at least tell what *direction* the caster had been in, but they couldn't. Which meant that the officer who shouted could no longer do anything but scream at the Generator to tell him.

In contrast, the remaining Generators didn't get agitated—their mental functions for *being* agitated had been broken. They would not grow scared and panic, even if their partners were destroyed.

Number Fourteen sluggishly pointed to the hole in the wall. And past the hole, to the highest point in this city.

Another officer hastily reached for a sniper rifle. He put the digital optic scope to his eye and turned up the magnification. The upper body of a single boy appeared on the roof of Yokohama Bay Hills, illuminated by the waxing moon in the western sky. The man magnified the optical sight as far as it would go. He couldn't see the boy's eyes, as they were hidden under biker shades, but his lips were unconcealed, and he could see them distort into a derisive smirk.

As soon as he saw the twisted smile, the man cried out and hunched over. The scope had suddenly flown apart, disassembled, and a piece of it wounded his eye.

But the men didn't have time to be worried about their colleague moaning in pain with a hand over said eye.

"Fourteen, Sixteen, get him!"

More than one voice ordered the Generators to counterattack. However...

"It is impossible," said one in a robotic voice.

"It will not reach."

Machines would do only what was possible. Generators had been reconstructed so they could use magic stably in any situation; they had no function to muster strength beyond their limits in desperation.

"Don't talk back to me! Get him!"

The voice directed at Number Fourteen and Number Sixteen with a complete lack of intonation had come from the officer on his knees with a hand over his eye; his temper was shot.

A reply came from over the phone:

"Do you think I'll let you?"

Noise appeared all over the bodies of Fourteen and Sixteen. Then they met the exact same fate as their two partners.

A sneering laugh came before the next words of ridicule. *"Why not do it yourself rather than ordering tools to do it for you?"*

But the strength to get angry at the sneer had been stolen from them. Their assailant was too far away to see with the naked eye; they couldn't even make out the outline of a person. Nobody here had the skills to magically attack something they couldn't see or otherwise perceive.

One man jumped for a landline. Another desperately tried to make a wireless call on a portable terminal. But the only thing they received were disconnected signals.

And yet, from their terminals' speakers…

"That won't work. The only one you can connect to from that room right now…is me."

…came the same voice they'd heard on the first receiver.

"Impossible… Even the wireless…? How the hell…?"

"EM wave convergence. You don't need to know how it was done."

The men were smart enough to know what he meant by that. The knowledge only heightened their feelings of hopelessness.

"Anyway, on to business."

The demon's verdict ushered in more noise to the man holding his eye. His face twisted into a look of true despair. It continued to twist and contort—until he turned to dust and evaporated.

The humidity in the room had gone up from the three times the sprinklers had activated. At this point, no combustion happened to the atomized body. Their colleague simply disappeared without even so much as a ceremonial burial flame, and the other men's faces froze.

One rushed for the exit. Noise had appeared on his back, and his contours had broken apart and dispersed into the air.

The remaining three officers in No-Head Dragon's eastern Japan

branch then realized their lives were now in the devil's hands. They couldn't run away from that fact any longer.

"Wait…! Please, wait!" shouted the branch leader after snatching away the receiver.

"For what, exactly?"

He had shouted his plea in spite of himself. He didn't think the enemy would let them live—the enemy was deleting them like computer data; he had no pity or mercy. But unexpectedly, the man got a response. "We…we will not interfere with the Nine School Competition any more!" he continued into the pause.

"It ends tomorrow."

"Not only the competition! We'll leave the country tomorrow morning! And we'll never come back!"

"Even if you don't, others will, right?"

"No-Head Dragon will withdraw from Japan! Not just eastern Japan—I'll have the western Japan branch pull out, too!"

"Do you have the authority to make such a promise, Douglas Huang?"

Huang's heart stopped for a moment in shock. Desperately, he pushed forward, arguing his defense. "I'm a close aide to the boss! Even *he* can't ignore what I have to say!"

"How are you able to say that?"

"Because I've saved his life! Our rules state that life debts must be paid by granting just as many requests!"

"Did you plan on begging for your life with that debt?"

Two sets of eyes pierced into Huang. They were murderous, hateful eyes, turned on a traitor. But he didn't have time to be concerned about them.

"Don't you need that debt to buy back your own life?"

"No! I don't have to do that! The boss would never discard me!"

"Are you saying you have that much clout with him?"

"Yes!"

"Can you prove it?"

"I, well…"

"No–Head Dragon…you were not the ones who began that name. It was given to you by opposing groups, since its leader never appears before his or her subordinates. I hear it is very thorough—even when directly regulating subordinates, they are knocked out and brought to his or her room."

A different kind of shudder shot through Huang than the fear of death or destruction. This man…knew far too much about them.

Who the hell had they started a fight with?

"If you say you have that much clout, then you must have seen your leader's face before, correct?"

But he didn't have time to think. To survive, he would have to take advantage of this flight of fancy the devil was showing him. "I am permitted to have an audience with him."

"What's your leader's name?"

Huang closed his mouth. That was the highest secret in their organization. The fear and loyalty imprinted within him over many years won out over his fear at the current situation. But that only lasted a brief moment.

"—James?!"

Another of his partners had disappeared from this world. Extinguished, without even being allowed a human death. That seemed to him just as horrifying as the profanity toward the dead conducted by their leader.

"So that was James Zhu? That was unfortunate for the international police assigned to you."

"Wait…"

"Will you be next, Douglas Huang?"

"Please, wait! …The boss's name is Richard Sun."

"What is his public name?"

"…Gongming Sun."

"Where does he live?"

Huang told him everything he asked, from his residence in the upper-class residential district in Hong Kong to his office building's name to the clubs he frequented. "…That's everything I know."

"Good timing. I had just finished questioning you. Excellent work."

"You'll believe me?"

"Yeah. You are definitely a close aide to Richard Sun, leader of No-Head Dragon."

Huang had been overwhelmed, and his face was empty. Now, though, he felt a tinge of joy. But that tiny ray of hope he'd gotten…

"Gregory!"

…was completely erased along with his final colleague.

"…Why?! We didn't take any lives. We didn't kill anyone!"

◇ ◇ ◇

"…We didn't kill anyone!"

Over the voice communication unit he heard convenient reasoning—reasoning that only worked in hindsight. They had plotted mass murder, and it had been stopped by Yanagi, Sanada, and Fujibayashi. But Tatsuya didn't point that out. "That has nothing to do with it."

"What…?"

"Kill whoever you want. Don't kill whoever you want. I don't care."

Tatsuya was fed up with all this posturing. He couldn't do it anymore, and he stopped caring about making his words sound pretty. He'd heard everything he needed to. He no longer had to do it. "You made a move on something you should never have touched. That touch has incurred my wrath. That's enough of a reason for you all to disappear."

"…You're a demon!"

"Maybe I am. But you're the reason I can *use* this demonic power, Douglas Huang. Will draws out power—but emotion makes it stronger." Tatsuya gave a thin, self-deprecating laugh into the mouthpiece. Its sound dissolved into the night wind, and in its place he spoke cold, hopeless words. "You drew out my one and only emotion. That's how I can finally let this demonic power loose again."

"Demonic power...? This spell—wait, is it the Demon Right?!"

That was his final cry. Nobody would ever hear his voice again.

Douglas Huang's very existence had been erased from the world.

[13]

The Nine School Competition entered its final day. The only event would be Monolith Code. The first match of the finals tournament would be at nine, and the second at ten. The third-place match would be at one in the afternoon, with the final match being held at two.

After that, starting at 3:30, would be the awards ceremony and the closing ceremony, with the competition itself wrapping up at five.

Only the events in the stadiums would end, however. There would be a party at seven. And unlike the banquet from before the competition, the closing party would *actually* be a place for friendship among the schools—so much so that every year, more than a few long-distance couples were formed.

This was a chance for high school students to not only network but also to make acquaintances with influential people in magic society. Many of the seniors especially looked forward to the double-sided party.

But for the four high schools that had advanced to the tournament, the matches would come before all that. Yet none of the schools were busy any longer. Everything they needed to do, they'd done. Now, the players and staff all quietly awaited the final battle.

First High's tent was no exception. Katsuto sat at the center, self-possessed, eyes closed, with some around him wearing nervous expressions and others wisely holding back their impatience, as athletes and staff alike waited for them to be called to the second match.

The team consisted of Katsuto Juumonji, Koutarou Tatsumi, and Gyoubu Hattori, along with the technical staff assigned to the final event. Isori was one of those present. A few steps away were the officers, surrounding the student council—Mayumi, Mari, Suzune, Kanon, and Azusa. Then came other junior and senior players, starting with Kanon. Those who couldn't fit into the tent were waiting with bated breath in the cheering section for the players to appear.

But Tatsuya was nowhere to be found.

◇ ◇ ◇

"Shouldn't you go root them on?"

"...There's still a little time before it gets rolling," answered Tatsuya to Fujibayashi, after he took a sip of his drink. In accordance with last night's orders, he'd visited Kazama's room after breakfast.

However, the room's owner had left for a confidential meeting with someone early in the morning, and now Tatsuya was eating a second breakfast with his fellow operative while they waited for Kazama to return. Tatsuya had the same appetite as every other high school boy, so he didn't have any trouble adding a sandwich to his meal as dessert.

After making just enough conversation not to be rude, Tatsuya put away the last of the dishes. Kazama returned with Sanada and Yanagi in tow. Tatsuya and Fujibayashi rose and saluted; Kazama nonchalantly returned their salute, then waved for them to sit down.

Kazama took the seat across from Tatsuya, Yanagi was next to Fujibayashi, and Sanada was next to Tatsuya. (He'd already heard from Fujibayashi that Yamanaka had gone back to Kasumigaura Base, which had been elevated from a garrison years ago.

"Good work last night," said Kazama finally, after some hasty greetings.

"No, sir, I apologize for causing all of you trouble over my private affairs."

"It wasn't a private affair. I was attacked, too."

"And we got some valuable combat data last night, too. Four thousand feet, was it? We barely have any data on long-range magic that can successfully snipe a person from that distance. Your original style is super long-range precision attacks, and you can even do OTH, or over the horizon sniping, so it might not have been far enough to satisfy you. But the observation results were more than enough for me."

After Tatsuya stood and bowed in apology, Yanagi and Sanada offered words of comfort and appreciation.

"That's how it is," concluded Kazama, accepting the bow. "The COIA and Public Safety were happier than we thought with last night's little present, too. Even though some personal affairs happened to be involved, you accomplished your mission, so there's nothing really to worry about."

"…Was the intel on a mere crime syndicate really worth that much, sir?" Last night, personal revenge had been part of the reason he'd actually called up the enemy and tormented them for so long, but it *had* all unmistakably been ordered by Kazama.

"Well, that wasn't just any crime syndicate."

Tatsuya's lips pursed.

Upon seeing the silent reply, Sanada spoke. "Tatsuya, how much do you know about Sorcery Boosters?"

"I've heard of them before, sir. A revolutionary magic amplification device making its way through crime organizations over the last few years. To be honest, sir, I thought it was a sham…"

"No, Sorcery Boosters do exist. And in a way, they really *are* revolutionary magic amplification devices, too."

"Is magic amplification even possible in the first place, sir?" Tatsuya didn't think Sanada would start lying or talking about unreliable gossip, but he still couldn't shake the feeling of it being dubious.

Magic did include a process that output a "signal" magic program from the magician to the target eidos, so the concept of amplification wasn't completely far-fetched. But the process that output a magic program was a movement of *information* within the Idea. The magic program signal wasn't *physically* moving between the magician and the target as something in and of itself.

What part of the magic program constructed by the magician could be amplified...? That was the first question he had.

"It's not amplification in the normal sense. Let's see... It's more like a CAD with a function to support the magic program construction *process*, using the program's blueprint as a base, rather than directly supplying a stronger magical program, I suppose. It makes it possible for a magician to create magic programs that exceed their innate magical capacity."

"That...sounds more like additional memory than a Booster, sir."

"Well, yeah," said Sanada, laughing for a few moments at the way Tatsuya put it. "...It's not unusual for nicknames not to properly express what something is. Anyway, No-Head Dragon is a supplier of Sorcery Boosters. There's an issue with the materials used to create these tools, though. No respectable company could make such a thing. Even nations would be at too high a risk if it were revealed. So in reality, No-Head Dragon has a monopoly on supplying them."

"Then...did we need information on their leader so that we could buy these Sorcery Boosters, sir?"

"Nope. We needed intel on the target so we could *stop* the manufacturing and supply of the Boosters. They aren't something that should be allowed to exist. I would never want to use one, and I wouldn't want to make anyone in my unit use them, either... Tatsuya, you know how the central unit of a CAD, a Reaction Stone, is created, right?"

A Reaction Stone converted psionic waves into electrical signals and vice versa. Feeling a little confused at the sudden change in topic, Tatsuya nodded and spoke. "Reaction Stones are chemically synthesized at the molecular level, and created by crystallized neurons grown in a network structure. The networks' construction determines the rate of conversion, so some say the issue isn't the neurons' physical characteristics but the pattern of network structure. But right now, there are no reported successes of creating a Reaction Stone from anything but artificial neurons."

Sanada nodded, satisfied with Tatsuya's answer. "That's right. But the central unit of a Booster *is* a Reaction Stone, one made from something other than artificial neurons."

"What could that be, sir...?"

"Human brains."

Tatsuya was speechless.

"To be more specific, magician cerebrums."

"...But if they used animal brain cells, the reaction with the user shouldn't happen because of the residual psions inside the brain," he argued. "The same should go for using human brain cells, shouldn't it, sir?"

The obvious inhumanity wasn't the main reason he was dumbstruck. He knew of both animal experiments and human experiments conducted at the dawn of CAD development. The trial-and-error experiments ignored all ethics, conscience, and faith, not caring what it looked like. As a result, they established the manufacturing know-how behind Reaction Stones by chemically synthesizing them from neurons.

But now Sanada was saying that No-Head Dragon had defied the conventional wisdom of magic engineering. That was what surprised Tatsuya.

"This isn't to say their Reaction Stones function exactly like normal ones. One Booster can only be used for one specific spell. And that spell depends on the individual Booster. Still, it can be predicted to an extent. Residual thoughts in the brain during creation can be guessed in order to change the type of magic one can use. That means, if they give strong emotions of a certain variety during the creation process, they can create the same type of Booster every time."

"...For example, delivering great pain or fear right before removing the brain, sir?"

"Most likely."

"...It's like the theory behind poisoning."

"I agree. Boosters probably developed from the fundamentals of poisoning techniques. Our experimental unit's goal is to make magic a weapon and include magicians in military systems, but we don't make the magicians into actual *objects*. I'm a magician, too. And so are the major, Captain Yanagi, Lieutenant Fujibayashi, and almost all the members of the unit, including the noncommissioned officers and rank-and-file soldiers. I might be convinced to accept Generators, but I absolutely will not acknowledge the creation or usage of Boosters."

"Even leaving sentimentality aside, Boosters that expand a magician's capacity are a military threat as well. The NAIA feels the same way, and they've apparently requested the COIA's help. Mibu is very thankful to you, Tatsuya," added Kazama, ending the explanation here.

◇ ◇ ◇

As Tatsuya looked around restlessly for an open seat in the cheering section, a pebble made of ice flew at him from up ahead. Flustered, he caught it, lowered his hand, then met eyes with his sister. He gave up on the pretense of not having noticed her group and meekly went to a seat close to the front.

"...That was a violent greeting."

"My brother was the one pretending that he didn't see us."

Tatsuya had nothing to say to that.

Well, he had a proper reason for it (or at least, he thought so): He didn't want to stand out in the cheering section right before the match started. It was clear, however, that it wasn't nearly enough to convince his sister.

Their classmates sitting in nearby seats certainly didn't seem to think Miyuki was in the right here—but nevertheless, he was not the least bit thankful for their detached looks of sympathy.

"Oh, here they come."

"You got here just in time, Tatsuya!"

Tatsuya's murmuring had been answered not by Miyuki, but by Honoka, who was sitting on the other side of her. Miyuki, busy trying to repulse her halfhearted gaze with a demure smile and thus, unable to answer, sat herself a little closer to Tatsuya instead.

The first match of the finals tournament would be First High versus Ninth High. Uncannily, it was the same pairing as in the rookie competition.

Ninth High must have had payback in their minds, because all three of their players looked raring to go.

In contrast, the three from First High all had their usual distinct mannerisms about them. Katsuto stood calm and composed, Tatsumi looked somehow innocent, and Hattori was returning the enemy team's challenging stares with a super-serious scowl of determination. They were no different from how they always were, which exuded a sense of reliability.

"A sense of security... Well, that's something we had none of."

"That isn't true! I never felt anxious about your victory, Tatsuya."

"Your team was great, too! It was really impressive!"

Tatsuya had really only made a casual comment, but what immediately returned—hard to tell if it was consolation or encouragement—made him feel a bit taken aback.

It was right before the match, and the two had kept their voices down in respect, so nobody had started staring at them *this* time. But there was no guarantee it would go so well every time. An old saying went that words bore evil, so he braced himself, rid his mind of worldly thoughts, and decided to focus on cheering.

...Partly because the unamused look Shizuku was giving him hurt.

But then, without any relation to their little skit, the match began.

The field was the crag stage, modeled after a karst topography.

The starting buzzer went off, and Hattori immediately burst out of First High's base.

He plunged toward the enemy with speed one couldn't achieve with leg power alone: He was mixing in jumping magic here and there.

Ninth High's reaction came late. They had more readily apparent fighting spirit, but First High had been the ones to actually take the initiative. With how fired up they were, Ninth High had probably been planning to be the ones to make the preemptive strike. But now, forestalled by the resolute charge that exceeded all expectations, they seemed confused about how to respond.

Should they focus all their attacks on the approaching member and establish numerical superiority? Or should they leave intercepting him to their defender and raid the enemy's base as planned? Perhaps that very stagnation was First High's goal.

Midway across the field, Hattori stopped and fired a spell at the three Ninth High players lagging in their base, causing an updraft of white fog to appear over their heads. The fog immediately grew denser, and then, as though it couldn't hold up its own weight anymore, it fell to the ground.

A hail of dry ice rained down on them.

Dry Blizzard: a compound spell using convergence, divergence, and movement-type magic.

It was the origin of the spell Mayumi had used in Speed Shooting.

The spell pushed the cooling carbon dioxide to its freezing point and then transformed both the active and latent heat loss into kinetic energy, propelling the dry ice bullets the moment the CO_2 froze. Naturally, the more heat there was to lose, the faster the bullet would go.

And here, they rained down from outside magical defenses and from above them, so the players couldn't hide behind a boulder to shield themselves. Admittedly, they were wearing helmets, and the pebbles were only pea size, so the combatants wouldn't be seriously hurt. But it *could* result in a light concussion after enough time.

That would be a direct line to losing the match by team knockout, so one of the Ninth High players expanded a mana shield—a virtual wall that reduced falling speed to zero—above their heads as cover.

All the shield did was temporarily change the speed to zero. After stopping for a moment in midair, the bullets were pulled down by gravity. The dry ice made by Hattori cooled the air around it, causing precipitation, and it fell to the ground along with a drizzle of water—onto their heads and onto the marble under them. Then, the precipitation absorbed the emitted carbon dioxide, turning it into a fog of dissolved carbon dioxide gas.

Because the fog was enclosed by the boulders in the terrain, it couldn't be easily dispersed from the Ninth High base. It wasn't really dense enough to prevent them from seeing, but the chilly moisture was unpleasant once noticed. A different player than the one who had made the shield tried to create an air current to blow away the side effects of the Dry Blizzard.

But Hattori's next spell activated before it could.

The technique altered both the weak static electricity created from the minutely vibrating grains of sand and the electrical properties of that sand at the same time, increasing its volume and releasing it into the surface of the ground.

It was the same type of spell the Eighth High rookie had used on the same crag stage where he forced an electron release, but the power and polish on it were an order of magnitude higher.

A crescent-shaped section of the ground, sixteen feet wide and wrapping around Ninth High's magical defenses, began to shine. Countless small, flickering cracks of lightning wound together, looking just like a swarm of small snakes wriggling toward them.

The sand-mixed ground, the sparse patches of grass, and the randomly scattered boulders got soaking wet from the fog, whose conductivity had increased because of the carbon dioxide thawing. The squirming snakes of electricity on the outside of their defensive line traveled through the ground, independent of magic, and attacked the Ninth High players.

It was the combination spell Slithering Thunder.

A combination spell was not a single technique with multiple magic processes involved. Instead, it was when a caster linked together each phenomena created by multiple spells to create a bigger effect than the sum of each individual spell.

In exchange for not having ridiculously strong magic specialization, enough processing speed that nobody could catch up to him, nor multi-casting in a way nobody else could, Hattori's distinctive characteristic and forte was being able to retain stability as he cast a great variety of different spells one after the other, no matter the situation.

Myriad situation-dependent magic that linked together and grew more powerful through synergistic effects—this could be called Hattori showing his true worth as a magician.

One of the three Ninth High players jumped into the air to avoid the electrical current. But the player who made the shield and the one who had just compiled a spell to blow away the fog were a moment late as they tried to switch to a jumping spell. The lightning coiled around his feet. The boots that came with the protection suits were insulated, but the insulation on the suits themselves was simple. (After all, with *too* much insulation, they'd lose breathability.) And already, the fog with the carbon dioxide gas in it clung to their bodies and dripped.

The player preparing the gust spell immediately changed the variables to create a downburst of wind; blowing away the fog droplets weakened the electricity. The player holding up the shield, though, took the full brunt of Slithering Thunder.

As he fell face-first onto the ground, the one next to him fell to his knees. That one gave up on his legs—they weren't going to be moving—and his fingers flew across his CAD as he knelt.

Then he heard a cry of pain from the air.

The player who had jumped to avoid the electrical attack had been rocked by an invisible flying hammer and fell to the ground in a jumbled mess.

It was an acceleration spell cast by Koutarou Tatsumi, who prided himself on his excellent output (strength of influence) when using techniques of a single family. He had instantly applied more gravity in the downward direction and knocked the enemy player to the ground.

But in spite of that, the Ninth High player's convergence magic went off. He hadn't been distracted by his teammate's fall—perhaps that just went to show the caliber of player who could advance to the finals tournament here. Instead, he fired a compressed-air bullet at Hattori. Excluding special environments like underwater or outer space, air existed everywhere, so it had always been popular as a medium for combat magic. In addition, the rules restricting methods of attack and lethality meant that compressed-air bullets and cutting winds tended to be seen quite often in Monolith Code.

The highly pressurized mass of air created outside Hattori's zone of magical defense, however, slammed into an invisible wall before reaching him, and dispersed.

Hattori hadn't been the one to make that shield.

The spell that had blocked the compressed-air bullet had been Reflector, which Katsuto had set up from a quarter mile behind Hattori.

Whether solid, liquid, or gas, the area-of-effect spell created a field that reversed movement vectors. In general, area-of-effect magic was said to be more difficult than anti-magic. It was all about how difficult it was to specify the spell's target.

The difficulty of altering an event was not in altering an object's properties or altering its spatial properties. The issue was how to *mark off the area* you wanted to overwrite the properties of.

In instances where there were clear, visible dividers, like walls, ceilings, and fences, it was simple. But if you were in a free outdoor space with no natural boundaries, it was quite difficult to "cut away" a specific region to define your spell within.

If it were an attack spell, you could lower the definition by just describing the size of the target area in your activation program. But with defensive magic, which required you to determine a target area within an opponent's attack, when you didn't know how far away or how big that attack would be, there weren't many instances where you *could* write in the surface area, volume, or shape in the activation program beforehand.

For example, a shield to protect yourself or a wall to cover your entire team: In those cases, you could configure it to be very close to your own position using relative coordinates. Normally, that was as much as you could do.

But Katsuto had just created a perfect Reflector with only Hattori's body as the target of protection—on an open field without anything to use as a reference, without using any support devices to supplement his mental image, and from a quarter mile away. It was an incredible ability to judge spaces.

Magicians in the Juumonji family refined their already-innate spatial awareness to freely use all kinds of defensive area-of-effect spells. That's where their nickname "Rampart" came from.

Hattori activated his next spell. He hadn't taken any defensive measures at all against the Ninth High player's attack. He'd constructed his magic programs fully expecting Katsuto to block all attacks for him.

Sand whipped up off the ground. Wind took the sand away. The dust cloud Hattori created about thirty feet in front of him grew in size and speed as it advanced, hurtling toward the enemy player as a storm of mud and dirt.

It was the compound spell Linear Sandstorm, which used acceleration and convergence magic. A wide-area attack spell built to use the first pieces of sand as a core and grown in density using a movement process.

The dust storm converged further before plowing through the Ninth High player.

◇ ◇ ◇

"That was pretty high level..." said Tatsuya in quiet awe, as the music sounded to end the match.

The match itself had developed into a pretty one-sided contest. When he said "high level," he meant the spells that had been used and the *way* they'd been used.

The way Hattori in particular had used his magic was so advanced that it made him want to make sure his sister learned from it. (Tatsuya decided that he wouldn't be able to emulate it himself.) That said, he had never rated Hattori lowly. Tatsuya may have won a duel against him, but he was objectively aware that it had been because of a surprise attack and that they had only just met. He'd predicted that Hattori was more skilled at *using* magic than just having a lot of magic power, after seeing him use spells at a variety of different rhythms, but the true skill he'd just shown had honestly exceeded Tatsuya's expectations. *I still don't have good enough eyes...*

"The finals are finally here," sighed Honoka, without a care in the world for Tatsuya's thoughts as he sat there slightly shocked. For her, it was only natural that her upperclassman, who was the student council president, had high magical abilities. However, that innocence—seeming to be "only natural" to her—was like a gentle, cool breeze to his mind.

It's only natural I don't have an eye for others; I'm still in high school.

It was at that moment that Tatsuya Shiba's mind finally switched from its prolonged stay as last night's specialist in the Independent Magic Battalion to that of a high school student.

"The final match is at one, but it's still a little early for lunch..."

"Would you like to get something a bit colder, Tatsuya?" suggested Miyuki.

"Agreed. I want ice cream," Shizuku responded immediately.

He didn't have a single thing to do today as part of the staff. And he didn't need to be worrying about any crime syndicates right now, either. Tatsuya decided he should let himself spend his time in an easygoing manner. He was a high school student, after all.

"There was a truck out there before. Do you want to eat there?"

"Yes, that would be good!"

The one boy and three pretty girls—oblivious to how they might look to others—headed for the ice cream truck with Tatsuya in the lead.

◇ ◇ ◇

The final Monolith Code match was set to go on the canyon stage.

Mayumi paid a visit to the players' waiting room to convey the decision from the administration committee. One might have also thought relaying messages wasn't exactly the duty of a student council president. But the fact was, Mayumi wouldn't have come all the way here just to tell him of the decision.

"Juumonji, are you in here?"

Not a second after speaking into the intercom at the entrance, she heard his reply: "I'll be right there."

A few moments later, Katsuto parted the sheets of canvas acting as a door, wearing the bottom half of his protective suit and a tank top.

"Sorry I'm not presentable."

"Don't worry about it. It's not like you're naked or anything."

The faint smell of alcohol wafted from his body. It wasn't because he'd been drinking. It was the subtle hint of the alcohol in his deodorant. In the few moments before he'd come out, he'd probably been worried about smelling like sweat when meeting her. He wasn't overly chivalrous toward girls, but he was a gentleman through and through. And Mayumi thought the fact that he didn't try to appeal to such consideration in the slightest was his own way of showing courtesy.

"What is it?"

Mayumi snapped out of her incoherent thoughts and retrieved the important matter back from the mental shelf upon which she'd deposited it. "They decided what stage the finals will be on. Do you have a minute?"

That would have been all she needed to say if she'd only come to tell him about the finals stage. But Katsuto didn't ask what or why; he silently followed after Mayumi.

She brought him to the room she'd used to ask Tatsuya's advice three days ago.

And like three days ago, she put up a soundproofing wall and brought her lips close to Katsuto's ear after he sat at the table. "I got an encrypted message from my father. He said he has a notification from the Master Clans Council."

"Really?"

"I guess you haven't gotten it, then."

"No."

Katsuto's response was surprise, but it took a lot to work the cryptanalysis on Master Clans Council messages, so he would have to be alone for no short period of time in order to decipher and read it. Even here, they were talking only on break time, and Mayumi interpreted this as Juumonji not wanting to invite any doubts by leaving his position as leader for too long.

Mayumi and Katsuto were in different positions than the other members of the team. Not in terms of student council president or team leader—but their social standings. Mayumi was a direct descendant of the current Ten Master Clans.

And Katsuto's position was even more different: He was also a direct descendant of the current clans, but unlike Mayumi, he was designated as the next head of the Juumonji family. In terms of all the high school students competing at this year's Nine School Competition, only Masaki stood in the same position as him.

"Remember when Tatsuya beat Ichijou the day before yesterday?"

"...Yes, what about it?"

Katsuto's response hadn't been "now that you mention it..."—he'd cut straight to the point.

Well, actually, the response itself had been a formal one.

"The Ten Master Clans stand at the pinnacle of this nation's magicians. Those who bear the name of one of the clans must be the strongest of all the magicians in Japan."

Mayumi's voice sounded a little cynical. She was speaking not of her own opinions but of her father's, and of the council's doctrines. Her own thoughts on the manner were likely different. But right now, what he needed to hear wasn't her own philosophy but the council's doctrines.

"This may be high school students playing around, but they say they can't allow any results that leave any doubts as to the Ten Master Clans' future strength."

"I don't believe that match was 'playing around,' but I see." His words were a rebuttal, but his tone was unconcerned. "What you mean is the council wants the matches to display the clans' strength right now, right?"

"Yes... It's absurd, though, and I would rather not burden you with it."

"No...this is actually something I need to deal with myself as the next head of the Juumonji. Sorry for making you worry."

"Look, it's not a big deal or anything..." For once, Mayumi was seriously making meaningless complaints—maybe her emotions had nowhere else to go. "It's all so stupid... If Tatsuya were related at all to the clans, even by a branch family, we wouldn't have gotten stuck in this poorly written comedy..."

Katsuto made no comment to Mayumi's grumbling. "Leave it to me" was all he said, his face emotionless.

◇ ◇ ◇

The final Monolith Code match of the day was to be First High versus Third High. It was a grudge match for many reasons and, put another way, was perhaps a fated showdown. But the match itself ended up even more one-sided than the semifinal had. Perhaps it was karma. They did the same thing to Third High that Masaki had done to Eighth High in the rookie competition.

The canyon stage had been chosen as their battlefield. All manner of attacks, from flying ice pebbles to boulders dislodging from cliffs to boiling water, had been continuously fired toward Katsuto for a while now.

But all of them bounced off the magical wall Katsuto had up. It reversed the movement vector of objects with mass. It reflected electromagnetic waves (including light) and sound waves. It aligned particle frequency to set values. It stopped psions from breaching. Every single type of attack was being blocked by a multi-layered wall, each for one of those purposes.

There was nothing to prevent Katsuto's stride.

The multilayered movement barrier spell, Phalanx.

The true value in this spell—and in the casters of the Juumonji—wasn't the simple fact that they kept the magic wall up continuously. It was their durability in updating many types of defense without pause.

This spell in particular mirrored a close formation of heavily armored soldiers, who, by forming into several lines clustered into one pack to advance, inverted their attack power into a heightened group defense.

If a soldier in the front line fell, a soldier behind him would replace him—it was an ancient tactic that maintained a constantly tight defense, and one from which the spell drew its name. Its defensive power and the pressure it exerted did that name no shame.

Katsuto advanced through the narrow field step-by-step, slowly but surely. The Third High players could neither ignore it nor avoid it. If they let up on their attacks at all, wouldn't a decisive blow come a moment later?

The pressure mounted with each step he took, with the unreasonable, yet compulsive, idea of steadily taking their attacks. Their ineffective efforts would be wearing the enemy down, sure, but it should have been *exhausting* to the defender. But in contrast to the three from Third High, who were breathing heavily now, Katsuto didn't look the slightest bit tired.

And once they were thirty feet away from one another, Katsuto suddenly stopped walking.

He stopped inching forward step-by-step…

…and then dashed off the ground with force.

His rocklike body leaped through the air.

He aimed for the enemy players with a self-acceleration and movement spell, going in shoulder first for a tackle—with his physical object–blocking wall still up to prevent anything from getting inside.

One Third High player bounced off his wall and went flying as Katsuto charged toward him. Katsuto's huge body changed direction instantly and soared at the next enemy without pausing. The remaining pair's magical defenses and momentum alterations had no effect against the even stronger field of influence being projected by their opponent.

The third player was sent flying, without any means to combat Katsuto, and the final Monolith Code match came to an end.

First High had achieved a perfect victory, putting the icing on the cake of their overall championship win.

As Tatsuya applauded Katsuto alongside the rest of the crowd, he was speechless. Katsuto, for his part, was waving magnanimously to the crowd.

The word *overwhelming* didn't even begin to cover it. It was nothing but *tremendous*.

His tactic itself had been simple: It was essentially simple brute force. But that spell—that wasn't *simple* brute force. It was an amazingly *advanced* brute force, one that kept on creating the walls of each of the eight types while switching their orders in an irregular fashion.

"That was amazing... Was that the Juumonji's Phalanx?" Miyuki couldn't manage anything but ordinary impressions, either. It went to show how much she'd been taken aback by the match. He understood how she felt.

But he couldn't agree with what she'd said. "It wasn't... I don't think that was the original Phalanx."

The multilayered barrier spell Phalanx was sometimes used to refer to the Juumonji family itself. But people had surprisingly few chances to see it with their own eyes. Normally, they didn't need to deploy barriers of every type of magic at one time. And that was only natural: If multiple magicians were attacking one target simultaneously, then the more attackers and the more types of attack spells there were, the easier it was for magic interference to occur. Tatsuya had never actually seen this spell before, either.

The multilayered barrier spell Katsuto had just used certainly did include every type of magic. That meant it was definitely Phalanx.

But Tatsuya couldn't accept such reasoning. "That last attack... It didn't seem like what Phalanx was meant to be used for."

It was less of a conjecture based on logic than it was a gut feeling. But he couldn't help feeling like the real Phalanx was an even more terrifying spell.

"If you say so, Tatsuya, then it must be true. Then I will rephrase... Juumonji has amazing talent."

Tatsuya felt the exact same way. As they continued to applaud, still impressed, he suddenly got the feeling that Katsuto had looked at him. The young man stuck his fist into the air to celebrate his victory.

His eyes met Tatsuya's for a moment—and then Tatsuya thought he saw him smile for just an instant.

He felt like Katsuto's eyes were saying this: *I'm stronger than you.*

Some said it was the benefit of a ruler for people to follow him without him having to rely on physical strength. But when you got right to the point, that was nothing more than political sophistry. What a ruler *truly* needed was this kind of absolute deterrence, to make the enemy know that he couldn't resist and to make the enemy abandon the effort of rising against the regent entirely.

As Katsuto responded to the cheers, he had the appearance of such a ruler—one who knew the value of his strength and had purposefully demonstrated it.

[14]

In stark contrast to two weeks ago (more precisely, twelve days ago), the hall was filled with a peaceful air. Keeping your mind open and unbiased was easier said than done, and if someone said the young minds here *weren't* preoccupied with their wins or losses, it would be a lie.

But right now, they'd just been released from fierce rounds of battles that had lasted ten days. The recoil they felt to being exposed to such tension, and for no short period of time, had placed most of the students into an excessively friendly mood.

The unified party on the last night again had a dress code of school uniforms only. Now stuck back in his blazer that didn't quite fit, Tatsuya had to wonder that if people were going to be dancing, why not have the right clothing for it? He stood by the wall as he considered things that would probably dig his own grave if he ever said them aloud.

"Pretty popular, eh?"

Addressing him with a wry grin was Mari, who had been given the slip of approval of complete recovery one day sooner than expected.

"Thanks to you. I'd rather be letting her take it easy, but…"

Without finishing his sentence with *it can't be helped*, Tatsuya glanced over at his little sister, who was surrounded by a crowd several layers deep. There were students from other schools, tournament organizers, high officials on base that supported the venues, and corporation officers backing the competition...

Maybe it really *was* inevitable, but there were even media professionals (from studios that created television programs, commercial production companies, and performing arts production houses) following her about. It made him want to demand of the party's organizers what was going on.

He would have liked to eschew all courtesy and physically kick the annoying hangers-on out the door, but Suzune was guarding against such an impolite approach with those sagacious (or just indifferent?) eyes of hers, so he refrained from intruding.

"I wasn't talking about your sister," said Mari to Tatsuya's honest answer, letting out a suppressed laugh and looking like she couldn't stand it anymore. "I was saying *you're* popular, Tatsuya."

Tatsuya frowned at her remark, clearly fed up with *that* idea. He wasn't often compared to Miyuki, who had never-ending crowds pressing down upon her, but people had been coming to talk to him as well for a while now.

Most of them were adults he'd never met before. Not ones who were unknown to him, though. In being freely associated with his father's company, Tatsuya knew the faces of a lot of businessmen for a high school student. But he knew them only on a high school student level. He lived in a laboratory and didn't touch any of the management or business affairs. Compared to regular company employees in the same business, he was only a little knowledgeable. And more than half of the people coming to talk to him were ones whose faces he knew.

"Wasn't that Rosen's Japan branch manager? Wouldn't that be the first time he's ever spoken to a freshman?"

"I don't know whether he has in the past or not. This is the first year I've actually been at the Nine School Competition."

"Oh, that's right." Mari wasn't trying to hide her grin. It was getting on Tatsuya's nerves a little—mostly because of pent-up anger. "...Well why bother being angry? I don't know why you're so negative about your name getting out there. But you can't fool a smart person by showing them a rock painted like a gemstone, and if you show a gemstone painted like a rock to someone, they're gonna know."

Tatsuya's jaw tightened.

"Don't look so sullen. The dance is about to start. After that'll be smooth sailing as a student. Just hold out a little longer."

She patted him on the shoulders, then walked over to the table with the drinks. For some reason, she appeared to be in high spirits. After she was injured, she seemed like she was forcing herself to act the same as usual, but now she looked like her mind had completely recovered.

Having a boyfriend has some pretty tremendous effects... Though he knew he couldn't understand things of that nature, he still couldn't help talking to himself about it. *With the way she's going, she's probably going to slip out of the party to see Naotsugu*, he thought, his imagination uncharacteristically turning to gossip.

That was just how he avoided the urge to sigh. Mari was right—all this barefaced trickery the adults were pulling would be over soon.

But it would be replaced with something he was just as unwilling to face: the dance.

However, students like Tatsuya were actually exceptions. As the big shots withdrew, the hall grew more gentle and restless. The soft sound of wind instruments began to play.

The boys reacted right away to the zeal of the organizers for having live music here. Taking the hands of the girls they'd succeeded in deepening friendships with via clever use of conversation, they headed to the center of the hall.

It was unfortunate the girls weren't in proper dresses, but the dancers didn't seem all that concerned about it. And besides, the silk organza inner gowns (the sleeveless gowns they wore under their outer bolero jackets), which were common to all nine schools, fluttered every time the girls turned, creating a splendor not all that different from full-length dresses.

As expected, boys clustered to Miyuki from all schools and grade levels. But nobody had succeeded in taking her hand yet. She had been surrounded by guests until just moments ago, so they probably hadn't talked very much yet.

Unlike Tatsuya, Miyuki had been formally trained in ball etiquette (it wasn't a dance party!), so she wouldn't stubbornly refuse a dance from a partner who was courteous (not to say she'd dance with *anyone*, of course), but the boys looked like they were being timid anyway.

Then, a face Tatsuya recognized came to Miyuki from out of the crowd. Not only did he recognize him—it would be fine to say he was acquainted with him.

Tatsuya left his spot at the wall and walked toward the crowd. He was certainly not of slender frame, but he skillfully slipped through the swarm of boys and walked up next to Miyuki.

"It's been two days, Masaki Ichijou."

"Oh. Tatsuya Shiba."

They exchanged relaxed greetings. They didn't think of each other as friends, but they also didn't think strict etiquette was necessary between them.

"Is your ear all right?" asked Masaki.

"There's no need to worry, and certainly no reason for you to worry on my behalf."

"Oh. Whatever."

Masaki's response couldn't be called friendly, though Tatsuya had at least *thought* he'd made his suggestion diplomatically. Still, for someone who'd suffered defeat at the hands of someone they could have beaten nine times out of ten, having that underdog worry about him wouldn't be pleasant. So Masaki's response was, in a way, justified in its cold brevity.

When Masaki noticed Miyuki looking at him uncomfortably, his mind was taken over by panic. "Wait, I... What? Shiba?!"

Masaki gave a little shout all of a sudden, saying Tatsuya's last name in a hysterical voice. Tatsuya looked at him strangely, as if wondering if he was all right in the head.

"Are you two siblings?!"

Masaki's words gave Tatsuya an indescribable feeling of exhaustion. "...You didn't realize that until now? Really?" he asked, irritated, implying that it was easy to see.

While Masaki stood there, speechless, a short, polite laugh came at him. Miyuki covered her mouth and looked away. "...So we don't look like siblings to you, Ichijou?" she asked, stifling her laughter and seeming happy about it for some reason.

"Uh, well, I... No."

Masaki gave up on making excuses and hung his head. Miyuki, in return, gave him a sweet smile. Tatsuya didn't know what she was so happy about, but Ichijou seemed to suit his sister's tastes—though only on the level of being an acceptable dance partner.

"Staying put here forever is going to get in the way, so why not dance with Ichijou, Miyuki?"

Masaki's face suddenly shot up at about the point when he said "dance with Ichi..." His eyes sparkled in anticipation.

Miyuki giggled for a few moments and then tilted her head at him, as if to ask what he wanted to do.

"Yes...may I...have this dance?" he asked, desperately restraining his high-pitched voice and respectfully offering his hand to Miyuki.

"Yes, you may," said his sister, also giving a respectful response and taking Masaki's presented hand.

Just before they got into position, Masaki shot Tatsuya a look of gratitude.

Tatsuya saw it and thought, *How devious.*

For Tatsuya, the charming romantic comedy with Masaki in it had nothing to do with him. (He hoped Miyuki felt the same about the comedy part.) That's why he could deal with it so easily. But if he'd been the dance partner concerned, just dealing with the situation passably, to say nothing of ideally, would have been beyond him.

Tatsuya fully realized his own inexperience as he watched Honoka stealing glances at him with hesitant, upturned eyes.

"Sir, at times like these, the man must take the lead."

I already can't deal with Honoka. And now someone's making fun of me. Who could blame me for wanting to run away? thought Tatsuya, complaining to nobody in particular—though not mentioning any of this aloud, of course. "Erika…why are you a waitress?"

"Because that was the condition for staying here in the first place," she said, smoothly ignoring his troubles.

Leo and Mikihiko had been called to the party as champions as well. Erika and Mizuki were offered honorary staff spots, too, but all four had turned them down. Right now, they were working diligently at their side jobs in the kitchen and hall.

Mikihiko had been placed in the kitchen like he originally wanted, but Erika was again going in and out of the hall in the same frilly waitress costume as before.

"…Then I don't think you should be wasting time in a place like this…"

"One of my jobs as hall monitor is to give appropriate advice to our esteemed guests."

Turned away once again by a composed expression, Tatsuya felt the urge to groan. Leaving aside the whole "jobs as hall monitor" bit, he knew her insistence bore some truth to it.

Honoka was waiting for Tatsuya to ask her to dance. He knew *that* much without having to be told. But he didn't know what to do about it. He had an absolute lack of experience inviting girls like this.

"Sir? I don't believe there is anything that requires such careful thought."

Erika had just been fooling around with him before, but her words were sounding more and more irritated. If he let her keep going, then she'd probably actually get mad before much longer.

And Tatsuya thought that would be a little—no, very—pathetic of him to do.

"...Honoka?"

"Yes?!"

Tatsuya steeled himself. "...Want to dance?" Despite that, though, there was a significant pause before he got the words out, and they came out as an unsure question, to boot.

"Gladly!"

Still, Honoka seemed more than happy to hear it.

After that, Tatsuya was forced into hard labor, dancing with Shizuku, Eimi, and Mayumi in turn. When it was all over, he slumped against the wall, exhausted.

Mayumi had been especially hard to dance with. Her sense of rhythm was...unique.

Nobody could call Tatsuya a good dancer, even as flattery. He hadn't ever practiced, so that was only natural. But he didn't make the mistake of stepping on the girls' feet or bumping into anyone else. In fact, he never missed a step. When Shizuku danced with him, she had actually told him he danced like a machine; he wasn't sure if that was a compliment or an insult. He was simply changing the speed of his motions based on the music, replicating a memorized dance while omitting the finer details. So leaving the beauty, elegance, and grace of his dancing aside, he at least had perfect precision.

On the other hand, Mayumi was, in a way, the exact opposite. She was not stepping in time with the music. It wasn't that she had no sense of sound, but she seemed to have a rather creative purpose in mind—although each of her steps was slightly off, she was actually dancing very gracefully if he considered the flow of the song.

Thanks to that, Tatsuya had been forced to jump through hoops to align his own steps with both the music's rhythm and hers. If he'd been a normal person, he wouldn't have had so much trouble getting in line with his partner, but Tatsuya was only reproducing movements he had in his head rather than letting his body do the work. Applying *that* was a lot of trouble.

Afterward Mayumi, herself rather elated, had left the utterly exhausted Tatsuya and gone to find a new dance partner, but there had actually been a lot of female students wandering around "aimlessly" in front of Tatsuya. After Masaki finished his dance with Miyuki, he'd been in great demand among the female upperclassmen. It hadn't been *that* bad for Tatsuya, but there was no lack of girls who had seen him in Monolith Code and gotten interested in him.

But when they saw him standing there like all his willpower and energy had been drained, they all sent him the same look of sympathy and passed him by. He didn't even have the mental power to reflect on how unfortunate that was for him. Just as he was thinking about getting back to his room, someone held a glass out to him, as if they'd timed the opportunity.

"Tha...thank you." He paused in the middle because of how completely unexpected the person who'd approached him was.

"You seem tired."

"...Yes, well."

"Can't do it like your matches?"

"Well... No, you're right. This may be forward of me, but you don't look like you have trouble with either of those things, Chairman."

"I'm used to it."

The one to talk to him was Katsuto. He gulped down his non-alcoholic drink in one go. Tatsuya got the feeling he needed to match him, so he downed his own glass in the same way.

But the real talk came after that. "Shiba, come with me for a minute," said Katsuto. No sooner had the words left his mouth than he had handed his empty glass to a passing waitress (not Erika) and turned his back.

That meant he didn't have any right to refuse. Tatsuya handed over his glass as well and silently followed along.

The courtyard where he'd caught the armed trespassers the night before the competition's opening ceremonies was silent tonight, with no signs of anyone sneaking around. It wasn't completely silent, though; someone must have opened a window, because he could hear the faint sound of the music. But the soft sounds seemed to only deepen the silence here all the more.

"Is this all right? I think the victory celebration is starting soon," asked Tatsuya politely to Katsuto's back once he stopped walking.

After the party, the hall had been reserved for First High's victory celebration. It was a trivial privilege given to the school that won the overall championship. Katsuto, both an officer of First High's team and a main player, would obviously need to be in attendance.

"Don't worry. This won't be long," answered Katsuto, turning around abruptly.

Is it not that important? Then why would he have to bring me outside during the party? he thought. Or maybe…it was something that would be settled in a short period of time.

…It seemed, at least, that Katsuto's plan involved the latter.

"Shiba, you're a member of the Ten Master Clans, right?"

The sudden attack almost put Tatsuya on guard against danger. That wasn't a metaphor—he nearly assumed a combat stance. At this stage, anyone knowing his true identity was taboo. "No, I'm not part of the clans."

There was a powerful insight in Katsuto's gaze, one that wouldn't permit lies or concealment. Tatsuya had been able to give his decisive question a denial only because it was the truth by the letter of the law. He *wasn't* part of the Ten Master Clans. He might have had their blood in him, but he wasn't recognized as a member. That was the undeniable truth.

"…I see." Katsuto stared at Tatsuya for a few moments, then nodded impassively. Tatsuya couldn't tell if it was because he believed him. "Then allow me to give you advice as the Juumonji's representative magician to the Master Clans Council. Shiba, you *should* be part of the clans."

Tatsuya stared.

"Let's see… How would Saegusa sound?"

"…Are you referring to her as a marriage partner?"

"That's right."

Katsuto's spell, Phalanx, was basically the natural enemy of Tatsuya's original magic, Dismantle. He could dismantle one thin barrier, but then more would come out at him. It would be an endless cycle. Tatsuya had felt a shudder at his prediction of such a thorough battle of attrition while he was watching the final match…but he hadn't predicted this at all, and now he felt himself shuddering again but with a conviction that was firm.

Katsuto was, without a doubt, his natural enemy.

—For many more reasons than he'd thought.

"…Wouldn't *your* name be at the top of the list to marry President Saegusa, Chairman?"

"That is another possibility."

"…Is President Saegusa not your type?"

"That's not it. Why? Saegusa is still quite charming in certain respects."

"…Ah." Tatsuya couldn't find anything to say to that.

"…Oh, are you worried about age, Shiba? Hmm… What about her younger sisters, then? I last met them two years ago, but they looked like they would be beautiful in the future."

"…I'm sorry, but unlike you and the president, I'm just a high school student, so all this talk of marriage and engagement seems premature…"

"Does it?" Katsuto tilted his head a bit. "…But you can't be too carefree for much longer. Beating the next head of one of the clans in a one-to-one match is a lot more serious than you think."

Tatsuya wanted to retort, *I don't want to hear that out of you*, since Katsuto had been the one who'd actually forced him into fighting Masaki in the first place.

"…We should get back. Don't be too late, Shiba."

He couldn't believe it—or at least, he didn't want to. *Is he…is he actually an airhead…?*

But as Tatsuya watched him stride away majestically, he earnestly felt that Katsuto was terrifying.

"Tatsuya?"

It was as he stood there in the night, overcome with surprise, that his little sister's voice snapped him out of it.

"What's the matter? It's unusual for you to be so absent that you don't realize I'm coming."

"No, well…I just saw something a little unexpected…"

"Like what?"

"It's, well, really not important…"

"Hm?" Tatsuya's words were inconsistent, but Miyuki just tilted her head in confusion and didn't pursue the topic. "…The party is ending soon."

"And the victory celebration is after that…" grumbled Tatsuya, his face scrunching up reflexively at the suggestion. "Guess I can't pass up on that…"

Miyuki put a hand to her mouth and giggled. "I think you just need to give up. If you go back to your room, I think you will only be attacked by Honoka and Erika."

"I can understand Honoka, but…?"

"Erika was captured by the president," said Miyuki. She laughed at it like it was funny. "The president is one step in rank above her," she added. "And besides..." With another smile, but restraining her laughter, her eyes a little serious, she peered into her brother's eyes. "I will not let you run away, Tatsuya."

Tatsuya heaved a sigh. But rather suddenly, Miyuki's ears perked up. "...Ooh, the last song is starting."

"Is it?" Tatsuya could tell the song had changed, but he wasn't aware this was going to be the last one.

"Tatsuya, would you share this last dance with me?"

Under the light of the moon and the stars, Miyuki asked him to dance, with a clear smile that he had barely ever seen before. The smile wouldn't permit any resistance from him.

"...Then let's get back before it ends."

"No, we'll just be wasting time, then." Miyuki took his hand. "We can hear the music from here." She brought her body in close enough that he could feel her breath. "And I can dance just fine on the grass with these shoes."

Tatsuya said nothing and put one hand on his sister's back. She leaned on it and put her hands on his shoulders.

Their bodies touched.

Gently clasping her hand and holding her back close to him, Tatsuya took the first step.

They spun and spun under the starry sky.

And as they spun around, Tatsuya's face was always right in front of Miyuki.

Miyuki's face was always right in front of Tatsuya's.

The scenery, the stars, the moon, the darkness...

With everything in the world spinning around them, they looked only at each other.

Chapter 2 Fin

AFTERWORD

This book is a work of fiction.
The world in which the story takes place is a different world, but
one much like our own. Any and all present or historical figures, organiza-
tions, nations, regions, and other unique names mentioned therein have no
relation to any real-world counterparts, even if they have the same name.

—The fourth volume made me want to include a proviso, but it should be implied regardless. Anyway, how did you all enjoy the story? Whenever I use a name that *happens to be the same* as a real one, I always feel indecision somewhere in my mind. And when it happens to be the name of an enemy, I can't help but be uneasy about it... I understand how shameless I'm being about this, so no witty retorts, please.

Speaking of unique names, I honestly find it difficult to come up with names for foreign characters. I worry especially because this story is set in a world close to the real one. There are plenty of examples of names from western Europe out there, but when you start getting into Southeast Asian, India, Iran, Africa, and South America...what do I do? It's fine so far, but I think this is going to be a big wall for me eventually. Is there any good way to go about this?

...Anyway, I will leave my griping nonsense at that for now and extend a thanks to everyone involved in this novel. Mr. M, thank you very much for all the appropriate advice you always give me. I think his suggestions have made the siblings into *deeper* characters. Ms. Ishida, Mr. Stone, I asked a lot of you with this tight, consecutive publishing schedule. I made a lot of requests again…so I truly apologize. Ms. Suenaga as well—I think I've put a lot on your shoulders in terms of scheduling, too. Thank you from the bottom of my heart to all the staff involved in the creation of this book.

And I deeply thank you once again, for the second time in two months, for reading the afterword like this. The fifth volume will be published because of all the support everyone has given me. The next volume will be a compilation of short stories. There will be six episodes in it. Two of them are newly written, too. The other works haven't been serialized commercially, so maybe I should just call them all-new works. Two of the "all-new works" will be slice-of-life episodes. I want you to enjoy peaceful moments before an even more difficult battle begins.

I pray from the bottom of my heart that you will read *The Irregular at Magic High School* again like this.

And once again, thank you all very much.

Tsutomu Sato